The Lace Reader

The Lace Reader

Brunonia Barry

HARPER LUXE

An Imprint of HarperCollinsPublishers

HarperCollins books may be purchased for educational, business, or sales promotional use. For information please write: Special Markets Department, HarperCollins Publishers, 10 East 53rd Street, New York, NY 10022.

FIRST HARPERLUXE EDITION

HarperLuxe™ is a trademark of HarperCollins Publishers

Library of Congress Cataloging-in-Publication Data is available upon request.

ISBN: 978-0-06-166826-5

08 09 10 11 12 ID/RRD 10 9 8 7 6 5 4 3 2

TO MY WONDERFUL HUSBAND, GARY,

and to my sister-in-law Joanne's magical red hair

PART ONE

The Lace Reader must stare at the piece of lace until the pattern blurs and the face of the Seeker disappears completely behind the veil. When the eyes begin to fill with tears and the patience is long exhausted, there will appear a glimpse of something not quite seen.

In this moment an image will begin to form . . . in the space between what is real and what is only imagined.

—THE LACE READER'S GUIDE

Chapter 1

My name is Towner Whitney. No, that's not exactly true. My real first name is Sophya. Never believe me. I lie all the time.

I am a crazy woman. . . . That last part is true.

My little brother, Beezer, who is kinder than I, says the craziness is genetic. *We're from five generations of crazy*, he says, as if it were a badge he's proud to wear, though he admits that I may have taken it to a new level.

Until I came along, the Whitney family was what the city of Salem fondly refers to as "quirky." If you were old Salem money, even if that money was long gone, you were never referred to as "crazy." You might be deemed "unusual," or even "oddball," but the hands-down-favorite word for such a condition was "quirky."

Throughout the generations the Whitney men have all become famous for their quirks: from the captains of sea and industry all the way down to my little brother, Beezer, who is well known within scientific circles for his articles on particle physics and string theory.

Our great-great-grandfather, for example, parlayed a crippling preoccupation with ladies' feet into a brilliant career as a captain of industry in Lynn's thriving shoe business, creating a company that was passed down through the generations all the way to my grandfather G. G. Whitney. Our great-great-great-grandfather, who was a legitimate captain in his own right, had a penchant for sniffing cinnamon that many considered obsessive. Eventually he built a fleet of spice-trading ships that traveled the globe and made Salem one of the richest ports in the New World.

Still, anyone would admit that it is the women of the Whitney family who have taken quirky to a new level of achievement. My mother, May, for example, is a walking contradiction in terms. A dedicated recluse who (with the exception of her arrests) hasn't left her home on Yellow Dog Island for the better part of twenty years, May has nevertheless managed to revive a long-defunct lace-making industry and to make herself famous in the process. She has gained considerable notoriety for rescuing abused women and children and turning their lives around, giving the women a place in her lace-making business and home-educating their children. All this from a raging agoraphobic who gave one of her own children to her barren half sister, Emma, in a fit of generosity because, as she said at the time, there was a need, and besides, she had been blessed with a matching set.

And my Great-Aunt Eva, who is more mother to me than May ever has been, is equally strange. Running her own business well into her eighties, Eva is renowned as both Boston Brahmin and Salem witch when, really, she is neither. Actually, Eva is an old-school Unitarian with Transcendentalist tendencies. She quotes Scripture in the same breath as she quotes Emerson and Thoreau. Yet in recent years Eva has spoken only in clichés, as if use of the tired metaphor can somehow remove her from the inevitable outcomes she is paid to predict.

For thirty-five years of her life, Eva has run a ladies' tearoom and franchised successful etiquette classes to the wealthy children of Boston's North Shore. But what Eva will be remembered for is her uncanny ability to read lace. People come from all over the world to be read by Eva, and she can tell your past, present, and future pretty accurately just by holding the lace in front of you and squinting her eyes.

In one form or another, all the Whitney women are readers. My twin sister, Lyndley, said she couldn't read lace, but I never believed her. The last time we tried, she saw the same thing I saw in the pattern, and what we saw that night led her to the choices that eventually killed her. When Lyndley died, I resolved never to look at a piece of lace again.

This is one of the only things Eva and I have ever vehemently disagreed about. "It wasn't that the lace was wrong," she always insisted. "It was the reader's interpretation that failed." I know that's supposed to make me feel better. Eva never says anything to intentionally hurt. But Lyndley and I interpreted the lace the same way that night, and though our choices might have been different, nothing that Eva says can ever bring my sister back.

After Lyndley's death, I had to get out of Salem and ended up in California, which was as far as I could go without falling off the end of the earth. I know that Eva wants me to come home to Salem. It's for my own good, she says. But I can't bring myself to do it.

Just recently, when I had my hysterectomy, Eva sent me her lace pillow, the one she uses to make the lace. It was delivered to the hospital.

"What is it?" my nurse asked, holding it up, staring at the bobbins and the piece of lace, a work in progress, still attached to it. "Some kind of pillow?"

"It's a lace maker's pillow," I said. "For making Ipswich lace."

She regarded me blankly. I could tell she had no idea what to say. It didn't look like any pillow she had ever seen. And what the hell was Ipswich lace?

"Try holding it against your sutures if you have to cough or sneeze," she finally said. "That's what we use pillows for around here."

I felt around until I found the secret pocket hidden in the pillow. I slipped my fingers in, looking for a note. Nothing.

I know that Eva hopes I will start reading lace again. She believes that lace reading is a God-given gift, and that we are required to honor such gifts.

I imagine the note she might have written: *"Of those to whom much is given, much is expected—Luke 12:48."* She used to quote that bit of Scripture as proof.

I can read lace, and I can read minds, though it isn't something I try to do; it is something that just happens sometimes. My mother can do both, but over the years May has become a practical woman who believes that knowing what is in people's minds or their futures is not always in anyone's best interest. This is probably the only point upon which my mother and I have ever agreed.

When I left the hospital, I stole the pillowcase off one of their pillows. The Hollywood Presbyterian label was double stamped on both sides. I stuffed Eva's lace pillow inside, hiding the threads, the lace, and the bonelike bobbins that were swinging like tiny Poe pendulums.

If there was a future for me, and I was not altogether certain there was, I wasn't going to risk reading it in the lace.

Each Reader must choose a piece of lace. It is hers for life. It might be a pattern handed down through the generations or a piece chosen by the Reader for its beauty and familiarity. Many Readers prefer the handmade laces, particularly those of old Ipswich or the laces made today by the women of Yellow Dog Island.

—THE LACE READER'S GUIDE

Chapter 2

When the phone call comes in, I am dreaming of water. Not the warm blues and greens of the California beach towns where I live now, but the dark New England Atlantic of my youth. In my dream I am swimming to the moon. Like all dreams, it seems logical. The idea that there is no pathway between sea and moon never occurs.

I swim my own combination: part breaststroke, part drownproofing: slow and purposeful, a rhythm remembered from another lifetime. The movement is all efficiency, with just nose, ears, and eyes protruding above the water, mouth submerged. With each forward stroke, tiny waves of salt enter my open mouth, then recede again as I slow, mirroring the larger surrounding ocean.

I swim for a long time. Past Salem Harbor and the swells. Past any sight of land at all. I swim until the sea becomes still and clear, too calm to be any real ocean. The light from the full dream-moon etches a clear path on the black water, a road to follow. There is no sound save my own breath, slow and steady as I swim.

This was once my sister's dream. Now it is only mine.

The rhythm of movement gives way to a sound rhythm as the telephone rings again and then again. This is one of the only phones that actually rings anymore, and part of the reason I agreed to take this house-sitting job. It is the kind of phone we might have had on our island. That's the one interesting thing about what has happened to me. I am encouraged to rewrite my own history. In the history I am writing, May actually has a phone.

My therapist, Dr. Fukuhara, is a Jungian. She believes in symbols and shadows. As do I. But my therapy has stopped for the time being. *We have come to an impasse,* was the way Dr. Fukuhara put it. I laughed when she said it. Not because it was funny but because it was the kind of cliché that my Aunt Eva would use.

On the fourth ring, the answering machine picks up. The machine is old also, not as old as the phone, but the kind where you can screen calls and hear a little bit of the message before you decide whether it's worth it to actually speak to a live person.

My brother's voice sounds tinny and too loud.

I stretch to pick up, pulling the surgery stitches that are still inside me, the ones that haven't yet dissolved.

"What?" I say.

"I'm sorry to wake you," Beezer says.

I remember falling asleep on this couch last night, too tired to get up, hypnotized by the smell of night-blooming jasmine and the sound of Santana playing over the hill at the Greek.

"I'm sorry," he says again. "I wouldn't have called you, but . . ."

"But May's in trouble again." It's the only time Beezer ever calls these days. At last count, May has been arrested six times in her efforts to help abuse victims. Recently my brother informed me that he'd put the number of the local bail bondsman on his speed dial.

"It's not May," he says.

My throat tightens.

"It's Eva."

Dead, I'm thinking. *Oh, my God, Eva is dead.*

"She's missing, Towner."

Missing. The word has no meaning. "Missing" is the last word I expected to hear.

Palm fronds clatter against the open window. It's already way too hot. Clear Santa Ana sky, earthquake weather. I reach up to pull the window shut. The cat runs scratches across my legs as it lunges for the freedom of the canyon, leaping through the window as it slams, catching just a few tail hairs, the last trace of what was here just moments ago and is now gone, that fast. Immediately the cat scratches on my legs begin to welt.

"Towner?"

"Yeah?"

"I think you'd better come home."

"Yeah," I say, "yeah, okay."

It is called Ipswich lace, or bobbin lace, or bone lace. It is made on bolster pillows held on the laps of the women. The pillows are round or elliptical and most resemble the muffs that Victorian women later carried to keep their hands warm while riding in their carriages. Each woman makes her own pillow, and those pillows are as individual as the women themselves. In old Ipswich the pillows were pieced together from bits of fabric, then stuffed with beach grass.

—THE LACE READER'S GUIDE

Chapter 3

The *Salem News* has already picked up the story about Eva's disappearance: "Elderly Woman Missing Ten Days" and "Lace Reader of Salem Vanishes." Eva used to send me the Salem paper. It was around the time that May started making the headlines. For a while I actually read them. My mother's clashes with the police over her tactics for saving abused women were becoming famous and made for good copy. Eventually I stopped reading the papers and would leave them on the porch in their wrappers until my landlord would get fed up and take them to Santa Monica for recycling or, if it was winter, roll them up tightly and burn them in her fireplace like logs.

The paper speculates that Eva just wandered away. A woman interviewed from the Salem Council on Aging suggests tagging the elderly residents of Salem. It evokes an interesting image—cops with ear tags and tranquilizer guns rounding up old people. Realizing she's gone too far with her suggestion, the woman goes on to say: "This kind of thing happens all the time. Salem is a small city. I'm sure she couldn't have gotten far."

The woman clearly didn't know my aunt.

The ferry from Boston lets me off on Derby Street, a few blocks from the House of the Seven Gables, where Nathaniel Hawthorne's cousin grew up. I am named after Hawthorne's wife, Sophia Peabody, although the spelling is different; my name is spelled Sophya. I was brought up to believe that Ms. Peabody was a distant relative, but I found out from Eva that we weren't related to the Peabodys at all, that May simply found

Sophia interesting, and appropriated her as our own. (So now you see which side of the family the lying thing comes from.) By the time it would have bothered me, May and I were hardly speaking anyway. I had already moved in with Aunt Eva. I had changed my name to Towner and wouldn't answer to anything else. So it didn't matter all that much.

I'm walking for a long time. The estrogen patch on my arm begins to itch. I have a rash from it, but I don't know what to do about that, short of ripping the damned thing off. I figure the rash is probably from the heat. I'd forgotten how hot it can get in New England in the summer, and how humid. Ahead of me tourists swarm. Buses line the lot at the Gables, jamming the side streets. People move in groups, snapping photos, stuffing souvenirs into bags that are already far too full.

Around every corner of Salem lurks a history lesson. Dead ahead as I walk is the Custom House with its gold roof. This is where Hawthorne worked his day job, an appointed position as clerk. Using the locals as subject matter, revealing their secrets, Hawthorne basically wrote his way out of this town, escaping west to Concord before the townspeople remembered their talent with the old tar and feathers. Still, now they celebrate Hawthorne as their own. The same way they celebrate the witches, who never existed at all in the days of the witch trials but who thrive here in great numbers now.

A kid steps in front of me, asking directions to the common. There are three kids actually, two girls and a boy. All in black. *Goths,* is my first thought, but no, definitely young witches. What gives it away finally is the BLESSED BE T-shirt worn by one of the girls.

I point. "Follow the yellow brick road," I say. Actually it's a tour line painted on the street, and it's red, not yellow, but they get the idea. A man in a huge Frankenstein head walks by, handing out flyers. I want to call for the continuity person, but this isn't a movie set. A cruiser slows, the cop looks at the kids, then at me. The boy spots the witch logo on the side of the police car, gives the cop a big thumbs-up. Frankenstein hands each of us a Freaky Tours flyer and sneezes inside his big hollow head. "Universal tours without the budget" is what Beezer calls this place. I heard from my brother that Salem is trying to shed its image as Witch City. He told me last year that they were attempting to pass an ordinance to limit the number of haunted houses that can be erected within one city block. From the look of things, the ordinance didn't pass.

The second girl, the shorter of the two, grabs the side of her head, pulling it slowly until her neck cracks. Celtic-knot tattoo on the nape of her neck, hair way too dark for her pale skin. "Come on, let's go," she says to the guy, and grabs his arm, leading him away from me. "Thanks," he says. Our eyes meet, and he flashes a quick smile. She steps between us then, turning him wide like a big ship she's trying to keep on course. I follow them, walking in the same direction toward Eva's house but leaving a safe distance so she won't think I'm after him.

It's a long walk toward the common. I hear the music before I see the crowd—it's nature music, New Age. We could be back in Woodstock except for the preponderance of black clothing. I'm wondering what holiday it is, what Pagan celebration. I count the days and realize that it's some kind of summer-solstice thing, though it's about a week too late. Living in L.A. has made me forget the seasons. Here the arrival of summer is something for everyone to celebrate, Pagan or not.

Salem Common, with its huge oaks and maples and the Gothic cast-iron fence, triggers a lost school memory. There used to be tunnels under the common, sometime after the witches but before the Revolution. The shipping merchants probably used the tunnels to hide trade bounty from their English tax collectors; that was the theory anyway. After the war for independence finally started, the tunnels were used by the privateers, who were the same thing as pirates, really, but with the government's permission. Not England's permission—it was the British ships they were stealing—but permission of the new government. I'm told they also hid ammunition there, and saltpeter. Beezer and I used to search for the tunnels when we were little, but Eva told us that they're all filled in now.

I turn the corner by the Hawthorne Hotel and see the low blue flame from the old glassed-in popcorn machine, which is still on the corner across from the hotel, as it has been every year since my mother was a little girl. There's also a makeshift stand selling wands and crystals, but that's new. Across the street stands the imposing statue of Roger Conant, who, after failing to realize his original goal in Cape Ann, ended up founding the city that would become Salem. I'm reminded of the cliché Eva used to repeat at least ten times a week: *There are no accidents.* And the one that inevitably followed. *Everything happens for a reason.*

The cops are everywhere: on bicycles, talking to people, asking for fire permits. "You can't do that here," I hear one of them say. "If you want to have a bonfire, you have to go up to Gallows Hill, or to the beach."

I cross the street. I open the gate to Eva's house, catching a whiff of flowers, peonies, coming from her gardens. There are hundreds of them now, tree peonies on small bushes that die back every winter. Eva has done well with her gardens. She used to leave a key for me in a peony blossom when she knew I was coming. Or she would place it in one of the daylilies if it was later in the season and the peonies were no longer blooming. I'd forgotten that. But there are too many flowers now. I could never find a key here, and of course she hasn't left a key this time, because she wasn't expecting me.

The brick house is much larger than I remember. More imposing and older. Huge chimneys list to windward. Off the back, away from the crowds of Salem Common, is the coach house, which is connected to the main house by the winter porch. The coach house is more damaged than the main house—probably from the weather or from neglect—and it seems to be leaning on the porch, which is showing its age and sagging under the weight. Still, its windows with their wavy old glass are sparkling, not spotted with salt from the sea air, which means that Eva washed them not too long ago, as she does with all the windows she can reach (eighty-five years old or not), the same way she washes them every April when she does her spring cleaning. She gets to all the first-floor windows and the insides of all the upper floors. The outside windows of those upper floors remain filmy and salted, because Eva has the frugality of an old Yankee and refuses to pay anyone for services she thinks she should be able to perform herself. When Beezer and I lived in town with Eva, we offered to wash the windows, but she wouldn't buy a ladder and said she didn't want us climbing up on ladders anyway, so Beezer and I got used to distortion and haze. If you wanted to see clearly, you had to either look out the first-floor windows or climb all the way up to the widow's walk.

The perfect line of first-floor windows gleams back at me from the winter porch. I catch my reflection in the wavy glass, and I'm surprised by it. When I left here, I was seventeen. I haven't been back for fifteen years. I knew my reflection in the glass when I was seventeen, but today I don't recognize the woman I see there.

The hours of Eva's tearoom are posted on the front door. A sign that reads SORRY WE ARE CLOSED leans against one of the side panes.

A young girl sees me walking to the house. "There's no one there," the girl says, assuming I'm one of the witches. "I already checked."

I nod and walk down the stairs. When she's out of sight, I walk around to the back of the house, figuring I'm going to have to break in and not wanting to be seen.

When we were kids, my sister, Lyndley, and I could break into any house. I was a master at picking locks. We used to break into people's houses just to sit in them—"like Goldilocks tasting porridge and sampling beds," Lyndley used to say. For the most part, we limited our break-ins to the summerhouses. Down at the Willows one time, we broke into a house and actually cleaned it. That's the kind of thing only a girl would do. Outlaw certainly, but homemaker, too.

I walk around the back of the coach house to a less visible spot half hidden by the garden. There is a small pane in the door, bull's-eye glass, already cracked. Once I'm inside the coach house, getting into the main house is a snap. I pick up a rock, wrapping the sleeve of my shirt over it. A quick tap and the crack spreads. I pull the glass fragments out carefully and wedge my hand through the small space, twisting the dead bolt that has been the only thing holding the door in alignment. Either because the lock is so rusty or because I am, I don't anticipate the way the door heaves as it opens. It pulls my arm with it, cutting through my cotton shirt, drawing blood. I watch the blood pool. It's not too bad; there's not very much of it, not after what I've gotten used to anyway. "Just a flesh wound, Copper," I say aloud in my best Jimmy Cagney. Then, ridiculously on cue, a police cruiser actually pulls up, and, even more ridiculously, the father of my first boyfriend, Jack, climbs out of the car and walks toward the house. This is strange, since Jack's father is not a cop, he's a lobsterman. I'm having one of those moments when you're pretty sure you're dreaming but you don't want to count on it. I regard Jack's father as he approaches me, his face screwed up into half concern, half joy, looking stranger than anything in my dream life ever did.

"You should have called the station," he says. "We have a key." It is not Jack's father's voice but his younger brother's that I finally recognize.

"Hi, Jay-Jay," I say, getting it, remembering now that Beezer had told me Jay-Jay was a cop.

He hugs me. "Been a while," he says, thinking, I'm sure, how bad I look and running through a list of possibilities in his head. I fight the urge to tell him I've just had my uterus cut out, that I almost bled to death before the emergency surgery.

"You're bleeding," he says, reaching out for my arm. The cops here aren't as scared by blood as the cops in L.A. are.

"Just a flesh wound, Copper," I say too loud. He leads me inside and makes me sit down at the kitchen table. I'm bare-armed now, holding a paper towel to my forearm.

"You need stitches," Jay-Jay says.

"It's fine."

"At least get some Neosporin on it. Or some of that herbal crap Eva sells."

"I'm fine, Jay-Jay," I say, just a little too sharply.

A long silence. "I'm sorry about Eva," he says finally. "I wish I had something new I could tell you."

"Me, too."

"That Alzheimer's stuff is all crap. I saw her a week before she disappeared. She was still sharp as a tack." He thinks a minute. "You need to talk to Rafferty."

"Who?"

"Detective Rafferty. He's your man. He's the one who's handling the case."

He looks around the room as if there's something here, something he wants to say, but then he changes his mind.

"What?"

"Nothing. . . . I'll tell Rafferty you're here. He'll want to talk to you. He's in court today, though. Traffic court. Whatever you do, don't drive with him. He's the worst driver in the world."

"Okay," I say, wondering why Jay-Jay thought driving with Rafferty was even a possibility. We stand there awkwardly, neither of us knowing how to follow that last thread of conversation.

"You look good," he says finally. "For an old lady of . . . what? Thirty-one?"

"Thirty-two."

"For thirty-two you look great," he says, and laughs.

I don't go into the main part of the house until Jay-Jay leaves. As soon as I open the door, I realize that everyone has made a big mistake.

Eva's right here in this house. I can feel her. Her presence is so strong that I almost run after Jay-Jay to tell him to call off the search, that she has come back, but the cruiser has already turned the corner, so I'll have to call the station.

But first I have to see my Aunt Eva. She must have gone on a trip and not told anyone. She probably doesn't even know the whole town's looking for her.

"Eva?" I call to her. She doesn't answer. Her ears aren't very good, not anymore. I call again, louder. Still no answer, but I know she's here. She's up on the widow's walk or down in the root cellar mixing up a new kind of tea, something with bergamot and kum-quat essence. Or maybe she never left, is what I'm thinking, though I know that's not possible. They must have searched the house. At least I assume they did. Didn't anyone come in here, for God's sake? Didn't May? No, she wouldn't, damn her. But the cops would.

Or my brother. Of course Beezer would have looked. Of course that's the first thing they would have done. Eva wouldn't have been reported missing unless she actually *was* missing, right? But now she's back. *It's as plain as the nose on your face,* I think, laughing out loud because I'm still channeling Eva's clichés.

"Hey, Eva," I call to her, knowing how deaf she's gotten, but giving it a try anyway. "Eva, it's me."

I'm not sure where to start looking. I stand there, in the foyer. Ahead are two matching parlors with black marble fireplaces facing each other from the ends of the long rooms. One of the rooms is closed off; that's the one Eva uses as her tearoom. I enter the other one. It's more like a ballroom than a parlor. The fireplaces look empty with neither flames nor Eva's usual arrangements of flowers in them. Chairs are placed symmetrically and strategically, like pieces on a chessboard. I look at the huge suspended staircase. I know that my next move should be up, but I decide to check the tearoom first, then the other kitchen, and the root cellar, where she blends the teas. I'm calling to her, talking as I go, speaking loudly so that she'll hear me. I don't want to sneak up and scare her into having a heart attack or something.

She's probably upstairs. I'm not supposed to be climbing stairs yet, but I'm yelling to her now, and I realize I'm going to have to get up there. I use the railing to pull myself, but it's easier to climb now than it was a few days ago, even though I can still feel the pull of the stitches with each step. When I reach the second-floor landing, I'm dizzy and have to sit down on a bench and wait until everything stops spinning. Finally I make my way to Eva's room. Old canopy bed in the corner, fireplace, armoire. The bed is made, the pillows fluffed. I pick up a pillow and smell it, expecting Eva's scent. Instead it smells of orange water, which is what Eva uses to rinse her linens. She must have changed the sheets recently. I check the walk-in closet. Everything hangs perfectly on the hangers. There is no laundry in the bins, which means that she has already washed the old sheets.

I spent a lot of time in this room when Eva took me in, a lot of time in this closet, actually, which Eva probably found odd but which she never mentioned. Eva is not my blood relation; she was my grandfather G.G.'s second wife, and no relation at all. Still, she understands me in the way a mother should and my own mother never has.

There are six other bedrooms on the second floor. She keeps all but one of them closed up for the winter. Actually, she rarely opens any of them now unless she's expecting company, which happens more and more infrequently—or so she tells me every week, when she calls. Slowly I move through each of the rooms, looking for her, talking as I go. The ghost furniture stands pale, covered in sheets against the dust.

Exhausted, I climb to the third floor. Even now, at eighty-five, my aunt has more energy than I do. Somehow I know she is up here on the third floor. "Eva," I say again. "It's me, Towner." I ascend the narrowing stairs heavily, holding both railings. I'm so tired.

This third floor is my floor. Eva gave it to me the winter I moved in with her, partly to appease me for having to move off Yellow Dog Island, which I loved so much, and partly because the third floor had the widow's walk, and she knew I could use it to keep an eye on things, like May still alone out there on the island, refusing to come in. Except for an occasional climb to the widow's walk, Eva doesn't use these rooms at all now, and, as she tells me often, she hasn't changed them since I moved. "They'll be ready when you are," she always says, and follows with some other zinger such as, "There's no place like home."

I climb the widow's walk first, because I know it's the only place Eva would go if she came up here. But there's no sign of her. The only thing up here is a gull's nest; I can't tell whether it's a new one or something left behind. I stand alone at the top of what was once my world. How many nights have I sat up here, checking on May, making sure her kerosene lamp went on in early evening, then off again when she finally went to bed? Every night of that one winter I spent here.

Salem Harbor has changed. There are a lot more boats than there used to be, and more houses around the perimeter on the Marblehead side, but Yellow Dog Island looks the same. If I squint my eyes and look past the harbor, I can imagine that I am a kid again and that at any minute I'll see the sail from Lyndley's yacht as it rounds Peach's Point and heads toward our island for the summer.

I go back down to the third floor, where my rooms are. This is the only place I haven't yet looked for Eva and the only place left where she could be. There are four rooms on this floor, which is gabled and smaller than the second floor, but the furniture up here is not covered with sheets, which seems odd, since Eva didn't know I was coming. One room is a small library filled with all my school things: my desk, cotillion invitations, report cards. There were books required for school, and books that Eva required me to read when she didn't think the school curriculum went far enough, old leather-bound books from the big library on the first floor: Dickens, Chaucer, Proust. Across the hall is the room that Beezer slept in on Christmas and during his winter vacations from boarding school. The last two rooms were my private suite, a sitting room with two fluffy couches and a little Chinese table between them. At the far end of the room, through French doors, is my bedroom. Since I've looked everywhere else, and since I know she's got to be in the house somewhere, I figure this is where Eva has to be.

I push open the door, scanning the floor first, suddenly afraid. Maybe she didn't come back. Maybe she's been here all along, and they just didn't check well enough. Maybe she has fallen somewhere up here and she's just been lying here in horrible pain the whole time. "Eva," I say again, dreading what I'm going to find as I open the door to what is the last room in the house, the last place she could be. "Eva, answer me."

I'm afraid I'll see her sprawled on the floor with broken bones, or worse. I close my eyes against the thought. But when I open them, there is nothing. Just the room as I left it the year I turned seventeen: the same Indian-print bedspread that Lyndley bought me in Harvard Square, one of Eva's patchwork quilts folded into a triangle at the bottom of the bed. On the wall across from the bed is a painting that Lyndley did for me the year before she died, all shades of blues and blacks with a golden path leading into deep water. It is a painting of the dream we shared, entitled *Swimming to the Moon.*

I walk over and stare at the painting, and I remember a lot of other things then, like the time Lyndley stole a huge bunch of flowers from Eva's gardens and got in trouble for it, too, because she almost wiped out Eva's annuals. She had my whole room on Yellow Dog Island completely decorated with those flowers when I got home that day, and she'd really overdone it; they were everywhere. May said it was too much, that it smelled like a funeral parlor. It made her sick to her stomach, she said. Lyndley thought that was an accomplishment in itself, making anyone sick with her artistic renderings. For some reason she found that very funny. It gave her an idea. She made me put on a dress and actually lie down on the bed like a corpse holding flowers on my belly, like Millais's painting of Ophelia, and she said I looked beautiful as a dead person, and she started sketching me, but I ruined it because I couldn't stop laughing, which made the flowers shake too much to draw.

I am jolted back to present time by the sound of footsteps on the stairway.

"Well, there you are," Eva says, not even winded. I reel around. She's wearing an old flowered housedress, one I remember, and she doesn't look a day older than the last time I saw her, the year she came to L.A. with some garden-club group to see how the Rose Bowl floats were made.

I start to cry, I am so relieved to see her. I take a step toward her, but I'm dizzy from turning so quickly.

"You'd better sit down before you fall down," Eva says, smiling, reaching out a hand to steady me, leading me toward the bed. "You look like something the cat dragged in."

"I'm so glad you're all right," I say, collapsing onto the bed.

"Of course I'm all right," she says, as if not a thing has happened.

She covers me with the quilt. Though it is far too hot, I do not protest. This is a ritual of comfort; she has done this more than once.

"I thought you were dead," I say, sobbing now, with relief and with exhaustion. There's so much to say, but she's shushing me, telling me she's "right as rain" and that I should get some rest now, that "things will look better in the morning." I know I should tell her to call Jay-Jay and also Beezer and let them know that she's okay, but her voice is hypnotic, and I'm starting to fall asleep.

"Rest your weary bones," she says, reading my mind the same way she's always been able to read my mind, pulling the concerns right out of it, putting peaceful images in their place. "Things will look better in the morning," she says again.

She starts toward the door, then turns back. "Thank you for coming," she says. "I know this must have been difficult for you." Then she takes something out of the pocket of her dress and lays it down on the bedside table. "I meant to send this with the pillow," she says. "But I am old, and memory isn't what it once was."

I struggle to see what she put on the table, but my eyes are heavy with sleep. "Pleasant dreams," she says as she walks out the door.

On her command I begin to dream, drifting up the stairs and out the widow's walk, then out over the harbor where the party boat is coming back from its cruise to nowhere, carrying a load of sunburned tourists. The sun is going down, and a new moon is rising behind Yellow Dog Island, our island, and I can see some women there on the dock, though I don't recognize them. Then I hear the blast from the party boat as it makes its turn, and I'm grounded back in the bed again, sleeping there. Two blasts as it heads into port. You can set your watch by those horns. Three times a day, you hear the horns as the boat comes back to Salem after each run—at noon and six, and again at midnight, on its last run of the night.

Like the muffs they resemble, the lace pillows were gathered and tied on each end. Traditionally, each pillow also had a pocket, and the women of Ipswich used the pockets to hold their treasures. Some held beautiful bobbins imported from England or Brussels, too precious to ever use. Other pockets held small pieces of finished lace, or herbs, or even small touchstones. Some hid poetry written in the owner's hand, or love letters from a suitor, which were read over and over until the parchment began to tear along its creases.

—THE LACE READER'S GUIDE

Chapter 4

When I wake up, I look on the bedside table, expecting to find a note. Instead I see my braid where Eva left it last night. Almost waist length the day Eva cut it, today it would reach only to my shoulders. I pick it up. The hair is fine, more like Lyndley's hair than my own. The length shows bands of color like the rings of a tree, a summer's sun, a winter's darkness. At one end is a faded ribbon, tied in a double-knotted bow. At the other, fine hair curling up around it, is a dried-out rubber band Eva put on after she cut the braid from me. It is wound very tight, as if to hold everything still and together.

Hair is full of magic, Eva always says. I don't know if that's true for everyone, but at least it's true for my mother, May.

May would never leave Yellow Dog Island for long. For this reason she didn't take us to Salem for haircuts, but to a barber in Marblehead who had a shop only a few feet from the public landing.

Old Mr. Dooling always smelled strongly of stale whiskey and fried food and vaguely of camphor. He was likely to wound you anytime before noon. Rumor had it he'd once slashed a kid's ear right off. My mother insisted she'd never believed that story. Still, May always booked our hair appointments in the afternoons, when the barber's hands were steadier and his alcohol haze had burned off along with the harbor fog.

May's haircuts were Marblehead's version of a magic show. The townie kids used to form lines up and down Front Street to watch as Mr. Dooling pulled the rattail comb through my mother's hair. With each pull, the comb would snag on something, then stop. As he reached into the mass to unwind the tangle, he would find and remove everything from sea glass to shells to smooth stones. In one particularly matted tangle, he found a sea horse. Once he even found a postcard sent from Tahiti to someone in Beverly Farms. On it were two Polynesian women, bare breasts covered discreetly by long, straight hair. I never figured out if he was sighing because of the girls and their various attributes or because of their straight, untangled hair that—although it might not have yielded treasures like my mother's—wouldn't have required a full bottle of conditioner for a single haircut.

The day my mother and I began to break apart was over a haircut—not hers, but mine. My mother had finished. Beezer had gone next, getting the Whiffle Deluxe, which cost $4.99 and came with a tube of stick-up for the front.

I had never liked having my hair cut, partly because of the wharf rats hanging around outside watching the whole thing and partly because Mr. Dooling's hands shook so much. On one occasion I covered my ears with Band-Aids before we got to town, figuring they'd be harder to lop off if the barber made a mistake. But May caught me and made me remove the bandages.

Although I wasn't fond of haircuts, they had never actually hurt me until that day. I watched as Mr. Dooling fished the scissors out of the blue gook and wiped them on his apron. The first cut sent a jolt through me like an electric shock. I let out a cry.

"What's wrong?"

"It hurts!"

"What hurts?" May examined my scalp, my ears. Finding nothing amiss, she asked again. "*What* hurts?"

"My hair."

"The hairs on your head?"

"Yes."

"Individual hairs?"

"I don't know."

She examined me again. "You're fine," she said, motioning for him to continue.

Mr. Dooling picked up a lock of hair, fumbled, dropped it. He stopped, put down the scissors, wiped his hands on his apron, then reached for the scissors again, this time dropping them on the floor.

"Jesus Christ," Beezer said. May shot him a look.

The barber went to the back room to get another pair of scissors, unwrapping them from their brown paper and making several practice snips in the air before he reached my side.

I gripped the chair arms, bracing as he picked up another lock of hair. I could hear him breathing. I could feel the chafing of cotton against cotton as his arm reached forward. And then I had what the doctors would later cite as my first full-blown hallucination. Visual and auditory, it was a flash cut to Medusa and thousands of writhing snake hairs. Snakes screaming, still moving as they were cut in half. Screaming so loudly that I couldn't make them stop; terrible animal screams like the time one of the dogs on our island got its leg caught in the tractor blade. I covered my ears, but the snakes were still screaming. . . . Then my brother's face, scared, pale, pulled me back, and I realized that the screaming was coming from me. Beezer was standing in front of me calling my name, calling me back. And suddenly I was out of the chair and lunging for the door.

The group of kids on the porch parted to let me through. Some of the smaller kids were crying. I ran down the stairs, hearing the door behind me open and slam a second time and Beezer yelling for me to wait.

When he reached the Whaler, I already had the bow and stern lines untied, and he had to make a running jump to get into the boat. He landed facedown, his wind knocked out. "Are you okay?" he wheezed.

I couldn't answer him.

I saw him looking back at May, who was out on the porch with Dooling, arms folded across her chest, just watching us.

I had to choke the engine three times before it caught and started. Then, ignoring the five-miles-per-hour limit, I opened it up, and my brother and I headed out to sea.

We talked only a few times about what had happened that day. May made two ill-fated attempts to get me to see reason, taking me to town once to talk to Eva about it and the other time calling someone at the Museum of Science in Boston and asking him to explain to me that there were no nerve endings in hair and that it couldn't possibly hurt when it was cut.

Sometimes, when you look back, you can point to a time when your world shifts and heads in another direction. In lace reading this is called the "still point." Eva says it's the point around which everything pivots and real patterns start to emerge. The haircut was the still point for my mother and me, the day everything changed. It happened in an instant, a millisecond, the flash of a look, the intake of breath.

For two years no one cut my hair. I went around with one long side and one short.

"You're being ridiculous," May said to me once, coming at me with a pair of scissors, attempting to finish the haircut and take back her power. "I won't have it." But I didn't let her near me then or anytime after that.

We had family dinners every night, sandwiches mostly, because May would shop on the docks only once a month when she went to town. The sandwiches were always served in the formal dining room on the good china and were followed by a small Limoges plate of multivitamins, which my mother referred to as "dessert." This final course could take a long time to finish, because May required us to eat the vitamins with a dessert fork, all the while practicing polite dinner conversation, something she had learned from Eva.

"I have a question," I said, balancing two vitamins on my knife.

May gave me "the look." I put my knife down. "Yes?" she said, waiting for me to ask in the small-talk style we had developed in order to keep from really talking about anything.

"Why did you give away my sister?"

Beezer's eyes widened. It wasn't the kind of thing we talked about. Ever.

May started to clear the table. I thought I could see a tear forming in the corner of her eye, but it never fell.

After dinner I went to my room. My haven. No one came in anymore. Every night I wore a ski hat to bed with one of May's nylon stockings under it, covering my scalp, so that she couldn't come in and trim my hair at night. I rigged my room with booby traps:

strings, bells, crystal glasses I'd stolen from the butler's pantry—anything that would wake me at the first sign of an intruder. It worked. My mother gave up. Once, my dog Skybo, whom Beezer had given to me for protection the summer before, got so badly tangled in the strings that we had to cut him free, but no one else bothered me. After a while May stopped coming into my room at all, but I never let my guard down, not for one minute.

It was Eva who finally fixed things. One day in late summer, I went to see her at her shop, begging for a lace reading. Except on my birthday, which was a family tradition, I didn't usually ask Eva to read for me. I didn't really like to be read—it made me feel creepy—but I was desperate. I'd lost Skybo. He was an unfixed male, and he had a tendency to wander. He was one of the island golden retrievers, trained by Beezer as a puppy, so even though he was tame enough for the house, he still had a wild streak. He was a great swimmer. Whenever I swam or took the boat, he followed me. Sometimes he set out all by himself.

I was a mess. I'd looked everywhere on Yellow Dog Island. I took the Whaler to town. I searched the wharf, the marine-supply store, and even some of the fishing fleet but turned up nothing. Finally I headed for Eva's.

She was working on a piece of pillow lace, sitting beside a fireplace that was filled with chrysanthemums instead of flames.

It was late in the season, and the water was really cold. I was frantic. I told her the story, told her I feared the worst—hypothermia, maybe, or that he had been caught in a shipping lane and run over. Eva looked at me calmly and told me to get myself a cup of tea.

"I can't drink tea. My dog is missing," I snapped.

Like May, Eva had also mastered "the look." I made the tea. She kept working. Every once in a while, she would glance up and gesture to the tea. "Don't let it get cold," she said. I sipped.

After what seemed a very long time, Eva put down the lace pillow and walked over to where I was sitting. She had a small pair of scissors in her hand, the ones she used to cut the lace free when she finished a piece, a technique Eva had invented. Instead of cutting lace, she reached over and cut off my braid.

"There," she said. "The spell is broken. You are free."

She put the braid down on the table.

"What the hell?"

"Watch your mouth, young lady."

I stood and glared at her.

"You can go now," she declared.

"What about my dog?" I snapped.

"Don't worry about your dog," she said.

I walked back to the Whaler, wondering if everyone I knew was crazy. I knew I was. May was pretty far gone, getting more reclusive by the minute. And Eva, whom I usually found so logical, was not acting the way she should, not at all.

When I got to the Whaler, Skybo was sitting in the bow. He was wet and tired and covered with burrs, but I was so happy to see him that I didn't even care where he'd been.

The women created their own patterns made of parchment, but thicker parchment than for the love letters, more enduring. Pins were pressed into the parchment, creating a pricking pattern that could be used over and over. For the lace making, the pins stayed in, holding the patterns to the pillow, and the lace was woven pin to pin. If there was any limiting factor to the production of more intricate laces, it was the expense and scarcity of pins.

—THE LACE READER'S GUIDE

Chapter 5

It is just after sunrise. I cannot get back to sleep. Placing the braid of hair in the drawer of the bedside table, I quietly make my way downstairs. I start to dial Beezer's number, then decide to wait an hour. I want to tell him that Eva's all right. Beezer has been great. He doesn't need this, not now. My brother and his long-time girlfriend, Anya, are about to be married. As soon as exams are over, they will be flying to Norway, where her parents live. After the ceremony they are going to travel around Europe for the summer. They will be so relieved, I think, both that Eva is okay and that they don't have to change their wedding plans.

I'm making mental notes. Call May. Call the cops. Although none of them deserves a call. I don't know how any of them could be so stupid that they couldn't find an eighty-five-year-old woman in her own house.

I let myself into the tearoom, with its frescoed walls painted by a semifamous artist my great-grandfather had flown in from Italy. I can't remember the name. Small tables crowd the room. Lace is everywhere. Some of the pieces bear May's company label, The Circle, but most of them Eva has made herself. A glass counter in the corner holds canisters with every kind of tea imaginable—commercial teas from all over the world, as well as several flower and herb potions that Eva blends. If you want a cup of coffee, you won't find it here. My eyes scan the teas looking for the one she named after me. She gave me that tea as a present one year. It's a blend of black tea and cayenne and cinnamon, with just a hint of cilantro, and some other ingredients she won't reveal to me. It has to be drunk strong and very hot, and Eva tells me it is too spicy for some of her older customers. "Either you'll love it or you'll hate it," she told me when she gave it to me. I loved it. I used to drink whole pots of it, winters when I lived with Eva. On the canister it's called "Sophya's Blend," but its nickname, just between Eva and me, is "Difficult-Tea."

Behind the canister is a notebook, its cover a poem I recognize, the Jenny Joseph poem that is getting so popular. *"When I am an old woman, I shall wear purple / With a red hat which doesn't go, and doesn't suit me. . . ."* Stuck inside the notebook are some photos, one of Beezer and May and one of me when I first got to California, my forced smile slackened from the Stelazine I was still taking.

From the look of things, Eva has a children's party set up for today. I check the calendar on the wall, but it's a lunar calendar, not a regular one, and it's difficult to read. The slivered phases of the moon are printed in shades of gray on the corresponding dates. Just when I begin to think I have it figured out, I spot a different kind of moon, a bright red full moon stuck halfway through the month. It's a little larger than the other moons and doesn't correspond to any of their cycles. It takes me a minute to realize it's not a moon but a hat. I remember Eva telling me about the Red Hats who were inspired by the poem. The ones who wear purple and come for tea and lace readings here at least once a month.

The tables are already set. Each table has a different pot, with different teacups and saucers set on individual circles of lace. The pots are very fanciful and colorful. If you choose to come for tea on a regular day, one that's not already booked for a private party, the lace at your table setting, once you use it, is yours to keep. You pay for it, whether or not you have a lace reading done. Many people just take their lace pieces home and use them as doilies. This never bothers Eva, even though I've always thought it was a waste, that the lace circles are pieces of art and should be framed.

Most of Eva's customers come for tea really hoping to get a lace reading. Eva never does more than two readings a day anymore; she says it wears her out, particularly now that she's getting older. She does not keep any money from her readings. All the money she collects for the lace and the readings goes directly to the Circle.

She'll do more than two readings if she has to. And if she senses real disappointment, or something urgent that the seeker should know, she'll even do the reading for free. But what she's most interested in is teaching the women to read for themselves. "Pick up the lace and look at it," she says. "Squint your eyes." If you follow her instructions, you start to imagine that you see pictures in the lace, the way Eva does. "Go ahead," she encourages them. "Don't be afraid. There is no wrong answer. This is your own life you're reading, your own symbols."

I find a teaspoon with the Whitney monogram and look around for my favorite teapot, which is actually an old china coffeepot that Eva has converted. I warm the pot, then brew the tea. I grab a cup and the lunar calendar and go to the only table in the room that isn't already set. On the table is Eva's worn first edition of Emily Post.

Before my great-aunt opened the tearoom, she taught manners classes to the children of Boston's North Shore. Kids from Marblehead, Swampscott, Beverly Farms, Hamilton, Wenham, and as far away as Cape Ann came to Eva for refinement. She'd set one of the tables in the parlor for a formal dinner, and the children would arrive in their little suits and dresses to brush up on their table manners. She taught polite dinner conversation, tricks to avoid the shyness that descends on children during such events.

"Keep asking questions," she advised. "It gets the conversation going and keeps the focus off you. Find out what they're interested in and what their preferences are. Offer something of yourself in the question; it's more intimate that way. For example, appropriate dinner conversation might be to turn to the person next to you and say, 'I like soup. Do you like soup?'"

She made the kids practice asking each other if they liked soup, invariably prompting giggles because the question was so inane. But it broke the ice. "There," she would say after such an exercise. "Don't you feel more comfortable already?" And the kids had to admit they did. "Now ask another question, and make sure you really listen this time for the answer," she would say. "One of the secrets of good manners is learning to listen."

I drink a whole pot of tea. At seven o'clock I call Beezer. No answer. I make another pot of tea.

I try Beezer again at eight. Still no answer. I decide to make Eva a pot of tea and take it up to her.

Someone knocks on the tearoom door. At first I think it's Beezer, but it's not. A girl, not much older than eighteen (if she's that), stands there, backpack across her shoulders, greasy hair parted on the side and hanging shoulder length, half covering a huge strawberry-colored birthmark that runs down the left side of her face. My immediate thought is that this is just another kid looking for a room or a reading, but when I glance out at the common, the festival is over. The only people left out there now are dog walkers and some Park & Rec guys cleaning up. I start for the door, wanting to answer it quickly, to keep things quiet for Eva, but then the teapot screams, and I rush back to silence it, burning my hand as I grab the handle.

She bangs again, louder this time, more urgently. I start back toward the door. I can see her through the wavy glass. There is a look on her face that reminds me of my sister, Lyndley. Or maybe it's the way she bangs on the door, pounding it hard, as if she might punch right through it. As I hurry toward the door, I spot the police cruiser patrolling, trying to find a space to pull into. I see the girl look over her shoulder at the cruiser. By the time I reach the door, she is halfway down the steps. As she turns to go, I see that she is pregnant. I open the door, but she is too fast for me. She slips down the alley away from the street just as the cruiser pulls in.

I put the teapot and cups on the tray and start upstairs when there's another knock at the door. Cursing, I put the tray down on the step and go to the door. My brother stands in front of Jay-Jay and some other guy I don't recognize.

"I've been calling you," I say to Beezer. I'm trying not to look excited, trying not to give it away.

They come in, and Beezer hugs me, holding it too long. I pull away then, to tell him that everything's all right, that Eva is here.

"I was just going to try you again—" I tell him.

"This is Detective Rafferty," Beezer says, interrupting me.

There is a long pause before Rafferty speaks. "We found Eva's body," he says finally, "out a little past Children's Island."

I stand still. I can't move.

"Oh, Towner," Beezer says, hugging me again, as much to keep me standing up as to commiserate. "I can't believe she's dead."

"Looks like she drowned," Rafferty says. "Or went hypothermic. Sadly, it's not uncommon at her age, even outside the water." His voice breaks slightly on that last part.

I run up the stairs, doubling over in pain as I reach the first landing, leaving them all standing there looking startled, not knowing what to do. I stumble into Eva's room, but she's not there. Her bed is still made, untouched since yesterday.

As quickly as I can, I move through the maze of rooms. Eva is old now, I'm thinking; maybe she doesn't sleep here anymore. Maybe she's chosen some other room to sleep in, something smaller. But even as I'm thinking it, I'm starting to freak out. I'm moving frantically from one room to another when Beezer catches up with me. "Towner?" I hear his voice getting closer.

I stop dead in the middle of the hallway.

"Are you okay?" he asks.

Clearly I'm not.

"I just came from identifying the body," he says.

I can hear their voices, cops' voices, echoing up the stairs, but I can't hear what they're saying.

"May knows," he says, giving me practical details, trying to ground me. "Detective Rafferty went out there to tell her this morning."

I am able to nod.

"She and Emma are waiting for us to come out," Beezer says.

I nod again, following him downstairs. The cops stop talking when they see me.

"I'm so sorry," Jay-Jay says, and I nod again. It's all I can do.

Rafferty's eyes meet mine, but he doesn't say anything. I notice a quick reach of his hand, comforting, automatic. Then he catches himself and pulls it back. He puts it in his jacket pocket as if he doesn't know what else to do with it.

"I should have stopped her," Beezer says, his guilt overtaking him now. "I mean, I would have if I'd known. She told me she had given up swimming. Last year sometime."

Because they were imported from England, pins were costly. The fewer pins used, the simpler the pattern, and the faster the lace maker could work. The thread was imported, because although the New England spinners were very good, they could not achieve the delicacy of the fine European linen or Chinese silk thread. Still, on average, each of the Ipswich lace makers produced upwards of seven inches of lace per day, a higher rate than the Circle produces today, and the Circle has the luxury of its own spinners and all the pins they could ever want.

—THE LACE READER'S GUIDE

Chapter 6

Rafferty is a nice man. He gives us a ride to Derby Wharf so we can pick up the Whaler. He circles the block looking for a space, then finally pulls onto the public walkway, getting us as close as possible to Eva's boathouse. "I'd have one of the guys in the police boat take you all the way out," he said, "but the last time they went out there, May shot at them."

You've probably heard of my mother, May Whitney. Everyone else has. I'm sure you remember the UPI picture a few years back, the one with May leveling a six-gauge at about twenty cops who had come to her women's shelter on Yellow Dog Island with a warrant to take back one of her girls. That picture was everywhere. It was even on the cover of *Newsweek*. What made the photo so compelling was that my mother looked uncannily like Maureen O'Hara in some fifties western. Cowering behind May in the photo was a terrified-looking girl who couldn't have been more than twenty-two, with a large white bandage on her neck, rescued from a husband who'd gotten drunk and tried to slit her throat. Her two little children sat behind her playing with a litter of golden retriever puppies. It was quite a scene. If you saw it, you'd remember.

In fact, it was that picture, coupled with a flair for public relations—both seemingly out of character for May—that revived the entire Ipswich lace industry. In a series of well-chosen interviews, she condescended to speak to the press, not about the newly rescued girl, which was the story they came out there to get, but about the bobbin lace that the other women, or "island girls" (as the locals called them), created. They called themselves "the Circle," after the old-time ladies' sewing circles, and that was the name that appeared on their labels.

May took the press on a tour of the cottage industry that she and her island girls were re-creating. First she took them to the spinning room, which was located in the old stone kennel. It had been built by my grandfather, G. G. Whitney, in an effort to breed and domesticate the island dogs, but he could never get them to go near the place, so it had stood empty until May's girls took it over. Once inside the stone kennel (if you ignored the anachronism of jeans and other modern garb), you could have been in a medieval castle. The women sat at the old spinning wheels and at the bobbin winders, silent except for the whirring and occasional creaking and clicking. This spinning room was where the new girls came, the newly rescued, those who were still too skittish to join the others. May often spun with them. They wove flax mostly, to make linen thread, and sometimes May wove yarns from the yellow dog hair, but that was rare. Although some stayed in the spinning room, most of these abused women went on to join the circle of lace makers in the old red schoolhouse as soon as they felt strong enough to be with people again.

May ended her tours at the schoolhouse, where the women sat with their pillows on their laps, making lace and chatting softly or listening to a reader (often my mother herself, who had a beautiful speaking voice and loved to read poetry aloud). Enchanted by the world May had created and the spell-like web of lace May spun around them, the reporters ended up forgetting the story they came out to get. Instead they went back to their papers and wrote about the Circle. The story resonated with their female readers, and women all over the country began sending money to purchase this new Ipswich lace.

Beezer lets me drive the Whaler. When we get to the island, the tide is dead low and the ramp is up. We could land at the float, but we'd have no way to get onto the island with the ramp up like this. For just a minute, I consider trying to land at Back Beach, which is impossible at low tide and hardly possible at any other time. The tide would have to be turning high and the sea dead calm to even attempt such a landing. So I figure I'll just have to land at the float and sit there waiting until someone notices us and lowers the ramp.

People who live on islands like their solitude. I don't mean islands like the Vineyard or Nantucket. People on those islands are so far from shore that they need to attract tourists just to survive. But people on these border islands generally like to be left alone, and they pull up their ramps because they are vulnerable. An island is a landing point for anyone who happens by. People assume that islands are public property: They picnic, they litter. They walk up to your front door and ask to use the phone, never considering for a moment that you probably have neither phone nor electricity. And so island people learn to pull up their ramps. Usually it's only a few feet, but it makes all the difference. At high tide the difference between the float and the ramp may be only five or six feet. Most people could make it, if they are willing to take that leap of faith, but few will. When the tide is dead low, the ramp is another ten feet down, and that's when you really feel your privacy.

Yellow Dog Island is more private than most. The whole square-mile figure eight of it is set high on a granite plateau with spires of rock shooting up from the surrounding water, giving the impression of an ancient fortress. Unless you know about Back Beach, the island is impenetrable. Because of the sheer drop of the cliffs, the dock was built about forty feet in the air, which makes the distance from the ramp down to the float even longer. It takes a hydraulic winch to lower the ramp, and this is one of the only spots on the island that has a generator, which also runs the salt-water pump to the houses for the plumbing, such as it is. When we still attended school on the island and my mother would give us a reading assignment, I would sit in the pump house and read by the one lightbulb on the island until the generator ran out of gas or I fell asleep. That one bulb represented all of civilization for me, and I took good care of it.

There are several outbuildings on the island, but only two real houses, one on each end, belonging to May and to my Auntie Emma Boynton, who is Eva's daughter, May's half sister, and my sister Lyndley's legal mother. My aunt's house is the larger of the two Victorians, but May's is the only one that is winterized. Until Emma's "accident," while she and Cal were still married, Auntie Emma and her "daughter," Lyndley, were summer people, and I guess my Uncle Cal was, too, if you want to count him, which I don't.

These days the women of the Circle all live at May's house. They catch rainwater in cisterns for drinking. They grow vegetables for food and flax for the lace, and they even have a cow, which, according to Eva, had to be airlifted onto the island by the coast guard. They tried for a while to keep sheep on what used to be a makeshift baseball diamond, but the dogs kept running the sheep, so they had to give that up. Now they get by on vegetables and the occasional rabbit, and, of course, fish and lobsters. I don't know what they do in the winter. I've never asked. I know as much as I do only because Eva has written me letters about it.

Beezer and I have been sitting on the float for about twenty minutes before anyone comes to lower the ramp. Finally it is my Auntie Emma, and not my mother, who shows up. She walks with her head bent forward, moving more slowly than I remember, partly from her infirmity and partly from age. She is much older than the last time I saw her, almost fifteen years older, come August. My heart catches when I see her; and though she cannot see me, she suddenly realizes I am there. It's like the take Melanie does in *Gone with the Wind* when she sees Ashley come back from the Civil War and suddenly recognizes that beaten-down man as her beloved husband. My aunt doesn't rush to me—she cannot do that—but her feelings rush forward, and they knock the breath right out of me.

By the time we reach her, she is crying. We stand there for a long time, hugging each other. She is crying and saying things like, "I knew you'd come," and "I told her so."

My heart sinks for a moment. She is so happy to see me that I wonder if she thinks I am her daughter, Lyndley. In a way it would be more likely. Because even though I know the physical laws of this strange planet and the impossibility of such a thing, I also know that it would be less of a miracle for my sister, Lyndley, dead more than fifteen years now, to come back here than it was for me.

We walk together up the ramp in slow motion, frame by frame. She's too weak to walk fast anymore, and I'm having so much trouble catching my breath that I can't even speak. But that's okay, because I wouldn't know what to say if I could. Ahead of us, at the top of the ramp, some gulls knock over one of the garbage cans. It rolls several feet, then stops just before reaching the edge of the cliff.

"May is waiting for you," Auntie Emma says, pointing to the old schoolhouse at the crest of the hill. She starts to walk with me, then takes Beezer's arm. She rests her head on his shoulder and cries softly.

"I'm so sorry about Eva," Beezer says.

I am surprised to realize that she knows and understands what has just happened to Eva. The "accident" that blinded her also left my aunt with brain damage.

Sometimes Emma knows who I am, sometimes not, Eva told me more than once.

The door to the red schoolhouse is open. I can see the Circle. They are sitting with their lace pillows on their laps. Some are working hard, passing bobbin over bobbin, winding their lives into the patterns as they go. Others are barely working at all but are listening, staring off at something not quite there, captivated by the reader's voice, my mother's, strong and clear. Quoting from Blake's *Songs of Innocence and of Experience:*

Then come home, my children, the sun is gone down,
And dews of the night arise; . . .

Her voice catches when she sees me in the doorway. It is so slight she doesn't miss a single beat but goes on . . .

Your spring and your day are wasted in play,
And your winter and night in disguise.

As May closes the book and takes a step in our direction, I hear another voice, one that's even stronger than my mother's.

"*There are no accidents,*" Eva says as Beezer and I step through the door.

What distinguishes Ipswich lace from all other handmade laces are the bobbins. The colonial women could not afford the heavier decorative bobbins used by European women. Like everyone else in the Colonies, the lace makers had to make do with what was at hand. And so the bobbins they wound the thread upon were lighter, sometimes hollow, fabricated from beach reeds or occasionally bamboo that came in on the Salem ships as packing material, or even from bones.

—THE LACE READER'S GUIDE

Chapter 7

We're all at May's house now. Beezer's fiancée, Anya, got here last night. They were supposed to leave for Norway tomorrow, for the wedding (which is only a week away). However, the trip has been postponed for a few days, until after Eva's funeral. Anya is clearly not happy about it; really, why should she be? I think she's being a pretty good sport about things, under the circumstances. I know how uneasy this place makes her. She told me that when she accompanied Beezer to California on a lecture tour that included Caltech. I have a certain respect for Anya's honesty, but I still don't like her. I think that's partly because she doesn't like me—doesn't like any of us, really, besides Beezer. I wonder about it, about how much my brother has told her, but Beezer isn't a talker. When I asked him how things went—when he identified Eva's body for instance—he muttered something about it being very difficult and about "crustaceans." I knew if I wanted to know more, I'd have to ask him, point by point, but I was put off by his choice of words and decided I didn't want to know.

This morning Beezer and Anya are sleeping in, but the rest of us are here, in the red schoolhouse, waiting for the minister to get here to meet with us and make arrangements for the service at the Unitarian church where Eva was a member. Dr. Ward will be arriving by water taxi. He has come out of retirement for Eva's funeral. They were friends, those two. For a number of years. We can see the boat, still far away, but getting closer.

No one's talking except for two small children, a boy and a girl, who are seated on the schoolhouse floor in the far corner, playing jacks. The floor is tilted with age and disrepair, and every time they bounce the ball, it rolls away from them. The kids find this very amusing. They giggle and scramble to reach it before it rolls out the door.

A nervous young woman, presumably their mother, watches them do this two or three times before the sound of the bouncing ball begins to grate on her nerves. Unable to stand it any longer, she walks over and takes the ball away. The little girl begins to cry; this in turn makes the mother cry. Seeing this, the women of the Circle move in, comforting the young mother, surrounding her.

"Let them play," one of the older women suggests. "Play is good." The woman takes the ball from the mother and hands it back to the little girl, who looks at it suspiciously.

Then one of the women spots the water taxi at the float and someone getting out of it. I recognize the minister immediately, even after all these years, but this woman doesn't, and I see her tense.

"It's okay." May puts a comforting hand on her shoulder. "He's here to see me."

The nervous young mother lets herself be led back to the Circle. The women are talking to her quietly now, saying things I can't make out, until they finally coax a smile from her. The little girl doesn't resume playing but puts the ball down intentionally and watches it roll slowly toward the open door, where it stops momentarily, then bounces down the granite steps, popping up twice before it disappears out of sight. The only picture left in the frame of the open doorway is that of May hurrying toward the dock to meet the minister.

May thinks it's better if we bring Dr. Ward to the main house, away from the women, who are skittish (at best), plus "they're working on the lace anyway, and we shouldn't interrupt them with our business." When we get to the house, Beezer and Anya are finally up. He's had his coffee and now gets some for the minister. Anya doesn't help, but she is attached to him, as usual. He compensates for it, like someone with a disability does, learning to move with her, forgetting after a while that this isn't the way he has always walked.

"We're thinking of a change of venue," says Dr. Ward, stirring in another teaspoon of sugar, clinking the sides of the cup with his spoon. "Probably move the funeral down the street, to St. James's."

"Why would we do that?" asks May.

"Because there are just so many attendees. The Catholic church is the only place that can accommodate so many people."

"How many people?" May has a bad feeling about it already.

"We think about two hundred," he says, "give or take."

"Two hundred people?" Anya is amazed. "I wouldn't get two hundred people at my funeral if *I* died."

"Give or take," he says again.

I can almost see May's skin crawling at the thought of so many people. She can't stay seated but gets up and starts to move around.

"Two hundred people," Anya says again.

"Eva had a lot of friends," Beezer tells her, partly to shut her up. "All those etiquette classes."

"All those witches," May says, frowning.

The minister shifts uncomfortably. Some people, certainly the Calvinists, would consider May to be one of "those witches." Even more so now that they call themselves "the Circle." He remembered it from when they'd changed their name, their business name, officially from "the Island Girls" to "the Circle." He hadn't liked it then, and he'd told Eva so. It had a certain connotation, that name, and he thought they should stay away from it. He'd always wondered—well, everybody wondered, really—what actually went on out here. Some people would consider these women a coven. It was logical, with witches everywhere in Salem now, to consider any group of women a coven, especially a group that refers to itself as "the Circle." Eva had laughed at him when he'd told her that, telling him to get with it, that it wasn't named after witches but after the old-time ladies' sewing circles that women used to have. Still, he thought it could be misinterpreted. "Career-limiting" were his actual words, but they went ahead and did it anyway. And as far as he could see, it hadn't been limiting at all. Eva had started to sell the lace made by the Circle in her tearoom shortly after that, and it had been selling well ever since. Well, you'd have to be crazy, wouldn't you, to take business advice from a minister? Still, he was sort of relieved now, to realize that not only was May not a witch herself but that she didn't seem even to like the witches. In that way, he thought, she was like the Calvinists.

"Who are the Calvinists?" I ask, unaware until I say it that I have been reading him. He startles. Dr. Ward's mind is so easy to read, so open, that I can't help it. That's the way it is sometimes with holy people. Their thoughts are right out there for the world to see, not guarded like the rest of ours.

May was really agitated now. I thought at first that maybe she was angry because I was reading the minister without being invited; that was another of Eva's etiquette rules. You don't read anyone's mind unless they invite you—it's intrusive, like trespassing. But I knew that if I could read this man so easily, then May could read him as well; we are all readers to some extent, although May won't admit to it. She *will* acknowledge that she's incredibly intuitive, which I would argue is almost the same thing. So either she is still angry about the witches, which I don't understand at all, or she is angry at me for reading the minister. In any case, her anger is palpable. Even he can feel it.

"What do you think?" Dr. Ward is waiting for an answer.

"You already know what I think," May says. "I don't think we should have a funeral at all."

"I think Eva would have wanted *some* kind of a ceremony," Dr. Ward says.

"A ceremony would be nice." These are the first words that Auntie Emma has spoken.

"Eva was quite religious, you know," Dr. Ward offers.

"Eva? Religious?" May laughs out loud.

Although I'd rather side with Dr. Ward than May any day, even I have to agree with my mother on this one. Eva was a church member, but she wasn't what anyone would call religious. In the summertime she did the flowers for the First Church. And she could debate Scripture with the best of them. But she seldom attended services. She told me once that her idea of spirituality was working outside in her garden or swimming.

"Well, I think she would have wanted something," Dr. Ward says. His voice has a bit of an edge to it, which he quickly hides under a forced smile.

"Then I think you should be the one to do the planning," May says, and walks out. And now I'm angry, because this is just like May, to leave us all sitting here this way. My mother has been known to hold off the county sheriff, the Salem police, and a dozen aggressive reporters all at the same time. She can run a thriving business or give a great interview to *Newsweek,* but when it comes to family, she can't handle anything.

"I don't know why anyone is even asking her opinion." I say a bit too harshly. "I'll bet you ten to one she won't even show up for the funeral if we do have one."

"You showed up, didn't you?" Beezer's voice also has an edge. He quickly feels guilty. "I'm sorry," he says, "but can we please not do this?"

"Sorry," I say, and mean it.

"Maybe we should just have it at the Unitarian church as planned," Dr. Ward says. "On a first-come, first-served basis."

I am picturing a deli counter where everyone takes a number. I keep the image to myself.

There is a long silence.

"Are you all right?" Dr. Ward finally asks me.

"I'm sorry," I repeat, not knowing what else to say.

"We're all sorry," Dr. Ward says, his eyes tearing up just a little. He reaches out a ministerial hand to touch my arm, but the tears have thrown his vision off, and his hand grasps at empty air.

Later, when they think they're alone in the house, I hear Anya talking to Beezer. "You have the strangest family," she says. She means it affectionately; it's supposed to be a little joke.

I know his expression without seeing his face. He doesn't smile.

When I was in the bin, after Lyndley killed herself, I signed myself up for shock therapy. It was against Eva's wishes and certainly against May's (which was part of the reason I did it), but the doctors recommended it highly. I'd been in the hospital for six months. They'd tried all the standard drugs for depression, though this was pre-Prozac, so the drugs they had to work with weren't all that effective. Plus, they put me on an antipsychotic for the hallucinations. I was on so much Stelazine that I couldn't swallow. I could barely speak. And the medication didn't help that much. My waking images were still of Lyndley posed on the rocks, leaning into the wind like the figurehead on an old sailing ship, ready to jump. My night terrors pictured

Lyndley's father, Cal Boynton, being ripped apart by dogs. I had begun by this time to realize that this last image was hallucination, though when I'd been admitted, I actually *believed* that the dogs *had* ripped Cal apart, that he was dead. The doctors called it some kind of wish-fulfillment fantasy.

Well, Cal wasn't dead, but Lyndley was. And no matter how I tried, I couldn't get either image out of my mind. I thought, and the doctors told me, that they could finally rid me of the image with shock therapy, so I signed up. I was almost eager for it. May's response to this new development was to send me a copy of Sylvia Plath's *The Bell Jar.* She didn't bring it, mind you; she never once came herself to see me at the hospital. Instead she sent the book in with Eva, who had instructions to read it aloud to me if necessary.

"I'm doing this," was all I said to Eva.

It wasn't horrible; at least my experience of it was not. And it worked. It took several treatments, but eventually the images began to recede. The image of Cal went back to being a nightmare, one I could often wake myself from before things got really ugly. And although the image of Lyndley didn't go away completely, it shrank down to the size of a little black box that stayed fixed in the left-hand corner of my peripheral vision. It's not that it was gone, exactly; it's just that I didn't have to look at it directly anymore. I could look at something else if I chose to, and I did.

For the first time I could remember, I had a plan. I was going to move out to California. Since I had already applied to and been accepted at UCLA, I told the hospital that I was going to go to college as originally planned. The doctors were delighted. They took it as a sign that I was cured, that their new and improved electronic medicine had worked on me.

Before I'd had the shock therapy, in a final attempt to talk me out of it, Eva had said something strange. She wasn't upset by my visions. In her profession as reader, visions were what you wished for. "Sometimes," she said, "it's not the visions that are wrong, but the interpretation of those visions. Sometimes it's not possible to understand the images until you gain some perspective." She was advocating more talk therapy and no shocks—at least that's what I thought at the time. What she really meant, and what she told me years later, was that she had seen the same images herself. She had seen both images in the lace, the one of Lyndley and the one of the dogs. But she had seen them as symbols, while I saw them as real.

"I blame myself," Eva said, already starting to speak in clichés. "I should have known."

We all find means of anesthesia.

"Hindsight is twenty-twenty," Eva told me with a sad smile.

The shock therapy took away most of my short-term memory. It hasn't come back. I remember very little of what happened that summer. Which is probably just as well—it's what I signed up for. What it also did—what is really unusual, one in a thousand statistically—is that it took away a lot of my long-term memory, too. They assured me that it would come back, and much of it has. Unlike most people, who *lose* memory over the years, I remember *more* as time passes. It usually comes back in fragments, sometimes in whole stories. I wrote some of them down when I was at the hospital, but by the time I got to UCLA, I had run out. I didn't last past the first semester. I told Eva I was dropping out because of the Stelazine, that I had double vision and couldn't read, which was true. I took my first house-sitting job for a film director, and he got me a job reading scripts, first for him and later for one of the studios.

For a while Eva tried to talk me into going back to UCLA. Or into coming back and going to school in Boston.

Today the women of the Circle create their bob-bins from the bones of the birds that once lived on Yellow Dog Island. The lightness of these bones makes the thread tension uneven, and it is this, more than anything else, that gives this new Ips-wich lace its unusual quality and lovely irregular texture and makes it so easy to read.

—THE LACE READER'S GUIDE

Chapter 8

I would have won the bet. May never shows up for Eva's funeral. Auntie Emma is there, escorted by Beezer and Anya, one on each arm. But May doesn't even bother to come.

"May has her own way of paying her respects," Anya feels the need to explain. "This morning she scattered peony petals to the four winds."

I don't comment. Anything I could say would sound sarcastic.

When we get to the church, people are lined up outside waiting to get in.

Rafferty's there, standing in the back of the church, under the organ, which extends two stories to the roofline. He looks awkward in his dark suit, more awkward in his knowledge that everyone is staring at him. Actually, it's only the women who are staring. Rafferty is a good-looking man, a fact that just makes him more self-conscious in this mostly female crowd.

This is an old church, the First Church in Salem, but Puritan in its origins. Two of the accused witches were in its congregation. This is also the church that excommunicated Roger Williams after he went on strike and refused to act as pastor or even attend services unless it cut off all dialogue with the Church of England. He fled not only the church but Massachusetts Bay Colony, escaping banishment and going on to found Rhode Island, the test state for religious tolerance.

Today Salem's First Church is Unitarian and about as far from its Puritan roots as a church can get. Still, those roots go deep. The last in a succession of meeting places, the Essex Street structure has changed considerably over the years. In the mid-1800s, when substantial shipping money came to Salem, the church was rebuilt in stone and mahogany, with hard wooden pews down the middle and soft, velvet-covered boxes (private seating for the shipping families) lining the walls. The light comes mainly through the huge, almost floor-to-ceiling Tiffany windows, which cast a film of ashy rose over the interior, making everything look beautiful, if slightly surreal.

The church has the kind of stark elegance found only in this part of the New World.

We sit off to the side in the Whitney box, with its horsehair cushions and dusty velvet covers, once a deep wine color, now a crushed, fraying pink. The seats in the center of the church have been restored, and that is where the congregation sits. Even today, when it is so crowded that people are forced to stand in the back, the only box open is ours. This is probably due to liability issues rather than segregation, but it seems somehow to be a way of setting us apart from the crowd. Because we face the people and not the pulpit, it feels as if we're sitting in a display case. I see people stealing glances at us when they think we're not looking. Maybe that always happens at funerals, those looks, maybe it happens all the time, but the families never notice because they're facing forward, looking at the coffin and not the congregation.

Already it's almost ninety degrees outside. "Too early for this," I hear one woman say as she comes in.

Her tone is mildly accusing, and I turn around to see who she's talking to, but it's a general comment meant for no one in particular, or maybe for God, whose house this is supposed to be. It's as if she's documenting something, going on record. People do that in this part of the country—they register weather extremes the same way they balance their checkbooks, making sure they get credit for everything and don't incur any charges that don't belong to them, as if the weather itself were controlled and obliged to produce a finite and determinable number of hot, snowy, or rainy days that must not be exceeded.

The church is filled with women, all wearing hats and linen sundresses, almost southern-looking, out of place here against the cold stone architecture. My eye is drawn to the center of the church and a group of women, each one dressed in a different shade of purple and wearing a red hat. These are Eva's regulars at the tea shop, a group she considered friends.

People fan themselves when they first come in, using whatever they can find: a sun hat, a program from last Sunday that has fallen to the floor. Their sighs are audible. The stone church is not air-conditioned but holds the dank feeling of a New England fieldstone cellar, damp and cool, with a memory scent of apples from last fall's Harvest Days and spruce left over from

Christmas. The people get calmer as they finally begin to cool down; they stop fanning and fidgeting. There are even some momentary smiles of recognition tossed back and forth and then covered with the more appropriate somber demeanor. "Try to act as if you're wearing black," I once heard a Hollywood director say to one of his actors. That's what these people are doing.

The only people who actually *are* wearing black are the witches, but they wear black all year. They are also the only ones who are not treating this as a solemn occasion. They talk quietly among themselves, greeting others as they come in. Death isn't the same for the witches, Eva told me once; she said it was because they don't attach the prospect of eternal damnation to it.

Dr. Ward gives the eulogy. He talks about Eva's good works, about all the people she helped. "People are defined, finally, by the good works they do." He runs through a list of Eva's works, things I never knew about my aunt, things she might have boasted about if she'd been another type of person. I realize the selfishness of children. We love them, and we revolve around their universes, but they don't revolve around ours. I left here when I was a child, and in some ways I haven't grown up yet. That I didn't know these things about my aunt speaks to that fact. I feel sorry about that as I sit here. I feel sorry about a lot of things today.

Dr. Ward clears his throat. "Eva Whitney swam every day, beginning in the late spring. Before many of the boats were in the water, she would be there. People started putting their boats in when Eva started her daily swims, because they knew that the weather would stay warm, that the season was upon us. Eva's first swim of the season was this town's version of Groundhog Day. When she went into the water that first time, we held our collective breaths. If she went back again the next day, we'd put away our snow shovels for good—spring had sprung." He looks around the room, making eye contact. "And now the season has changed. Summer is here again, but Eva is no longer among us." He looks at Auntie Emma, then at Beezer and me. Beezer shifts uncomfortably in his seat. "'To every thing,'" Dr. Ward says, "'there is a season, and a time to every purpose under the heaven.'"

He doesn't finish the verse but steps down, gesturing to Ann Chase, who moves toward the pulpit, her speaker's notes in hand, black robes brushing against the corner of our box as she passes. Dr. Ward remembers his manners, extends an arm to her, helping her up the steps, a polite gesture from an old gentleman. As she takes his arm, I can see that her hand is the supporting one. She's helping him down more than he's helping her up. Dr. Ward walks slowly to the front row and takes a seat facing the coffin. He looks straight ahead.

I haven't seen Ann Chase since the summer that Lyndley died. She is a little bit older than I am, maybe four or five years. She looks slightly muted but otherwise unchanged these last fifteen years. Her features are less clearly defined, like a copy of an old master done by an art student, one off, more suggestion than reality.

She doesn't introduce herself. She doesn't have to. With the exception of Laurie Cabot, Ann Chase is the most famous witch in Salem and a direct descendant of Giles and Martha Corey, who were once prominent members of the First Church (until they were executed as witches during the hysteria). They were *not* witches, of course. Their pardons hang now in the back of this church for everyone to see, pardons issued by Queen Elizabeth II at the end of this century, way too late for Giles and Martha and (some people would say) too late for Ann as well. *"The sins of the fathers,"* someone whispers, loud enough for everyone to hear. But if Ann hears it, she doesn't flinch.

Most people in this town think that Ann became a witch as some kind of family protest taken to the extreme, a "can't beat 'em, so join 'em" kind of justice, an "I have the name, so I might as well have the game" type of thing. I'm not sure about that. Ann Chase was already practicing witchcraft by the time I left town, living in a hippie house down by the Gables, growing herbs, and brewing magic-mushroom tea for all her friends. She didn't wear black then; she wore long, flowing Indian-print skirts made out of the same kind of material as the bedspreads Lyndley and I bought in Harvard Square. She usually went barefoot and had henna tattoos across her knuckles and a toe ring that wound all the way up her ankle like a silver vine. Part of the time, Lyndley and I thought she was very exotic. The rest of the time, we thought she was just plain strange. Like that day we saw her way out at the end of Derby Wharf standing huge against the tiny lighthouse, incanting love spells for her girlfriends, who followed her around like puppies. We used to spy on them from out in the harbor, from the Whaler parked on someone else's mooring. We would laugh as we watched them, covering our mouths so they wouldn't hear us. But those spells must have worked in the end, because Ann's friends started having little hippie babies, which they dressed in tiny tie-dyed T-shirts and nursed in public places. Never mind that the sixties were long over by then. "The sixties didn't arrive in Salem until the seventies," Lyndley used to say, and of course she was right. But when the sixties finally did arrive in the old port of Salem, Ann Chase was one of the first to jump on board. And when that ship sailed away again, Ann stayed behind waving from the beach. She had found her home port.

Back then everyone could do a little magic, but Ann took it to a new level. Instead of reading tarot cards or throwing the I Ching, she took up phrenology. She could tell your fortune by reading the bumps on your head. She would grab your head with both hands and press it as if she were buying a melon at the market. In the end she could tell you when you were going to marry and how many kids you were going to have. Lyndley went to her a couple of times, but I never did, because I didn't like having my head touched, and besides, I had Eva to tell my fortune if and when I needed it.

What Ann was best at were the oils. She grew herbs in window boxes and began brewing remedies and distilling essential oils. One by one, as her roommates moved on, turning into yuppies first, then later into soccer moms, Ann replaced them with cats. She opened an herbal shop down at Pickering Wharf before it was a high-rent district, and she was successful enough to stay on when it became the fashionable place to shop. Eventually, as the shop got more and more successful, she stopped trying to grow her herbs in the window boxes and started purchasing them from Eva instead. That was when they became friends.

Ann's evolution into "Town Witch" was gradual. To hear Eva tell it, you'd think that Ann just woke up one day and realized that she was a witch. In fact, it wasn't a decision; it was an evolution. But her family history was what made her famous. The witches of Salem—the locals who have taken up the practice or the ones who've been practicing and have come to Salem because it has been declared a safe haven for witches—have all rallied around Ann Chase. They wear their association with her like a badge of courage, one that proves that the Salem witches really did exist here all along, a kind of "look how far we've come" thing. It proves nothing of the sort, of course (because Giles and Martha Corey were not witches, just unfortunate victims), but the connection, once made, was difficult to erase. I wonder as I sit here how Ann feels about being their mascot.

She has been talking now for several minutes: about Eva's gardens and her plant conservation, which has been written up in magazines I've seen over the years. I want to hear what Ann has to say, but that same person is whispering again, and it's interfering with my concentration. I look around, but I can't find the source, and so I try again to concentrate on Ann's speech and on the details of my aunt's life.

"Eva saved at least one plant species that I know of from extinction," Ann says.

"Wild exaggeration, load of malarkey," the same voice whispers, loud enough for me to hear this time. I reel around, shushing the women to my left, thinking it's one of them. They look at me strangely. *"As if you have two heads,"* the voice whispers in my ear, louder this time, much closer. I recognize the voice. It is Eva. She is speaking loudly enough to fill the church, or at least to be heard in the rows around me, but it is clear that I am the only one hearing her voice.

"Eva Whitney was one of us," Ann begins, and some of the witches clap. "Not officially, of course, but she was."

I'm looking at the reverend now, which is where Eva wants me to look. I don't know how I know this, but I do. He was a good friend. I have memories of him at the house, discussing Scripture and literature late into the night.

I look at Dr. Ward. I can tell he's distraught. He's trying to hold himself together for the sake of the congregation.

"I am reminded of a quote that was a favorite of Eva's," Ann says. "'The grass will grow green again next year. But you, beloved friend, will you return?'" Ann looks right at me as she speaks that line.

Ann is stepping down now, and Dr. Ward is heading back toward the coffin. As Ann descends the stairs, her dark robes inflate, and I am reminded of flight, and of witches on broomsticks. Then Eva tosses me a snippet of memory, of us all sitting here—Beezer, and Eva, and me—"the day the man flew," or at least that's how Beezer always referred to the incident.

It was Christmas Eve. Dr. Ward was new then, and Eva was showing her support for him by making sure everyone attended services. Beezer had been selected to play the bells that year, along with twelve other children, who all wore matching red robes. Each child had one bell, and together they played an oddly timed "Ode to Joy," each child lifting his bell on cue and shaking it as if his very salvation depended on it. When Beezer finished, he made his way back to the booth. He was blushing from all the attention and from the heat, which Dr. Ward had cranked high to make sure the children stayed warm in the drafty old building.

The pews in the center aisle are slightly elevated, about six or seven inches, which is unusual, and if you forget about it for even a minute, it can be treacherous. I remember sitting in this box with Beezer that night. The service was ending. The choir was singing, just as it is now. An older gentleman, in a hurry to get home and seeing a break in the procession, violated protocol and jumped in line, but he must have forgotten about the step down. What I remember most is the look on Eva's face as the man came hurtling into our box, headfirst, as if he were flying, his legs almost parallel to the floor. Beezer spotted it before the rest of us and yelled "Holy shit!" which was something Eva would have slapped him for if we'd been at home, but before she could reach him, he was down on the floor of the box pulling me with him. Everyone in the church turned in time to see Eva reach both hands up over her head and grab the old man midflight, like a gymnastics coach spotting a vaulter. It changed the man's trajectory and probably saved him from a broken neck. And for a moment, before he came down, the man was weightless and flying. I remember thinking he'd be okay if he could just believe he was really flying and not that he was about to get hurt. But the old man lost it, his face contorted, bracing. He landed hard, half on Eva's lap and half on the gate to the box, shattering the mahogany as he did. By some miracle the man wasn't hurt. And neither was Eva. I remember how impressed Beezer had been by Eva's catch and by her courage. He talked about it for days.

"Holy shit!" the voice whispers then, and I see Beezer smile. I realize that this memory was meant for him, not me. He's half laughing now, half crying as he remembers. Then the soloist begins to sing "Raglan Road," which is an odd choice but a good one, one that my brother picked out and that I know Eva would have liked.

I see Ann smile as she passes, her robes still flowing, and there's movement as Eva's spirit jumps from our box to Ann. I look at Beezer to see if he has noticed, but he's up and moving toward the coffin along with the other pallbearers, and he hasn't seen anything.

We follow the coffin then, all of us. As the massive church doors open, the cool inside air condenses into a fine mist, steaming as it releases us to the burning pavement below. But before we go, there's a moment when everything stops. No one wants to go back outside. A step outside is the end of something, a huge change. We can all feel it. Never mind that it feels like about ninety-seven degrees out there. This is something else. For a moment the threshold seems too high to step over, not only for the pallbearers but for everyone else as well. No one wants to be the first to take that step. Eternity is in this one moment, and we are all suspended in it. It is finally Dr. Ward who breaks the spell and steps outside.

Waves of heat rise off the asphalt driveway, distorting the figures of the people as they step into sunlight, blurring everybody's edges then, not just Ann's. It's as if we were all spirits and the coffin with its dark horizontal lines is the only thing that has any true weight and mass. People move slowly, deliberately, down the steps, their eyes adjusting to the bright sun.

There is no hearse waiting. Instead the pallbearers have opted to carry the coffin to the graveyard—Beezer, Jay-Jay, and some other young men I don't recognize, friends of Eva's, maybe.

A few doors down at the Witch House, a group of day-camp kids, preschoolers, is lined up on either side of a thick yellow rope with loops every few feet. Each child holds on to a loop with one hand; some are absently sucking thumbs with the other. A few of the older ones, more used to the buddy system than to the rope, clutch a loop with one hand while holding hands under it, not taking any chances. It would be difficult to walk this way, but they're not walking now, they're just standing in line waiting to get inside. I wonder at their teachers, bringing them here to the house of Jonathan Corwin, who was one of the hanging judges, though he was far more skeptical and less committed to the sad practice than were the rest. The kids won't get it. They'll think, as I did at their age, that the Witch House is a place where witches lived. If they think of anything, they'll think of Halloween and candy and what their costumes are going to be for next year. They won't get the rest of the dark story, which is just as well. Some are sleepy with the heat, distracted, looking for something to pull them out of their dazed state. Their eyes catch the coffin as it moves slowly out of the church driveway, and they watch as it bobs down the street, locking onto it, going for a ride with their eyes, unaware that they shouldn't. They have no frame of reference for death; to them it's just part of a tour they got tickets for, or perhaps they think we're like the street performers they've seen wandering the town doing skeleton skits, trying to lure you to the Salem Witch Museum or the Witch Dungeon or even one of the haunted houses.

We pass the gardens of the Ropes Mansion. The cars are stopped in both directions as we cross Essex Street and head up Cambridge toward Chestnut Street, which was Eva's favorite street in town. The Whitneys had originally lived on it, before politics drove them down to Washington Square with the rest of the Jeffersonian Republicans. It is Beezer's intention to turn right on Chestnut Street and pass the old Whitney house before turning up Flint Street and down Warren, then looping back up Cambridge Street again toward the Broad Street graveyard. It's an idea that sounded good at the time (and would have made Eva happy), but it is far too ambitious. The heat makes it almost impossible. Already I'm exhausted and out of breath. I'm thinking it would be better if they went straight and didn't make the detour at all. I try to send Beezer that thought, but when the procession gets to Chestnut Street and Hamilton Hall, Beezer steers them right, as planned, and the coffin follows, the back end swinging wide like the stern of a boat.

Chestnut Street is decked out for summer with window boxes and flowering planters on the front steps of the old Federal houses. It's beautiful at any time, but it's never been the easiest place to walk. The old brick sidewalks are like waves dipping up and down to accommodate the twisted tree roots and frost heaves of the last two centuries. It's a moment in time, this street, but it's as uneven as Salem Harbor in a storm tide, and the coffin bobs along as if it were floating on the water. A tourist trolley pulls around the corner, and some of the visitors, sensing a photo opportunity, lean out to snap pictures as they pass. As the trolley rings its bell, an older man playing solitaire at a window table shoots a look of tolerant annoyance at the trolley, only to be surprised as the coffin floats by his window at eye level, our entire parade behind it. He gets up, walks to the window, and closes the Indian shutters.

Broad Street Cemetery sits high on a hill and falls in a subtle slope toward the church. It is not far "as the crow flies," but it is too distant for the pallbearers in this heat. I can see the strain of it on Beezer's face;

he is wondering if this was a bad idea. We are coming to the burial hill now, the relatives in front with some of the hatted ladies. The cemetery is just up ahead, but the road dips down before it rises up again. Although I can see the gravestones on the hillside, I can no longer see the entrance to the cemetery, so I have no idea what everyone is looking at until I'm almost on top of it. The witches, who are on the rise behind us and can still see the whole picture, have stopped cold and are staring at something in their path.

"What's going on?" the pastel woman asks her friend. "What are they looking at?"

I can feel the protesters before I see them, and it feels like a wall, or a locked gate. Then I spot the signs: big ones, handwritten on poster board with Magic Markers: NO CHRISTIAN BURIAL and SORCERY IS AN ABOMINATION UNTO THE LORD.

Detective Rafferty, who looks as if he's been expecting trouble all along, is already on his cell phone, calling for backup. One of the pallbearers, who managed to navigate the sidewalks of Chestnut Street without a false step, stumbles now, although we're back on solid pavement. He almost falls but recovers at the last second. The ripple of unbalance moves through them, and for a quick moment I think they're going to drop the coffin right there on the sidewalk.

"Move along," Rafferty is saying to the protesters as another squad car pulls up. Two officers jump out, blocking the way of the protesters so that the coffin may pass. The pallbearers start up the hill, but it is steep. I can see the sweat soaking through their jackets.

"I don't understand," one of the women in pastel says to one of the Red Hats. "Who are those people supposed to be?"

"They're Calvinists," the Red Hat replies. I'm suddenly feeling the way Beezer looks. I realize I probably should have eaten something before we came, but I couldn't. It's as if I'm looking at the whole thing through binoculars held wrong side out, so that everything in view moves far away into the distance.

"As in old-time Puritans?"

The Red Hat moves carefully past the protesters, sidestepping so she doesn't get in their way but not daring to turn her back on them.

"You've got to be kidding," the pastel woman says, both to the hatted woman and to the demonstrators. Getting no response, she hurries to catch up. In the distance the sound of a siren draws closer.

"Let them pass," Rafferty says again, tougher this time, now that reinforcements are on the way. "You want to protest, that's your right, but you're not doing it inside this cemetery." Rafferty steps between the

Calvinists and the witches. The witches move together in a silent group, and I can feel something shift. One man crosses himself as they pass, an old superstition from his previous Catholicism, as if he's not sure (in a pinch) that this new religion he has adopted will hold. Even I can tell that these men are afraid of the witches. Their fear shifts the balance of power, and now the witches feel strong enough to pass; they know that these guys are afraid of them, especially in such a large group.

Anya takes Auntie Emma's arm, directing her up to the top of the hill, where the Whitney family plot is. I walk behind, keeping an eye on the Calvinists. From below I can see more police cars pulling up.

The wind is blowing off the water. Once we're at the top of the hill, the air finally begins to move. It smells of salt ocean and low tide. I can feel the stitches from my surgery, still undissolved, throbbing from every uphill step. I look around for a place to sit down, but there is nothing. I want to cry, know I *should* want it, but it isn't possible for me, not here with these people who are all watching us. Watching me.

In front of me is the tall Whitney monument and then the small markers that surround it. I look down at the marker in front of me, my grandfather's stone, G.G. Whitney. Everyone you meet in Salem can tell you a story about my grandfather. But it is not G.G.'s marker

I am looking for today, it is Lyndley's. By the time my sister was buried, I was already in the hospital. I glance down at the end of the row, to the newest-looking stone, hers.

Eva's marker stone has already been cut. It lies on its side next to the open grave. Anya is ranting about it. She is very angry, because they got the name wrong. They spelled it "Eve," not "Eva." It may be an honest mistake, but she wants someone to pay for it. "And look at the way they spelled the word 'died,'" she says. "They spelled it with a *y*. Like hair dye. Where did you find these people?"

She isn't talking to me. Or to anyone who can do anything about it. The same family has done the Whitney gravestones for years, stonecutters from Italy, marble cutters G.G. brought over. I've known them since I was a little girl. They did the intricately carved center monument. They did all the granite sculptures in Eva's gardens: carving delicate rose petals and ferns from the hard New England granite that was so different from the soft marble they were used to. They are great stonecutters, if not great spellers, and I won't have Anya saying anything bad about them.

I walk down the rows of Whitney markers. When I get to Lyndley's, I stop and stare. Lyndley's name is spelled wrong, too. They got the last name right,

Boynton, but they spelled her first name with an *s* instead of an *l* ("Lyndsey" instead of "Lyndley"). I feel a bit sick, standing here. And dizzy.

When I get back to the group, Anya is holding Auntie Emma's arm. She has remembered herself and has stopped ranting.

Dr. Ward is reading prayers at the graveside. He keeps glancing at Auntie Emma as he reads, directing the reading to her. But she doesn't seem to notice. She is not looking at the minister but at the piles of dirt by the open grave. Still, I don't think she has any idea that we are burying her mother today. The day I arrived, she seemed to know. But today she seems oblivious. Her eyes remain fixed as we recite the Twenty-third Psalm. She does not appear sad or even terribly curious about what we all are doing here.

The ceremony is over now, and some of the people are leaving. But none of us wants to leave Eva here above-ground, not with the protesters still out there below. So some of us stay behind, waiting until she is lowered, each taking a ritual handful of earth or flowers and putting them down with Eva.

And then, when it finally is over, when we all turn to go, there is a gasp from one of the red-hatted women.

I reel around in time to see one of Cal's disciples walking toward the cemetery. He's robed and sandaled, and his hair is long and flowing. He has a beard. Even Dr. Ward cannot help staring. Then I see Rafferty step in front of him, blocking his way. The group of protesters moves in, and the police cars converge. I can see Rafferty's face all twisted up as if he'd just tasted bad fish or something

"Jesus Christ!" the pastel woman says.

"Hardly," says one of the Red Hats.

"That's not Jesus, that's John the Baptist," another Red Hat chimes in.

"And that's Cal Boynton," says a second in a far less jocular voice. She gestures to a man wearing a black Armani suit.

"How dare he!" says one of the other Red Hats.

The crowd goes still as Cal passes. He stops in front of my aunt.

"Hello, Emma," he says to my aunt. She stiffens. "And hello, Sophya," he says to me without turning, without having to look at me. "Welcome home."

The ground spins, and Beezer grabs my arm.

Before I can think what to do, Rafferty is there. "Move along," Rafferty says to Cal, who doesn't budge.

"Relax, Detective Rafferty," Cal says. "I've just come to pay my respects like everyone else."

Anya has taken Auntie Emma's arm and is leading her away from the crowd. "Come on," Anya says. "It's over." Beezer looks at me. He stays by my side as Anya walks my aunt down the other side of the hill and out the back gate of the cemetery toward the harbor.

Beezer gestures for me to go ahead of him. "Let's go home," he says.

Rafferty stays behind, keeping an eye on Cal, making sure he doesn't follow us.

Chapter 9

Anya accompanies Auntie Emma back to Yellow
Dog Island. When Anya gets to Eva's house, she
goes directly to the pantry and pours herself a drink.
Besides May and my aunt, Dr. Ward is the only one
who doesn't come back to the house. He sends his
apologies via note, explaining that he's not feeling very
well and promising that he'll stop by later in the week
to see me. All the rest of the mourners show up at the
house, including all the witches. The Calvinists might
just as well have shown up themselves, because they
are everyone's main topic of conversation. *The nerve
of them,* everyone says, *showing up like that at the
cemetery.* I'm still stunned by the whole thing, and I

can tell that Beezer's angry at me for it, or at least frustrated. He keeps insisting that I shouldn't be surprised about this. He says I knew about Cal and how he had all these followers who dress up like the apostles and think he's the Second Coming. Even though it was shocking and sick and everything, Beezer said, it really shouldn't surprise me that much, because I knew about all of it already. We had talked about it more than a year ago, he said, and I'd told him it didn't bother me.

I have no recollection of any such conversation, and I tell him so.

"Remember Eva sent you all those newspapers?" he said, as if that should do it. "She sent them to you because they had articles about Cal in them."

I'm still looking at him blankly.

"For God's sake, Towner, it was ATH."

That's how Beezer and I refer to my history. BTH was "before the hospital," and ATH was after. When I first got out, Beezer helped me reconstruct my memories. A lot of the stories and images I have come directly from my brother, his own memories superimposed on the thin skeleton of my own. He came to California that next summer, on his school vacation, and he tried to help me. He was even thinking of staying out there for college, applying to Caltech, but then one day the whole thing got to be too much for him, and he had to leave.

He only had a week left before he had to go back to prep school. He told me that Eva wanted him to come back early to get ready. I could tell he felt bad about it. I could also tell that it was a lie. Remembering was a difficult process. It got worse as it went on, especially when we started to talk about Lyndley. I remember suggesting that maybe we should have known about the abuse, or known at least that Lyndley was in trouble, that maybe we could have helped her. There were signs everywhere, I told him: the bruises, the precocious sexuality, the acting out. I could see Beezer's face tighten as I went on and on about my sister. I could see him shutting down from it. This wasn't something he could talk about; it was too much for him, as it might have been for any healthy person, anyone who wasn't obsessed with the whole thing the way I was. I wanted to let it go, but I was powerless in the face of the scraps of memory I did have. I clung to them as if they were a life raft, and it was just too much for my brother to handle.

Beezer is very patient with my BTH lapses, but he cannot tolerate any lapses ATH. I had no shock therapy ATH and no more extended hospitalizations, with the exception of my recent surgery, but that was physical, not mental (although my ex-shrink might be the first one to dispute that point). The newspapers, the ones my brother kept referring to as proof that I knew about Cal's new vocation, were the ones I had never opened. So Beezer's *proof* meant nothing to me. I don't remember talking about Cal with my brother at all. It is starting to piss me off, actually, the way Beezer keeps telling me how I feel and that it doesn't bother me. I know he needs me to be okay with it, and I respect that, but come on. For God's sake, I think I would have some recollection of being told that my uncle, Cal Boynton, was a fundamentalist preacher whose followers believed he was the new Messiah. I think I would have remembered something like that.

When the crowd thins out a bit, Beezer goes down and raids Eva's wine cellar, coming back with some sweet sherry, a dusty Armagnac, and some amontillado.

"Oh, goody," Anya says, "how very Poe."

The pastels and the Red Hats are glad to see the sherry, and they pour tiny glasses for everyone. I put on some tea in Eva's honor, and people settle around the little tables with their lace doilies as if it were a regular day at the tearoom and not the day of Eva's funeral. I'm thinking I should make cucumber sandwiches with the crusts cut off, the way Eva would have, but there isn't any food in the house besides the things that people brought, plus the sherry and the tea. Looking back,

I realize that Eva forgot to teach me death etiquette, because, with the exception of Lyndley, no one in the family has died since G.G. and my grandmother, but both happened when I was a small girl and too young to attend services. I didn't go to Lyndley's funeral because I was in the hospital by then, but I suppose that they must have had one and that they probably came back here afterward. Where else would they go?

One of the pastels has had too much of the sherry. Her face is red, and she is starting to cry. She is talking about Eva and how she helped her son. She's talking about dancing school and how hopelessly clumsy he was as a boy, and somewhere in her rambling monologue I realize that her son has "passed on," that he died in the Gulf War. "Friendly fire," she says, smiling strangely, "as if there is any such thing." And then she turns to me. "You can't let her gardens die," she says urgently, grabbing my arm. "Promise me you won't let them die."

I nod because I don't know what else to do, and because the two are somehow tied together in her mind, Eva's gardens and her dead son, but I can't quite figure out how they are connected, so I just nod stupidly and promise.

The whole group is quiet. One of the Red Hats takes the crying woman's hand, and then Ruth, the only one who is still wearing her hat, takes it off and presents it to the crying woman, holding it out, offering it like an old-fashioned elixir guaranteed to cure any ill. I don't know if it is the hat itself or the childlike innocence of the gesture, but it works. The crying matron doesn't put the hat on her head but runs her hands over it, as if it were some beloved cat who had just jumped up on her lap to be petted. It seems to calm her. After a minute she manages to smile through her tears.

"You can put it on," the Red Hat says.

And before the crying woman has a chance to refuse, Ruth takes the big floppy pastel hat off the woman's head and replaces it with the oversize red one. And then, like the Circle (the women on the island), the group surrounds their new friend.

When the Red Hats leave, they go in a group, the same way they arrived. The women wave as they go, their voices chorused together in condolence and compliments, fading like music, then splitting into single notes as they move to their separate cars. I don't notice until later the lone hat propped against the mantel. I don't see it until the grieving woman has already driven away, but by then it is too late, so I leave it there.

Someone has switched on the radio, looking for NPR, but the radio is old and the signal is weak, and WBUR has been hijacked by some stronger station, one that favors show tunes. This one's playing *South Pacific*, Ezio Pinza singing "Some Enchanted Evening."

By the time Rafferty stops in, most of the people are gone. He walks over to Jay-Jay, the only person here he really knows. I watch Jay-Jay trying to straighten up as Rafferty approaches. By then both Jay-Jay and Beezer are getting pretty drunk, because while everyone else has been drinking one form of sherry or tea, Beezer and Jay-Jay have appropriated the Armagnac for themselves and are carrying the bottle around refilling their snifters. I've never seen Beezer drunk, and it has never even occurred to me that he *might* drink, but Anya seems comfortable with it. She's walking again as if she were attached to his hip, carrying her drained glass of sweet sherry upside down like a little dinner bell she's about to ring to summon her guests to the table.

Jay-Jay pours himself another drink.

"Where are the tea ladies?" Rafferty asks.

"You've just missed them," I say, and he looks relieved.

"Have the Calvinists gone back to their cages?" Jay-Jay wants to know.

"Trailers," Rafferty corrects him, "and yes, they have, for now."

I detect a trace of a New York accent.

"Your mother's not here?" Rafferty asks me, eyes scanning the room. Considering he's a cop, it takes him a while to notice things.

"No."

He seems surprised. Obviously he doesn't know May very well. "You're not staying in this house all alone, are you?"

I don't answer that kind of question, even from a cop.

"Anya and I are staying with Towner," Beezer says, jumping in to rescue me.

"Oh, of course," Rafferty says, suddenly realizing how it sounded. "Sorry."

"Were you asking as an officer of the law or merely a concerned citizen?" I say, trying to make light of it.

"More like an attempt at small talk," he says.

"Then you need a drink." Beezer goes for a glass, offering the Armagnac.

Rafferty holds up a hand, declines.

"AA," Jay-Jay mouths in exaggerated pantomime to Beezer, but we all catch it, including Rafferty, who rolls his eyes.

"Tea?" I offer.

"God no," he says, horrified, and we both laugh.

Beezer figures I've got it covered and turns back to Anya and Jay-Jay.

Rafferty is looking for something to say to me. His eyes scan the room. Finally he settles on the obvious. "I'm sorry about your grandmother," he says. "She was a nice lady."

"She was my great-aunt, actually," I say, and I can tell he doesn't know what to say to that, "but thank you."

We stand there awkwardly, neither knowing what to say next.

"How did you two know each other?" I finally ask.

"I used to come here for lunch," he said.

I think of the lunch fare on Eva's menu: finger sandwiches, cucumber and dill on dainty white crustless bread, date-nut bread with cream cheese. It seems unlikely.

"I'm a big fan of the fancy sandwich," he explains.

It's the last thing I'd expect him to say, and it makes me smile.

I seem to remember Eva mentioning that she was good friends with a cop. For some reason I had pictured her friend as much older.

Rafferty is trying to figure out what I'm thinking. He looks at me strangely.

I'm searching my Eva training for something to say when I notice that he still has nothing to drink. "How about a soda?" I offer. "I think I saw some in the pantry. I don't know how old it is, though."

"Any vintage after 1972 is okay with me."

I go to the kitchen and get some ice, coming back with both glass and soda. Jay-Jay has started pulling boxes of old photographs out of the bottom drawer of the buffet. He and Beezer have them spread out on every available surface, and there's no place to pour. I hand the glass to Rafferty and unscrew the cap of the soda. It snaps when the seal breaks, so I know it's still good—too good, actually. When I start to pour, it fizzes up and over the side of the glass. I don't know if it's because it is so hot in the pantry or because I've put too much ice in the glass, but before I reach the halfway point, it's fizzing up and over the rim of the glass and is about to land on the Aubusson when Rafferty sticks a finger in the glass to stop it.

We stand there stupidly, Rafferty with his index finger in the glass up to the second knuckle, me looking around frantically for something to put under it. "It's okay," he says. "It stopped."

"Sorry," I say to him. Then, looking at his finger, I comment, "Nice trick."

"I used to be a beer drinker," he says, "in my last life."

Beezer and Anya take a pile of the old photos to the window seat, begin shuffling through them. Jay-Jay, who's invasive by nature, walks around the room, opening up cabinets and picking out objects he remembers from childhood. He spent a lot of time in this room when he was younger. He and Beezer played board games and poker in here when Beezer was home on vacation. They'd clear off one of the bigger tables and spread their stuff out, and I remember that it would drive Eva crazy. They would get rid of all the lace in the room, hiding it in drawers and under cushions, and she would still be looking for pieces for weeks after Beezer had gone back to boarding school.

"Remember this?" Jay-Jay says, holding up a teapot in the shape of a bird.

"I remember when you broke it," Beezer says, looking it over, pointing out the crack.

"She made us work off the debt serving high tea." Jay-Jay goes back into the cabinet, digging deeper.

"You got a search warrant to do that?" Rafferty says to him.

"Oh, Towner doesn't mind," Jay-Jay says.

Rafferty looks at me, checking. I shrug.

"Curiosity killed the cat," Rafferty says, then smiles.

"And satisfaction brought it back," Jay-Jay retorts.

Rafferty shakes his head.

"It probably makes him a good cop, though," I say to Rafferty.

"You'd think that, wouldn't you?" It's so genuine and unfiltered that I can't help but laugh. He looks immediately sorry. The doorbell rings.

"Saved by the bell," he says, and rolls his eyes again. It's as if Eva were in the room, channeling clichés through us.

It's the woman who forgot her hat. I grab it, head to the door. *Here's your hat, what's your hurry?* I think, but I don't say it out loud this time.

"Sorry," the woman says. "I got all the way to Beverly before I realized I'd left it here." I walk her across the porch. "Eva would have been so happy you came back," she says. "I hope you don't mind me saying so." She doesn't wait for an answer.

It is finally cooling. Somewhere in the park, someone is playing a violin.

They're telling stories about Eva when I return. Prompted by the photos. Every picture is a story. They're one-upping each other, Beezer and Jay-Jay, playing to Anya or to Rafferty or to anyone else who will listen.

"It's starting to sound like an Irish wake." Rafferty hands me the empty soda glass, not wanting to put it down amid all the photos.

"More?" I ask, surprised that he's finished it so fast. He holds up a hand—he's had enough. "Eva was part Irish," I say.

"You're kidding," he says, and I can tell he is surprised.

"On her mother's side." I remember that Eva used to tell us that our Irish blood is what made all of us good "readers," that all Irish people have the gift of blind sight, or at least all Irishwomen do. But I don't have any Irish in me. My grandmother was G.G.'s first wife, Elizabeth, who died giving birth to my mother. May is quite psychic as well, though she goes out of her way to deny it. So the *gift* must come from both sides of the family.

The stories from the other end of the room are getting too loud for us to carry on any other conversation.

"Remember the time she told the Republican candidate for governor not to run?" Jay-Jay says, and Beezer does a spit take. "What was it she said to him?"

"No good could come of it," Beezer says.

"Yeah, that's it." Jay-Jay turns to Anya. "The guy had a ton of money. People thought he actually had a shot at winning. A week before the election, he slipped on one of his glossy four-color campaign flyers and ended up spending six weeks on his back in some Podunk hospital out in East Cupcake that he didn't dare leave because he was afraid he would, quote, 'alienate his constituents.'"

"Who voted straight Democrat anyway," Beezer tells Anya.

"So he lost?" Anya asks in disbelief.

"A Republican? In Massachusetts? Of course he lost. Doesn't take a psychic to predict that one." Jay-Jay is laughing his ass off.

"You think we should tell him about our recent run of Republican governors?" Rafferty asks, then decides against it. Anya and Beezer are laughing so hard they can't tell him either.

"What?" Jay-Jay says, but Beezer's got his whoop laugh going now, and no one is immune to it.

Rafferty looks at me. The whole party is laughing now. Beezer laughs silently, his face in a grimace that looks like something out of a horror film. The only noise he makes is on the intake, a big whooping wheeze that sounds like he's kidding, but he's not. People start to calm down, and then he whoops, and they are off again, weak with laughter and release.

Jay-Jay's girlfriend, Irene something-or-other, comes running up to us.

"Where's the bathroom," she says urgently. "I think I'm gonna pee my pants."

"Great," I say, pointing to the hall, and I follow to make sure she gets there.

Rafferty follows me out into the hall.

"The last door," I point, and she goes in.

Rafferty and I are in the hallway then, where it is slightly quieter, the voices muffled. He seems grateful for the quiet. He looks relieved, then awkward, searching for words.

"This was a hard case," he says.

"What do you mean?"

"This case. Eva's. Usually when somebody disappears without a trace, it's Eva I go to."

"Really?"

"She's helped us more than once, actually."

I remember Eva talking about her friend the cop. How she had done a reading that helped him find a missing boy. So I was right; the friend she'd talked about was Rafferty.

"She was a hell of a lady."

"I'm glad you knew her."

"She talked about you all the time."

I hate the thought of Eva talking about me, and he can tell. I try to cover, but it's too late.

"All nice things," he said, but I can tell he knows more than all nice things. Everyone in this town knows more than nice things about me; they're public knowledge. I can't imagine the discussions he might have had about me with Eva—about my hospitalization. God, if he got curious and looked up my police records, he'd have enough material to talk about me for the next year.

"I need to sit down," I say, realizing it's true only as I say it. I feel a little sick. It's been a long day, and I'm not supposed to be having long days. My head is reeling with the noise of everything in this room that isn't being said. I have no more strength to push away people's thoughts. I can hear all their unspoken questions: *Why the hell did she come back? How crazy is she, do you think?* Before Rafferty has a chance to protest, I escape back inside.

I cross the room, putting distance between us, going to a table in the bay window. Rafferty comes in a minute later. He scans the crowd until he sees me, then walks over and leans down.

"I'm sorry," he says. "That was another poor attempt at small talk."

I don't have it in me to smile.

"Eva kept telling me over and over how bad I was at this kind of thing."

I feel some compassion for him. He is trying. I look at him and realize that his secret thoughts, whatever they might be, are probably the only ones in this room that I'm not reading tonight.

"She kept telling me she'd give me a discount on one of her manners classes," he says.

There is a long pause. He shifts awkwardly. "I guess I should have taken her up on it."

I'm still trying to think of something to say back to him, something polite but not personal. Finally I get it. I speak to him in Aunt Eva's own words. "I like soup. Do you like soup?"

It is a test. To see how much he knows. If he has talked to Eva as much as I suspect he has, he will know the expression. It was one of her favorites. Especially if they were talking about the skill of making small talk or his lack thereof. Learning to talk about soup was the first lesson Eva taught.

He looks at me curiously. I'm watching his eyes, waiting for signs of recognition. He shows nothing. "Excuse me?" he says slowly, deliberately.

I'm staring at him now, trying to read his thoughts. His mind is either intentionally blank or unreadable. His eyes are steady. He might be telling the truth, or he might be just a hell of a good cop. I can't decide which.

Irene comes back into the room then, fluffing her skirts down as she goes. "What'd I miss?"

"Tell her about the statue," Jay-Jay says to Beezer. "Hey, Reenie, you gotta hear this one."

"I was telling Anya about the time Cal tried to get the statue of Roger Conant removed," Beezer explains.

Irene smiles, remembering.

"Because it looks like a witch?" Anya asks.

"Because it looks like it's masturbating," says Irene.

"What?" Anya says, peering out the window at the statue of Salem's founding father, which is right across the square. "Oh, please, it does not."

"Swear to God." Jay-Jay crosses his heart.

Irene goes to the window and tries to point it out to Anya, who's squinting into the gathering darkness, trying to make herself see it.

"Where?" Anya says.

"Right there. The way he's holding his staff."

"More like his rod," Jay-Jay says, and even Irene thinks he's gone too far.

"I've gotta get back to work," Rafferty says then. I start to get up to walk him to the door. "You want me to take him with me?" He gestures to Jay-Jay.

"He's okay," I say.

Rafferty shrugs.

"Thank you for coming," I say.

"We'll see each other again."

"Yes," I say.

I walk him to the door, watch as he walks down the steps to the black unmarked car. He sits there for a minute, then starts the engine and does an illegal U-turn on the square, barely missing a parked car.

Ann Chase is cleaning up, gathering dishes off the tables, taking them to the kitchen. I follow her.

"See? There? It really does look like he's jerking off."

"Does not," Anya says, but she's laughing now, a hearty Norwegian sort of laugh.

"Does too," Lyndley's voice says in my mind, flashing a random memory. It was the summer before Lyndley died that she discovered the statue of Roger Conant. I don't mean she literally discovered it— we'd been looking at that statue all our lives. But that summer when she looked at it, she saw something completely different. She was laughing so hard she almost couldn't tell us what she was laughing at. She stood on the curb directing us, making us walk around and around the statue, looking at it from all angles until we saw what she had seen. It was Beezer who saw it first, and his face turned bright red. He was so embarrassed he actually went back inside the house, although I'm sure he wouldn't remember that now. It took me a lot longer. By the time I saw it, cars were stopped, tooting their horns at me, and Lyndley was laughing, yelling back at the cars, telling them not to "get their panties in a wad," a southern expression she'd picked up over the winter and one she used for everything. Finally a driver laid on the horn; and Lyndley gave him the

finger. It was then that I caught the right angle on old Roger Conant, and I just started laughing hysterically. I don't know if it was the expression on the driver's face or on Lyndley's or the sight of our distinguished founding father all robed and holding a staff that from the back right angle looked like an erect penis. I don't know which thing set me off, but I didn't stop laughing until Eva came and got me off the sidewalk and made me come back to the house. She didn't ask me what I was laughing at. I had the impression that she didn't want to know.

"I'm not seeing it," Anya says.

"You can't see it so well from here," Beezer says to Anya. "It's better from outside." Then he tells her the story about how Eva single-handedly saved that statue and how it pissed Cal off royally but made Eva a town heroine from that moment on.

I grab some more dishes and follow Ann Chase to the kitchen. She is standing at the sink, carefully peeling off a piece of lace that has gotten itself stuck to the bottom of a saucer.

"She's having fun with us tonight, I'd say," Ann says to me.

"Who?" I ask, thinking she means Anya, or maybe Irene.

"Eva," she says.

I don't say anything, don't know what the correct response would be.

She peels the lace, looks at it. "Do you read?" she asks, meaning the lace.

"No."

"How come?"

I shrug.

"She told me how good you were."

"I guess I don't find lace reading very accurate."

"Really," she says, half question, half declaration. She's not buying it.

"For one thing," I say, not knowing why I feel the need to prove anything but unable to stop, "Eva told me I was going to have a daughter."

"And you're not?"

"Not a chance in hell," I say. I was only trying to throw her off the track. I had wanted to avoid talking about Lyndley, but now there is an edge to my voice.

Ann clearly doesn't know what to say. "Eva taught a group of us to read the lace," she says. "I'm afraid I'm much better at reading heads."

She squints her eyes at the lace, then gives up, folding it. " 'Well, sometimes the magic works, sometimes it doesn't.' "

I look at her strangely.

"It's a quote"—she looks at me—"from *Little Big Man.*"

"I know what it's from," I say, hearing the edge sharpen further. "I'm sorry. I didn't mean to say anything I just said."

"My bad," she says. "I'm nosy by nature."

We both smile. She hands the lace to me. "She was my friend, you know," she said. "Long before it was fashionable to be my friend." She's extending her hand, still holding the lace.

"Why don't you keep it?" I say, not taking it.

She looks doubtful.

"I'm sure she'd want you to have it," I assure her.

"Thanks," she says, and starts back to the parlor, stopping at the door.

Another woman comes in then, a Realtor, I think. Someone that Jay-Jay introduced me to earlier. She looks around the kitchen. I can tell she was hoping to catch me alone, since she seems a little disappointed. She decides to take her best shot.

"Quite a discussion they're having out there," she says to me.

Ann turns back to her dishes.

The Realtor pulls out her card, hands it to me. "I was wondering if you'd thought about what you were going to do with the house."

"The house?" I ask stupidly.

"I mean, I know it's premature, but I didn't know if your family had thought about selling."

"Selling the house."

"Yes."

I can feel Ann's energy shift. She doesn't like this woman.

I clearly don't have an answer.

"Maybe I'm a bit premature," the Realtor says.

Ann has turned around now. She stands there facing us, holding the dish towel. "You think?" Her tone is sarcastic.

"I'm sorry," the woman says, fumbling in her purse, pulling out another business card, forgetting she has already handed me the first one. "I'll call you later," she says. Then, seeing Ann's look, "Or you call me."

She leaves the room.

"Lovely," Ann says.

Ann makes us a cup of tea. We sit at the kitchen table. She can tell I'm too weirded out to talk about it, so she just sits with me, refilling my cup, wiping down the table with the dish towel, polishing it, just to have something to do. Finally one of the other witches pokes her head in. "You ready?" the girl says. Ann motions for her to wait outside.

"I have to go," she says. "I'm their ride."

"Thanks," I say.

"You'll be okay," she says to me. "Just take it slow."

I nod.

"Call me if you need anything," she says. "I'm in the book."

"Thanks," I say again.

I finish cleaning up the kitchen. She hasn't left much to do, but I straighten up a little. I realize how tired I am then, realize also that the back steps are blocked with boxes and that I have to go through the front hall to go up the stairs. I push through the door, gathering strength.

The party is still going strong. They're back to Eva's clichés, one-upping each other.

"The truth will out," Jay-Jay says.

"It'll all come out in the wash," from Beezer.

"Oh, what a tangled web we weave," again from Jay-Jay.

"Possession is nine-tenths of the law." Beezer's.

"A high tide floats your boat," Jay-Jay misquotes.

Beezer laughs. "Don't throw out the baby with the bathwater."

"Water, water everywhere . . ." Jay-Jay.

"He's not operating with both oars in the water," Beezer says, using Eva's cliché but gesturing toward Jay-Jay.

"He's not playing with a full deck," Jay-Jay volleys back at him.

"He's crazy as a loon." Anya.

"Two bricks shy of a load." Jay-Jay.

"Not the sharpest tool in the shed." Anya again.

"Two bricks shy of a load," Beezer says, and they're hysterical again, both of them. They're also starting to have trouble talking.

"You said that one already," Jay-Jay says. "Dumber than a box of rocks."

"Are you just quoting, or do you mean me?" Beezer turns to him in mock agitation.

"If the shoe fits," Jay-Jay says, and falls down laughing.

"If it doesn't fit, you must acquit," Irene says.

"That's not Eva, that's Johnnie Cochran," Beezer says.

"None of them is Eva." Anya comes to Irene's defense. "If you want to get technical about it."

"They're not?" Beezer says in mock horror. "Don't tell me that. Don't destroy my childhood illusions." Anya is drinking the Armagnac now, pouring it into her little glass.

"There's another one," I hear Beezer say from the other room. "One she used to say all the time. I can't remember it."

"What one?" Jay-Jay likes this game.

"You know the one," Beezer says to me, trying to pull me in.

"I'm going to bed," I say, picking up one of the boxes of pictures, taking it with me.

"That's not it," Beezer says.

"Party pooper." Irene's getting bolder.

"She definitely didn't say 'party pooper,'" Jay-Jay says, and makes a buzzing sound like a game-show blooper.

"I didn't mean Eva, I meant Towner," Irene says, cracking her-self up.

She doesn't know me well enough for this.

"I've got it," Beezer says, popping up. "It's something about sewing."

"Sewing?" Jay-Jay is laughing. "I don't remember her saying anything about sewing."

"Sewing," Beezer says. "Something about needles."

"It is easier for a camel to go through the eye of a needle . . ." Anya starts.

"A stitch in time," I interrupt. I'm halfway up the stairs now, and my voice echoes down the spiral, a message from above.

"Right! A stitch in time! A stitch in time!" Beezer is delighted.

"Yeah, I remember," Jay-Jay says. "There was more to it, though."

"No there wasn't," Beezer says, and they're at it again.

"A stitch in time . . . does something," Jay-Jay says.

"Towner?" Beezer's calling for a tiebreaker.

"'Night," I say, not wanting to get into it.

"Saves nine," says Irene.

"What?" Beezer looks at her.

"Saves nine," she says. "That's the phrase. A stitch in time saves nine."

"Nine what?"

"Nine stitches, I guess."

"That's stupid."

"I didn't make it up."

"I think she's right," Anya says.

"Why nine stitches? Why not eight? Or thirty-two?" Beezer's not sure.

"It's nine." Anya's very sure.

"You're Norwegian," Beezer says doubtfully.

"What? I'm Norwegian, so it doesn't count?"

"It rhymes," Jay-Jay suggests.

"If anything, I should get extra points for being Norwegian," she says.

"What points? We're not playing for points," Beezer says, and shakes his head.

"We will sell no rhyme before its time," Jay-Jay says in his best Orson Welles.

"You're shut off," Irene says to Jay-Jay.

"You're both shut off," says Beezer.

When I reach the third floor, they're all heading for the door. Anya, doubting Beezer totally now, wants to see the statue of Roger Conant for herself, and Beezer has agreed to show it to her. Jay-Jay wants to be there when Anya "gets the whole picture." And Irene is going along just to keep an eye on Jay-Jay.

All I want is to get to the bed and lie down. But things are distant again, and though the bed is only a few feet from the door, it seems like miles. Sounds distort, echo. Every step takes forever. I'm walking through water.

I sink into the bed, grateful for it, for the peace of sleep, but then I feel suddenly as if I can't breathe. I'm afraid if I go under, I'll never surface again. I need air.

I make my way up to the surface, up the ladder to the widow's walk. I can sense the air above me, in the tiny glassed-in room leading to the outside. I push the ceiling hatch, but it's stuck, much heavier than it was the day I was searching for Eva. My stitches pull. I shove my shoulder against it, standing on the ladder, expelling my last breath with the effort. The hatch bursts open, displacing a huge gull, lifting her into a hover above the widow's walk. Her wingspan is expansive, probably six feet across. The wind from her ascent comes back at me, warm and fetid. She must have been nesting here, laying her eggs; it is the season. She hangs in the air above me, blacking out the stars, and for an instant we're together in time and space. There is a moment of understanding between us, this huge creature and myself, but then, before I can define that moment, it is over. She lifts up and she's gone with it, leaving me behind with the nest and the guano and the stink. I stand there stupidly, able to breathe finally, but unable to sit down the way I usually would, unable to settle here. Instead I lean on the railing and look out over the town, taking in everything for the first time since I've been here, *knowing* it somehow.

I see Anya and Beezer across the common, walking around the statue of Roger Conant, trying to spot the offending gesture. Jay-Jay stays on the sidelines coaching them, giving directions. Their laughter stands out, echoing from the quiet streets below.

Beyond land's end the black water stretches past Peach's Point in Marblehead to Yellow Dog Island. I can see the light on in May's bedroom. Two lights, actually. That's new. The brighter light, the kerosene lamp, has always been visible from here, and that is the main reason Eva gave me these rooms so long ago, so that I could check on May's light, so I'd know that she was all right, that she was alive out there and hadn't slipped on the rocks and hurt herself or frozen to death over the winter. Eva told me I could climb up here and check on May anytime I wanted to. I used to check that light every night, more than once a night. I checked it so often, in fact, that the checking is still part of my sleep ritual, in my mind's eye at least, something I must do each night before I can drift off. Even three thousand miles away in California, as far as I can get from this place without falling off the edge of the earth, I can still see May's light. This is comforting, actually, because I realize that's what drove me up here tonight. It wasn't so much that I couldn't breathe as that I needed to see that light, not in memory but for real, before I could sleep. That's all it was.

But the reality is different from the memory. Tonight there is not just one light, there are two. I wonder how long May has had that new light, and I think it's odd in a way, that the two images don't match. It's just as odd that they don't make sense. Like Eva, May is frugal. Burning two lamps would be a luxury she wouldn't permit herself.

And then I remember the Stelazine they gave me at the hospital and how after I took it for a while I had double vision. I didn't get the twitching thing some people get (the dead giveaway, my doctor called it), but I remember I had trouble swallowing (which has never entirely disappeared). I also remember seeing two of everything. I remember coming up here then, when I got home, and it looked as if May had two lamps burning, but that was all an illusion.

"Two if by sea," a voice says, and I can't tell if it's Eva's voice or my own, but I'm thinking that it's good I am alone, because talking to myself or talking back to my voices is not something I can afford to do in public. It's more of a dead giveaway than twitching, if you ask me.

Still, things have changed a lot since the hospital, and, for the most part, time and common sense have taught me to tell reality from illusion. I know that the lights I'm seeing tonight are real even if the voices in my head are not. I think of the phrase "two if by sea," trying to find a deeper, more symbolic meaning, but then my mind wanders off on this Paul Revere thing. He's hanging the lamp in the church in Lexington or Concord or wherever the hell it was, and I'm wondering where this movie reel came from, some old summertime history lesson from the red schoolhouse probably, when it was still our school, before they closed it down for good and made Beezer and me move to town and live with Eva.

From below I can hear the sound of my brother laughing.

And I start to cry. I cry for Eva, and for Lyndley, and for everyone who has died, and for me for having to come back to this place, and even for Beezer and Anya and their belief in their future. Because what were their odds, really, when you thought about it? What were Beezer's odds of succeeding in marriage? Anyone's odds were pretty bad these days, but ours were a lot worse than most. I cry for a few minutes for everybody. I'm set to cry all night, I'm settled in for it, but after a while the tears stop coming. I'm too dried out from the plane and from the surgery and from grief itself to cry any more tears. I'm too dried out for tears to even form.

Their voices echo from below. They're all laughing now, Jay-Jay and Beezer watching as Anya gets the right angle on the statue and finally sees old Roger Conant doing his thing. They are racked with laughter, with the absurdity of the sculptor's mistake. It occurs to me that this is Beezer's bachelor party, since he and Anya are leaving for Norway tomorrow. They probably had something else planned. His colleagues from MIT would have taken him out, probably, at least to some bar in Cambridge or maybe even to Route 1 to the Golden Banana or something (though that is hard to picture, all those geeky professors at a place like that). Anyway, it never happened.

Instead they're all in the park tonight: Beezer and Anya, Jay-Jay and Irene. Tonight the floor show stars old Roger Conant, he's taking the place of the Golden Banana, and I find myself thinking that Ann Chase was probably right, that Eva really *is* having fun with us tonight.

When George Washington came to Ipswich, it was not for any political purpose but because Martha fancied some black lace for a shawl she was having made. It was a phenomenon. This industry created and run by women was thriving like none before.

—THE LACE READER'S GUIDE

Chapter 10

I keep a Stelazine pill in my pocket. It's old and expired, and it might kill me if I took it. More likely it would do nothing at all. Still, it is my insurance policy, my lifeline to sanity. In case of emergency, pop pill. I find myself checking my pocket on the way out to Yellow Dog Island. Just to make sure the pill is still there.

We are going out today for the reading of Eva's will.

Our island was originally named Yellow Island, for the fever. It was the spot where the Salem vessels dropped off sick sailors on their way back to port.

At the time they still believed that yellow fever was contagious, and many sailors died on the island, some as a result of the fever but even more from exposure.

The island didn't become Yellow Dog Island until much later, when someone dropped off two golden retrievers from the mainland. Whoever it was dumped them into the channel between our island and the Miseries, probably expecting them to drown, but the wind and tides were right for once, and the dogs swam in. Because there were wild rabbits all over the island, as well as water rats and thousands of gulls, the dogs thrived and became great hunters. Like the coyotes in L.A., the dogs seldom come near people. Except for my mother. The dogs go tame for May—they lie down and roll over and stick their feet in the air when she approaches, as if they're waiting for her to scratch their bellies, which she almost never does.

It would have been more convenient (and more logical) to read the will in town, at Eva's attorney's office or even at her house, but May, of course, would not go to town.

No one is happy to be here. Beezer, Anya, and I took the Whaler. It was calm inside the harbor, but once we passed Peach's Point, the wind picked up and the swells were as high as six feet in some places.

"I don't know why we need to be here," Anya says to Beezer. "We already know she's going to leave everything to Emma."

Beezer doesn't answer but lands the boat perfectly at the float like the island boy he is. If Anya isn't impressed, she should be.

The lawyer comes out with Dr. Ward. We are at the top of the dock when we see the water taxi slowing to make the turn into the channel. Beezer goes back down to meet it.

"I miss Eva," Anya says, standing there looking toward town.

"Me, too," I say. I can tell she doesn't believe me. Especially since I never came to visit. Not once. From Anya's point of view, we're all no good. May didn't come to the funeral. And I never came to see Eva. She doesn't understand any of us. She thinks we didn't love Eva. She's wrong about that. I loved Eva more than anything. And even though I'm mad at May for not going to the funeral, I know she loved Eva, too.

We walk toward the house in silence.

From the rise by the tower, I can see the red schoolhouse and the lace makers working. There are about twenty women, chairs in a circle, with the reader in the middle. Several children sit off to the side in a smaller circle. It looks as if one of the women is leading them in daily lessons.

The laws have changed. Homeschooling is legal now. I find myself wondering what would have been different if Beezer and I had been allowed to stay here for our lessons. If we hadn't had to go to town that fall to live with Eva.

Anya stops short. She is trying to say something to me, but the wind blots out all sound. She is pointing to the rocks. The dogs appear from everywhere, coming out from their caves to see what is going on. It's like the puzzles they used to have when we were kids. *How many hidden dogs can you find in this picture. Five? Ten? . . . More?* I see them all around us, their eyes tracking each step the lawyer takes. I can tell that Beezer sees them, too, but he keeps on walking, pointing out areas of local significance, leading everyone's eyes away from the cliffs. Eventually the dogs lose interest and head back to their caves.

By the time we get to May's house, the four of us are walking together. The wild dogs have gotten bored with us, but two of May's favorites, the ones she allows near the house, are sunning themselves on the porch. They are posed on either side of the steps, their manes fluffed, front paws stretching out in front of them, like a matching set of stone lions.

The first, a female, seems nonplussed. The male doesn't move, but he meets the attorney's eyes. The attorney thinks the dog is being friendly and is about to reach down to pat him when May steps between them and shoos the two dogs off the porch. The first goes easily, but the one who was staring doesn't move.

"Byzantium . . . go," May says, and the dog reluctantly drags himself off the porch and down the steps. He throws a look back at May as if he doubts her good judgment, which immediately makes me like him.

"Interesting name for a dog, Byzantium. Did you make that up?" the lawyer wants to know.

"Golden retriever," Anya says.

The lawyer looks at her strangely.

"Gold? The Byzantine Empire?" Anya has reverted to art-historian mode and is prompting him as if he were one of her students.

"Actually, it's after the poem by Yeats," May says, correcting Anya.

Typical May. Can't let anyone be right. The dog may be named after the poem, but the poem was about the Byzantine gold. That's what I mean about my mother.

We are seated at the big mahogany table in the dining room, the only place where there is natural light on this dark day. I see the lawyer expect May to turn on a lamp, then realize there aren't any. I hear his thought process; he's hoping he remembered his glasses, reaching into his pocket for them, finding something else, keys. *Damn it. Supposed to remember to leave them for her. Glasses . . . glasses.* He tries the other jacket pocket. *Bingo.*

He is thinking that we're all going to be shocked. That he wishes his partner had come on this mission instead of him. *Tried to bribe the guy, but no go.* Thinking he's never been good at delivering bad news. *Especially not to a crazy family like this one. I tried to tell the old lady. A hundred times I tried to tell her. "You have to provide for the invalid. She is your daughter, for God's sake." Never done well with these old-money families. Even if they are my bread and butter. I will never understand their ways.*

"Are you all right?" Anya says to me. She takes my arm.

I have been staring at the attorney. I think my expression reads.

There is anxiety in the room. Not just from the attorney. Everyone's picking up the energy. Or maybe it's the occasion.

"Would you like some water?" May bends over and asks me. She and my aunt are the only ones in the room who are not nervous—my aunt because she is oblivious and May, I realize only now, because she already knows what the attorney is going to say.

She pours me a glass, slides it across the table to me as if it were a piece on a chessboard. Although I'm thirsty, I do not pick it up.

The room goes silent as the lawyer reads the document aloud. When he finishes, no one speaks for a long time. He clears his throat. Then, as if our shocked collective expressions indicate a lack of understanding, he does the color commentary, paraphrasing what we just heard. "The will is simple in its intent," he says. "With the exception of the family land in Ipswich, which will be left to the First Church for the express purpose of constructing a camp for blind children, the bulk of the estate has been left in trust to Sophya . . . to disburse as she sees fit."

"What . . . ?" Anya says. She is the only one unguarded enough to say it aloud. *What about Auntie Emma?* is the last part of that thought. To her credit, she stops midsentence.

I look at May, who meets my eyes but does not waver. "You knew about this?"

"Yes."

"And you approved?" I am as shocked as Anya.

"It was Eva's money. It is not up to me to approve or disapprove."

"Actually, May was a witness to the signing." The lawyer shows me May's signature.

"Why?" I ask.

May looks away.

"She obviously expects you to stay and take care of Emma," Beezer answers.

I see the look on my Aunt Emma's face.

"No one has to take care of Emma," May says. "Emma takes care of *us* most of the time. Isn't that right?"

Emma tries to smile.

"Emma *is* her daughter," Anya says. "I would have imagined a trust or something."

"You seem to have thought this through." May's tone is icy.

"I just meant . . ." Anya starts.

"I would *like* you to stay," Emma says. "It would be so nice."

I cannot speak.

"You don't have to stay," May says. "You can always refuse the inheritance."

"What would happen if I refused?" I ask the attorney.

"If you refuse, the entirety is to go to the church."

"Not to Emma?"

"Eva was very specific."

Dr. Ward looks alarmed. "I don't think that was Eva's intention. I am sure she would want to see Emma provided for." He turns to May for confirmation.

"Don't look at me. It's all up to Sophya."

Check and mate.

In 1820 the first machines for making lace were brought to Boston, and for a few years the two lace industries thrived together. By 1825 it was all over. The tide of industry had turned, just as the sands of the Ipswich River had drifted in and closed the mouth of the harbor, leaving the shipping trade to towns like Salem and Boston. Ipswich turned back then to its agrarian beginnings and the women of Ipswich to being the wives of farmers, and lace making became simply a pastime to be handed down to daughters—like sewing and bread baking (though less important than either).

—THE LACE READER'S GUIDE

Chapter 11

I stay up all night packing the lace. I take every piece off each table and out of every drawer. The only piece I don't get is the canopy off Eva's bed, because that is where Anya and Beezer are sleeping, and I don't want to wake them.

When I am finished, I wrap the lace pieces in white paper and tie them with a silver ribbon I found in Eva's closet. It looks like a wedding gift. I put their names on it.

"What am I supposed to do with this?" I hear Anya asking Beezer as I come down the stairs.

Beezer makes a face. Anya realizes I'm there, turns to me.

"It's nice of you, Towner, it really is. It's just that I'm not a lace person."

She hugs me. I try to smile.

The cab is late. Beezer tries to get the cab company on the phone, hangs up frustrated.

A horn blasts from outside. "They're here." Anya starts for the door.

"You sure you can't come to the wedding?" Beezer is asking me.

"I don't have a passport." I told him that just last night.

"Nobody doesn't have a passport." Beezer smiles. "Except you."

"And probably May," I say.

"Yeah, probably."

I hug him again, then her. "Best wishes," I say to her, aware that it sounds formal but remembering what Eva told me, that you never congratulate the bride.

"It's okay to sell the house," Beezer said. "I know that Eva was trying to get you to stay, but it was a bad idea."

He can always read me.

"No one will blame you," he says.

"Think about it anyway," he says after a minute.

I nod and say, "Call me after the ceremony." He's got all three bags, and is still managing to hold the door for Anya to pass through.

The wrapped lace remains on the table in the hall.

PART TWO

There is lace in every living thing: the bare branches of winter, the patterns of clouds, the surface of water as it ripples in the breeze. . . . Even a wild dog's matted fur shows a lacy pattern if you look at it closely enough.

—THE LACE READER'S GUIDE

Chapter 12

Old houses catch threads of the people who have lived in them in the same way that a piece of lace does. For the most part, those threads stay quietly in place until someone disturbs them. An old cleaning woman reaching for cobwebs reveals the dreamy dance of a girl home from a first cotillion. Dance card still dangling from her wrist, the girl closes her eyes and twirls, trying to hold the moment, the memory of first love. The old cleaning woman knows the vision better than the girl herself does. It's the one she has longed for but never lived.

In the web of threads, it is possible for the two worlds to come together. For the girl who lived it, grown now, all but the feeling is forgotten. She cannot recall the name of the young man. Her memories hold other things, things more important to her, finally: the man she married, the birth of a child.

But for the cleaning lady, the thread is stronger. It is part vision, part the fulfillment of a wish long gone but never forgotten. She finds herself breathless and has to sit for a minute on the girl's bed. Eva's bed.

The place where the threads connect has tied the two women together. The cleaning woman has no way of knowing that the young girl was Eva, now middle-aged. The woman is not from here. She did not know Eva as a girl. But even without this knowledge, something has changed between them. When the cleaning woman finishes and comes down the stairs, for the first time ever, Eva offers her a cup of tea. The old woman doesn't take it, of course; it wouldn't be proper, and even if it were, she is a shy woman and not given to conversation. It would be uncomfortable, if not impossible, to change their relationship this late in their lives. Still, something *has* changed, and they both know it.

Today Eva is showing me many of her memory threads, at least one from every decade of her life: the farm in Ipswich where she grew up, her wedding to G.G., Emma's birth. The creak of an opening door becomes Eva's voice with its Brahmin accent. The voice poses questions, as if Eva were trying to read the lace to find out what has come to pass. *"I died? I am gone? My life has ended?"*

"Yes," I say aloud, and the answer pings around the room, echoing off the walls. "You have died. I am here to go through your things so that no one else will. No stranger will touch those things you most treasured. I am doing this not because I want to—what I want is to leave this place and never look back. No, I am not doing this because I want to but because I know that it is what you would have wanted."

The Reader must first clear the lace, then the Seeker, then herself. This step is taken to remove both past influences and future expectations. It is into this clear space that the question is cast.

—THE LACE READER'S GUIDE

Chapter 13

I have been in Eva's closet for most of the morning, sorting through her things. It is my ritual, something I have done every day for the last few weeks. I have boxes piled everywhere in this house: some for Beezer and Anya, some for my mother, and some for the Circle, the women of Yellow Dog Island. Today I have packed a small box, a final one, light enough for me to carry. In it are the things I will take with me.

To a stranger cleaning out this closet, Eva would have been defined by the things she left behind, though it would be impossible to tell whether those things were treasures or simply miscellaneous items tucked away because she could never find a place for them. To a stranger they would take on meaning. They might appear to be the signs of dementia. Which is why I have to do this job before I go. I can't bear the thought of anyone judging Eva. I know what it feels like to be judged.

The shoe boxes are a great example. There are at least sixty of them in this closet. I find the shoes that my grandfather, G.G., had given to each of us that last Christmas he was alive. The memories flood back: all of us standing in the bathtub together in our new shoes, soaking them. "Let them dry around your feet," G.G. ordered. We walked through the house wet all day, making squishing sounds, leaving little snail trails of wet across the marble floors and the Oriental rugs. When they hadn't dried by nightfall, he made us stay. We went to bed with our shoes on, waking in the morning to perfect custom fits and more than a few sniffles.

In the back of the closet, on the floor, are other shoe boxes, all alike, bearing the label of G.G.'s shoe factory but otherwise unmarked. Inside are the gifts we gave Eva as children. Christmas and birthday gifts. There's the comb-and-brush set I decorated with rhinestones. Far too garish for Eva's refined tastes, but I remember her telling everyone how beautiful it was and how creative. I find a sculpture I made for her another year, a topiary, covered with shells and beach glass. It's nothing Eva could use, but nothing she could bear to part with either. "We have a budding artist in our midst," is what she said when she unwrapped that gift. But she'd been wrong about that. Lyndley was the budding artist, not me. Still, the topiary had held a proud place on her mantel for years, until its glue dried up and shells began to fall off, leaving strange spaces of framed neon-looking green where the Styrofoam showed through. When too many of the shells had fallen off, Eva wrapped the topiary in the same colored tissue paper she had used for her Bible markers and placed them in pretty boxes tied with French ribbons. The fallen shells lay in the folds of the tissue paper, next to the body of the dead topiary, like favorite items placed by loved ones in the coffin of the deceased.

I open the next box, which is full of photos. There are many more matching boxes, and I lift the lids of the next two to see if this is the only box of photos, but no, all these boxes are full of them. There are pictures of my mother, May, from the time she was a little girl. And a photo of May's mother, my grandmother Elizabeth, G.G.'s first wife, who died giving birth to May. My mother's wild hair, tamed with ribbons and braids, still manages to escape and curl around her head like a halo. There are more pictures of my grandmother and several of her husband leaning up against his car or playing golf. Later there are photos of G.G. with Eva, his second wife and Emma's mother. In one box are group photos, even a few with Cal in them, in the early years when he was married to Emma, before all hell broke loose.

There is a box of photos of Eva's flowers: her roses, lacecap hydrangea, peonies. At first I think there is no order to the pictures, but as I open the fourth box, I realize that they are actually quite organized. Each box contains one theme. When the photos are of family, each box focuses on one of us, or primarily one, along with the people who surround us. Planets in little solar systems. Like the one of my brother, Beezer, at his second birthday party, with all of us there and with him sitting at the head of the table, his tiny hand sunk up to the wrist in the cake frosting and the rest of us laughing as if it were the funniest thing we'd ever seen.

I haven't found Lyndley's boxes yet, or any pictures of Auntie Emma except for the one with Cal. And not really that many of me yet either. There are far more of Beezer and my mother. I know how Eva's mind worked; I know there must be full boxes dedicated to each one of us.

I reach for another, larger, box. It weighs more than I anticipate, and it falls to the floor, raising dust in a little cloud as it lands. It is filled not with photos but with books.

I recognize the old family Bible, its passages marked with bits of faded tissue paper that protrude above the binding. I pick it up. It's heavier than it looks. In fact, you need two hands to lift it properly. I misjudge its heft, and it flops from my hand, tumbling over, sending the papers falling soundless and weightless as October leaves.

I open the Bible to the marked passage.

John 15:13: "No greater love hath any man than this, that a man lay down his life for his friends."

I put the Bible aside. Someone in the family should have this—Emma, probably, or maybe Beezer and Anya. There are two other books, matching red journals with leather covers. Both look familiar. I open the first. It is written in Eva's hand. I have seen it before. It is full of Eva's thoughts and of readings she has done. It is part journal, part fancy, part instruction manual. On the front inside cover she has scrawled a title: "The Lace Reader's Guide." I open to a random page.

Reading the Bride on Her Wedding Day

The bridal veil is the most joyful of lace to read. Every possibility is in it. Because of the sacramental nature of marriage, there is seldom anything disturbing in the bridal veil; rather it is possible to see the beauty of a life as it stretches only forward. The children's faces can often be seen in the lace at this time and sometimes even the grandchildren the couple will have.

Where there is a long train of lace that needs to be carried, it is often possible to see the full figures of the ancestors carrying the train, which appears to float in places where the laws of gravity would dictate otherwise. A bride's excitement on this occasion will often correspond to the number of persons attendant on the veil.

It all seems so familiar. I have read it before. I must have. I flip through the rest of the book. Sometimes Eva details specific readings, sometimes she writes about different types of lace. If tea was served with a particular reading, the tea blend is sometimes described in detail, with brewing instructions. Interspersed with the readings are daily notes, usually about her flowers. There are observations about her hyacinths and her Cornish roses. There are also bits of the old sayings, written into the margins. Lines of poetry: Goethe, Spenser, Proust. Clichés blend with news of weather and tides, but each entry always ties back to the lace like a thread moving through a piece of intricate Belgian lace, then returning with symmetry to its center.

I feel Eva with me. I am crying again. Maybe this packing thing isn't such a good idea. It is too much. I feel a hand on my shoulder. Comforting. I do not turn to look. I know it is Eva. She directs my gaze to the second red book. My hand picks it up. Though they are twins in color and size, this book seems much heavier than the first. Too heavy to hold. I almost drop it. The hand reaches to help me. I open the journal.

It is the journal I wrote at McLean. Dosed with Stelazine, my face hanging and drooping, I wrote my history as I remembered it. The handwriting is the opposite of what you might expect—small and forced, controlled. The history was my ticket out of the hospital, as it turned out. I have no idea how much of it was true. When I didn't remember something, I made it up. I filled in the gaps.

I cannot read the journal. It is too painful. Instead I take it, along with Eva's journal and the family Bible, and hide these books with the other things I will bring with me when I go: the lace pillow, Lyndley's painting, and a canister of Difficult-Tea.

When the Realtor finally arrives, she has brought the house inspector with her, "just to make sure there are no surprises," she says. I spot a For Sale sign in the back of her Volvo.

"I don't want a sign," I say.

"It's much easier to sell the house if you have a sign."

"Nevertheless . . ." I say in a voice I recognize as Eva's. She doesn't notice but shrugs and leaves the sign in the car. The inspector stays outside walking the perimeter, looking at the house from all angles.

Five minutes of small talk follow. She says it's a shame to sell a house like this, that someone will probably condo it. Then, realizing she might be talking herself out of a sale, she adds, "I wouldn't move back either, not if I lived in sunny California."

Outside, the inspector pulls a ladder from his truck and carries it to the building, stepping over flower beds.

"The perennial gardens are great," the Realtor says, "a real selling point." She makes a note of it, as well as some other things she sees, including the slate roof.

"How many bedrooms?"

"I don't know. Ten? Twelve? Some of them she was using for other things."

"How many closets?"

I'm totally blank.

"That's how we define a bedroom, by whether or not it has a closet."

"Oh," I say. It doesn't help.

"FYI," she says.

I follow her around the house. She looks in every closet, writes "7" in the blank next to bedrooms. She looks in cabinets, under eaves. She stops short of opening Eva's drawers.

I must be making a face. "It's not easy," she says, "when it's someone you love."

The inspector finds water in the basement. There's just a small puddle in the wine cellar, next to the wall where Eva has hung some of her dried flowers. He inspects it, curious about its origins.

He looks at the wine bottles to see if any of them are broken. Not finding anything, he turns to me. "Is there a sink above this?"

"No," I say.

"I don't think it's anything too serious," he says, "maybe just a spill of some kind."

The Realtor picks up a dried bouquet and smells it. It's lavender, I can see that from here. She makes a face as if she were smelling bad cheese. "Who in the world would dry flowers in a basement?" she wants to know. "Get rid of these and you get rid of half the problem." She gestures to the drying flowers. "They're all mildewed."

I think it's odd that Eva *would* dry flowers down here, but she has them everywhere, little bunches hanging upside down drying, so maybe she just ran out of room upstairs. Or maybe the cellar was dry at the time.

"I'll throw them away," I say, and the Realtor smiles, erasing her bad-cheese expression. I know I should write this down, or I'll probably forget to do it.

"Anything else?" she says to him.

"Some of the windows need reglazing. But the house is in pretty good shape considering its age."

"What more can you ask for than that?" The Realtor turns to me. "I wish someone would say that about me."

I try to smile.

The Realtor finishes her list. "Is any of the furniture for sale? Or the wine?"

The inspector takes this as his cue to exit.

"I don't know. I hadn't thought about it."

"You probably need to get an appraisal. You've got some nice things here."

She gave me a number for someone at Skinner's, for the antiques. "We have a guy back at the office who's pretty good with wine," she adds. "Collecting it, I mean, not drinking it. Although he's pretty good at that, too, come to think of it."

I walk her out. The peonies are flopping in the heat. I don't think anyone has watered them since Eva died, so it's amazing they're even still alive. When I get back inside, I look up Ann Chase's phone number and dial.

"Hi, Towner," she answers, "I've been expecting you to call." She speaks in a low, spooky-mystic voice. Before I have a chance to fall for it, she laughs. "I was only kidding. I wasn't expecting you. I just sprang for caller ID."

I can hear some voices in the background. "Is this a good time?"

"It's tourist season. There won't be a good time until after Halloween, and that's months away. But that shouldn't stop you from calling. . . . How are you holding up?"

"I have something for you."

"Sounds intriguing."

"Maybe I'll come by."

"I came by there this morning, to see if you needed any help with the garden. You must still be on California time."

"Probably," I say.

"I watered them a little for you."

"I didn't even hear you. Thanks."

"You need to give them a lot more water. A good soaking."

I hear the sound of an old-fashioned cash register *cha-chinging* as she rings someone up.

"Water the whole garden," she says. "But don't do it until late afternoon or you'll scorch the leaves. This sun makes the water into a magnifying glass. I'll come over tomorrow morning, and we can figure out the rest."

"Thanks."

"No problem. How're you holding up other than that?"

"I'm okay," I say.

"Okay is good," she says. "Sometimes okay is real good."

I don't know what to say.

"So drop by the shop if you want. Otherwise I'll see you tomorrow."

I realize I'm starving. There's nothing in the house. I need to go out, but first I have to find something to wear. I have no clean clothes. Because of my surgery, I couldn't lift a suitcase when I came here, so I only brought the pillow. I go to my closet, but I've already worn all of my teenage stuff. I put on an old pair of cut-offs that Lyndley and I bleached one summer. I cinch them tight with a beaded belt that reads WOLFEBORO, NEW HAMPSHIRE across the back. Then I raid Eva's closet for shoes and a short-sleeved shirt.

My feet are bigger than hers, and the only shoes I can find are the sandals I bought her my last summer here. Frilly white ones with daisies on the strap. I figured she'd like them because they were flowers, but they're still in their original box. I scratch up the leather soles with a metal nail file I find in one of her dresser drawers, because they're too slick for me to walk down the stairs in them as they are.

I walk over to Red's Sandwich Shop. It's packed. There's a line half-way down the block. I get in, but then a seat at the counter opens up and no one wants it, so I grab it. I order everything I can without going over ten dollars, which is what I have in my pocket.

"Coffee?"

"Tea."

"With milk?"

"Straight up."

They're grilling English muffins and piles of potatoes and eggs in groups of a dozen at a time. I'm wondering where all these people are coming from, and the waitress answers me as if I'd asked the question out loud.

"Fleet's in," she says.

The cook groans.

"Twelve o'clock tour bus," the waitress explains, pointing to the Trolley Stop.

The crowd stirs, and a group of tourists moves together toward the windows. Outside, a young woman in Puritan costume is running down the street, trying to escape from a crowd. They follow, finally catching her, holding her while a man berates her, reading a list of accusations in a loud voice. I recognize Bridget Bishop and check my watch. She was the first of the accused witches. They put her on trial once every few hours in the summertime, recruiting the tourists to sit on the jury. Poor Bridget is often condemned and sentenced to hang all over again . . . often, but not always.

I hear some whispers and turn around. Two women sit in a booth, a mother and a daughter. They stop talking as soon as I look at them. The daughter picks up her coffee, sips.

I pay the cashier and have to walk through the line that is all the way out the door.

Rafferty's coming in as I'm going out. He takes one look at the line, swears under his breath, and heads back outside, stopping when he recognizes me, grabbing the door at the last minute before it hits me.

"I thought you went back to California," he says.

"Nope."

"May told me you did."

"Maybe I did, then," I say, shrugging. "God knows May Whitney is always right."

He laughs. "According to her, anyway."

I see him struggling to think what to say next.

"I'm selling the house," I volunteer. "That's probably what she meant."

"You're selling the house?" He sounds surprised.

"It's too much." I feel stupid explaining, feeling the need to explain.

"It's a lot of house." He is trying.

I nod.

"Does that mean you're going back to California?" he asks.

"Pretty much," I say.

"Too bad."

It seems an odd thing to say, but he doesn't elaborate.

"Nice meeting you," I say, extending my hand to shake his. It is good Eva etiquette, but not really in character for me. I can tell he gets a kick out of it.

He grins. "You're not leaving today, are you?"

"No. I've got to finish cleaning out."

"I'll see you before you go."

I get all the way up the street before I think of asking him for the key. I remember Jay-Jay saying they had one, and not only do I not like the thought of a key floating around, even if it is with the cops, but I'd told the Realtor I'd make her a copy. It occurs to me that the only key I know of is in police custody. I rush back down the street.

"You okay?" he asks me as I catch up with him. "You look a little pale."

"Fine," I say. "How about you?"

"I'm Irish. I always look a little pale."

I ask him for the key then, and although he clearly doesn't know what I'm talking about, or remember that they even had a key, he tells me he'll look into it and get back to me.

I return to the house, intending to do more packing. But I catch sight of myself in the mirror and think better of it. I do look a little pale—not surprising, really. I feel slightly queasy and decide to slow down a bit. It's getting too hot to do any work on the second floor. Instead I decide to walk down to Ann's shop. I pick up the box of lace that Anya left on the table and head out.

The store is crowded, and Ann is in the back doing a reading on someone's head. She motions for me to wait a minute.

It's a nice store, not too touristy. I notice the Ipswich lace and pictures of Yellow Dog Island. In the far corner, there is a marketing display, a good one, eye-catching, with a rocking chair, a spinning wheel, a braided rug. Very New England, very homey. Rounds of bobbin lace hang from a makeshift mantel, the old fireplace is filled with bobbins. A lace pillow sits on the rocker, as if someone had left for just a minute and would be coming right back. I recognize the chair from the island. It used to sit in our den. This is a display of lace made by the Circle. On the mantel are framed photos of the women and a pile of brochures telling the story of how the Circle started and why, complete with order forms. In front is a pile of brochures and a hand-written sign: TAKE ONE.

The brochure is lined with photos: women making lace, a beautiful golden retriever lying at their feet, a long shot of the spinning room, skeins of yellow yarn made from the dog hair, and everywhere the pieces of lace.

The main photograph, the one on the front of the brochure, is the archetypal Early American home. It looks the way you'd imagine settlers' lives to look if you didn't know the hardships they really endured. Still, there is something wrong with the pictures, and it takes me a while to figure out what it is. When you look at them carefully, you realize that there aren't any faces on the women. Not that the faces have been rubbed out or erased or anything, just that the photos have been taken from a perspective that never allows the faces to appear in the shot at all. Precautionary, I'm thinking, but still oddly disconcerting.

"They say their yarn has magical powers." A salesgirl is at my side, standing a little too close. I am guessing she works on commission.

Ann finishes with her customer and hurries over, catching the last part of the sales pitch.

"It's dog hair," Ann says to her, "not the Golden Fleece."

The salesgirl shrugs. "I'm just telling you what they say," she says to me, and huffs off.

I hear Ann sigh.

"I can't stand her, personally," Ann says, "but she's the best salesperson I've got."

I hand Ann the package I've been carrying. She opens the box. Inside are twenty or thirty pieces of lace. "You're not giving this to me," she says in disbelief.

"I tried to give it to Beezer and Anya as a wedding present, but they wouldn't take it."

"I won't take it either," she says. "This was Eva's lace. She'd want you to keep it."

"If you don't take it, I'm donating it to the Peabody Essex."

She puts the package behind the desk.

"Consider it a thank-you gift in advance."

She looks at me blankly.

"For helping with the gardens."

She is clearly delighted. But then she remembers. "I can't come until the day after tomorrow," she says. "Is that okay?"

I grab the gift as if to take it back. She laughs.

"Thank you," she says. "I will treasure it."

"You're very welcome."

Ann takes a break between readings to get a cup of tea with me. When the tour bus pulls in, she gets up, sighs, walks back inside. "See you Thursday," she says. She stops before the door. "You'll have to water them before that. Otherwise we'll have to deadhead the entire garden."

"I'll water," I say.

Ann stops to pose for some photos on her way back inside. She fluffs her black robes and smiles mysteriously for the camera.

I take the rest of my tea out to the bench and watch as the first mast of the *Friendship* is raised. It's a replica of a ship that sailed from Salem in the old days. Eva told me half the town is working on it. Over by Eva's boathouse is the rigging shed where the volunteers re-create history. A crowd gathers to watch as the huge crane lowers the top third of the mast into place. I watch for almost an hour before I have the energy to walk back up the hill and water Eva's gardens.

Eva has over an acre of gardens, carved out wherever there is room, between the house and the coach house, along the path. Every available space is filled with flowers or vegetables, not segregated but growing together—tomato vines next to snapdragons next to daylilies.

The summer porch has been turned into a potting shed. I drag a few of the smaller container plants inside and put them in the sink to soak. It's hot in here, and it's dry. The sink spits air before it comes on, and the first water that runs is too rusty and hot to use. This is Eva's drying room—the main one anyway. Scents of lavender and coriander permeate the old wood. Flowers and herbs are tied with ribbons into bundles that have been hung upside down lining the beadboard walls. There's still some room left on one of the far walls, which makes me wonder why Eva risked ruining bunches of lavender by hanging them in the cellar to mildew. I decide that maybe she wanted to keep them out of the sunlight, because of the fading. Besides, she didn't know they would be there so long, did she? When she went for her swim that day, I'm sure she thought she was coming right back. It freaks me out more than a little to think about it.

I drag in all the containers I can, but the bigger ones are too heavy for me, so I go for the hose. I can't lift anything much. I can still feel the pull of the stitches. *I should walk,* I think. The doctor said walking is good. And swimming—I think he said I could swim. It occurs to me that I am going to miss my follow-up appointment, if I haven't missed it already. I'll have to remember to call.

I wait until four o'clock, and then I start to water the garden. It takes over an hour, and by the time I finish, I'm wet and dirty. My sandals are slippery—they are actually soaking—so I leave them midstride on the path, footprint art. I cross to stretch the hose to one last patch, the one where the fuchsias are, all pinks and purples, and there's a lone passionflower crawling up the side of a potted bougainvillea. The hose won't stretch that far. It tangles back on the edges of one of the raised flower beds, and I know I should walk back and untangle it, but I'm too tired. Instead I pull, not using my stomach muscles but my full weight, and after stretching to the breaking point, the hose lets go and I go with it, taking a tumble over the marjoram and into a bed of young tomatoes and eggplants, which Eva has labeled TOM and EGG, respectively, as if they were little people. I look around to find that I've wiped out the first two rows of baby plants, and I feel bad about it, and careless. I'm too tired to get up right away, so I just sit there.

It is here that Rafferty finds me, covered with dirt and murdered vegetable matter, surrounded by the fuchsias where the hummingbirds are feeding. I must have wiped out some mint, too, on my way, because I can smell it on me. The mint will take over the flower beds if you let it. I remember Eva telling me that. You have to be careful with mint. You have to confine it to its own space.

Rafferty's looking down, following the green hose trail to its logical end where my sandals are splayed. He stops, looks at me, then up at the hummingbirds.

"I'm not even going to ask," he says, swatting one of the hummers away as if it were a bee as he leans over to pull me up.

I brush myself off, checking the scratches. He reaches into his pocket, draws out the key. A bunch of things fall out with it, including nicotine gum, one piece, old, its package fraying. He hands me the key.

"I hope this is the right one," he says, bending over to pick up two very wet coupons, which he waves in the air to dry. He looks at them. "Darn it," he says. "What's today's date?"

"I think it's the third," I say.

"Okay," he says, looking at the coupons. "I'd forgotten these." He shows them to me. Free dinner for two. I can't quite make out the name of the restaurant.

"It expires tomorrow, part of the Salem Bribe-a-Cop program. You want to go?"

"Tomorrow?"

"Sure. Tonight, tomorrow, whatever. I just don't want these to go to waste."

"Tomorrow's probably better."

"Yeah, they'll probably have fireworks tomorrow," he says.

"Okay," I say.

"Tomorrow, then." He gathers and stuffs the rest of the things back into his pocket. "Seven." He starts to the gate. "You'd better check that key. It's the only one I could find, but it's not labeled."

"Will do," I say.

He starts to leave. Turns back. "What were you doing anyway? Before the attack of the killer hummingbirds?"

"Watering the plants."

"Interesting technique," he says, starting down the path again.

I try the key on the way back inside. The door opens. I'll have to have a copy made for the Realtor. And I'll have to fix the broken glass, I think, turning to look at it, assessing the damage. And move the moldy flowers. I decide I'd better start that list but can't find any paper.

As if by magic, Rafferty's face appears where the glass should be. I'm startled by it, and I jump.

"Sorry," he says.

"What's up?"

"It has to be tonight."

"What?"

"You got the date wrong. *Today* is the Fourth of July." Firecrackers pop in the background, proving him right. "I'll understand if it's not enough notice."

"It's okay. Give me an hour."

"I'll give you two," he says.

I fire him a look.

"I didn't mean that the way it sounded," he says. "I don't get off work until seven, is what I meant. Then I have to pick up the boat."

"The boat?"

"Did I forget to tell you that the restaurant is in the middle of Salem Harbor?" He grins.

"I think I would have remembered that."

"Sorry . . . the restaurant is in the middle of Salem Harbor."

"I'll dress accordingly."

He looks at what I'm wearing, and, to his credit, he decides not to comment.

Firecrackers suddenly pop and snap. Everyone has come out. Across the park one of the proselytizing

Calvinists is watching the house. Or maybe I'm being paranoid, and he's just looking this way because he's seen Rafferty's car and, like everyone else, he's trying to figure out what's going on at Eva's house now.

I'm on time. Rafferty is late. He's apologetic, says it's pathological. He has called for a reservation at least, but now he's afraid they're not going to hold it. When we get to the middle of the harbor, not only is there no reservation, there is no restaurant. It's gone. Rafferty pulls out his cell phone, has to wait a minute for service. I can tell he doesn't like to wait.

"Yeah, this is Rafferty. Has anyone reported a missing restaurant?"

I can hear laughter on the other end of the line.

"I'm serious, the Rockmore is gone. . . ." More laughter. "Well, where the hell did it go?"

"Uh-huh . . . Forever, or just for tonight?" He nods into the phone. "I see." He hangs up, turns to me.

"They moved the restaurant to Marblehead for the evening."

Now I am intrigued.

"Something about the harbor illumination." He thinks about it. "Do you still want to go?"

"Do you?"

"Sure, why not?" he says. "A free meal's a free meal, right?"

"There's no such thing as a free lunch," I say, quoting Eva. And even though I agree, I still wish I hadn't said it out loud.

"True enough," he says. "But this isn't lunch, it's dinner."

"Good point," I say.

"Hang on," he says, and I take him at his word, grabbing the gunwales as he roars off, ignoring the five-mile-per-hour limit.

We pass the tiny lighthouse at Winter Island. We turn to starboard, toward Peach's Point, cutting close to Yellow Dog Island. It's getting dark. May is down on the ramp, securing it for the night. In the grove of pines is a meditation circle. Or tai chi. We get closer to the rocks than most people would dare, as close as I would if I were piloting the boat, which is impressive because it means that Rafferty knows these waters well. One of the women in the Circle hears the engine, looks up at us, annoyed by the interruption. She recognizes Rafferty first, then me.

"That ought to start a few rumors," he says, loud enough to be heard over the engine.

It takes half an hour to get to Marblehead—not because of the distance but because of the crowds.

By the time we reach it, there are so many boats tied up to the floating restaurant that it is hard to find a spot.

The Salem police must have called for Rafferty, because they seem to be expecting us. The owner is waiting, and helps us tie up. "I thought you knew about the move," the owner says to Rafferty by way of apology. "We do this every year."

When we go inside, the owner holds the chair for me to sit down. I can feel people looking at us; I don't like the feeling. I sit as quickly as possible, but I can still feel their eyes. A wave of paranoia spreads over me. I turn to see who's looking, to send it back, but the light is fading and it's difficult to see.

"Something wrong?" Rafferty asks.

"No," I answer, glancing around. I am feeling watched again, but I don't want to *seem* paranoid.

"Would you rather sit on this side?" Rafferty asks.

"No, this is fine," I lie, picking up the menu, trying to cover.

He follows my lead, looks. "I hope you like fried food."

I order a fisherman's platter and a side of onion rings. Plus a Diet Coke, which I can tell amuses Rafferty.

I feel the eyes again, then hear someone's thoughts: *Hey, when did crazy Sophya get back to town?* I move my chair to get out of the range of vision. Rafferty moves his chair slightly, blocking my view of the back deck, acting as if it weren't calculated. It does the trick. I start to relax.

"You ready to order?" the waitress asks, placing a red plastic basket of rolls in front of me.

"Is the scrod haddock or cod?" Rafferty asks.

"It's neither," the waitress says. "It's scrod." She shrugs, looking at him as if *he's* crazy. I can read her. She is thinking how much she wants to go home.

"I'll have the swordfish," Rafferty says.

The waitress heads toward the kitchen.

"So." He turns back to me. "Eva told me you're a writer."

Here comes the small-talk portion of our program. All right, I'm Eva-trained. I can survive this. "No," I say. "I'm not a writer. I'm a reader."

I can tell he doesn't understand.

"You read for a living?"

"If you can call it a living."

"Lace?"

"Not lace, no." I sit back in my chair, moving away from the thought. "Scripts." I hold out the basket of rolls. He takes one.

"Movie scripts."

"Yes."

"Cool," Rafferty says. It isn't a word he would normally use. If I read it in a script, I wouldn't buy it.

"And you live in Hollywood?" He looks around for butter, doesn't find it.

"Sometimes."

He regards me strangely.

"I move a lot. . . ." This was tough. "Am I under interrogation for something?"

He laughs out loud.

"I moved up from New York," he volunteers. This is good Eva stuff. Offer something about yourself to get the conversation going. It isn't soup, but it's a start.

"Cool," I say.

He grins. "Date much?"

Now I have to laugh. "Not very," I say, stating the obvious.

"I meant me, not you." His face goes red.

We both start to laugh.

"Oh, man," he says. "At least one of us is supposed to be good at this."

It finally occurs to me that this is a date. I don't know what I'd thought. That it was an afterthought of some kind, a kind gesture. Date much? The truth was, I didn't date, ever.

"I'm sorry," he says. "Maybe this wasn't such a good idea."

My mind races, searching for something to say. *Come on, Eva,* I beg, *give me something I can use.*

"How long ago did you move up here?" I ask. The voice is weak, barely my own.

He knows I'm trying and looks grateful.

"Two years ago," he says.

"Why?" I ask, realizing how it sounds.

We laugh again.

"I like to sail," he says.

"That makes sense," I say. It does. I'm starting to relax.

"You sail?" he asks.

"Not well," I answer.

"Liar." He laughs.

He knows more about me than I thought he did. I realize that Eva must have told him. I almost tell him then that Lyndley was the really good sailor in the family, far better than me, but something keeps me from saying it. "It's been a long time," I finally say.

He nods and sits looking at me. I realize then that Rafferty is someone I cannot read. Not that I would ever try. I spend most of my time trying not to read people, hoping to avoid the intimacy of invading their private thoughts. Rafferty can be read, but only if and when he allows it.

"What?" I finally say.

"I was thinking that you look a little like Eva."

"Really." He can tell that I don't believe him.

He nods. "To me you do."

"You were good friends," I say, realizing that I am only slightly more comfortable with that idea than I was the other night.

He grins. "Eva always liked to help the underdogs and strays."

"That she did."

"Maybe a bit too much sometimes." A shadow crosses his face.

"What does that mean?"

He quickly covers, forcing a smile. "It means that she befriended me when I was new in town, and she fed me like any stray, and then she couldn't get rid of me."

"Fancy sandwiches?"

"Right." He laughs.

"Good food for a stray."

I am relieved when the harbor illumination begins, the crews lighting flares around its perimeter.

As soon as it gets dark enough, the fireworks start. They're good. Better than I remember. With each burst you can see the people on the shore: miles of them in lawn chairs on the sprawling front yards of the neck or lining the town docks or the yacht clubs or way over by

Devereux Beach. The harbor is so thick with boats that you could almost walk across it. They are tied double and triple on the moorings, bumpers out. With every show of light, the boat horns blast their approval and people onshore cheer, their voices carrying across the water.

The sounds make me jumpy. I can feel someone's eyes on me. I am being watched again.

I'll bet she's doing him.

"You okay?" he says to me. It's obvious I'm not. Sweat runs down my face. My hands are shaking.

She's doing the cop.

I don't know who I'm reading. I don't want to know.

"Seasick?" The boat is clearly moving.

"No," I say. I've never been seasick. A creeping sense of panic travels up my spine and across my shoulders.

He picks up on it, looks around. "We can leave if you want."

"No," I say. "I'm all right." I am trying to calm myself. Working every trick my shrink ever taught me. Breathe. Use the senses. Smell, touch—anything to stay in the here and now.

I feel myself beginning to calm when a fight erupts.

I hear it before I see it. The sound builds slowly amid the bigger blast of fireworks, but it is distinctive and different, a slamming. I don't realize what it is until they come to get Rafferty and he goes with them to break it up. I don't know if they come to get him because they've forgotten they're not in Salem, where he would be the logical authority to summon, or because he's the only cop in the place. The Marblehead police boat is all the way at the other end of the harbor. With the boats so dense, it would take them ten minutes to get over here, and by then the damage would be done.

The fight is perfectly timed, starting just before the fireworks finale. In the extended light show, I can see Rafferty holding one of them, a big guy; the other, a yacht-club type, stands bleeding from the mouth. It's an old story, the townie versus the preppy, except that these guys are far too old for this. The preppy looks vaguely familiar, someone I once met at cotillion, maybe. I cannot see the townie's face. They're no longer throwing punches, but the words are still flying. Rafferty has to tighten his grip on the townie, who's ready to take another swing. Rafferty holds him for a full minute before he finally lets him go.

The preppy sits back down at his table. One of his friends pours some ice out of his glass, into a napkin, hands it to the guy to put on his mouth, but he won't take it.

Instead he is looking in my direction. They are all looking.

"You're a fucking moron," I hear the townie say, lunging for the guy again. Rafferty catches his arm before it connects.

I recognize that voice and watch as my childhood boyfriend, Jack, throws some money down on the table and takes off, jumping into his boat, the way a cowboy in an old western would hop onto a moving horse.

Rafferty says something to the preppies, who go back to their designer beers.

When he gets back to the table, Rafferty grabs a napkin and wipes himself down.

"What was that about?" I ask, trying to keep my voice calm but knowing, paranoid or not, that I was somehow part of it. It was about me. My shrink would say that not everything's about me. My shrink is full of Eva clichés. Usually my shrink would be right. But not this time.

"What's it ever about?" He's trying to cover. His pants are beer-soaked, and he swears under his breath as he mops them off. "Let's get out of here," he says.

On the perimeter of the harbor, the flares are still glowing red, but they are starting to go out, and the glow is intermittent now around the shoreline, leaving big gaps of darkness in between.

Whatever ease we had with each other is gone. Rafferty ignores any speed limits, which is fine with me. All that either of us wants to do is end this evening as soon as possible.

I can hear the sounds of religious music, the sizzle of a bad microphone, as we pass Winter Island. Rafferty speeds up.

We don't speak again until we are in the police car in front of Eva's house.

He turns off the engine and turns to me.

"I'm sorry I took you there," he says.

"It's okay," I say.

"I know Jack LaLibertie is a friend of yours."

"Was," I say.

"I know you two have history," he corrects himself.

I don't know what to say, so I don't say anything. I am clearly uncomfortable.

The police radio pops and echoes.

"Hey, Rafferty?" the voice from the radio says. "You find the restaurant?"

"Leave me alone, Jay-Jay," Rafferty says. "It's my night off."

"Someone just filed a missing-persons report."

"I'll see it tomorrow." He reaches for the dial.

"It's Angela Rickey."

"Shit," he says, picking up the phone so it won't broadcast the details. "Not again."

I don't know what this is about, but I can tell it's important. I start to reach for the door handle. He holds up his hand to stop me. "Get a warrant signed," he says into the mike. "I'll come by and pick it up." He covers the mouthpiece.

"This was a disaster," he says to me.

"It was okay."

"Let's give it another chance."

This surprises me.

"Tomorrow night," he says. "We'll go sailing."

The radio is still blaring. "All right, all right," Rafferty says to it. "I'm on my way."

He turns the volume down and looks at me. "I'll pick you up at Derby Wharf. Seven o'clock, sharp." He turns back to the radio before I have a chance to say no. He picks up a napkin, dabs at his pants. "Shit," he says again.

To clear the lace: the presence of joy.
To clear the Reader: meditation or prayer.
To clear the Seeker: breath alone.

—THE LACE READER'S GUIDE

Chapter 14

Ann was reading her fifteenth head of the night when Rafferty caught up with her. It was almost ten. She conducted her readings in the back of the store, where she blended the essential oils. She kept a cauldron back there as well, but that was just for looks. Behind the velvet curtains that sectioned off the fortune-telling booths, it looked more like a chemistry lab, with beakers, tubing, and Bunsen burners for brewing the oils and other potions she sold.

Ann caught sight of Rafferty as he entered. She motioned for him to wait while she finished up with a mother and daughter who had come in for a reading.

"I'll need some kind of personal item," Rafferty heard Ann say to the older woman. "A ring, a set of keys, something like that."

"Give her your ring, Mother," the younger woman said.

"Your mother is the one who needs to decide what to give me," Ann said. The older woman thought about it for a minute, then reached inside her handbag and pulled out a scarf. Awkwardly she handed it to Ann.

"Thank you," Ann said, then closed her eyes and held on to the scarf, breathing slowly, taking it in. When she opened her eyes again, she handed the scarf back to the woman, who put it into her purse.

"What happens now?" the older woman asked.

"Now I will do my reading," Ann said, standing up and moving behind the woman's chair. She placed her hands gently on the woman's head and began to massage.

The woman sighed. "This is lovely," she said, finally, closing her eyes.

Rafferty watched in fascination.

When the older woman's breathing slowed, Ann began to move her hands in a different fashion, stretching the woman's face into bizarre expressions as she felt for bumps, dents, and other imperfections that would predict her future. Rafferty's eyes went to the phrenology chart on the wall. This bump determined longevity, that one indicated artistic leanings.

Rafferty stopped observing them when Ann started to read. Though the daughter was taking notes, this was a private moment. Instead of listening, Rafferty browsed the store, stopping to look at little packages of herbal sachets and spells: rose and vervain to help you sleep, yarrow and ginger to find lost love. There were sachets for prosperity, for protection, for health, even one for winning elections. Ann kept a huge section of incense. The scent was overpowering. Rafferty moved quickly by it to the even larger section of self-help books. He picked up a few and flipped through the pages. Then he moved on to the crystals. Rafferty ran his hand through a bin of rose quartz, then through another of obsidian.

He was elbow deep in fire agates when Ann finally caught up with him.

"Those are good for potency," Ann said, and Rafferty quickly pulled out his arm.

"Sorry," she said. "I couldn't resist."

She led Rafferty into the back room, brushing a cat or two off the futon bed she kept there. A lunar calendar hung on the wall. It was the same one he'd seen at Eva's house, except without the Red Hat symbols. It was the Red Hats who had reported Eva missing. They were her regulars. When she hadn't opened the tea-room on their scheduled day, they had driven directly to the station to report her missing.

"Everyone's gone missing," Rafferty said, mostly to himself. Two in one month, that was strange enough, but it wasn't difficult to see that these two were connected. Eva had helped Angela more than once, giving her food and sometimes shelter. And Eva was the one whom Angela went to when she got herself in trouble. At least that's what she'd done the last time. That time Eva had sent her out to the shelter, to May. And Cal had hated Eva for it. Actually, Cal hated Eva for a lot of things.

"Strange year," Ann said. "You're not allergic to cats, are you?"

"Just dogs," he said.

"Sit." Ann gave the command as if speaking to a dog.

Rafferty couldn't help smiling. He liked Ann and her sense of humor. It was subtle most of the time, and most of the time people didn't get it at all. Rafferty moved a third cat out of the way and took a seat.

"You filed this?" Rafferty held up the folder. Ann was the one who had filed the missing-persons report on Angela, if you could call it that. It was more of an "I haven't seen her around the docks lately" report, a general sounding of the alarm. Angela had disappeared before, about six months ago, after being beaten by the Calvinists. She had gone back to them voluntarily, and against everyone's better judgment.

Angela fit the profile of a kid who would end up in a cult. She was sixteen, a dropout, and a runaway. Definitely fucked up. Probably abused early on. Anything that promised any kind of safety or salvation would be seen as the perfect fix for a kid like that.

The thing that stood out most to Rafferty wasn't who *had* filed the report about Angela but who *hadn't*. The last time Angela took off, the Calvinists had called the station every day, accusing the witches first and then Eva of kidnapping Angela. Rafferty's friend Roberta, who worked at Winter Island, had told him that Angela had been thinking of moving on, maybe to warmer climes.

"I heard she was thinking of heading south," Rafferty said.

"South? Yeah, I guess so, if you consider Eva's boathouse south." Ann pointed out the window. "She's been staying there for the last few weeks. Hiding there, actually, I'd say. She just came out at night. Did a little Dumpster diving behind Victoria Station, from what I hear. I only found out because I caught her picking tomatoes out of my pots over there."

"Jesus," Rafferty said.

"I started leaving things in the pot for her. Fast food. Healthier stuff when I could find time to cook. I feel sorry for her. She's a good kid."

"Why didn't she come to me?"

Ann just looked at him. "Right."

"Or go to the shelter at least."

"Her eye was black when I saw her. She had bruises all the way down the side of her face. She made me promise not to tell anyone I'd seen her."

Rafferty nodded. May was right. She should have stayed on the island. He should have made sure she stayed rather than letting her return to Cal and his group.

"You couldn't have stopped her." Ann knew what he was thinking. "And she hated Yellow Dog Island."

Rafferty shivered.

"I couldn't live out there," Ann said. "Milking cows, growing flax. I'm as crunchy granola as they come, but I couldn't do it."

"When was the last time you saw her?"

"Three days ago. She was on the docks that night, and I was open late. I saw her walking down toward Shetland Park. Sometimes she used to sit on the rocks over there. But the Calvinists were down on the docks that night. Proselytizing. Picking through the tourists, looking for new recruits."

"You think the Calvinists dragged her back?"

"I don't know what I think. She's not at the boat-house. Maybe they dragged her back. Maybe they just scared her off. I don't know. I don't know why she didn't file charges the first time they beat her up. I sure as hell would have."

"Food, shelter, lodging." Rafferty's list sounded like a highway sign.

"What?"

"Old story," he said. "Power, dependence. If you add saving her soul, it's the total package." He had a really bad feeling about this. But nothing he felt like sharing. "Did Eva know she was staying at the boathouse?"

"Eva gave her the key . . . after the last time she got herself beaten up." Ann hesitated before saying the last part. It was a sore subject for him, and everybody knew it.

Rafferty pulled the flashlight from his glove compartment. He left the cruiser double-parked in front of Ann's shop and walked across Derby Wharf toward the boathouse.

If Angela had left in a hurry, she had locked up as she went. Rafferty shone the light through the windows, but they had been boarded from the inside. He started down toward the dockside, where the boathouse faced the harbor. High tide. He scrambled over slippery pilings only to find the first-floor opening closed and boarded up. Without a Sawzall, the only place to get in was the wooden doorway to the second-story loft. He cursed a couple of times. Then he went back to the cruiser for a rope.

Some boaters watched as Rafferty climbed the rope. There was applause as he reached the top, then more as he swung back and kicked through the loft door.

It was dark in the little room above the boathouse. Rafferty trained the flashlight on each of the four corners. Somebody had been staying here all right. The place was a mess. Full of fast-food wrappers and old rat droppings. No big surprise there. The water rats on the wharf were as big as cats. They were a diverse population: Indian, Chinese, Caribbean rats whose lineage dated back at least three hundred years to a time when Salem imported goods from all over the world. The restaurant owners complained about them a couple of times each summer, but they were a hardy bunch.

Rafferty scanned the room, noting everything: A wine bottle with a candle. Dusty. Candle burned out. An old pack of cigarettes stuck into a corner nook. Cot in the corner, unmade, covered by a faded Indian bedspread with a hole burned dead center.

A sound echoed from downstairs. Rafferty turned. Shone the light. "Angela," he said, "it's me, John Rafferty." No answer. He pointed the light down the stairs. Heard the lapping water. He started down the stairs into the full dark below, the flashlight scanning like a lighthouse beam, highlighting an old sailboat, an oarlock, an ancient Boston Whaler with a hole in its bow. He knocked a spiderweb aside, spit part of it out of his mouth, then spit again.

The bottom stair was rotted, and it collapsed under his weight, sending him sprawling, throwing the flashlight out of his hands. He watched it roll crazily toward the water's edge. He started to curse.

The light caught a loose board nail and stopped rolling. Rafferty got to his feet, realized his hand was bleeding. He cursed again.

Something smashed. The noise silenced him. Rafferty grabbed the light, spun around, and shone it toward the sound. The sound was coming from the water, or below the boathouse floor, he couldn't tell which. He pointed the beam into the water along the far wall of the boathouse, revealing a small half-moon indentation just above the waterline. Tidal erosion, probably, but then he spotted a rat, the size of a small car, he thought—well maybe not a car, but it was huge. The rat looked back, and the beam of light caught his red eyes, and then he scrambled into the hole, which was not tidal erosion at all but a giant rat hole. His tail hung out for a second, then slithered snakelike into the hole and disappeared. "Enough," Rafferty said, starting back up the stairs. Hard to believe that Yellow Dog Island was worse than this.

Rafferty stood at the top of the loft window, looking out over the harbor. Jack's boat was back in its slip; he could see the light on in the cabin. Jack was facedown on the bunk. Passed out, Rafferty thought, noting the empty bottle sidewise on the galley table. Then, for some reason, Rafferty looked toward the island and noticed the two lights, May's signal. She might think she was moving someone tonight, but Rafferty knew better.

He went out the way he'd come in. Not with the rope this time; he looped it up and tossed it down to the wharf before he jumped out the window. High tide, he thought gratefully as he dropped into the cold black water, thankful he wasn't going to smash himself to pieces on the rocks.

Rafferty changed clothes, then stopped at the station to pick up the warrant, and finally headed over to see the Calvinists.

Winter Island was at the mouth of Salem Harbor. The only thing beyond it was Salem Willows, where Rafferty lived. This was a different part of Salem, more island life than port city, a Victorian enclave set apart by a thin stretch of road that skirted the power plant with its huge pile of coal and the freighters that brought it into port.

Winter Island faced the harbor and Derby Wharf and downtown on one side, open ocean on the other. It connected to the mainland by a small causeway. On the ocean side stood the Plummer Home for Boys. Imposing, Victorian style, it looked like an old hotel. One of Rafferty's pigeons had grown up there. That's what they called the newcomers in the AA program, pigeons. Because when you tried to help them out, they'd invariably shit all over you, then fly away. AA humor. Still, Rafferty's latest pigeon was a good enough kid, and Rafferty had taken him under his wing—no pun intended—because the kid had asked him to, and you didn't say no to a kid like that even if you knew how much trouble he was going to give you.

The Plummer Home was an old mansion with arguably the best oceanfront location in town, so it wasn't horrible by anybody's standards, but it was still a place where unwanted kids ended up. Both brothers, Jay-Jay and Jack LaLibertie, had done a stint there after their mother died, when their father had taken off to work his traps up in Canada and didn't bother to come back for almost a year. Those kids had turned out okay. At least Jay-Jay had. He was annoying as hell, but he was a good kid. Jack was another story. A drunk like his father, Jack had tried AA a number of times, but he just couldn't stick with it.

Jack LaLibertie had other problems besides the drink, not the least of which was what had happened with Towner Whitney. Like a lot of alcoholics, he had the victim role down. The old wound had never healed, and Jack kept picking at the scab, making it bleed and fester until, when it got bad enough, he would show up at a meeting drunk as hell and start ranting about Towner and what she did to him, as if the whole thing had happened just last week and not almost fifteen years ago. Obviously tonight had been one of those nights.

But Rafferty didn't want to think about tonight. He didn't want to think about Jack LaLibertie or about his own failed date with Towner, if you could even call it that. Hell of a date. Home before ten. He would have laughed out loud if it weren't so pathetic.

Rafferty's mind kept coming back to Angela. It was a bad situation all around. It had only been a question of time until something happened. He realized now that he'd been waiting for it. Rafferty couldn't help wondering whether things would have been different for Angela if she had stayed at May's place on Yellow

Dog Island. Or if when she first came here she'd been able to stop one driveway sooner, if the Plummer House had been a home for unwanted kids and not just boys. Maybe Angela would be here now if she had been welcome there and hadn't gone that one step further, to Winter Island, where Cal and his crazies were waiting to save her soul.

Rafferty had a bad feeling about Angela. And apparently so had Eva. She'd been the one who called him when Angela had first taken up with the Calvinists. "Can't you do something about this?" she asked. Rafferty knew her history with Cal Boynton. Eva had been Cal's mother-in-law. She had reported him more than once for his abuse of her daughter, Emma. There was no love lost between Eva and Cal.

Tonight Rafferty was very worried about Angela. He couldn't shake the feeling that something was really wrong. His cop's instincts had always been spot-on, the exact opposite of his dating instincts.

When Rafferty pulled into Winter Island Park, the revival meeting was still in full swing. He checked his watch a second time—10:47. Thirteen more minutes and he could shut them down for disturbing the peace. He'd done it before. Several times. Used to make a practice of it last summer if the weather was good. He'd take the cruiser over to the Willows and walk around, stopping to play a few games of pinball at the arcade and maybe get a chop suey sandwich. Then he'd come back to Winter Island and raid the place promptly at eleven o'clock. It worked for a while, until Cal got wise to it and bought himself a Rolex.

Rafferty stopped at the guard shack and rolled down his window.

Roberta opened the slider without looking up from her *Cosmo.* "Twenty-five dollars a day," she said, still not looking up. "And yes, that includes the holiday." She was reading an article entitled "Make His Summer Sizzle."

"Cash only," she said, reluctantly closing the magazine.

"Just put it on my tab," Rafferty said.

He watched her turn over the magazine so he wouldn't see the cover.

"Too late," he said, laughing. "Busted."

She didn't think it was funny. "I thought you were out on some date," she said, not even trying to disguise her sarcasm.

"Jesus," Rafferty said, incredulous. "You gonna tell me what I ordered for dinner, too?"

She didn't answer.

Roberta was wearing her new park uniform, with a white jersey top she had intentionally purchased one size too small. Her bleached-blond hair was spiked with gel, still growing out from a cut she'd tried to give herself one night a few months ago when she'd temporarily fallen off the wagon.

He knew her from AA. She was one of the first people he'd met when he came to town, his first friend besides Eva. She had a thing for cops, she'd told him as they stood by the coffee machine. He'd poured a half inch of coffee, greasy black stuff that had been sitting way too long. The styrofoam cup shocked his teeth with static electricity as he brought it to his mouth. He made a face, then threw the whole thing into the trash and took a seat by himself in the back of the room, wondering how many other potential new friends he'd just managed to offend.

The next meeting Roberta had brought him Dunkin' Donuts coffee. He could see her losing her confidence even as she'd handed it to him. "Did I mess it up? You're not a Starbucks snob, are you?"

"No," he'd said, laughing. He was worse than a Starbucks snob, but he didn't tell her that. He didn't even drink Starbucks coffee. Used to. Then, last year, his daughter had saved up her allowance and bought him a French press for Christmas, and now he couldn't drink his coffee any other way.

Still, Rafferty had appreciated the gesture. He'd taken the cup and thanked her, and he'd even gone out of his way to sit next to her, pretending to sip the coffee all through the meeting and taking the still-almost-full cup with him when he left.

They'd gone out only a few times. Mostly because she'd done the asking. Rafferty was still new to town and lonely. He'd tried his best to turn it into friendship. In his favor, he'd never slept with her, though her bed would have been an easy one to fall into.

"How was your vacation?" he asked her.

"It pretty much sucked," she said. "My mother backed out of baby-sitting, and my sister had to bring the kid."

Rafferty nodded. He'd never met her sister or the kid, but he'd heard her stories. She talked about her sister a lot at AA meetings. Not in a good way. Whenever Roberta fell off the wagon, it was usually after spending time with her sister.

"So what are you doing here?" Roberta asked, partly curious, partly just annoyed. "You two didn't hit it off?"

"Angela Rickey has been reported missing."

"What? Again?"

"You seen her?"

"Contrary to popular opinion, I am not her keeper."

"I didn't ask you to take her in again. I only asked if you'd seen her."

"Negative," Roberta said, thinking about it. "Not for a while."

Roberta had told him very little about the few weeks Angela had stayed with her. Only that she'd gone back to the Calvinists. And good riddance.

"You didn't see anyone fighting? Or hear anything unusual before she left?"

"Define 'unusual,'" she said.

As if on cue, the wind pitched easterly and the screams echoed up from the deserted coast guard hangar where Cal was preaching. The sound of human agony chilled the already cooling air. What night was this? Thursday? Thursday was teen-exorcism night. It was a family outing, drawing crowds from as far away as Rhode Island. It was one of Cal's most popular family events.

And one of the noisiest. Evidently the demons didn't depart from their teenage hosts without putting up a good fight, one that echoed across the parking lot and up out over the water, startling even the nesting gulls, who quickly relocated. Even the wind rejected the sound, trying to shift directions again, throwing itself in circles with its efforts, knocking things about wildly: an old metal sign, the limb of a dying tree. Finally it caught and grabbed the breeze that held the big brass-band music from the pavilion and blended the two sounds until it seemed as if John Philip Sousa had written a score to march the demons right out of their victims and blow them out to sea.

Rafferty could just hear the calls coming in back at the station. Sound carried far over the water, even on a windy night like tonight. The townies were used to this by now. Most of the calls came from the summer people. Usually they thought it was some freaky tour that stayed open too late. Or one of the haunted houses. Rafferty had instructed the officer on duty to say, "We'll take care of it," or "We'll look into it." He had discovered from experience that telling callers the real source of the screaming did little to calm their already fraying nerves.

"This is too weird," one particularly perturbed woman had complained. "Can't you people do anything?"

Truth was, they couldn't. As long as the services didn't exceed the prescribed decibel level or continue past 10:00 P.M., the Calvinists were within their rights. The one time Rafferty had tried, Cal had countered by having his church members call the station six times to report a disturbance by a late-night folksinging traveler down on Winter Island's Waikiki Beach who was trying to master Bob Dylan's "My Back Pages," then, failing that, had moved on to several rousing choruses of "Kumbaya."

There wasn't much to be done. The campground at Winter Island was a public place. The Calvinists paid their fees up front. And they paid for the entire season. They weren't going anywhere until Columbus Day, when the park closed down for the winter. But by then the summer people would be gone, and windows would be closing against the chilling autumn air, and the people who were left would be looking forward to Halloween, when screaming of any kind simply added to the festivities.

Something registered in Rafferty's peripheral vision. His eyes followed the figure of a man moving along the ridge. As he focused, he realized he was looking at the Calvinists' robes hanging on a makeshift clothesline. Twisting in the wind. Tethered to their ropes, they filled with air, taking human form and spinning about. Ghost dancers. Hypnotic. It seemed to Rafferty that at any moment they could break free and dance down the hill and into the ocean, disappearing forever into the blackness below. Then, as suddenly as it had made them appear, the wind shifted again, and the life force flowed out of them, and they became once again what they were all along. Not dancers, not ghosts, just somebody's laundry.

I've been in Salem too long, Rafferty thought.

Several more screams could be heard. Then Cal's voice, rising above the others. "Name yourself, demon!" he bellowed.

Rafferty had seen it at least a hundred times. If the demon didn't depart, and it usually didn't, at least not on the first try, Cal would grab the kid and shake him until the kid either stopped screaming or passed out, whichever came first.

Rafferty couldn't believe that anyone would fall for this crap. People would believe anything. Bible-thumping born-agains were one thing. At least they'd read the book. But this was ridiculous. Cal's sermons were plagiarized from Cotton Mather, old movies, and any number of late-night televangelists. Cal picked pieces of his favorites, mostly hell-and-damnation stuff. It was like choosing food off a Chinese menu. Hellfire from Column A, eternal salvation from Column B. The best ones he'd gotten from the Catholic Church, the early years, before they went all ecumenical. But clearly the Thursday-night exorcisms had become his bread and butter. Hey, what parent doesn't think his teenager is possessed? Rafferty had spent enough time with his daughter, Leah, last summer to kid her about bringing her down to see Cal if she didn't shape up. "Hey, I live in New York City," she said to him. "You don't scare me."

Evidently imitation wasn't considered flattery by the Catholics, who had enough trouble of their own these days and didn't want to be reminded of past indiscretions. It was Father Malloy over at St. James's who'd called the meeting of churches to discuss what could be done about the Calvinists. "Whatever happened to tar and feathers?" the priest had joked when the local churches voted unanimously to form a council that would meet monthly until the issue of Cal Boynton was resolved. "I mean, can't we at least ride him out of town on a rail?" Father Malloy had only been half kidding. The Episcopal minister had seconded the motion, and Dr. Ward from the Unitarian church had called for a vote.

"Seriously," a representative from the Methodist church had said after the laughter finally died down, "isn't there anything we can do?"

"I'm afraid there isn't a lot," Rafferty had informed them. Everything he could do, he'd done months ago. Like getting the fraud unit on it. Problem was, the parents were almost always satisfied. And the kids didn't want to talk about it.

Roberta squashed a mosquito, smearing a trail of blood down the window screen. She made a face, wiping her hands on her shorts.

"She's crazy like the rest of them," Roberta said. She hadn't intended to say it, but here it was.

"Angela?" Rafferty asked.

"Towner Whitney."

Rafferty searched his mind for a response, but he couldn't come up with a thing. He wanted to say he was sorry, for tonight's date, for somehow giving Roberta an impression that he'd never set out to give.

"I'm sure you've heard the story." Roberta couldn't let it go. "Sophya, or Towner, or whatever the hell she calls herself these days." She spit the words. "She's a certifiable nutcase."

Rafferty remained silent.

"I'm just telling you because you weren't here when it happened. I'm not sure you've heard the stories."

"I've heard them."

"She confessed to a crime that never happened. She had the whole town out searching for a body." She looked toward the revival tent. "Three different search parties. He wasn't dead."

"Obviously," Rafferty said, looking down the hill.

"She never touched him. He wasn't even in the fucking state at the time."

It hadn't been three search parties. It had been two officers and a dog. Listening to stories about Towner Whitney was like that old children's game. Telephone or Gossip, something like that. The story changed as it was passed from person to person. Everyone's version was a little different. So different, in fact, that Rafferty had actually pulled Towner's police record himself, to get some kind of sense what the truth was. He had his own ideas about what had happened that night, ideas he wasn't about to discuss with Roberta.

"Let's stick to the subject at hand," Rafferty said.

"Whatever," Roberta said.

A Mini Wini with Kansas plates pulled up behind him. "I'm gonna go down and have a look around." He put the cruiser in gear, ending any possibility of further conversation.

Rafferty pulled into the parking lot and killed the engine.

Winter Island was an old coast guard station turned national campground, a strange mix of industrial compound and beautiful seaside retreat, complete with its own miniature lighthouse. The two sections were separated by an expanse of asphalt parking lot and boat launch ramp. A huge deserted airplane hangar flanked the parking lot, with long-abandoned barracks and commissary, a casualty of the post-Vietnam defense cuts. Cal had strategically planted his revival tent at the end of the hangar, which was lit with carnival lights he'd bartered from an errant carny who'd robbed his employer blind before the show left town. The lights and tent, plus the ne'er-do-well's pocket change, were the price Cal extracted for the man's soul. The demons evidently didn't depart, but the carny did, leaving behind his ill-gotten gains, which Cal considered the ultimate gift from God, a portable church complete with lights and a fog machine that Cal set up inside the hangar to create an eerie feeling for the unsaved. Ever the showman himself, Cal pitched the tent with its opening facing the hangar so that sinners had to make the long trek toward salvation through the deserted cave, their footsteps echoing in concert with the sounds of the screech owls and other night creatures who had nested in its high rafters, as the penitents hurriedly made their way toward the light of Cal's revival meeting. Only when the meeting was over did he open up the flap at the other side of the tent and let the newly saved go back to terra firma.

Cal was in rare form tonight.

Rafferty sat on top of the cruiser and listened to the next three exorcisms. Some of the demons had deep voices, some shrieked, and one talked in pig latin. At the end of the last one, Cal asked his penitents to dig into their souls and their pockets and make a contribution to the ministry. Anything would be acceptable, he said, but special prayers of deliverance would be spoken aloud for everyone who paid at least 125 dollars.

The collection took more than twenty minutes, after which Cal's choir of redeemed witches sang a rousing chorus of "Bringing in the Sheaves" while the congregants began to file out.

Rafferty was fanning himself with the search warrant when the service broke. People stumbled, dazed, into the parking lot. The teenager who had spoken in pig latin walked held up by his father. The mother, who was still crying, walked several feet behind. "Glad to have you back," Rafferty heard the father say to his son. Rafferty wasn't sure the kid was back. It looked more like he was simply in shock.

Rafferty watched as the crowd thinned out. He nodded to a man he recognized from the boatyard, but the guy seemed embarrassed to be caught here; he wouldn't meet Rafferty's eyes.

Disturbed by the crowd, a wharf rat scrambled out of its hiding place. A barn owl that had been perched on a high rafter swooped down after the rat, flying just over the heads of the penitents and causing one of the women to swoon and drop to her knees, sobbing and swearing that she had just seen the Holy Spirit.

There was a clicking sound and a sizzle, and then the place went dark. Rafferty thought for a moment that he might have missed Cal, but then the preacher emerged from the hangar side, dressed in his usual Armani, though it was far too hot. Still, Cal knew his audience. Evidently the devil was more likely to stick his neck out for Italian silk than for Holy Land muslin.

Two robed disciples stood watching as Cal emerged. Rafferty recognized them as Cal's bodyguards. One was an ex-marine he used to see at AA, and the other was the one they called "John the Baptist." Cal motioned for them to go ahead without him. He paused briefly to allow a female penitent to kiss his ring. After offering the woman his standard blessing, he walked over to Rafferty's car.

"Lovely evening, Detective." Cal drew out each syllable of the last word hitting each consonant hard. "I expect you have come to inquire about our prodigal daughter."

Rafferty would have chosen a different parable to describe Angela. But that was Cal. Already putting his own spin on things.

"I have a warrant," Rafferty said, handing it to him.

"That won't be necessary," Cal said. "We have nothing to hide."

The tourists in the Mini Wini were roasting marshmallows over a propane grill. The woman looked up from her s'more with mild interest as the two men passed.

"Which one is Angela's trailer?" Always start with a question you already know the answer to.

"Was," Cal said. "Angela left the order almost a month ago."

"Any idea where she went?" Rafferty asked, watching Cal's face for the answer.

"She went home," Cal said. "At least that's where we agreed she should go. We try to encourage runaway teens to reunite with their families. It is God's way. And of course she needs her family now more than ever. With the pregnancy and all."

Not bloody likely, Rafferty thought. He'd already called Angela's family. Home wasn't a place she would go unless she had no other options.

"Mind if I look around?"

Cal ushered Rafferty to the old Airstream that had served as Angela's quarters since she'd gone back to them after the last time she "disappeared."

"Mind your noggin," Cal said, pointing to the low overhang. Noggin. The word was all wrong coming from a man wearing Armani. It was more like something from an Andy Hardy movie. It was a word consciously appropriated by Cal to make him appear harmless.

The Airstream was ancient and tiny, but he could see Angela's touch. Candles everywhere. And angels—the warrior angels, Michael and Gabriel. Around the perimeter of the room, jammed into every available spot, were the *milagros:* tiny pieces of disjointed miracles—a head, an arm, a heart. Though her family was a loose mixture of native Maine and French Canadian, Angela had a thing for Spanish artifacts, which she usually picked up at the shops in the Point. A black lace mantilla hung in the corner. The kind old women used to wear to Mass back when hats were required. This one hung suspended in front of a picture of the Virgin, more veil than hat. For just a moment, Rafferty wished he had learned to read lace.

The trailer smelled like Ann's shop. Essential oils of some kind. Sandalwood, maybe patchouli.

Cal frowned at the scent. As his expression changed, his scalp tightened, revealing his graying roots. Rafferty's gaze dropped to the tiny white sink. It was stained, a deep brown color. He touched the cold porcelain, drawing his finger across the stain. It was in the wrong place for a rust stain. And too dark for blood. A close match for Cal's hair, he realized. Angela was the one who dyed his hair. For some reason this got to Rafferty. He assumed that the baby was Cal's. And it bothered him, of course it did. But this was worse, somehow. Rafferty remembered Angela's father telling him she'd gone to beauty school for a few months after she'd dropped out of high school. Yes, it was Angela who dyed Cal's hair all right, a shade too dark for the age of his fading skin. He wasn't old by any means, but the hair was the wrong shade. It was like everything about Cal. Perfect to some eyes, maybe. But when you looked closely, everything was just a shade off.

"You mind if I take this?" Rafferty picked up Angela's toothbrush.

Cal flinched. He obviously did mind. But what he said was, "Suit yourself."

Rafferty carefully placed the toothbrush in an evidence bag, sealing and labeling it.

He looked around the room for more items, making a list. Under the bed he found her backpack. He'd seen it with her before. She'd had it on the island. It was the only piece of luggage she owned. It was big and bulky, and Roberta complained about it during the short time Angela had crashed with her.

"She obviously left in a hurry," Rafferty commented, pointing to the backpack.

"I told you it was planned," Cal said. He was clearly lying. He was good at it, Rafferty thought. Psychopaths usually are.

He'd argued with Eva over that one. She had called Cal a sociopath. His religious fundamentalism seemed so out of the ordinary to her. So "beyond the fringe of polite society" was the way she had put it. Looking at it one way, she was right. But looking at it another, Eva was the one who was beyond the fringe. Rafferty had been a cop for a long time, long enough to know that two people looking at something with two different sets of eyes seldom saw the same thing.

Rafferty thought of Cal's followers, the ones he'd "saved." They were a diverse group of misfits: the ex-marine who credited Cal with his sobriety; the one they called "John the Baptist," a schizophrenic that Cal had taken off his meds. Ten people could tell you ten different stories about Cal. And they'd all be right—and wrong at the same time.

Rafferty walked to the end of the trailer and looked back from this new perspective. Viewed one way, the trailer was the room of a penitent. Looked at another, with its velvet-curtained bed and candles, it was something else entirely. Madonna and whore. The classics. The saved and the sinner. Everything and its opposite. No wonder Angela had hung the veil in front of the Virgin's face. She didn't want Mother Mary to see the kind of sins that happened here.

And yet, by her own admission, Angela had been "saved." That's what she kept saying to May when Rafferty went out to Yellow Dog Island the first time to get her back. She had to go back to Cal, she cried over and over while May paced the dock. She had made a terrible mistake coming here, she said. Cal had never beaten her, she insisted. It was the others, the women in particular, who hated her and accused her of falling back into witchcraft.

"But you were never a witch," Rafferty had said.

"I don't know." Angela seemed confused. "Reverend Cal says I was." She rolled up her sleeve, revealing a large birthmark. "I have the devil's marks," she said. "Here"—she started to undo her blouse—"and here."

"Stop," May said. "If she wants to go, let her go."

"Praise Jesus," Angela said.

Rafferty had expected more of a fight from May.

"I have enough trouble with the ones who *want* my help," May said.

She turned and walked up the dock.

He didn't know what to do. The girl was obviously delusional.

"I am saved," Angela said.

Saved? Rafferty scoffed. Statutory rape? Or was it child abuse? Saved? Then, in a flash, it came to him. He understood the attraction. Rafferty with all his lapsed-Catholic guilt. And the list of amends he kept trying to make. To his ex. To his daughter. In this moment he understood the draw of redemption. He understood why people wanted to be born again. Accept Jesus and you get a free ticket to heaven. No matter what you did in the past or would do in the future. When you were saved, you were saved. No penance. No Hail Marys, no moral inventories, no ninth-step amends. The Calvinists preached fire and brimstone, but only to the unsaved: the Catholics, the Jews, the Wiccans. The insiders were protected. A few indulgences and some tithing bought you an insurance policy.

Who the hell wouldn't want to join a religion like that?

In a round piece of lace, the still point is found at the center. All patterns emerge from it. In the laces of Ipswich, the still point is not as easy to find. The Reader must rely on intuition. Within the still point, past, present, and future exist simultaneously and time, as we know it, disappears completely.

It is from the still point that the reading must begin.

—THE LACE READER'S GUIDE

Chapter 15

Ann laughed aloud when he presented her with the toothbrush. "You trying to tell me something, Rafferty?"

"It's Angela's."

"And?"

"And I heard you tell that woman you needed something personal. So you could read her. I figured a toothbrush was pretty personal." Rafferty grinned.

"You're something else," Ann said.

She pulled the curtain, took a seat across from him. On the floor under the table was a dimmer, which she pushed with her foot, bringing the lights down to a faint glow.

"Very impressive," Rafferty said.

"Shut up," Ann said. She took the toothbrush, held it for a few minutes. She twisted it. She felt the bristles. She closed her eyes. Then, suddenly, she dropped it on the table and glared at Rafferty.

"What?" he said.

She stared at him, assessing his intentions.

"Do you know why I asked that woman for something personal before I would read her?"

"I assumed it was because it had some kind of energy."

"Everything has some kind of energy," Ann said. "That wasn't the point. When I asked her to give me something, what I was really asking for was permission to read her."

"I don't get it. Didn't she pay you for a reading?"

"Her daughter was the one who paid me."

"So?" Rafferty was confused.

"So I thought her daughter might have some kind of agenda."

Rafferty looked at the toothbrush.

"Was this a trick?" Ann asked him.

"What?"

"You know it's not her toothbrush." Ann made a face. "It's Cal Boynton's."

"I had my suspicions. I needed confirmation."

"And they think psychics are duplicitous." Ann excused herself and walked to the sink. She turned on the hot water and washed her hands all the way up to the elbows. Then she dried them and put on petitgrain oil for protection.

She came back and sat down again. "Haven't you just destroyed your own evidence?"

"It's a toothbrush, not a murder weapon. I was only looking for verification of their relationship."

"Not to state the obvious, but I would think her appearance of late would be your verification," Ann said.

"I needed more," he said. Not wanting to piss her off any further than he already had, Rafferty continued: "I really do want a reading on Angela. I mean, if you can do one."

"You have some other personal item for me? Used dental floss or something?"

"No," Rafferty said. "Nothing else."

Ann looked at him again. He was sincere.

"I'm not going to do a reading," she said. "But I'll help *you* do one."

"Right," he said.

"I'm serious," she said. "If you want my help, you're gonna have to work a little."

"I don't know," he said. He had absolutely no talent for this kind of thing.

"A guided meditation," she said. "I'll lead you in it."

"I don't know," he said again.

"Take it or leave it," she said. "I've got a busy day today."

"Okay," Rafferty said. "What do I have to do?"

"You can start by breathing," she said.

"Yeah, I seem to do that on a regular basis."

"Slowly."

He looked at her.

"Either you believe in this stuff or you don't."

Rafferty tried to slow his breathing. He felt ridiculous.

"Anyone can learn to do readings," she said. "Eva must have told you that."

Eva had in fact told him that, though she also told him that some people had a natural talent for reading. Like Ann. And Towner.

"Okay, okay. Help me a little here," Rafferty said. He was starting to hyperventilate.

"Take a deep breath and hold it," Ann said.

Rafferty's first deep breath made him cough. He fought the urge to laugh. He took another breath and held it for a long time.

"Okay," she said. "Now exhale."

Rafferty repeated the breathing until he felt himself relax. For a minute he felt as if he were slipping off the chair. It occurred to him that he should open his eyes to check, but he didn't.

"We're going to do a little meditation now." Ann's voice seemed far away.

Rafferty nodded.

"Picture yourself in a house. It can be any house. One you're familiar with or something you just imagine."

Rafferty pictured the house he grew up in, a sprawling postwar ranch in need of a paint job.

"Open the door," Ann said. "Let's go inside."

Rafferty did as he was told. He closed his eyes. He breathed deeply.

"We're going to climb a flight of stairs," Ann said. "Seven steps."

Rafferty breathed. There were no stairs in the house he grew up in. There was no second floor. He'd already fucked this thing up.

"Slow, relaxed."

Rafferty tried to picture another house. Nothing came.

"At the top of the stairs is a corridor with several doors."

Rafferty was trying, he really was.

"Choose one of the doors. Open it."

Nothing came to him. There were no stairs in this house. Well, there were stairs, and there was a door, too, but the stairs went to the basement. Not knowing what else to do, he imagined himself going down those stairs. He walked to the door. He was trying to match his breathing to Ann's, trying to sync up.

"Walk through the door. . . . Stay for a while. . . . Look around. Take in everything and try to remember it. Don't judge, just observe and try to remember."

Ann was silent for a long time. When she spoke again, Rafferty wondered if he'd dozed off for a minute. He felt calm and relaxed. And completely blank.

"Okay, now slowly, slowly, descend the stairs. Hold the railing as you go. When you get to the bottom of the stairs, step outside into the light. Feel the warmth of the sun."

Rafferty tried to picture himself doing the opposite. Coming up the stairs, moving outside into the light.

"When you're ready, open your eyes."

He opened them.

He felt embarrassed, and completely inept. He'd totally failed.

"Describe what you saw," Ann said.

Rafferty didn't speak.

"Go ahead," she said. "You can't make a mistake."

"Well, first of all, I didn't go up, I went down."

"All right, maybe *you* can make a mistake."

"It was a ranch house," he said, trying to explain. He expected her to end the exercise right there. Or tell him to stop wasting her time. Instead she took a breath and continued.

"What did you see when you went down the stairs?"

"I didn't see anything," he said. "Nothing at all."

"What did this nothing at all look like?"

"What kind of question is that?"

"Humor me," she said.

"It was black. No, not black, but blank. Yeah. Dark and blank," Rafferty said.

"What did you hear?"

"What do you mean, what did I hear?"

"Were there any sounds? Or smells?"

"No. . . . No sounds. No smells."

He could feel her eyes on him.

"I didn't see anything. I didn't hear anything. I kept trying to go back up the stairs. I failed Psychic 101," Rafferty said.

"Maybe," Ann said. "Maybe not."

"What's that supposed to mean?"

"I went into the room with you," Ann said. "At least I thought I did."

"And what did you see?"

"Nothing. It was too dark."

"I told you," Rafferty said.

"I heard something, though . . . a word."

"What word?"

" 'Underground.' "

"Underground as in hiding? Or underground as in dead?"

Ann didn't answer. She had no idea.

POLICE REPORT
August 21, 1980

At approximately 9:55 P.M., a teenaged girl entered the station. The officer on duty was Darby Cohen. Also present was Officer Margaret Kowalski. The girl, who was approximately 17, identified herself as "Towner Whitney." She was very distraught, her appearance was disheveled, and her clothing (which appeared to be a nightshirt) was wet. She wore no shoes, and there was a deep wound on her right foot between the first and second toes. Officer Kowalski recognized her as a resident of Yellow Dog Island. When asked to state her name again, the girl revised her previous statement, saying that, "for the record," her first name was really "Sophya."

The girl was very agitated. There were scratches on her legs, and there was a cut on her head, although neither of the wounds appeared to be fresh. When later questioned about them, she stated that the wounds had been received "about a week ago," when she was trying to save her "sister, Lyndley Boynton, from drowning."

When asked the nature of her visit, the girl reported that she had come to turn herself in. She said that she had "just killed Cal Boynton." When questioned further, as to the location and method of Mr. Boynton's demise, she reported that Mr. Boynton was "torn apart by the dogs on Yellow Dog Island."

The police boat was dispatched to Yellow Dog Island at approximately 10:16 P.M. At the recommendation of Officer Kowalski, the Salem paramedics were summoned to examine the girl. Sophya was bandaged and reported healthy at approximately 11:00 P.M. She refused both stitches and a tetanus shot, both of which were recommended. She was issued a change of clothes (Tyvek suit), a blanket, and some decaffeinated hot tea. Although no determining tests were given, it is the opinion of the paramedics that she was not under the influence of alcohol or any illegal substances. There was no sign of concussion, and she did not appear to be physically hurt beyond the above-mentioned wounds.

The police boat arrived at Yellow Dog Island at approximately 11:32 P.M. The responding officer was Paul Crowley, the harbormaster. Officer Crowley reported that when he arrived on the island, the ramp was down. He reported that the Boynton house was boarded up and that a lamp was on at the Whitney house, but that no one appeared to be home. All entries to the house were secured, with the exception of one open window.

Officer Kowalski stayed with Sophya. When questioned further about the events, Sophya reported that

Cal Boynton had landed at Back Beach in a Boston Whaler and had proceeded to "head up the cliffs toward his house." She reported that Mr. Boynton was "looking for his daughter." She admitted to being confused by this, because there was no one at his house, which had been boarded up for the past two years. She said that Mr. Boynton's daughter "died about a week ago, in a *drowning accident.*" She also said that to the best of her knowledge Mr. Boynton had already been informed about his daughter's death. She speculated that he might have been "in denial" and perhaps that was why he had come here "all the way from California" to look for her.

The witness then informed the officer that she had been in fear for her life, when she saw Calvin Boynton, and when asked to elaborate, she went on to say that the alleged victim's wife, Emma Boynton, had been recently hospitalized in San Diego after receiving a severe beating from her husband. This story was later verified. Sophya then told the officer that her "great-aunt, Eva Whitney," had flown to California the day before and that her "mother, May Whitney," was on the island waiting for news of Emma's condition. She then broke down in tears.

She said that she had been "very frightened" by the appearance of Cal Boynton on Yellow Dog Island,

and that he was "very agitated." According to her, he said, "I'm here for my girl." When asked to elaborate, she could not, but only described his intentions as "ominous."

The girl reported that the dogs then "just started to appear." She told the officer that they "came out to see what was going on." According to her first report, there were "hundreds of them, all over the cliffs and the beach and everything," but when asked how many of the dogs actually attacked Mr. Boynton, she answered, "Ten or twelve, I think."

Sophya went on to say that the dogs had "never liked Cal" and that he "used to beat them" and had "actually killed one of them a few summers ago with a baseball bat," although she said that has never been proven. "Tonight it all happened very quickly," she said. "The dogs just attacked him." When asked for more information, she said that she had "wanted the dogs to go after Cal."

The girl reported that when the attack was over, Cal Boynton lay motionless on the ground, "dead." When asked if she was certain that he was dead, she said she was, although she said she did not examine the body because she "did not want to get near him in any way." When asked why she did not go to May Whitney for help, she said that she had not gone to May because it "hadn't occurred to me." When further questioned, she revised her story, saying it was because she knew that May Whitney "would not have helped."

Officer Crowley awakened May Whitney, who was "very concerned" about the girl. May Whitney told Officer Crowley that it was "improbable, if not impossible," that Cal Boynton had been on the island that night. She told police that Cal Boynton was lost at sea somewhere off the west coast of Baja, California. After severely beating his wife, Emma, Mr. Boynton had reportedly "stolen a boat from the San Diego Yacht Club" (from which he had recently been fired), and his boat had "gone down off the coast of Rosarito Beach in Baja." She said that both the San Diego police and the Mexican authorities were searching for the boat and that "when and if they found him," he would not be returning to New England but would be arrested and arraigned in San Diego for the theft of the boat and for the severe beating of his wife, Emma Boynton, who had been hospitalized in San Diego and was in "critical condition." Upon further investigation, May Whitney's story was confirmed. San Diego police reported that Cal had been found two hours earlier off the coast of Baja. He was delirious and severely dehydrated but expected to recover.

Sophya insisted that both the San Diego police and May Whitney were "liars" and once again insisted that

Cal Boynton had been "ripped apart by dogs." She became more agitated as she reiterated the story, and neither police nor May Whitney were able to calm her down.

Addendum, August 22, 1980. At 11:45 A.M., Sophya was admitted to Salem Hospital for observation. At the family's request, she was transferred later that day to McLean Psychiatric Hospital and admitted to that facility at 4:32 P.M.

When reading the lace, the Reader must look for one of two things: something that enhances the pattern or something that breaks it.

—THE LACE READER'S GUIDE

Chapter 16

Rafferty grabbed the pages off the copier as they came out. A black stripe ran down the final page of the report, obscuring the signatures of the three officers.

Rafferty had read everything he could find on Angela, which wasn't very much.

And now he'd begun to go back through the old records, pulling everything on the Whitney family and most particularly on Eva and her problems with her ex-son-in-law, Cal Boynton.

Rafferty had checked every hospital and every morgue all up and down the coast. He had called Angela's parents, who insisted they hadn't heard from her. Then he'd checked five local shelters. He had even called HAWC, the local group that helped abused women and children. No one had seen anyone matching Angela's description.

Angela Rickey had disappeared. Again.

Rafferty went to his office and shut the door. He poured himself more coffee and sat down to read all the reports one more time, looking for something, anything, he might have missed. His mind was fuzzy. He hadn't been to bed at all last night. And it looked like he wouldn't be getting there anytime soon.

He read Towner's report again. And anything else he could find on the family. There were two restraining orders against Cal, one forbidding him to go to Yellow Dog Island and the more recent one that kept him away from Eva. There were two older reports of beatings, one filed by Eva and the other by May and Eva the night Cal broke Emma Boynton's jaw. There was the other beating, too, of course, the one that had blinded Emma, the one that happened in San Diego the night Cal disappeared at sea.

Eva had told him the rest of the story. About how some Mexican fishermen found Cal off the coast of Rosarito Beach. Spotting his orange life preserver bobbing out near the horizon and the line of gulls following closely, they had gone over to investigate. Cal was almost dead when they fished him from the water, Eva told Rafferty.

When Cal was well enough to leave the hospital, he was taken to a San Diego jail. For stealing the boat. And for the beating that blinded Emma Boynton.

According to Eva's story, Cal had been let go from the San Diego team, ending any hope he'd had of winning the America's Cup. He'd gone to a waterfront bar and drunk away the afternoon. Then, as was his habit, he'd gone home and taken the whole thing out on Emma.

The severity of his normal beatings wasn't enough to satisfy Cal, who had just seen his life's dream dashed. He hit her harder. He smashed her face into a mirror. She wouldn't stop staring at him, he later told the judge. He cried as he told the courtroom the story. When he saw the extent of her injuries, Cal fled. Hiding out until nightfall, he sneaked back into the club and stole the boat they had built for him. His boat. Somewhere south of the city, Cal had run the boat aground.

While Emma fought for survival with her mother, Eva, by her side, Cal fought for his own life. Unable to untie the life raft, Cal grabbed a vest. He was not found until forty-eight hours later.

When he recovered, Cal seemed a changed man. He claimed to have seen God. Out in the ocean, without hope of survival, Cal had seen the face of Jesus. He was redeemed.

When he was finally rescued, Cal decided to devote his life to spreading the Word.

He told his story to anyone who would listen. He had seen his own death. Cal told them his body had been torn apart. He had felt the fires of hell.

Through the power of the Lord, Cal had stopped drinking without a struggle. Anyone who saw him had to admit that he was a changed man.

Cal's work with recovering alcoholics led to a reduced sentence in his conviction for the beating of Emma Boynton. She had been relocated to New England due to the severity of her injuries, she was neither available nor reliable as a witness, and Cal's sentence was reduced to time served plus six months' community service and two years' probation.

While in San Diego, Cal founded and incorporated his own church. Known as the Calvinists, his members included the severely disenfranchised and previous domestic abusers. Some of his converts were local street people, including schizophrenics and the alcoholic homeless who responded to the religious message preached by Cal and trusted him as one of their own. To this day the City of San Diego cites Cal Boynton as an example of successful rehabilitation, where "previous

offenders utilize their own histories to make a difference in the lives of others." In his campaign for reelec-
tion, the mayor commended the group's success as one
of his accomplishments while in office.

Cal did not acquire his robed disciples until he came
back home to New England.

He had come home to reconcile with Emma, or so
he claimed. When Eva took out the restraining order
on him, Cal was livid. How dare she keep him from his
home and family? He spent what money he could get
his hands on hiring a team of attorneys to win his half
of Yellow Dog Island. He wanted to build a church on
what he considered was still his marital asset. But Eva
and May were way ahead of him. The island had been
put into trust long before, the first time Cal had raised
a hand to Emma. It didn't take a reader to know that
the marriage would end badly.

"How dare you!" Cal shouted at Eva from in front
of her house one snowy night in mid-December. He
picked up a rock and heaved it at a second-story window
but lost his balance and slipped on the icy sidewalk. He
broke his leg in two places.

When asked to comment on the incident for the local
papers, Eva shrugged and said, "I guess the Good Lord
prefers my prayers to his."

It was the first time Cal had been known to speak in
tongues. His rant lasted several hours, until the doctors

prescribed a strong sedative. Cal reportedly slept for days. When he woke up, he filed his first formal accusation against Eva. Not for the slippery sidewalk in front of her house but for witchcraft.

Rafferty went through all of Eva's files. Cal had made several complaints against her: sorcery, witchcraft, kidnapping. That last one had been crossed out and over it were the handwritten words *"making a girl disappear."* It read like something you'd pay to see in a Vegas magic show. Vanishing Act. Rafferty read through the complaint again, looking for something he'd missed the first time. The tie was there. Eva/Angela. Angela/Eva. For a crazy minute, Rafferty thought of dragging the shoreline out by Children's Island, looking for a second body. But Eva's death had clearly been accidental. There had been no sign of foul play. And he'd been looking. There was nothing Rafferty would rather do than arrest Cal for the murder of Eva Whitney. But there was nothing to support it. Except for the fact that Eva was found so far away. That was the one thing everyone kept pointing to. Eva hadn't given up swimming; she had lied to Beezer about that. But for the last few years, she had always confined her swims to the harbor. Eva was a woman who knew her limits.

God, he missed her. He wondered sometimes if he didn't miss her more than her own family did. She was like family to him. Better than, actually. She was his friend. He still couldn't believe she was gone.

"'**Facts are** the enemy of truth,'" Eva quoted Don Quixote.

"If you were twenty years younger, I'd marry you," Rafferty said to her the day she quoted that line.

"If I were twenty years younger, I wouldn't even look at you," Eva said.

He'd laughed all afternoon about that one.

It was about that time she'd started talking about Towner. Or maybe his mind was playing tricks on him. But at some point in their friendship, Eva had started to talk about her and about the surgery Towner kept putting off, about her almost bleeding to death. She had tumors, Eva told him. Benign, yes, but still dangerous. Something a woman couldn't afford to ignore.

"There are many ways to kill yourself," Eva said.

Rafferty nodded in agreement. As a drunk he'd had firsthand experience with at least one of them.

It was the second time that Angela had disappeared. The third if you counted the original, when she ran away from home. But it was only the second time that anyone had been looking for her. The first time Angela had disappeared from the Calvinist camp was before she got pregnant. Rafferty had been called by Cal to search Eva's house.

Rafferty had already known about Angela. Everyone in town was talking about her. She was one of the few pretty women in the Calvinist camp, which had few women at all, really. The Calvinists were a notoriously antifemale bunch. Not only did they fervently fear bewitchment, but beauty of any kind caused them to pray aloud for deliverance. And Angela was a beautiful girl. At least she had been when she'd first arrived.

Angela was also a runaway. She had hitched a ride down Route 1, all the way from Maine, ending up in Salem just in time for one of the Pagan festivals. It was happy coincidence; she wasn't a witch herself, but it was a fun place to be, so she stayed. She hung out in the common for several days, sleeping on a park bench and panhandling near the tour buses. Angela stayed after the Pagans disbursed, and Eva more than once took her a plate of food or let her sleep in her garden or in the gazebo if the weather got bad. Toward the end of the summer, Eva had started to come up with odd jobs for Angela: some windows to be washed, a children's birthday party she needed a waitress for. Somewhere along the way, Angela happened upon one of the revival meetings down at Winter Island. Cal singled her out, which was not too difficult to understand. She was the only pretty face in a sea of despair and addiction. He accused her of witchcraft on the spot. He prayed for her demons to depart. By the end of his exorcism, Cal had convinced Angela and his congregation that her particular demons were much stronger than most and that it would take his personal dedication and unusual methodology to remove them.

No one except Angela ever knew what his unusual methodology entailed. But with the exception of the true-believer Calvinists, no one in Salem thought for a minute that it was Angela's immortal soul Cal was interested in saving.

It didn't take much to convince Angela of her sinful nature. Maybe it was convenience. The weather was getting cold, and she needed a better place to spread her sleeping bag than either the park bench or Eva's gardens. Or maybe it was something inside her. She was running away from some kind of abuse, Rafferty was certain of it. It was never difficult to convince the victim that it was somehow her fault, that there was something evil in her nature that brought out the worst in the abuser. Cal was an expert at that kind of convincing. He'd certainly convinced Emma Boynton of it for years, and probably their daughter as well. Dressed in Armani with his Bible in hand, Cal became persuasive enough to make Angela believe that he was the only one who could save her.

When Cal accused Angela of witchcraft that night, she fell to her knees and confessed to it on the spot.

After Angela admitted practicing witchcraft, the Calvinists paraded her all over town. Even in old Salem, the confession of a witch called for public celebration. In the 1600s it was only the ones who insisted on their innocence who were hanged.

While the Calvinists celebrated her salvation, the witches were getting pissed off. She'd annoyed them before, by panhandling in front of their shops or dressing in black and posing for pictures with the tourists. She never said she was a witch, but she certainly acted the part. Angela was an opportunist. The witches put up with it. They were an entrepreneurial bunch, so her business acumen was not lost on them. They even gave her some charms, a pack of incense, or a free meal once in a while. Ann let her pick herbs from her window-box garden. Usually they had a peaceful coexistence with Angela—some of them even felt sorry for her—but she wasn't one of them. Wicca was a religion as much as any other, and it had its own course of study and ritual before you could call yourself a member. While Angela had been hanging around the shops, she had never even expressed an interest in the religion itself.

Like most people, Angela had an image of witchcraft that was a Hollywood one or, worse, one that came from the hysteria itself. The truth was, there were no witches in old Salem, but they thrived here in great numbers now. It was the ultimate irony, and one that didn't escape a single one of the witches—the fact that they owed their success today to one of the most terrifying religious persecutions in history. It was an uneasy legacy. So when Angela publicly confessed to witchcraft, a nervous shiver ran through the community.

"What do you want me to do about it?" Rafferty had asked when Ann and some of the other witches complained to him.

"I don't know. . . . Something," Ann said.

"First Amendment rights," Rafferty said. "Angela can go around claiming she's the Second Coming if she wants to."

"I'm afraid that role has already been taken," Ann said.

"And we haven't been able to stop Reverend Cal even with God on our side, have we?" Rafferty was referring to the council of churches who'd been trying to find a way to run Cal out of town for the last two years. "The Calvinists are making it their goal to rid Salem of the witches," Rafferty said.

"I don't get it," Ann said. "What kind of weak, lily-livered god are they worshipping if they're so afraid of a few witches?"

"They'll step over the line one of these days, and we'll nail them," Rafferty said.

"That makes me warm with security," Ann said.

But Cal was getting too smart to step over the line. He went right up to it, but he was careful not to cross.

The Calvinists paraded Angela all over town, proclaiming that the witch had been saved. They took her over to Pioneer Village and put her into the stockades. Cal sent photos to the *Salem News* and the *Boston Globe.* He printed brochures listing group rates for exorcisms. The Calvinists distributed them on street corners.

When the Calvinists began to identify other witches in the community, the council of churches called an emergency meeting.

"It's 1692 all over again," Ann said.

"God, save me from your followers," said Dr. Ward.

A month later someone set one of the witches' houses on fire. Everyone assumed it was one of the Calvinists, though no one could prove it. The insurance company attributed the fire to a dirty chimney flue and paid the claim.

Over the winter the Calvinists moved down the coast to a campground somewhere in Florida. When they returned, they had added a new trailer full of women to the entourage. They were a scary-looking bunch. Drunks. Drug addicts. Meth and crack whores. All confessed witches. All supposedly saved.

According to Angela's report, the first time she went to Eva for help and then somehow ended up on Yellow Dog Island, it had been those reformed witches, and not Cal, who had beaten her so badly.

"Stoned," Eva corrected the report. "They didn't beat her, they stoned her."

"Did she tell you that?" Rafferty tried to keep the horror from his voice.

"No," Eva said. "I saw it in the lace."

"So Cal didn't do it," Rafferty said. He *couldn't* keep the disappointment out of his voice.

"Make no mistake," Eva said. "This is Cal Boynton's work, all right."

"You think he told them to do it?"

"I think he *inspired* them to do it. And that's much worse. . . . At least in the old days, he used to do the deed himself. In the old days, you could tell who the bad guys were."

Rafferty stood and looked at her. He could see her pain. Almost as if, for this one moment, he were a reader himself. Eva was letting him see her.

"Cal ruined your family."

"He did," she said.

"Your daughter, Emma," Rafferty said. "And others."

"None of us was left unscathed." Eva looked at him.

He stared at her. Something about her tone quieted him. He didn't dare speak.

"Do you believe in redemption, Detective Rafferty?"

He couldn't answer. The truth was, he didn't know what he believed. Not anymore.

"You'll need to decide that," Eva said. "And quickly."

Cal swore he wasn't around when the beating occurred. Later Angela herself would swear to the same thing. The women had hurt her, she said, because they had found some of the trinkets she'd gotten from the witches. And a piece of lace. It was a piece that Eva had given to Angela months earlier. It was the kind of lace the island girls made. The kind of lace Eva used to do her readings.

When Angela didn't come back to the camp, Cal had gone to the police. Some of his disciples had followed her to Eva's house.

"Don't you mean chased her?" Rafferty asked him. He was already getting phone calls about the Calvinists. He'd been on his way over there before Cal showed up at the station. There was a mob gathering in the park, and in front of Eva's house.

"I want you to search the house," Cal said.

"I have no intention of searching the house." Rafferty stood on Eva's top step with Cal right behind him. "If Eva says Angela's not there, then she's not."

"She's lying."

"I have nothing to hide," Eva said. "Feel free to search the house if you like, Detective Rafferty. Mr. Boynton can come, too, as long as he is in your company."

"If I'm not mistaken, that's a legal invitation," Cal said, stepping over the threshold.

Rafferty started to protest as Eva moved back to let Cal pass.

Eva held the door for Rafferty. "I know what I'm doing, Detective," she said. Her eyes shifted for just an instant to the lace on the window. "Come in."

Rafferty walked inside.

They searched the house. Cal had learned every inch of this house in the days he'd been married to Emma. Even Eva seemed surprised by how familiar he was with the floor plan. He led the search, taking them room to room, sometimes checking a place more than once. Cal was very agitated. He searched the cellar twice and was headed to the widow's walk for the third time when Rafferty finally called off the search.

"Enough," Rafferty said. "She isn't here."

"No," Eva said. "I regret that she isn't."

"She came into this house," Cal said.

"Yes. . . . She did."

"We have witnesses that say she never left."

"Your witnesses need to have their eyes examined," Eva said.

The word of witchcraft spread quickly. Eva had made Angela disappear. The Calvinists were convinced that Eva had magic powers. Even the witches seemed impressed.

"Angela went into the house, but she never came out," Ann told Rafferty. "I know that for a fact. I don't know how Eva did it, but she did."

The next morning Cal and a group of his followers showed up at the police station to file a formal complaint accusing Eva of witchcraft. It was a decent attempt, hand-lettered in old script with *s*'s and *f*'s interchanged, an academic Middle English. It was the first formal complaint of witchcraft filed in Salem since the 1600s.

The Calvinists sent a copy of the complaint to the *Salem News*, which, not knowing how to treat it, printed it in their editorial section.

It had taken Dr. Ward to point out the obvious plagiarism. "See for yourself," the minister said. "It's pure Cotton Mather, down to the 'plan to countermine the devil in New England.' If you don't believe me, you can look it up. The whole account of the witch trials is on display at the Peabody Essex."

"What year is this? What century?" Ann Chase wanted to know.

"I don't understand why we're even taking his report," the police chief said to Rafferty. "Witchcraft isn't even a crime. In this town it's a profit center."

"I'm just building a case," Rafferty said. "For future reference."

"Not against Eva?" The chief seemed shocked.

"Please," Rafferty said.

It was almost three weeks before anyone found out where Angela was.

She radioed Rafferty from Yellow Dog Island. "You have to come out here and get me." Angela's voice was urgent. "I've made a terrible mistake."

The chief stood over Rafferty's shoulder as the message came in.

"I didn't know she was out there," Rafferty said. He could tell the chief didn't believe him.

The two men looked at each other.

"What do you want me to do?" Rafferty asked.

"Go out and get her," the chief said.

Rafferty took the police boat out to the island. May was waiting on the dock with Angela. Her backpack leaned against the ramp.

"You could have told me she was here," Rafferty said to May.

"Not my policy," May said.

"So Eva helped you," Rafferty said.

"Eva told Angela her options. She came here on her own."

"And now I want to go back on my own." Angela's tone was sarcastic.

"Good," Rafferty said. "Because if you tell me you're going back to Cal Boynton, I'm leaving you here."

"She will," May said.

"Reverend Cal never hurt me." She turned to May. "I told you what happened. The women threw stones at me."

"They stoned you?" Rafferty was amazed by Eva's accurate reading.

"Reverend Cal never touched me," Angela said.

"Well, he must have touched you at least once," May said.

Angela turned red.

"She's pregnant," May said.

"Is that true?" Rafferty looked at her. She wasn't showing. Not yet.

Angela started to cry. "This is why I'm leaving," she said. "I told you that in confidence. You're not supposed to tell."

"I don't keep confidences that might endanger you."

"I told you, he wasn't the one who hurt me."

"I'm not talking about physical abuse. I'm talking about sexual abuse."

Angela looked horrified. "He didn't abuse me."

"Right."

Angela went on with her explanation. Cal had never been anything but good to her. Angela went on and on. Talking about the accusation of witchcraft, the devil's marks. And how Cal Boynton had saved her from the fires of hell. She said she was lucky to be chosen. Lucky to be saved.

Rafferty watched May give up on Angela.

"She came too early," May said to him later. She had seen it before. "They never make it if they come here before they're ready."

Rafferty could see the toll it took on May. She was used to girls going back. But May didn't like losing one of her girls. Especially to the man who started the whole thing, the man who'd ruined May's family.

Rafferty gave Angela a ride back to town, but, true to his word, he refused to take her back to the Calvinists. "You shouldn't stay here," he said. "Don't you have friends somewhere?" He knew better than to mention her family.

She ought to file charges, Rafferty told her. If not against Cal, at least against the women who stoned her. She said she'd think about it.

He called around, looking for a room for her. But it was late October, and there wasn't a room anywhere.

He called Roberta and explained the situation. He told her Angela was pregnant. He said he knew that Roberta was looking for a roommate, someone who could help with the rent. Rafferty said he would cover the first month, while Angela looked for something to do for work.

"Why would you do that?" Roberta was already suspicious. "It's not your baby, is it?"

"Funny," Rafferty said.

It didn't last the month. By the end of the first week, Angela was back with the Calvinists. Not in the women's tent this time but in the tiny Airstream parked conveniently next to Cal's RV.

Rafferty knew that it was only a question of time until she showed. He wasn't sure whether Cal knew she was pregnant or not. Unless they were going to try to claim a virgin birth, Angela was about to become a major inconvenience to all the Calvinists. And especially to their leader, who had made a small fortune preaching his own set of commandments, the second of which was celibacy.

No two Readers will ever see the same images in the lace. What is seen is determined entirely by perspective.

—THE LACE READER'S GUIDE

Chapter 17

Rafferty's eyes were beginning to sting. He thumbed through the remaining files. Cal's file was thinner than Eva's, and older. It went back to the seventies, documenting each reported beating of Emma Boynton, most of them uncorroborated or denied altogether by Emma. Until the broken jaw. When questioned at the hospital, Emma would not say anything about her husband. Only that she had fallen down the stairs. At May's insistence the emergency-room doctor had called the police. These days it would be a matter of course. HAWC had their posters everywhere, as did the state. It was unusual *not* to suspect abuse. These days you got a hangnail, they took you into a room with an abuse counselor. A lot of his coworkers thought it excessive. Rafferty wasn't one of them. He remembered the old days. When everyone pretended not to notice until someone ended up dead.

In his own way, Rafferty's views weren't all that different from May's, though she'd never believe it. To May, Rafferty was the enemy. In fact, they usually ended up on opposite sides of the law.

Rafferty radioed ahead to tell her he was coming out to Yellow Dog Island. And why. He stuffed the files into an old sail bag along with his jacket and the rest of his thermos of coffee. He went out the back door and down the steps, leaving the cruiser where it was. Parking spaces near the harbor were hard to come by this time of year, even for a cop.

He decided to walk. He needed the air. Truth was, he needed every advantage he could get. Especially if he was going to match wits with May Whitney.

May was waiting for him on the dock. More angry than concerned. It wasn't a good day for a visit, she told him for the second time.

"Too bad," he said.

Clearly pissed off, she turned and started to walk up the dock.

"You can cooperate," he said, "or I can get a warrant."

She stopped. She spun to face him. "I told you, Angela Rickey is not here."

"When was the last time you saw her?"

"You ought to know. You were here."

"And she hasn't tried to contact you."

"No."

"And you'd tell me if she had."

"Right," May said.

"Just like you did the last time."

"No comment."

"You mind if I look around?"

"I told you, it's a bad day." May was losing patience.

"I need to look around."

"If I were trying to hide Angela Rickey on this island, you wouldn't find her."

"And you haven't moved her," Rafferty suggested.

"What?"

"You were trying to move someone last night. I saw your signal."

"What are you talking about?" Her voice had all the requisite frustration, but her inflection was just a little bit off.

"Two if by sea," he said. "I saw your lights."

"I don't understand."

"If you don't want the whole world to know what you're doing out here, you'd better pick a better signal. Given the time and the inclination, any schoolkid could figure that one out."

"I don't know what you're talking about, Detective Rafferty."

"Was it Angela Rickey?"

"I don't know what you're talking about, but I can assure you that we didn't *move* anyone."

"I know you didn't. I know it because your driver was passed out in his boat at the Derby Wharf."

May stared at him. "I think you're losing it."

"He got into a drunken fight at the Rockmore over a disparaging remark someone made about Towner."

That one stopped her. "Is she okay?" She meant it.

"She's fine," he said. "But Jack LaLibertie is a loose cannon. It's only a question of time before he does something really stupid, and when he does, everyone's going to know what you're doing out here."

May stared at him.

"So I'll ask you one more time. Was it Angela Rickey you were trying to move last night?"

"No," May said.

"You'll pardon me if I don't take your word for it."

Several worried-looking women had started to gather at the top of the dock.

"Is everything okay?" one of them yelled down.

May flashed the okay sign. "Fine!" she yelled back.

They stood unconvinced, watching the police boat.

"Come with me," she said to Rafferty.

She started up the dock toward the island. He followed. At the top of the pier, she turned left toward the far end of the island, past the Boynton house, all boarded up now. They crossed the baseball field and walked in silence toward the stone kennel.

"Watch out for the rabbit holes, Detective," May said as they approached the old building. "You could easily break your leg."

Rafferty was extra careful as he walked down the path. Just like her Aunt Eva, May had powers beyond the normal, even if she didn't care to admit it. "Watch out for rabbit holes" might sound like a warning about furry creatures and sprained ankles. But if Eva had been alive, she would have called it better. May had just fired the proverbial shot across his bow.

Rafferty took in the details: the stone kennel with its blue door, the picnic table outside where two children sat. A worried-looking woman, obviously their mother, watched.

"I'm going to introduce you as a friend," May said. "Not a cop. You think you can pull that off?"

"I'll give it my best shot."

"Make it work," May said. "She's been through enough already."

He could see that.

"This is my friend John Rafferty," May said to the woman. "John, this is Mary Segee."

Rafferty waited. The woman nodded to him but did not extend her hand. He could see the scars on her wrist. Cigarette burn marks. Bent and broken nose. She saw him looking. He looked away. Packed bags. An old suitcase in a corner. He turned his attention to the two children.

"And who might you be?" Rafferty held out his hand to the girl.

"I might be Rebecca," the girl said.

"She might be, but she's not," May said. "Her name is Susan." The little girl remembered herself, looking scared for just an instant. "We were playing a game," she said. "That's my brother, Timothy." The little boy didn't look up.

"Nice to meet you both," Rafferty said. Now the boy looked up, then at his mother, then down again.

"Going on a trip, are you?" Rafferty said.

"We're going to Canada," the little girl said before the mother was able to stop her.

"Canada is beautiful this time of year," Rafferty said.

"I'm going to have my own bike," the boy said.

"That's great," Rafferty said. "Fantastic."

"Mr. Rafferty has to go now," May said. "He just wanted to say hello."

"You're not going to Canada, are you?" the girl said, glancing toward his boat.

"I'm afraid I'm only going to town," Rafferty said, and shook her hand again. "You have a nice time up there, okay?"

"Okay," the girl said.

Rafferty walked behind May to the dock. He was glad for the ruts in the road. Glad for the silence. Grass matted in tangles. Gulls overhead. Up by the baseball diamond, some kids had started playing softball with some of the women. Others worked the garden. A cow grazed at the far end of the field. A couple of cows. And some sheep. And the dogs. Everywhere the dogs. He watched as one of them stalked and killed a rabbit. It was violent, but it wasn't personal, unlike the kind of violence that had happened to the human inhabitants of Yellow Dog Island.

They stopped at the top of the dock. "Satisfied?" she said.

"Yes."

"You didn't really think she'd come back here, did you?"

"No," he said.

"You think Cal killed her?"

"I don't know what I think."

"You think he killed Eva?"

He didn't answer.

"Everybody else thinks so."

"Good," Rafferty said.

The Reader must be certain, as she asks the question, that the Seeker is prepared to receive the answer.

—THE LACE READER'S GUIDE

Chapter 18

Rafferty had been fighting a headache all afternoon. He'd stopped by the old Chinese acupuncturist down by the docks and had some needles put in, but then he'd gotten a call and had to cut the session short. He didn't realize it was a migraine until he was bringing the boat around.

He was late. Well, what else was new?

Towner was waiting for him on the wharf. The sun had just dropped behind the Custom House, lighting up the sky behind her with every shade of color, intensifying the aura that began over the city and carried all the way outside the harbor over the open ocean, until the sky and the water became indistinguishable, cut only on the vertical by Towner herself and the halo of light that played around her.

To say that she was a vision would be accurate, but not in any normal sense. Ethereal glow yes, but that was from the sunset and the migraine aura that was short-circuiting his brain cells.

As the boat moved past her and came toward the dock, the shimmering light show shifted. Now he had to focus his eyes and concentrate just to see her, and in this new half-light his cop's mind filed the images he saw. Cutoffs, bare feet. The same T-shirt he'd seen her in at Red's. Another of Eva's old sweaters draped around her shoulders and clipped with a granny chain.

"I was beginning to think you stood me up," she said.

"Sorry." He pulled in.

The beginnings of a migraine were odd for Rafferty. Sounds echoed. His cotton shirt scraped his skin like sandpaper. He felt as if he could see nothing and everything all at the same time. He couldn't focus on her face at all, but he could see the tracing line of the tan she'd gotten in the garden today, the shadow under the fingernails where she couldn't quite scrub away the dirt from the garden.

Something told him to go home. To call this off. He'd talked her into it, hadn't he? It wasn't something she'd wanted.

She was in the boat before he had a chance to say it. He was still a few feet from the dock. Planning the perfect landing, showing off a little, maybe. He expected her to grab the side of the boat; instead she jumped in. He reached his hand up, and she grabbed it to steady herself, but her aim was dead-on and she didn't need him. This was a woman who was comfortable at sea. Maybe only at sea, he thought. Well, she came by that naturally, didn't she? As soon as he had the thought, he tried to erase it. The last thing he wanted to think about tonight was her family.

"A 110," she said, admiring the boat. Old, wooden. Painted brown. It looked like a chocolate cigar with its tapered ends. "My first boat was a 110."

"You're kidding me," he said.

He realized he was already heading out toward open ocean, away from the lights of town. It just happened. Any question he'd had of turning back was gone.

"Did you race her?" Again Rafferty realized that it was a question he already knew the answer to. He'd seen a photo of Towner as a kid, racing at the Pleon Yacht Club in Marblehead. The photo was on Eva's wall.

She seemed to think about it for a long moment before answering. "No," she said finally. "I never raced."

It stopped him.

"Gaps" was the way Eva had put it. Towner had gaps in memory. He hadn't been too thrown by that. Who didn't have gaps? In AA they called them blackouts. He liked Eva's word better.

Tonight there were gaps in Rafferty's vision, he noticed, holes and empty spaces that were getting larger. The glow was gone, but the sky was too clearly divided. Too sharp. For a minute it was a tiny knife cutting through his vision, slicing it almost perfectly in half before the blade went into his scalp. He wasn't going to avoid the headache this time. Sometimes he did. But it was coming. He pulled the sheet in tighter, had to move the boat faster to keep the nausea at bay.

"Do you mind if we don't talk for a few minutes?" he asked.

Towner seemed relieved not to have to make conversation. Instead she sat in the bow, hands holding the sides. She was turned away from him, looking ahead, north toward the black water, never back at where they'd been.

It might have angered another woman. The not-talking thing. But she seemed comfortable with it.

They fell into the rhythm. The wind. The swells. There was something hypnotic about it, and something in the moving air that made it easier to breathe.

He knew she felt it, too. This date was already better than the one last night. It was better when they didn't try to talk.

Somewhere past Manchester he lost all vision. Partly it was the darkness. At first he thought they were off course, much farther out to sea than they were. But then he heard the gulls and knew they were near land. He had never before lost his vision so completely. Usually it was just one side or the other, and you could see nothing by directly looking at it; you had to look past to see what was right in front of you.

He didn't know if it was the darkness or the migraine. All he knew was that he couldn't see. Postphasic, he thought. Usually the visuals came first. They had come first in this case. Then gone away as the headache came on. But then the visuals returned. The worst he'd ever experienced.

"Are you all right?" He heard her voice.

"Migraine," he said. "I can't see. You're going to have to take over."

He stayed low in the boat as they traded places. He was dizzy.

"You want to head back?" she asked.

"Yeah," he said.

Twenty minutes, he thought. Twenty minutes to a half hour. That's how long the visuals lasted. He would time it. If it went on any longer, he'd think it might be something worse—a stroke, maybe.

Rafferty sat facing her, his back pressed into the bow.

"You get a lot of migraines?" she asked.

"Yeah," he said.

She sailed easily. The wind was against them on the return trip, but she was skilled. They weren't moving as fast as coming out, but she was keeping a good clip.

"You take anything for them?" she asked.

"Sometimes," he said.

He found himself counting. Realized it was silly. By the time they passed Beverly Harbor, he took his hands down. It was fading. He could see the lights along the shore—intermittent and ringed, but there. He made himself breathe.

"I didn't get a lot of sleep last night," he said when he could speak again. "And I drank too much coffee." He said it aloud as much for himself as for her. The sound of his voice seemed stupid. He wished he hadn't said anything.

By the time they reached Salem, his vision was back. The pain was mostly on the right side.

"You're better," she said.

He wasn't sure how she knew. He hadn't moved much.

"Yeah," he said. He leaned forward, rubbing his neck.

"Do you want to sail her in?"

"No," Rafferty said, pointing. "Take her in toward Shetland Park. The mooring's back there."

She nodded.

He sat in the stern and watched her sail. The harbor was full, a slalom course of boats. She moved among them like a skier, confident enough to cut it close.

"You sail in California?" he asked.

"Not even once," she admitted.

He could see it surprised her. How familiar and easy it seemed.

"Like riding a bicycle," he said, and she smiled.

He kept his eyes leveled. She would have been embarrassed if she thought he could see, but she wasn't. He watched her shift. He watched the muscles in her arms.

It occurred to Rafferty that his senses had never been this acute. He could smell the air. Smell the citrus on her. From Eva's sweater. Her hair moved independently in the breeze. Some things in it. Shapes. A shell, a sea horse. Migraine images. Phosphorescence trailed behind the boat, marking their course.

"Which one's your mooring?" she asked as they got close.

"There," he said. Starting to get up. He realized that it was a trick question. She knew he was watching her. She'd probably known it all along.

She grabbed the mooring in one pass.

They sat in silence for a minute. "Thanks for sailing us in," he said finally.

"No problem," she said.

He had no idea what else to say to her. He reached over and grabbed the horn. Gave it three quick blasts to summon the launch.

They sat another minute, neither of them speaking. Then he heard the sound of the launch as it was approaching.

"How's your head?" she asked.

"Hurts like a son of a bitch." He tried to laugh.

"Poor baby," she said.

He didn't know if she meant it or if she was making fun of him.

"Are you okay to drive?" she asked as he held the passenger door to let her in.

"I'm okay," he said.

He took her to the house. He walked her to the door.

"I'd invite you in, but . . ."

Rafferty put up a hand. "I've got to get home," he said, gesturing at his head. He was disappointed as hell, but there was nothing he could do about it.

She nodded. "I hope you feel better," she said.

"Twenty-four hours," he said. "Or a good night's sleep. Whichever comes first."

He started down the steps. Halfway down he turned around. He walked back.

"I need to tell you to lock your door," he said.

"What?"

He was standing too close. It made him dizzy trying to look at her this close. And it scared her a little; he could tell it did. He stepped back down a stair. "Cal is going to try to see you. Sometime. I'm not trying to scare you. I'm just telling you to keep your door locked."

"Okay," she said. Her voice cracked slightly when she said it.

"I'm not trying to scare you," he said again.

"Okay," she repeated.

Rafferty waited on the step until she was inside and he heard the click of the lock.

He wondered if he had any Imitrex left. This was going to be a bad one.

It is important to ask the right question of the lace. This may be the Reader's greatest responsibility.

—THE LACE READER'S GUIDE

Chapter 19

I lean against the door to steady myself, waiting for the rush of adrenaline to fade. Rafferty wasn't trying to scare me, but he did. I know he's right. Cal will try to see me. I've seen it in my dreams a thousand times. My nightmares. I know how it will go. The scene has played through me so often that it seems almost rehearsed.

It may not freak me out anymore, not on a daily basis anyway, but it's a bad place for me to go.

I'm not all that disappointed that our evening ended early. Though I feel bad that Rafferty has a headache, the truth is that I'm not feeling all that great myself. I can't tell if it's physical or psychological, but I make a mental note to call my surgeon in L.A. and have him set up some kind of postsurgical follow-up with someone in Boston.

It takes me a few minutes to realize that I've left Eva's sweater in Rafferty's car. I hear the sound of the engine starting as I race down the steps. By the time I reach the brick walkway, the cruiser is rounding the corner.

I climb back up the front steps and turn the handle of the front door. It spins but doesn't engage. The door is locked. I can see the key on the front table where I dropped it.

I could pick the lock. It's an easy one. All I need is a hairpin, something wiry. I look around the porch for something, anything. But it's too dark, a moonless night, and the porch is trellised and ivy-covered. I'm too tired to spend a lot of time looking. If I'm going to have to break in again, I figure I should walk around back to the window I've already broken. Why add another window repair to the Realtor's list?

The iron gate of the garden creaks open. I close it behind me and step into the formal gardens. My footsteps crunch on the pea stones and crushed shells of the path to the back door.

I am halfway across the garden when I feel his presence. It jumps down on me like a cat into a baby's crib. It is thick and oppressive, and it steals my breath.

I reel around.

The figure of a man sits motionless on the bench. Hunched over. Illuminated by the reflection of the streetlights through the barred iron fence. Only the eyes are moving. I can feel them on me as I walk.

My legs are nightmare heavy. I am stuck.

Rafferty's warning comes back at me. *Cal is going to try to see you.*

I can hear him breathing.

I cannot move.

I close my eyes and try to summon the dogs. In the nightmare—or the hallucination, as my doctors insisted on calling it—there were dogs. But my nightmare takes place on Yellow Dog Island, not here in Eva's garden. There are no dogs here to help me.

For the first time in my life, I hope I'm having a hallucination. I close my eyes. When I open them, he will not be there.

Slowly, so slowly, I open my eyes. He is still there. This is real.

"What do you want?" I try to growl the words.

His eyes burn into me. I have been here before.

"Go away," I say. But the growl is gone, and my voice sounds thin, tinny. I have already lost.

The world stops. We are suspended. When I finally hear the voice, it shocks me.

"Sophya," his voice says. It is barely a whisper.

I am surfacing through water. I am being pulled out of something dark. I can breathe.

"Jack," I say.

My eyes clear, or adjust to the darkness, and I see him for the first time. My childhood love. Inside, a few minutes later, under the harsh electric light, I will see the years on him. The anger. The betrayal. But here, lit only by moon and stars, he is eighteen again.

*The beginning Reader must resist the urge to inter-
pret the images seen. These images belong entirely
to the Seeker.*

—THE LACE READER'S GUIDE

Chapter 20

I awaken in a sailing ship. Floating on open ocean
with no land in sight. My skin cracked open from
sun. Tongue thick with dehydration. I am dying.

I try to clear my head. I have been here before,
dreamed it at least.

I force myself to sit up.

What is real?

Force of will clears my head.

What is real?

I am in a room. Eva's room. I have been staring up
through the lace of the canopy. I jerk my head away,
and my vision fades, leaving traces along the walls as it
disappears.

What is real?

Eva's bed sits dead center in the room, a sailing vessel surrounded by open ocean. Its four carved posts lift upward like the spires of a miniature cathedral. The mahogany was brought back as ballast on one of the Whitney ships that traveled the Madagascar run. It was then carved by a Salem mast maker who was more aspiring artist than shipwright. The headboard is rough-hewn, but as the posts ascend, they curve and twist in symmetrical perfection, lifting to the billowing canopy, which Eva fashioned from rounds of bobbin lace she made over the years, then patched together into a crazy quilt of lace. The bed hovers somewhere between cathedral and sailing ship, but more of the latter, because there is definite movement to it, as much from its canopy sail as from its four masts.

I realize I've been staring up through the canopy. The pictures I'm seeing are in the lace.

My head hurts. Not just my head. Every muscle in my body aches. If this is a hangover, it is a bad one. I am not a drinker. At least I wasn't until last night.

We finished the bottle, and then one from Eva's cellar, before Jack had the courage to say what he'd come here to say.

"I am a dead man," he said.

"No," I said, mistaking his anger for grief.

"It wasn't Cal you killed," he said, his eyes burning into mine. "It was me."

I had gone to McLean Psychiatric Hospital because I thought I had killed Cal. That was a hallucination. A wish-fulfillment fantasy is what the doctors called it. Seeing Cal Boynton ripped apart by dogs. But Cal was still very much alive. I may have wanted to kill Cal for what he'd done to my sister and my aunt, but my aim was off. It was Jack that I ended up hitting.

While I was in McLean, Jack had come to see me almost every day. He had driven his father's truck, lobster traps in the back. He parked in the back lot, away from the other, fancier cars.

When they started the shocks, I began to lose memory.

"She may not know you," the doctors told him. "Sometimes the short-term memory disappears for a while."

He waited for me to ask for him. The weather got cold. Still he waited.

He walked against the wind, his collar up, head down, coat drawn tight around him. I watched him coming through the trees.

He came every day until the first snow. Until the night his father got drunk and totaled the truck on some black ice.

"He won't be coming back," Eva said. I turned my head toward the wall and stared at the trees. For weeks I stared. I stared at them as the leaves finally fell away and they revealed their lacy black branches underneath. I looked for Jack in the web of lace. He wasn't there. I looked for Lyndley, too, but she was nowhere. There was one leaf left on the tree, one still hanging on to the very end of a branch, and I watched that leaf, too, until I woke up one morning and found that it had released its hold. I walked to the window and looked down, thinking I would know the leaf in the pile, that I had stared at it for so long I would be able to recognize it anywhere. But it was a leaf like any other now. Browning, dying. Soon they would come and burn it with the others.

I saw Jack just one more time after that. Almost a year later. It was the day I was leaving for UCLA. They had released me from McLean only because I had a plan. I had submitted my stories to UCLA and been accepted into their writing program. Everyone seemed to agree that it was a good thing to do. Everyone except Eva.

I stood in the Whaler as Beezer cast off. Jack's boat was pulling in as we pulled out, both of us standing as we passed each other. He was trying to read my face, looking at me for signs of recognition. I looked back at him, trying to keep my expression blank. I held my breath.

I actually thought I had fooled him. Until last night.

My head hurts. The canopy moves and swirls. To get away from it, I roll over in the bed. The motion turns my stomach. I am going to be sick.

I hoist myself up, holding the bedpost. I move slowly, grabbing onto furniture for balance, pulling myself along until I get to the old marble sink in the corner of the room. I turn on the faucet and wait until it runs cold. I douse my face, then pour a glass and make myself drink the entire thing. Then I throw up.

I am drenched with sweat.

I need air.

I walk to one of the windows and lift it open, but it is too heavy, its sash cord broken and dangling. I look around for something to prop it up with, find an old ruler. I walk across the room to open its opposing window. It holds for a moment, then comes crashing down, just missing my fingers. It slams hard, cracking two panes almost symmetrically in half. It jolts me awake.

I move carefully window to window, opening them all. The hot breeze fills the room, bringing up street noise.

The curtains billow and snap like old sails, and the lace canopy furls and fills with air, catching my attention with the sound. There's a rush of salt air, and then the room is full of sailing ships. I am back in time to the Salem of the China-trade era. The huge ships move slowly by one another in the harbor. The merchants in the streets sell spices to the local mistresses, who fight over them, paying a fortune for a small amount of pepper that they will take home and keep locked up in ornate boxes and almost never serve to anyone.

I make my way to the edge of the bed. I stretch for the low-hanging border of the canopy, pulling it down. I stuff it under the bed. My head spins and reels. I turn on my side and put my hand against the headboard to still the room. I wait for sleep.

When I wake up again, it's noon. I feel a pain in my stomach.

When was the last time you ate? I imagine Eva asking. She would be right. The pain is hunger.

I get up. I'm thinking I should try to make my way downstairs for charred toast and tea. Eva's cure for anything.

I hear a sound. A voice.

At first I think I am hearing Eva's voice again, and then I recognize the Realtor's nasal twang.

She told me about the showing, but I have completely forgotten. She didn't say that I wasn't supposed to be here when she showed the house. She just assumed that I would be aware of such protocol.

They are coming up the stairs. I hear the Realtor telling the couple about the suspended staircase and how the beams are cantilevered into the walls so that the stairs seem to have no visible means of support. I can tell she doesn't know I'm in the house, because the story has changed since I told it to her. She stops at the landing window to highlight the gardens below, adding new hybrid flowers to Eva's collection, not only the one new rose named for Eva but two or three others that I've never heard of and that she seems to be making up on the spot. She has also added something about the French doors on the third floor, something that is totally untrue, but I can see that would be a selling point if it were not such an embellishment. Still, I can tell even from here that the people aren't interested in the house, that her performance is a total waste of time.

"I died for you."

I stop still. It is Eva's voice. It is so loud I am certain they must have heard.

They keep coming up the stairs.

I have to get out of here, right now.

Before I have a chance to make my exit, the Realtor and her clients have reached the landing. I move toward the back door. I'm dizzy, feeling my way along the walls as if the room had gone dark, though I can see every object. Sweat pours down my face. The Realtor catches the movement in her peripheral vision and looks up. I see her notice me and then lead their eyes to the Samuel McIntire woodwork, giving me time to make my escape out the back door and down the servants' stairs.

I wait for the Realtor in the garden. I am very tense. I can overhear snippets of their conversation as they stand by the gate talking. I am trying to hear them, to ground myself by the sound of their voices, real voices. They are from somewhere in the Midwest. Chicago, maybe. The woman had been to Salem once before, she says, on a tour. She tells the Realtor that she remembered the architecture and thought of Salem when she learned that her husband was about to be relocated to the Boston area.

I can tell that her husband is less than enthusiastic, both about the house and about Salem.

"So do they still burn witches in this town?" He is trying to be funny.

"They don't burn them, they hang them." The Realtor smiles. Then she moves the conversation back to the sales pitch. "The property values here are much better than on Beacon Hill," I hear the Realtor say, trying to charm him. "Or Back Bay for that matter. . . . You'd pay three to four million for a house like this in Back Bay."

The man asks about the commute. Says it took him forty-five minutes to get here from town. There is vague annoyance in his voice at having to be bothered.

"That's because of the Big Dig," the Realtor says to him. "You should have taken the bridge instead of the tunnel."

He's not buying it. I can tell that, and so can she. She tells him about the commuter rail, says it's within walking distance, twenty minutes to the North Station. What most people do is take the train, she says, but I can tell that this man is not someone who would ever ride the train. This is a man who likes to be in control of his own vehicle.

The whole showing is a waste of time. The Realtor tells me later that she knew it going in. "He wanted to take out the gardens," she says, "to put in a second parking space. Can you imagine?"

She says she has another showing at four and that really it would be better if I were not at home when she comes back. "The owner's presence tends to intimidate potential buyers," she says. "At least if they know you're there."

I make my way into the house. Put on water for tea. Regular Assam and charred toast. I make myself swallow. By midday, I am starting to feel a little better.

I've totally forgotten that Ann is scheduled to meet me on her lunch hour to help me deadhead the flowers. She shows up just as the party-boat horns blast noon. "You okay?" she asks. "You look a little pale."

"Hungover," I say. I feel stupid saying it, but it's convincing.

"Been there, done that," she says.

She doesn't have a lot of time, so we get to work immediately. We work together well. Moving down the rows, deadheading the huge blossoms. It's rhythmic, hypnotic: plucking, gathering, handing the basket back and forth. The heat of the sun is soothing to my aching muscles.

"Thanks," I say.

At the end of a long row of peonies, I see something white in the bushes. I lean over and pick up today's *Salem News* from where the paperboy has thrown it. I am used to seeing Eva's face staring back at me from these papers and am relieved for a moment to see that it has been replaced by another, younger face. Then not as relieved when I read the name—Angela Rickey. The hair is severe, pulled back in a style that could easily date to Puritan days. Angela's disappearance has replaced Eva's as front-page news.

I recognize her immediately.

"She was here," I say.

"What?"

"I saw her. The first day *I* was here. She came to the door. By the time I got there, she was gone."

"Where's your phone?" Ann asks. "We have to call Rafferty."

He arrives within ten minutes.

I tell him the story. About how I thought she had come back, but it was Beezer and Rafferty instead.

"Are you certain it was her?" Rafferty pulls out another photo, a better copy of the one the paper had been running.

"Except for the birthmark," I say.

"What birthmark?"

"She had a strawberry-colored birthmark down the side of her face." I pass my hand down my face from temple to chin.

Rafferty and Ann exchange looks.

"What?" I say.

"Was the girl you saw pregnant?" Rafferty asks.

"Yes," I say. "Quite."

"It's got to be her," Ann says. "Looking for Eva."

I watch Rafferty consider.

"Is it possible she didn't know that Eva was missing?" Ann asks.

"Anything's possible," Rafferty says. He is formal. Professional. His face is stone.

"Maybe she was trying to give Eva the key," Ann suggests. "Or looking for help."

"Okay," Rafferty says. "Thanks."

He turns to leave. It startles me.

"Wait," I say, putting down the basket. I walk him to the gate. "How's your head?" I ask.

"Fine," he says. "How's yours?" His voice is clipped, the tone sarcastic. "I've gotta go," he says, and walks away from me.

I go back to where Ann is working.

She sees the look on my face. "Lovers' quarrel?" she asks.

"What? No. . . . I don't know."

"Call me old-fashioned, but even when alcohol is involved, I believe it's customary for the new boyfriend to get upset when you spend the night with the old one."

I stare at her.

"It's a small town," Ann says. "News travels fast."

"It's not true," I say. "Jack was here, but I didn't sleep with him."

"Hey, it's not my business." Ann goes on deadheading.

I put my hands over my eyes, but the world spins and leans. I throw up for the second time, in the middle of the deadhead basket.

Ann leaves me on Eva's couch. I have a fever.

"Probably the heat," she says. "Or maybe from the surgery."

I tell her about the surgery. In case it is important. Also to explain why I couldn't have slept with Jack LaLibertie. Or anyone else for that matter. I want her to know.

"I'll come by after work," Ann says. "I have some herbs that will fix you right up."

I nod. All I want to do is sleep.

The fever dreams take hold. I dream about the climb. The one Lyndley made the day she jumped and the one I kept attempting later, when May was trying to keep me alive.

I had taken Lyndley's death hard; I had almost died myself. Even Eva thought I should be in a hospital. But May had said no. This was our business. Even the first day she caught me up on the rocks, she still thought she could handle it. She was wrong, of course. The same way she was wrong about a lot of things.

Her reaction was pure May logic. She called the locksmith to come put locks on all the escape routes from our house. And then she had him board up the Boyntons' house. The front door was locked, double dead-bolted. The locksmith had no problem installing a double lock on Auntie Emma's door (their house was deserted and boarded up), but he balked at installing one on ours. Double locks were illegal in Massachusetts, because they kept you from getting out in an emergency. He pointed that out to her, but he'd already put locks on all the first-floor windows and some other places, and May refused to pay him if he didn't finish the job the way she wanted it done. So in the end he gave in.

The locks weren't meant to keep anyone out; they were meant to keep me in. They had me on suicide watch. Even then, people knew that suicide runs in families, and May wasn't taking any chances with me.

But May was no match for me when it came to locks. I didn't even bother with the dead bolt. I had the window locks disabled within about thirty seconds. All it took was a paper clip from the drawer of her desk.

The moon was full, its pull strong. They were wrong about the suicide thing. I wasn't seeking peace, or not eternal peace anyway. What I was looking for was perspective. To see things through her eyes. Everyone blamed the abuse. They talked about what Cal had done to her. Everyone said we should have seen it coming. But I knew it was more than that. It was my fault as much as hers. Cal might have abused her. But I had taken away her only hope of escape.

And so I made the climb again. To try to see things as she saw them. It was something I had to do.

It was a long climb. Far more difficult than it looked. Some of the dogs came out of their caves to watch me. The birds circled and screeched. Halfway to the top, I cut my foot on a shell the gulls must have dropped. It slid in between my first and second toes, slicing them apart, making the space between them widen. It wasn't bleeding that hard, considering, but it was continuous, and I couldn't stop it, so I stopped trying. Instead I just kept climbing, leaving a Hansel and Gretel trail of blood drops behind me in case I couldn't find my way back home.

It took me what seemed like forever to get to the top, partly because of the shadows cast by the full moon, partly because of my foot.

I stood for a long time at the precipice where the rocks jut forward. The very spot she jumped from. I stared down at the black ocean below. Then I saw that my dress had changed. I was no longer wearing the cutoffs and T-shirt I'd left the house in, but the white nightgown Lyndley was wearing the day she died.

The dream shifts perspective again, and I am no longer on the cliff, but in Eva's parlor on Christmas morning, wearing the white lace nightgown that Eva had given us, one to Lyndley and one to me. And though the view of the water is the same, it is not real, but is the painting Lyndley made for me the last Christmas she was alive. The one she titled *Swimming to the Moon.*

I have just undone the wrapping, and I am standing over it, staring at the texture of the water and the figure of my sister, her hair wild and trailing behind, one arm extended, reaching for the path that stretches endlessly in front of her, narrowing as it disappears into the full moon just above the horizon. I am fascinated by the painting, more fascinated than by any other she has done. I am aware of the voices around me, Eva's and Beezer's voices commenting on the painting, telling me how beautiful it is. And I ask them how they were able to surprise me like this. I was notorious for discovering my presents before Christmas Day. How had they possibly kept this big package out of sight until Christmas morning?

The room goes dead quiet. The dream shape-shifts again. The people are gone. Even Lyndley's arm is gone now as my eyes move in close-up on the painting, examining the detail of the brushstrokes, the amazing colors that you can see only when you get close to the water. Every color is reflected, if you get near enough to see it. I lean in too far, the same way Lyndley did just before she fell from the rocks, and I lose balance, the way she did that night. I am aware then that it is a great distance down. And that I'm not where I think I am at all, not on the rocks Lyndley jumped from, and not in Eva's living room, but on the Golden Gate Bridge. I am watching my own death, a suicide cliché told in dream terms. Fingers of fog reach up and over the bridge, trying to grab me, to pull me in. But I am already tumbling end over end, and I'm aware that I can't possibly survive. I feel myself falling into the colors of the paint, but it is rock-hard dried paint, and I realize that it's too far to fall even if the paint were not already dry, that falling into plain water from this height is like hitting concrete. Unless you fall perfectly straight, you couldn't live through the impact. But even as I have this thought, the colors below me start to move and turn liquid again, and the perspective shifts once more, and I slide between the colors into the cool of the water.

I don't go under it the way Lyndley did. I am not in the water, but in the painting itself, and I'm swimming on its surface through a mist of colors. Swimming to the moon. I am trying to catch up to Lyndley, who is there ahead of me, her red-blond hair trailing behind her. She is swimming away from me, moving fast, and I am trying to catch her, but I'm not as strong a swimmer as she is, and the distance between us keeps widening. Off to the left is Children's Island, and dead ahead the moon path is replaced by fog.

Cold and exhausted, I call her name. The fog is everywhere now. I turn in each direction, but the colors have disappeared. The ocean is dark and empty. I am out of breath, but I keep swimming in the direction I saw her go, ignoring every sense that tells me not to.

I call to her again. "Lyndley!" And my voice cuts through the fog. I see the hair again, or just a glimpse of it, and some images it holds—a shell, a sea horse. I call her name again. She hears me, turns. But it is not Lyndley's face I am looking into. It is Eva's. Her expression is loving and kind. She is trying to say something. I stop swimming for just a stroke. I listen.

"Run for your life!" she yells.

Once again I am on the rocks. I scramble down them, aware of the blood. It is everywhere now, covering things. The rocks are slippery with it. It takes a while to get to the base.

I feel Cal's presence before I see him. His hand grabs my wrist.

Then the dogs start to appear, watching, waiting. Waiting for me to give them permission.

They are on him. Quickly. Tearing him apart. I could stop them; I know I have that power. But I don't. I want Cal to die.

The blast of a gunshot wakes me from my fever dreams. No . . . not gunfire. Thunder.

I am cold with sweat. But better. The heat has broken. Rain slaps the panes, then rolls in over the sills as if the house were a huge ship that's taking on water. I run around closing windows. Then I see the clock. I've slept for an hour and a half. Only ten minutes and the Realtor will be back with another client. I grab Eva's yellow mackintosh and rush outside into the rain.

The air is cooling. Not just because of the downpour. I can feel the cold front moving in. I cross the common, not fully awake yet, having no idea where I'm going, but heading out into the storm. I stop at the corner to let the Duck Tour pass. AMPHIBIOUS VEHICLE, it says on the side. The front of it looks more like an army tank than a tour bus. A miked voice identifies landmarks as they pass, asking if anyone knows who the statue is. Everyone guesses it's a witch. The tour guide tells them they're totally wrong but that they're in good company. The statue is of Salem's founding father, she says, but tells them not to feel bad if they didn't guess right, because a national magazine got it wrong, too. When their article on Salem came out, she says, it pictured the statue of Roger Conant with a caption that labeled our founding father as "a determined sorceress."

It's surreal. I'm still half dreaming, maybe. Tourists lean out the windows snapping photos as they turn, shape-shifting into tree limbs with waving arms, reaching out the windows to touch me as they pass. Or maybe it's the trees that are moving behind them, another trick of perspective.

The rain brings me back to life. I find myself down at Pickering Wharf, outside Ann's shop, looking at the window display. My eyes focus through the glass, the world behind the world. In the corner Ann's assistant sits at a round table, tarot cards spread out in front of her. A customer focuses attention on the cards, telling more with just her body language than the cards do, making them unnecessary. I could read the woman even from here: lost love, a sad slump of shoulders. This is a woman whose dreams have died. She has come here looking for hope. Let's see, a traveler, she will travel. Maybe I'm not really reading, because the traveling part is obvious; the woman is clearly a tourist, so she has at least traveled here. Still, I see more travel in her future. *Tell her that,* I'm thinking. *Give her something to hold on to.* "*Make voyages, attempt them, there is nothing else.*" Eva's voice, quoting. I don't know why anyone would want to do this for a living, telling people's fortunes. It would make me so sad.

Tourists bustle by. One very round man, who has forgotten his raincoat, wears a black garbage bag with armholes cut out. Tour buses park two across. I don't remember the wharf ever being this busy. People linger in doorways, under the overhangs, waiting for new weather. *If you don't like the weather in New England, wait a minute.* Six witch shops line this little alleyway. I see tourists inside, buying soaps, oils, little bags of potions before they get back on their buses bound for Nebraska and Ohio. Making the buses wait for them. "Oh, please, please wait. I need something for my granddaughter. I don't know when I'll get back this way again. Next year we're going to Atlantic City."

Ann's assistant is ringing up the customer she was reading. The deck of tarot cards sits next to the register. She looks up at me.

"Is Ann here?" I ask.

"She's in the storeroom," the assistant says. "She'll be right out."

The woman who just paid steps back, and I try to move to the side and out of her way, but I catch the tarot cards, spilling them onto the floor.

"Sorry," I say, stooping to retrieve them.

"Don't touch them!" the salesgirl says. She kneels down and picks up the cards. The deck is intact except for one card that has landed faceup at my feet.

The salesgirl looks up dramatically. "The death card." She lifts the card by the edges, as if it were hot or somehow contaminated. She places it on the counter. Then she walks slowly to a bin of crystals, pulls out an amethyst on a chain.

She presses it into my hand. "Wear this around your neck," she says. "Don't take it off, even when you shower."

"What?"

"You need protection," she says.

Ann comes back in then and must see the look on my face.

"What's going on?" Ann asks. She regards me doubtfully. "Are you all right?"

The salesgirl turns to her. "She drew the death card."

"You came in for a reading?" Ann finds it hard to believe.

"No," I say. "I knocked over the cards."

"The death card landed right at her feet. She needs protection."

Ann grabs my head and pulls it down, running her hands all over it, feeling and squeezing as she goes.

"She's fine," she pronounces. She hands the girl the crystal. "Put this back."

"Sorry about the head thing," she says. "It was the only way I could get her to leave you alone." She looks concerned. "You okay?"

I don't know what to say.

"Come on," she says, leading me to her office. "The death card means nothing," she says. "Well, it doesn't mean nothing, but what it usually means is transformation. One way of life ending, another beginning. It's usually a good thing," she says. "Plus, it has to be read in combination with other cards." Ann looks disgusted. "I shouldn't let her do any readings," she says. "Remind me to fire her."

I try to smile.

"You look better," she says, trying to be positive. "A little."

I sit on her futon for a long time. She feeds me warm tea with valerian root.

"It's natural Valium," she says. "I drink it all the time."

"I need to ask you a question," I say finally. It's what I came here for.

"You want a reading?" She seems surprised.

"Not that kind of question. Something about Eva."

"Okay." She looks at me.

"Do you think it's possible that Eva killed herself?" It's the question that keeps coming to me. The one I can't let go.

"You mean suicide?"

The word seems wrong. "I'm not sure what I mean."

Ann shakes her head. "Eva was the happiest person I've ever met. She wasn't the type to kill herself."

I nod.

"Why would you even ask?"

I don't want to tell her about the voices.

"She knew I was coming," I say. "I'm pretty sure."

Ann considers. "Well," she says, "Eva was a reader. She knew a lot of things, didn't she?"

"She sent me her pillow. The one she used to make the lace. Why would she do that?"

"Maybe she just wanted you to have it," Ann suggests. It's supposed to make me feel better, but it doesn't. "You didn't find a note or anything." It was more a question than a statement.

"No."

"I don't think it was suicide," Ann says. "That wouldn't make sense." She wants to say something else but thinks better of it.

I sip the tea.

I stay at Ann's office for a long time. I camp out on the futon. She brings in dinner. She feeds me more herbal teas. At eight o'clock she takes my temperature.

"It's not as bad as it was," she says. "But you still have a fever."

"I think I'll go home," I say, gathering my things.

"I'll give you a ride if you can a wait a little while," she says.

I look up at the house. I can see it from here.

"I'm okay to walk."

"I'll call you later," Ann says, hugging me good-bye. "Feel better."

The truth is, I feel better already. Much better than I felt earlier. Ann has seen to that. A little rest, I'll be okay.

I walk up the wharf, cutting diagonally across the common, crossing the street and going through the back gate into the garden. It is still light enough to see, and I notice a few blossoms that I missed right next to the back door. I lean over and pluck the first blossom, then, realizing that Ann must have done something with the basket after I got sick, I put the blossom in my pocket.

I bend to reach for a second one. My hand misses, and I grab stem instead of blossom, pulling it down low, then watching as it springs back like a tiny catapult, flinging something into the air.

I hear the sound of twanging as it falls on the bricks. The sound is metallic, a recognizable sense memory. Inevitable. I lean over to see what it is. I pick up . . . a key.

The key.

I stare at it. It is old, not one of the copies made by the police but Eva's key, the one she used to leave for me in a peony blossom when she knew I was coming.

I was right. She knew. She knew what was about to happen to her, and she knew it meant that I would come.

I am still leaning forward. I can't seem to right myself. A splitting pain cuts my head in two. The pounding of fever. A chill runs down my arms and legs.

As I struggle to stand up, I spot the Italian silk.

Cal is standing close enough to touch. His lips are moving, but no sound comes out. He is praying.

When he finally speaks aloud, it is a bellow. "Lord save this girl from the fires of hell." He raises his hands to heaven. His eyes stay on me, tracking every movement and twitch of muscle, the way I've seen the dogs do when they hunt their prey.

I am frozen.

He begins to speak again, but the words are indiscernible. He is speaking in tongues.

I am hallucinating. I must be.

But then the smell hits me. A memory sense. I know his smell. It is sickening.

I look for the dogs. This is the time they should start to appear. To help me. To kill him. This is the dream.

But even as I wish for it, I know that this is no dream. There are no dogs. This is what Rafferty warned me about.

I feel myself going under, losing consciousness. I dig the key into my palm, and the hard metal wakes me up. The key . . . the door. I gauge the distance. I start to run.

Cal follows.

I can feel him behind me. Closing in.

I struggle with the key. Finally get it into the lock when he grabs me.

He is shaking me. Imploring devils to come out. "Kneel and pray!" he demands. "Kneel and pray with me!" He tries to push me down, but I manage to stay upright.

"Who are you, demon?" he bellows. "Name your-self!" His eyes glow yellow.

I push the door hard, and it gives way. The portal opens, and I move into another world, Eva's world.

The loose hinge shifts the weight of the door, and Cal falters. I push the door against him, closing it.

"Jesus died for your sins!" he screams at me. "Jesus *died* for you!"

I can hear him through the broken bull's-eye of glass, still, imploring, demanding the demons to depart. "Kneel and pray!"

He reaches through the cut glass, grabs a fistful of hair, and pulls my head back, slamming it against the door.

"Demon, depart!" he yells, smashing my head hard enough to drive them out. I feel a piece of glass slice my scalp.

Sparks ring around my vision. We are inches apart through the shards of the glass, the same glass I broke the first night I came here.

He is trying to kill me. He is trying to save me.

"I died for you." It isn't Cal's voice now. It is Eva's. It wakes me up.

"Kneel and pray," he demands once again, and this time I obey, grabbing his hand in mine as I drop to my knees, forcing his wrist down on the broken glass.

His screech is like a wounded animal's.

It stops time.

"Run for your life," I hear Eva say.

I run for the phone, dial 911.

I yell for Rafferty, and then I drop the phone, severing my connection to everything that is real.

PART THREE

Hold the lace to the visage. If the person you are reading is unavailable or has passed on, some belongings or even a photograph of the person will sometimes do—though the life-force is always more powerful than any rendered image.

—THE LACE READER'S GUIDE

ITEMS REMOVED FROM CRIME SCENE

Two matching red journals
with red leather covers

First journal: "The Lace Reader's Guide" by Eva. Contains lace readings, recipes, daily observations. Appears to be primarily a manual for telling fortunes by reading lace.

Second journal: Written by Towner in 1981 and used in psychiatric treatment as some kind of therapy. Contains one short story, which appears to have at least some basis in real events. The story continues by way of dated journal entries. Some speculation about events as fictional; the journal was part of a creative-writing class for inpatients sponsored by McLean Psychiatric Hospital in 1980. Further study is needed to determine if any of this material can be used as evidence against Calvin Boynton in either case.

1981 McLean Hospital, Creative Writing

FLASHLIGHT TAG
BY TOWNER WHITNEY

We played every summer, sometimes two and three times a week, but never before Lyndley arrived from their home in Florida, which was sometime between Memorial Day and the Fourth of July. They never called ahead, not even ship-to-shore, and when they finally came into port, it was always under full sail, and the kids from the mainland and the outer islands took it as a sign that the games were about to begin.

May had an "open-door policy" when it came to the game, and when we first started, before it got so competitive, she actually played it with us a few times. This was partly because Beezer wanted to play and didn't want to be the one "left standing," as we called it then, so she used to play with him as a team to kind of even things out. We allowed it only because Beezer was so little and because when you scared him, he had the greatest scream/laugh. It was a silent scream, and his face contorted like something out of a horror film; when he inhaled, he hooted like an owl, partly due to his asthma and partly because he was the funniest kid in the world. When you heard his hoots, you couldn't help giggling (no matter where you were hiding), so it often worked in his favor. He might be scared by one person running in, then flush three other players out of their hiding places just by laughing like that. As he got older, it became a tactic, and when he'd get close to where he thought you were hiding, he'd actually turn the flashlight off and sneak up and just hoot at you until you were laughing so hard you couldn't run in and save yourself.

The rules of flashlight tag are simple. I'm sure you know them. It's basically a variation of hide-and-seek, except that it's played in the dark and the only light allowed is the flashlight you get to carry when you're "it." When we first started playing, all you had to do to win was find a person who was hiding, tag whoever it was with the beam of the flashlight, and then, also with the beam, tag the big old oak tree, which was always "home."

But that got old fast, because really it was too easy for the person who was "it." All that person really had to do was to turn off the light and wait by the tree until people started to run in, then turn on the flashlight and tag them out. What ended up happening was that no one took a chance and ran in, so one round of the game could go on for hours, until everyone got tired of it and went home, leaving whoever was "it" out there alone for hours in the dark. That's what we referred to as "left standing." When you were the one left there all by yourself, it was pretty bad. It was crazy-making. You couldn't tell if everyone was just hiding really well or if you were all alone on the middle of the island with the seagulls starting to talk to you and saying your name like they always do if you're alone with them for too long. You'd end up sitting endlessly with your back against a tree, scared shitless, too afraid to move. Once I actually stayed out all night when it happened to me, but I got in real trouble, because May caught me sneaking in at dawn and decided we had to put an end to the left-standing thing.

"Why can't you just play like normal children?" she asked Lyndley and me when she started speaking to us again, which was sometime the following afternoon. I remember Lyndley bursting out laughing when she asked that, and it was such a ridiculous question that even May had to smile a little, although you could tell she was trying hard not to. But she ordered us to either change the game or stop playing. Those were our choices.

So we changed the game. And the change made it better. We made the game more difficult. Like in regular hide-and-seek, when you found someone, you had to race that kid home. It worked much better that way. It became more competitive. It was about this time that the other kids started coming to play the game with us. Lyndley told one townie kid about it, and Beezer told a kid he sailed with on Baker's Island.

Word spread. At the game's peak, we played four or five times a week from the Fourth of July until Labor Day weekend. We didn't stop doing the left-standing thing, though; it just evolved into something else. We modified it. Instead of a tactic, it became a rite of initiation. Every time a new kid joined the game, it was an unwritten rule that the new kid would be "it" for the last round of the game. Sometimes we had to quit earlier than we would have liked, just to make it happen. Other times we would run in early and tell where the new kid was hiding so he could be tagged out for the next round. Then the new kid, the new "it," would face the oak tree and count to a hundred. While he was counting, the game ended and we all went home. We left the new kid standing there until he either figured it out or got freaked out when it had gone on way too long and he was starting to think the worst—that maybe there was some killer out there who was picking us off one by one or that we'd been taken away in a flying saucer or something. Seldom did it occur to anyone that we had simply gone home. That wasn't something kids ever did, at least not voluntarily. But eventually they caught on to the joke, the betrayal. If the kid came back after that, if he came back for more, he was one of us. If not, we figured it was no great loss. No one ever mentioned the dirty trick. It was our unwritten rule, our rite of passage.

And, of course, it almost goes without saying that we had a "no wimp" policy. If you got scared or hurt, you'd better keep it to yourself. One time a kid from one of the other islands fell into a rabbit hole and sprained his ankle. He was such a trouper that he didn't even complain about it and played the rest of the game, even though his slowness running in made him the object of great ridicule. Better that than admit a weakness, because if you did, you wouldn't be asked back. As it turned out, that kid was on crutches most of the summer and couldn't come back anyway, but he earned our respect and played every summer from then on.

After his accident we tried, at May's suggestion, to put little flags in the rabbit holes, little white flags that could be seen in the dark, but it didn't work. There were too many holes, and one kid tried to jump over a flag and "almost impaled himself" on its point, as Lyndley put it when she told the story to May. So we stopped the flag thing. Besides, the truth was, we liked the rabbit holes. We figured it was a good thing that we knew the obstacles and they didn't, the same way it was good that we knew the best hiding places. These townie kids were pretty tough players, and we needed some kind of home-court advantage, if you know what I mean.

Our island was laid out with our house on one end of the figure eight and Lyndley's on the other. In the middle by the dock was the red schoolhouse and behind that, more on our side of the island than on Lyndley's, was the saltwater pond where we'd take baths and wash our hair in the summertime. In the winter May melted snow for washing, which we did once a week "whether we needed it or not," as Beezer liked to put it. There was an old copper tub in the upstairs washroom, and we'd put the pans of hot water on the dumbwaiter and pull them up to fill the tub. But in the summer May sent us down to the saltwater pond with a cake of Ivory soap and some puffy shaving cream to wash our hair. Beezer, Lyndley, and I would strip, dive in, pop up, lather, and dive back in, leaving a floating trail of soap suds all the way across the pond. You couldn't do that now, because it isn't good environmentally, but we were not conscious of such things then. Since it was salt water, we could never get really clean but walked around all summer with a whitish film over our tans. The only time you could get really clean was if there was a rainstorm, and then May sent us out with our soap and told us to dance under the raindrops until we stopped foaming or our lips turned blue, whichever came first. She never did this in a thunderstorm, of course, just regular rain.

Usually we bathed in the saltwater pond. I remember one time we forgot to bring home the Ivory soap, and May made us turn around and go get it, but it wasn't there. The next day we found it washed up on Back Beach, where we had found my dog Skybo after Cal killed him earlier that same summer. Cal always said it was an accident, but we all knew better. But that is another story, and a bad one, which I do not want to go into here. Suffice it to say that these occurrences led to a lot of speculation on our parts. That, and the fact that the lake was very deep, led Lyndley and me to the idea that the saltwater pond was bottomless and that it flowed out somehow into the ocean at Back Beach. We thought that the Ivory Soap Incident proved our theory, but Beezer insisted we were wrong about it all, because, of course, Ivory soap floats and does not sink to the bottom anyway. "It doesn't prove that the pond is bottomless," he said. He was disgusted with us and very upset at the same time, and he clearly didn't want to talk anymore about it to either of us, so we eventually dropped the subject and never talked about it again.

Beezer was so upset about the whole thing, in fact, that Eva had to talk to me about it. We ended up talking more about the differences between Beezer and me than we did about the saltwater pond. "There are mystics and there are mechanists," she said, "and they see things with different eyes."

The year we played flashlight tag with Jack and Jay-Jay was the year Lyndley began to change. Looking back, I realize I knew it before that night. When Lyndley arrived that summer, there was something different about her. Something I couldn't put my finger on. She didn't run off the boat and up the ramp and grab me and wrestle until we both fell into the water laughing and dunking each other the way we usually did. Instead she waved and smiled but walked up the dock like one of the grown-ups. She didn't fight with me at all; she just gave me a hug. "Oh, Towner, you're all grown up" was what she said to me, although it was clear that she was the grown-up, not me. She said it all sad, like some old lady or something. Even her voice was different that year. The hint of a southern accent she had at the beginning of each summer and lost by the end had crystallized; it was more affected. I called her on it, but she said she had no idea what I was talking about.

No one else had any idea what I was talking about either. May couldn't see it, and it wasn't something you could talk to Beezer about. It was like the Body Snatchers or something, like someone had replaced Lyndley with a pod person, and that person didn't know how to act. I knew what I was supposed to do. I was supposed to tell someone that this wasn't my sister and to demand that they bring Lyndley back, but I didn't know whom to tell. Auntie Emma and Cal were acting just as strangely as usual, so I knew there was no way that they had been replaced by pods. Later that year, after that whole weird summer was over, I told Eva about it, and at least she listened, although she didn't draw any conclusions, none that she told me about anyway. I knew she didn't believe in colonizing pods from outer space, never having even seen the movie or anything. Still, Eva is the one who seemed to come the closest to understanding, which was always the case.

"Who is Lyndley, really?" Eva asked me when I was finished ranting. She often asked strange questions like that, so it didn't surprise me. It wasn't the answer I'd wanted, though, so I didn't try to answer it then. Instead I just gave her a very frustrated look.

"Think about it" was all she said.

She had a way of reframing things for me, Eva did, a way of helping me sort things out. It truly did get me thinking. I thought about Lyndley a lot. It wasn't until a few days later that I figured out what Eva meant. The quick answer, the answer you'd tell anyone who asked, was that Lyndley was my twin sister and that I'd known her since the womb.

But the actual answer was not as clearly defined. Because the truth was, I didn't really start to know my sister until I was thirteen. My mother had given her away soon after we were born, gift-wrapped her and presented her to her half sister, my aunt Emma Boynton, who could not conceive a child of her own. Much as I longed to know my twin, I didn't know her at all. They lived south of here, where Emma's husband, Cal, raced sailboats for a living. So I didn't know Lyndley until the year I turned thirteen and the Boyntons started spending summers up here, when Cal began to race for the Eastern Yacht Club in Marblehead.

The Boyntons spent a total of five summers in New England, which amounted, in total time, to little more than a year. If you figured it out mathematically, as my brother Beezer might have if Eva had asked him the same question, the picture began to look a lot different. Most of Lyndley's life had occurred in places far away from me. So when Eva asked me who Lyndley really was, I thought about it a number of ways before I tried to answer the question, and I found, in the end, that I just couldn't answer. The things that were happening to my sister, all the formative and life-changing things, were happening while she was far away from me, in a life I had no part of. I would ask myself Eva's question several times in the years to come. By the time Lyndley died, I would come to wonder if I had ever really known her at all.

The summer we played our last game of flashlight tag was the same summer that Lyndley started seeing Jack LaLibertie. He and his brother Jay-Jay had come out a few times to play the game with us. There were a lot of town kids who played with us, six or seven of them in all including Jack and his little brother. If you counted the summer kids from Baker's Island, we usually had ten or twelve kids per game, mostly boys. Both Jack and Jay-Jay had already taken their turn at the left-standing thing, and on this particular night there was a new kid named Willie Mays, who was a baseball star from Beverly High. His name wasn't really Willie Mays, but he was a good runner, and everyone said he would probably turn pro, and he did, too, for a while, but he never got past the minors, and he didn't play much even then.

Everyone knew that Jack had a crush on Lyndley. She was sixteen that summer, and I think Jack was seventeen, although he looked older. Lyndley said it was because he spent so much time in the sun working on his father's boat. He was gorgeous. We'd seen him before—some of the LaLiberties' traps were near Back Beach, and Jack had taken them over after his father got in trouble for shooting a poacher, which was still legal in Massachusetts at the time but was still sort of frowned upon. He'd smiled at us once when Lyndley and I were spying on him from shore, and we both almost fell over.

Cal's drinking was out of control that summer, so we'd taken to playing the game "weather permitting." What we really meant was "Cal permitting," meaning that we played only when Cal was gone, which he was most of the time anyway. He had a room at the Eastern Yacht Club, and he stayed there most nights, because they comped his drinks as long as he was winning for them. They encouraged him to stay at the club, since that way they had some control over him and knew he'd at least show up for the next day's race. Also, that way they could dilute his drinks if he got too bad. Or that's what Lyndley told me. I'm not sure how she knew.

So "weather permitting" came to mean if and when the ramp was down, which the kids figured out pretty quickly. I don't know if they made the connection that the ramp was down only when Cal's boat wasn't tied up at our float. If they did, no one ever mentioned it, at least not to me.

As it turned out, we played the game most nights that July. The last time we played, we had sixteen kids, including a girl from another of the border islands, a sailor Beezer had met at Pleon, the children's yacht club. She was really too young to play, but we let her in anyway, just to have another girl to round things out. When there were two new kids, we usually tossed a coin to see who would be left standing, but this year it was understood that it would be Willie Mays, because the girl was too young and we would have felt bad leaving her standing all alone like that in the dark.

Jay-Jay and Beezer were fast friends. So much so that Beezer showed Jay-Jay some of his hiding places, which was totally against the rules, but we let him get away with it; we always let Beezer get away with everything. Besides, they weren't such great hiding places, because Lyndley and I had all of those tied up.

Unless we hid together, which we often did, Lyndley and I had different territories. She had the west side of the island, by the baseball diamond, and I had everything from the salt pond over. She did better, since her spots were farther away, and usually the person who was "it" would not go that far from home in case people started to run in. I had less square footage, but my hiding places were better. I had one tree limb I used to climb into where no one ever caught me, not even Lyndley. She used to walk back and forth under it looking for me, never even bothering to look up, even though I was sitting just a few feet above her head.

That night we'd already played six rounds, which was a lot for us, because we had so many players and it took a long time for them to run in. Although we had already decided that Willie Mays would be the one left standing, he was almost impossible to catch, so Jack let himself get caught so he could set Willie up. Jack instructed each of us to stay hidden until Willie Mays ran in. Then Jack counted to a hundred, turned off the light, then sat there by the tree waiting for Willie. It took a while, but he finally made a run for it, and when he did, Jack, who'd heard him coming, simply stood up right next to the tree, turned the light back on, and tagged him. Then, before Willie had time to protest, Jack called, "Olly, Olly, all in free," and we all stood up from our hiding places and walked in.

If Willie knew he was being set up, he never let on. Like the good sport he was, he just went to the tree and started counting. When he did, the rest of us exchanged looks that said, "This is it, the game is over," and we all just went home. The townie kids and the kids from the other islands headed for their boats. It was understood by the whole group that they had to row them out past the little island and into the channel before they could start their motors, because sound carries over water and we didn't want Willie Mays to catch on to our trick.

Beezer and I walked to the house without saying a word, but when we got there, May's light was on in her room, and I didn't want to go in.

"You go," I said.

"Where are you going?" I could tell that Beezer was worried. That was his MO this summer. Worry and frustration about me and everything I was doing.

"I just don't want to go inside the house yet."

"You can't go and take off, you know she hates that."

"She won't know."

"Her light is still on. She hasn't gone to sleep."

"She won't come out of her room, though."

"Yeah, but what if she does?"

"Tell her you came home early. Tell her I'm still out playing the game."

"I don't know," he said. "You're supposed to be staying here."

"I'm coming back, for God's sake."

I was starting to get pissed off now, and he knew it.

He was looking at Lyndley's house, figuring that's where I was headed. "You're not supposed to go over there at all," he said.

"Well, I'm going."

He flashed another worried look.

"He's not even home," I say, meaning Cal.

He knew, but it didn't erase his scowling. "I'll tell her you're still playing the game," he said, as if it were his idea to say it in the first place.

"That's a good boy."

"Don't be mean to me," he said. "I'm only trying to protect you."

I felt really bad then, because I could tell he meant it. I wasn't afraid of May's wrath, though. It had been a while now since I'd feared my mother.

He flashed a quick worried look toward the dock, then turned back and went inside, turning off the porch light as if I were already home. He was a smart kid, a good kid. I sat for a while on the porch, just to make sure the coast was clear, and then I decided to walk over to Lyndley's and see if I could get her to take a ride to the Willows with me. We occasionally did that, when we were both feeling daring enough to sneak out. Sometimes we'd ride the dodgems or win money at the cigarette game, because even though you have to be eighteen to play, the guys who worked there liked us and never checked our IDs.

I decided to take the back path, since I could see the flashlight beam crisscrossing on the trail, and I could tell that Willie Mays was moving around down there already, starting to look for us. When he headed up toward the saltwater pond, I cut across the dunes to the regular path, taking my sneakers off before I reached the Boyntons' porch. I could see Auntie Emma from there, sitting near the window reading by candlelight. Lyndley must be upstairs, I thought. I could easily have walked up to the door and knocked; my aunt would have been glad to see me. But I wanted Lyndley to sneak out, because Auntie Emma would never allow us to go to town, not this late anyway. Plus, Cal didn't allow Lyndley to go to the Willows at all. I tiptoed past the window to the back door. The screen door was latched. I looked around for a small stick, slipped it into the crack of the door, and pulled up the latch so smoothly it didn't even click.

I headed up the back stairs. I knew from experience that the third step from the top squeaked, so I skipped over it. By the time I reached the upstairs, I could see that Lyndley's room was dark. That was no big surprise. Lyndley never lit her candles—she wanted everybody to think she was already asleep. I walked to her bed. She wasn't there. I knew she wasn't downstairs, because I looked in the windows as I passed. I figured she was probably in the bathroom, so I sat down on the bed and waited for her to come back.

I'd been sitting there for about five minutes when I heard someone on the porch. I figured maybe Lyndley had gotten stuck and had to walk down by Back Beach to get around Willie Mays, but she'd given me the high sign and I'd seen her take off in this direction, so it seemed odd. Then I heard Cal's voice downstairs, and I froze.

His voice was loud, pissed off, and very, very drunk. He was ranting about something, and it took me a minute to realize that it was Willie Mays he was yelling about, demanding to know whose boat was tied up at the dock. Auntie Emma swore she didn't know, which didn't do anything to calm him down.

"Tell me who he is!" Cal's voice was raised now, making him sound like the jealous husband he was, one who thinks his wife is hiding a man in the closet or something. I was afraid he was going to hit her, which he had done before on more than one occasion, and I was wishing Lyndley would come back, because I had no idea what to do in this situation. I was thinking about jumping out the window—that's how much I didn't want to be here. I could tell what was coming, and I knew it wasn't going to make things any better if Cal found me here. I could probably make it if I did jump, but it was pretty far down, and there was a big ledge at the bottom. Still, I thought I should at least run and get May; down the back stairs would be best.

Then it happened. There was a loud cracking noise and then silence for a minute, and I was waiting for Auntie Emma to cry out, but there was no sound at all. Then some steps and then, real quickly, before I had a chance to figure out what had happened, Cal was upstairs in the hall coming toward this room, looking for Lyndley. I was taken by surprise. It was all so fast. I'd never seen Cal move so quickly, and I realized that his anger was propelling him. I could feel his fury even from where I stood. I could touch his thoughts with my mind if I wanted to, but that was the last thing I wanted. Even from here I could tell they were dark, horrible thoughts, and they made me feel sick to my stomach.

I fought the urge to break and run. It was too late. I couldn't reach the back stairs now, couldn't outrun him, but the window was open across the room, the curtains wafting gently in the breeze like on any other peaceful night when nothing unusual was happening. I could see the ocean through the open window, all shimmering black in the moonlight, and it was playing a trick of perspective on me. It looked as if I could just dive through that window into that beautiful water and be out of here, but of course I couldn't, because of the rocks. Still, I would rather have taken my chances with the ledges than with Cal and with the awful silence below, where Auntie Emma's voice should have been. For a quick second, I almost dove out that window anyway, I was so panicked, but something told me not to move, to just stand there in the shadows with my back against the wall next to the big old armoire. There was no light for Cal to turn on, no electricity in this house at all. I could see already that he hadn't brought a flashlight or anything, not even a candle. And I knew then that Lyndley was not in the house. Because if she were, she would be downstairs by now, or getting a knife or something and coming after Cal herself.

Don't make a sound, I heard the voice in my head say, and I knew then that it was my only option. I pressed my back against the cool wall, fixing my eyes on the window, wishing I were anywhere but here, when suddenly I felt him in the room.

Cal slammed across the room to Lyndley's bed and literally tore it apart, flinging blankets, pillows. Obscenities poured out of him, all the worst words I knew—and some I didn't. "Where the fuck is she?" he half screamed, half growled at my aunt, but no sound came up the stairs.

He hurled the cut-glass candle stand onto the floor, smashing it to pieces. A shard of glass hit my leg, and it stung for a minute, and then I could feel the wet where it started to bleed. I couldn't reach down or anything, and I remember hoping that Cal couldn't smell blood the way dogs could, or smell fear.

"Whore!" he yelled then at the empty bed. "Temptress and whore!"

He reeled around as if he'd felt a presence, and I tried to make my mind blank so I would be invisible. I closed my eyes tight to block out thought. *Don't move, don't even breathe*, the voice said, and then my mind did go blank.

It worked. The next thing I remember was Cal running down the stairs and out the front door.

I was down the back stairs and out of the house before he even hit the porch. I looked in the living-room window as I flew by and saw Auntie Emma on the couch, sitting up now but looking dazed. There was blood on the side of her face, and she was trying to stand, but tentatively, holding on to the couch arm for support. I could tell by the look on her face, by the dread in her eyes, that she was thinking about Lyndley and what was going to happen if Cal caught up with her. Even when she was hurt, her maternal instincts were strong. But she wasn't strong enough for this; she never had been.

She made her way to the door, to the porch, yelling after him, telling him to leave Lyndley alone, that it wasn't what he thought, that she had lied to him before when she told him that Lyndley was staying in tonight. She gave Lyndley permission to go out and play the game, she said, nothing more. "For God's sake," she yelled after the figure who was raging up the pathways, "for God's sake, they are just children!"

But the wind was against her, and her voice was weak anyway. It wouldn't carry. Besides, Cal was already gone.

I couldn't believe that Lyndley could be still playing the game. She had given me the signal that she was going home. We had waved good-bye to each other, and I'd seen her walk toward her house.

It didn't make any sense that she was still playing. Even Willie Mays had given up the game by now. From the porch I could see him making his way down the ramp, the flashlight bobbing as he got into the skiff and started the engine. I saw the running lights as he pulled away from the dock. I briefly wished Lyndley *had* gone with him, so she would be safe from Cal, at least for the moment. But she hadn't. Lyndley was still hiding someplace out there, and Cal was going to be the one to find her if I didn't do something fast.

I tried all the usual places: the cave at Back Beach, the one where the dogs live. I tried the saltwater pond, which wasn't even her territory but where she would go sometimes when she felt like cheating, which was most of the time. I even tried the stone kennel and the crawl area under the red schoolhouse, though that was a place I favored more than Lyndley did. All the while I was trying to send her messages with my mind, which usually worked with Lyndley if she was tuned in—but she wasn't listening, not tonight.

Finally I climbed to the top of the rocks by the water tower. I could see the gulls rising away from Cal as he passed by the garbage cans at the top of the pier. Cal headed up the path toward the pine grove, and I prayed then that Lyndley wasn't cheating for once and was hiding in her own territory.

I was desperate. I had to find her before Cal did, but Lyndley was the best of all of us at this game, and I had no idea where she would be. I did something strange then. Instead of looking down, I looked up at the stars. I stared at them until I lost them completely and everything blurred into a lacy pattern and then finally the stars disappeared altogether. Then, when everything was gone, I took that blur of vision and focused it back down. And when I did, when I focused my eyes again, I could see Cal at the red schoolhouse, and I could even hear him calling to her through the door. I could see my mother, May, who had fallen asleep reading in her room, and Beezer sitting in the living room at the table trying to stay awake until I came back in. I could see

Auntie Emma sitting on the top step on her porch, too dizzy to stand now, holding the railing for support. I saw the yellow dogs, hundreds of them in their sleeping places in the caves at Back Beach, all heads and tails piled together, their fur against the pebbles as if someone had thrown a big carpet on the beach. I could see the whole expanse of the island, the whole figure eight of it—the houses, the cliffs, and the ocean beyond. And then, past the baseball diamond in another grove of trees, I saw something glowing. I have no idea what made it glow. Maybe Lyndley had lit up a cigarette, because it was a place she used to go to smoke sometimes, an old abandoned car. Maybe it was the moonlight, which seemed to be illuminating the whole island. But it was definitely glowing. It couldn't have been more plain if a guiding star or even some cartoon arrow had come out of the sky and pointed at the car with a big flashing sign that said LYNDLEY! LYNDLEY! LYNDLEY!

I scrambled down the rocks and raced for the other end of the island and the car, running as fast as I could go, knowing that any minute Cal would abandon the red schoolhouse and head back in the direction of the baseball diamond.

I cut across the field. I couldn't breathe. I missed a step and twisted into one of the rabbit holes and almost went down, but I was moving so fast my foot didn't go that far in, and I was able to catch my balance and keep going. I was getting closer, and I could see the car clearly now, its two rear wheels stuck in the dirt. May's father and his friends got it out here on a barge, then got it stuck and abandoned it for good in the middle of the field. The grass was growing up around the flattened and long-rotting tires, into the wheel well, as if the car had just grown out of the earth and died there and nature was taking back her own.

When I got to the car, the windows were all fogged up. I reached for the car handle, the finish line. I threw open the door.

I didn't know at first what I was seeing. All arms and legs moving and trying to sit up. Then my eyes focused, and I realized that yes, it was Lyndley I was looking at and that she wasn't alone.

"Damn it, Towner, close the door!" Lyndley said, and I saw Jack struggling to find his clothes and cover himself.

"Cal's back!" I gasped. And by the way I said it, she knew that it was bad. Then, like an idiot, I actually closed the door and stood there waiting for them, more shocked by what I'd just seen than by the danger of Cal himself.

The baseball bat came down hard, smashing the front window of the car, shattering glass everywhere. Lyndley screamed, hurt, bleeding from it, and suddenly Jack was out of the car, ready to fight for her. Ready to kill Cal himself if it came to that, wanting it to.

Cal backed into the shadows, waiting to make his next move. I had to do something quickly. I'd seen Cal's rages. And I knew in my gut that if this was going to be a fight to the death between them, it would be Jack and not Cal who was going to die.

I ran faster than I'd ever run before. I ran to get May, to get her gun.

May stood, frozen in time and place, gun leveled at Cal.

"Get dressed," May said.

Lyndley and Jack scrambled for their clothes.

"He's the one you should shoot," Cal said.

But May wasn't listening to him; she was staring at the bat hanging at his side.

"You're all wrong about this," Cal said, looking for a crack. "I was just trying to defend her. You have no idea what was going on here."

Jack pulled on his shirt.

"Go home," May said to Jack.

Jack started to protest, but May wasn't having any of it.

"You are disgusting," Cal said to him. "You are filth!"

I could see the muscles tense in Jack's neck. He reeled around and moved toward Cal.

May kept the rifle leveled at Cal, but she was speaking to Jack. "Go!"

Jack waited for Lyndley's nod, grabbed his jacket, and walked toward the dock. It took everything he had to leave her there, but he did it.

"Go ahead and shoot," Cal said to May. "They'll string you up. You and your whole goddamned family."

Even as he said it, he knew he was wrong.

She cocked the rifle. She was going to do it.

And then I saw Auntie Emma. Moving over the rise. Having trouble walking. Willing herself forward. Her jaw hanging crazily to the side, bruised, blood running down the side of her face. She stopped dead when she saw us. "No," she said. "Oh, God, please, no."

Cal recognized his only shot. He played it perfectly. With remorse and concern. As if he couldn't believe his eyes. I almost expected him to ask who had done this to her. What monster? "Oh, God," he said. "Oh, my God, Emma." He was crying real tears.

Cal took a step toward my aunt.

"Don't you touch her," May said, aiming the rifle.

Cal froze. He'd gone too far, and he knew it.

Auntie Emma stepped between them, lunging for the gun with the little strength she had left, falling.

May was the one who reached for her. Not Cal. The gesture was automatic. Instinctive. Any right person would have done it.

I reached for the gun. I wanted to finish him. But by the time I picked it up, Cal was already gone.

"Don't you ever come back!" May yelled after him. "Or I swear I will kill you."

But it was far too late. She had missed her chance.

We stood together in the still point. Where past, present, and future all come together. For a moment we had a glimpse of the future. Of how we might have changed it if we had taken the chance we were given. But then, like all glimpses, it was gone as quickly as it had come, and we were left with reality.

And there was Auntie Emma on the ground, her jaw contorted, resting on her neck. There were things that had to be taken care of. Not in the future. But in the here and now.

Auntie Emma had a broken jaw, two black eyes, and multiple lacerations. She had seventeen stitches across her left eyelid and cheek. The doctors at the hospital referred her to a plastic surgeon, but she never went.

She refused to file charges. My mother tried to file for her, but May wasn't an eyewitness, and even though I'd been in the house and heard everything that happened that night, I was not technically an eyewitness either, especially since my aunt was denying the whole thing, telling the police that she had slipped and fallen down the stairs. Both Eva and May pressured the authorities, trying to at least get a restraining order against Cal, but without cooperation from my aunt there was no way. Cal was a local hero. The towns of both Salem and Marblehead were claiming him as their own; he was everybody's bet to skipper the next America's Cup. This would be good for Marblehead, which was fast losing its reputation as the yachting capital of the world to Newport and San Diego. Since Cal was heading back to Florida in a few days anyway, the police said they believed that the "trouble was over." They'd spoken to him, they said, and he'd assured them he would stay at the club until it was time for him to sail.

With Auntie Emma's permission, Eva pulled some strings and managed to get Lyndley into Miss Porter's School. Cal was livid. He threatened Eva, he threatened my mother. The police were called one night when a neighbor heard him yelling in front of Eva's house, but Eva told the police that everything was okay, that she and Cal were just "having a little chat." She took him inside and made him a cup of tea.

The "little chat" included a reminder to Cal that Eva held the second mortgage on his house in Florida, an unfortunate circumstance that had become necessary after Cal's financial dealings with some of his sailing buddies went bad. Eva assured Cal that Miss Porter's would help to discipline Lyndley, who was admittedly getting wilder by the moment. She also pointed out that Cal would hardly be able to keep an eye on his daughter while skippering the America's Cup team. She reminded him that this was his one chance at fame. "Opportunity knocks but once." That's what she told him.

She glanced down at the lace when she said it, and not even Cal could contain his eagerness.

"What do you see?" He had to know.

"I see that you can't afford any distractions, that this is your big chance to really distinguish yourself."

"But am I going to win?" He couldn't help asking.

Eva only smiled at him. "I'm not going to tell you that," she said. "It wouldn't be any fun if I told you that, now, would it?"

Cal finally agreed to let Lyndley attend Miss Porter's, provided that Eva pay the tuition and all other expenses, and she assured him she would. But, he said, next summer, after he'd won the cup, he was going to pull his daughter out of that school, and she could damned well finish her senior year at home.

"Of course," Eva said, as if she had no objection. "After you've won the America's Cup, you'll want the whole family to be together."

I don't know whether it was a slipup or whether she was being intentionally duplicitous, but it was exactly what Cal wanted to hear.

"Or," she said, "perhaps your fame may present new opportunities for you."

Now Cal was intrigued. "What kinds of opportunities?"

"You never know," she said. "It could be something out west. Or in the media."

He leaned in.

"We've got a whole year to figure it out," she said.

Cal left Eva's house smiling to himself. He left town a few days later under full police escort and with the requisite fanfare from the clubs who were sponsoring him, but without even a word of good-bye to any of his family, which, under the circumstances, was just fine with everybody.

But his new confidence didn't last long.

May prepared a room in our house for Emma, who was more like a real sister to her than a half sister. Auntie Emma's house was not winterized, and if she were going to stay up north, it would have to be with us or with Eva. My mother was so happy to have her as a houseguest that no one even dared suggest that Eva's place might be the more logical choice. After all, Eva was Emma's mother. But May nursed my aunt's wounds. She made frappes for Emma to drink until the wires came off her jaw. I've never seen May as happy as she was for those few weeks when she was taking care of my aunt. May might not have been a great mother, but she was (it seemed) a born nurse.

Then things began to change. The week before Labor Day, the yacht-club launch came out to the island with a letter. It was addressed to my aunt and sealed with wax and the yacht club's emblem. Thinking it was some kind of invitation, like the ones I got to Hamilton Hall or to other assemblies, I hand-delivered it to her.

It was an invitation all right, but not the kind I was expecting. *"Come back to me. As God is my witness, I will never harm you again,"* it read. *"I do not want to live my life without you."*

Cal's newfound confidence had lasted less than a week.

Auntie Emma was packed to leave by the next morning. She called the water taxi before May was even up.

My mother caught up with her on the dock. May tried to haul the bags back, and she and Emma actually struggled physically. It was like something out of a bad movie, and one of the handles on my aunt's leather suitcase ripped almost all the way off.

"Leave me alone," Auntie Emma said through clenched teeth. "Let me go!"

"You're crazy!" May said. "You don't know what you're doing."

"He's my husband."

"He's just trying to manipulate you."

"He needs me."

"Please."

"He loves me."

Women are so stupid. That's what May was thinking. I could read the disbelief in her, that it would come to this. She knew she had to raise the stakes. "The same way he 'loves' your daughter?"

"What is that supposed to mean?"

May's silence said it all.

"Tell me," my aunt said. "Tell me what you mean by that remark."

"Open your eyes," May said.

"You are a sick, perverted woman," Auntie Emma said.

May said nothing.

"You are disgusting," my aunt said.

"And you are blind."

The world seemed to stop for a moment as the impact of May's chosen word was taken in by my aunt.

"No wonder he hated it here," Auntie Emma said. "No wonder he had to get away. . . . You accuse him of horrible things. Unspeakable things."

"How long do you think it's going to be before he pulls her out of that school? A week? A month?"

"I don't want to hear this."

"At least think about your daughter."

My aunt grabbed her suitcase and threw it into the boat.

"All right," May said. "If you want to be an idiot, I can't stop you. But I won't have you putting your child in danger."

"What is that supposed to mean?"

"It means that if you try to take her back there, I will stop you."

"You're a fine one to talk about putting a child in danger." She looked past me toward Beezer, who had just appeared, inhaler in hand, at the top of the dock.

"Come on," May said to me, starting up the dock.

I didn't follow. I just stood on the dock looking at my aunt. I could not believe that she was really going; it seemed impossible. We stood there looking at each other, and she must have been able to read what I was thinking, because she broke the gaze first, going back to get the broken suitcase, dragging it over, pushing it onto the boat. The skipper grabbed it. I saw him notice the bruises on her face, which were starting to fade to yellow, like jaundice.

May turned around at the top of the dock. "Come!" she yelled to me, clapping her hands together as if I were one of the dogs. "Now!"

May walked ahead of us back to the house. Beezer waited for me. He took another hit of his inhaler.

Beezer grabbed my arm as we walked, just in time to keep me from falling into a rabbit hole. It was a hole I'd never seen before, right there in the middle of the path, and it was a dangerous one. It surprised me to see it there. I thought I knew where all the rabbit holes were, but this was a new one. The rabbits must have dug it sometime last night, while everyone was sleeping.

I heard the boat pull out, but I didn't turn back. I was trying not to think about what it meant. I couldn't believe that Auntie Emma was really going. I couldn't believe it was all going to end like this.

Winter to summer . . .

I like the hospital. I like being here. It feels safe. But I miss the smell of the ocean so much. I just wanted to say that.

I'm trying to remember what happened that winter, but I can't. Most of the memory has been lost to the shock therapy. I only remember being very cold and very lonely. I don't think I heard from Lyndley at all. I don't remember.

The next time I remember seeing Lyndley was the following summer. The weather was beautiful the day she arrived. I was finally warm.

When the school term ended, Lyndley came back to Salem by herself.

Since neither Cal nor Auntie Emma would allow Lyndley anywhere near May, my sister was officially staying with Eva in the rooms that later became mine. But Lyndley came to the island anyway. She spent her time moving back and forth between the island and the mainland, and no one ever really knew where she was staying on any given night, so no one really worried about her if she didn't show up, which suited Lyndley just fine. When she stayed on the island, she slept in the room that May had prepared for Auntie Emma.

It was the happiest I'd ever seen her. Lyndley was free. She had liked school and was looking forward to her senior year. She had a lightness I'd never seen in her, and her natural wild streak was unleashed. She had always been pretty, but now she was magnetic. In the same way May was. The beginning of legend.

Everyone wanted to be with her. I had to fight to get equal time.

"Let's go to Harvard Square," Lyndley suggested one day, and I jumped at the chance. "Bring your jacket," she said. "It's going to get cold later."

We rode the bus to Haymarket, which took forever, then the T into Harvard Square. It was hotter in town, and Lyndley traded my jacket to a hippie panhandler for a pair of huarache sandals, because her feet hurt, but the sandals were one size too big, so she went barefoot unless we went into a store, like this head shop she found. Then she'd put the sandals on and flop around, her feet making tiny farting sounds as she walked. The guys at the counter were getting a kick out of it, but guys always got a kick out of anything Lyndley did, because she was so pretty, and besides, their eyes were really bloodshot, so I think they were stoned, which makes anything funny. Every once in a while, when the sound was really outrageous, she would blush and say, "Excuse me," or *"Pardonnez-moi, s'il vous plaît,"* and they would about fall off their seats. By the time we left, Lyndley had gotten a 20 percent discount on a silk sari and a five-finger discount on some rolling papers that they pretended not to notice her pocketing. She got away with this only because she had promised one of the guys that she would give him her phone number, a good trick since she didn't even have a phone. She hoped he'd forget about it, but he followed us out of the store with a pen, and Lyndley ended up scribbling Eva's phone number on the guy's arm.

"Hey, what's your name?" he yelled after her, tripping over the curb as he tried to read his arm.

"Eva Braun," she said.

Lyndley thought this was very funny, but the guy didn't get the joke, and I wasn't laughing, because not only was it not funny at all, but I was starting to get pissed off about the jacket, although it wasn't one I really liked. Even I knew that you didn't give away a fifty-dollar jacket for a pair of ten-dollar sandals. That was just plain stupid.

By the time we got out of there, I could tell that Lyndley felt bad about it, too, because she took me into Marimekko, where she was going to buy me something, but the designs there were too cheery for her, or anyway that's what she told me, so we went to Pier 1 instead, and she bought us two Indian-print bedspreads. She was going to cut hers up and make pants out of them, she said, because Eva had a sewing machine she could use. But I didn't have to make pants with mine, she said. I could keep it as a bedspread if I wanted to.

At another head shop down the block, I saw a pair of earrings that were really pretty, and I pointed them out to Lyndley, who went ahead and bought those, too, but not for me, for her. It kind of pissed me off that I was the one who had found them—not that she hadn't bought them for me, she had already bought me too much, but that she had to buy them at all. When she asked me what I thought, I told her they looked good on her, but she could tell I was mad.

"Where are you getting all this money?" I asked.

"Eva gives me an allowance," she said. "She doesn't know how much kids should get, so she gives me way too much."

I looked at her. She could tell I was judging her. We are all readers, even Lyndley, who likes to pretend she isn't.

"Come on, let's go get some incense," she said, grabbing my arm.

Lyndley bought some frangipani incense and a purple tie-dye T-shirt. Then we stopped for oolong and Earl Grey at Tivoli, and she paid for that, too, but we both agreed that it wasn't very good, because they didn't warm the pots the way Eva did when she made us tea.

We took the bus back to Marblehead, getting off at Fort Sewall just at sunset, as the blasting cannons from the yacht clubs shot their echoes all around us. We ran down the stairs to the Whaler, which we had tied up to someone else's mooring, and luckily our boat was still there. We arrived back at the island just as May appeared at the top of the dock, Lyndley losing one of the sandals as she ran up the ramp, like Cinderella or something, but she ran back for it herself instead of leaving it for some prince to find.

"I thought you were in Salem," May said to us, and I could tell she'd been watching where the boat came from.

"Marblehead," I said.

"You told me Salem."

"No I didn't."

She looked at us, then at the bag and at Lyndley's one sandal. I was really scared for a minute that she was going to ask to see what was in the bag, and I was hoping that Lyndley had kept the rolling papers in her pocket and not transferred them to the bag or anything, but May didn't ask. Instead she started pulling up the ramp.

"Next time you're late," she said, "I'm just going to pull this up, and you can sleep on the float all night."

My mother was so weird.

It did get cold, and rainy. For the next few days, we stayed inside playing gin rummy with Beezer, who was starting to wheeze. Lyndley kept trying to cheer him up by drawing fake tattoos on his arms with a ballpoint pen, dotting the ink on—a phoenix on one arm and a killer shark on the other. Then she took out her sketch pad and drew pictures of Skybo lying on the rug, but he was dreaming and his feet kept twitching, so she finally gave up and just started writing her name over and over in different styles, trying to find a new style of penmanship that suited her.

By Thursday, Lyndley was itching to get out, and May needed some groceries and some ephedra for Beezer's wheezing, so we volunteered to go to town. Eva was on her way out when we got there, but she had the ephedra and some other herbs ready for us to take, as well as some tea, and then Lyndley asked if we could borrow some furniture from the coach house while we were at it.

"You want my furniture?"

"Just old stuff. Stuff you don't want anymore."

"For what purpose?" I could see Eva's wheels turning, wondering what we were up to now. She looked at me to a get a better read of the situation, but I clearly had no idea what Lyndley had in mind, so my thoughts told her nothing.

"We're going to redo the playhouse," Lyndley said. "It looks like a bomb struck it."

It was one of Eva's expressions, and Lyndley used it to get her favor. Still, you could tell that Eva was suspicious, since we hadn't touched the playhouse in years. I watched her mulling over the idea. "There's some old junk piled in the coach house. If you want to haul it away, that's your business. It'll save me paying somebody to do it."

Lyndley kissed her on the cheek. "Thank you, thank you, thank you," she said, and started out the door. "You are a wonderful woman and a great American."

Eva stopped, as if just remembering something. "By the way," she said, "some young man called here and asked me out last night. I assume he was looking for you."

It stopped Lyndley. "What did he say?"

"He said he met me in some store in Cambridge and that he can 'get ahold of a car next Thursday night' if I want to go out and 'shoot the shit.' "

"What did you say?" Lyndley was trying not to laugh.

"I told him I was grounded for the rest of the summer."

This cracked Lyndley up. "Good one," she said, "really good."

"Consider it done," Eva said.

"What?" Lyndley asked.

"No more trips to Boston," Eva answered. Then she thought about it. "More specifically, town limits to the island. And consider yourself lucky. If your mother finds out you're even going out to Yellow Dog Island, she'll kill me."

"Okay," Lyndley said, but her voice was quiet.

"And I want to know ahead of time where you're staying each night," Eva went on.

"Okay."

Eva was waiting. "Starting now," she said when Lyndley didn't pick up the cue.

"On the island," Lyndley replied. "For tonight."

"All right." Eva nodded and started toward the door, leaving Lyndley standing there, slightly stunned. "And, by the way, it's pronounced *Ava* Braun, not Eva Braun. And that reference is not even remotely funny." And I could tell that there was something else going on. I'd never seen Eva this edgy.

I held the door for Eva, and she went through it without a thank-you or a look back.

When she was out of earshot, I turned to Lyndley and said, "I can't believe you gave them the real phone number."

She shrugged. For someone so smart, Lyndley could be really stupid sometimes.

"Come on," she said finally, "let's go."

"Where?"

"To fix up the playhouse."

"We're really going to do that?"

"Yeah, what do you think we've been talking about all this time?"

I had to admit I had no idea.

"And why would I want to help?"

"Because you're my sister, and you love me, and I need your help."

"No sale."

"All right. How about this one? Because you're my sister, and I love you, and I know you haven't got anything better to do."

The playhouse was actually Eva's boathouse. It stood on stilts down by the docks right on the water. From my room on the island, Eva's boathouse looked like a huge open mouth facing out to sea waiting to catch whatever came into the harbor. It was originally built as a rigging shed when the Whitneys were in the shipping trade, but it had later been moved and placed on the stilts, and the huge opening was cut into the harbor side, exposing it to the elements and making it look as if it were always just about to fall down. Toward the rear of the building was a closet where we left the sails and oars in the winter. At the back of the closet was a tiny staircase leading to a loft. There was a barn window off the loft, but the window had not been there originally; like the door, it was cut in much later. When the tide was high enough, that window was a great place for diving into the water.

May says the original loft was probably built for smuggling or avoiding British taxes, as the tunnels under the common were, and only later used for more altruistic purposes, like the Underground Railroad, maybe, but it doesn't matter. The point is that the loft was our playhouse, and it was a great place. Eva had given it to Lyndley and me that first summer that Cal had gotten so bad, so she'd have a place to get away to, somewhere he couldn't find her.

No one from our family came anywhere near the boathouse in the summer, so it was very private. In the winter we left some of our boats here: Beezer's Whaler, a dory, and anything else we didn't want to leave out on the island to get slapped around. The water level varied with the tides, going from ten or twelve feet at high tide to just a few feet when the tide was dead low. That made it bad for anything with a keel, and even with a small boat you would have to pull up the outboard when you left, or you'd come back and the boat would be spinning around or even balancing on its propeller, which wasn't great for the engine. For that reason no one used it as a real boathouse anymore, so it became ours during the summer. It smelled of salt, mildew, old sails, and seagull guano, and you'd have to use a lot of bleach to get the place smelling halfway decent, but it could be done. At the height of summer, the whole building became a steam bath, and that's usually when we abandoned it in favor of other locations. But it was still a great place. When the loft window was open, you couldn't smell anything from down below even if it was ninety degrees out, which was almost never.

We made several trips to and from Eva's coach house, dragging chairs, a table, even an old horsehair mattress that was no good to anyone, really, but that Lyndley couldn't live without. Except for the chairs, we couldn't fit anything up the stairwell, so we had to go back and get some rope and pull the table and mattress up through the loft window. The sky was black to the north, and even though the thunderstorm was going to miss us, it was getting pretty windy, and we almost lost the mattress once into the water. When we finally pulled it through the window, it flopped onto the loft floor, kicking up years of dust. Lyndley dragged it into the corner and covered it with the new Indian-print bedspread she'd brought with her.

"I thought you were going to make pants out of that."

"I said *you* should make pants, I never said *I* was going to."

I hated it when she twisted the story like that. Usually I would call her on it, but I was so tired from hauling the furniture that all I wanted to do was lie down on the mattress. I was glad she'd covered it.

She'd brought two things with her in her backpack: the bedspread and a bottle of burgundy she had stolen from Eva's wine cellar, which was odd, because the one thing Lyndley didn't do was drink, and she hated anyone who did.

"What are you doing?" I said.

"You'll see."

She didn't have a corkscrew, so she took an old rigging stick and pushed the cork down into the bottle. The wine squished around it, up and over the top, and she got some on her T-shirt, and it pissed her off, but then she went to the window and dumped the rest of the wine into the water below. I watched as the deep red turned pink, then gray, then disappeared altogether. It was somehow satisfying to watch as the wine lost its power; I thought maybe I was watching some kind of healing ritual or something, Lyndley exorcising the power that demon alcohol had over the life of her family, something like that. But then she sat down on the mattress and rolled herself a joint, and my theory went out the window along with the wine.

I thought about pointing out the irony of the situation, but Lyndley wasn't as into irony as I was, and besides, I didn't really know what she'd been doing with the bottle anyway, so I didn't say anything. I was starting to get tense, not because I cared if she smoked a joint—I hardly knew anybody who didn't—but because I was one of the only straight kids left, and I was self-conscious about it. I'd tried smoking one last summer with Lyndley, and basically nothing happened. It just made me choke, which made me feel grouchy and very uncool.

I was getting kind of pissed off at Lyndley again. "Is this what we're building here? An opium den?"

"It's not opium."

"You know what I mean."

"Don't be so dramatic."

I'd moved across the room, sitting as far away as I could get, over by the window, in the better of the two chairs we had taken from Eva. It didn't have any caning left on the seat, so I sat balancing on the rim, trying not to fall through.

I frowned. Lyndley took another toke, drew it deep, then got up off the mattress and walked over to me. I figured she was going to breathe it on me. We'd tried that last summer, but it hadn't worked; my clothes and hair had just stunk of weed. Instead of blowing it, she leaned over and kissed me on the mouth. I say she kissed me because that's what I thought she was doing, and I pushed her off me, and she ended up laughing, choking out the smoke.

"Jesus, Towner, you are so damned uptight."

"Fuck you very much," I said, trying to prove her wrong.

She finally took the paper wrapper from the candles, made a little tube, and blew the smoke into my lungs, which I let her do.

I didn't choke, and after several tries I did get high. I only know this because I sat back down on the mattress and watched as Lyndley dumped a bag of candle stubs onto the table. Then she took the empty wine bottle, lit the candle, and melted the colored wax down the side in tiny drips. When one candle was finished, she'd light another and another, until the wine bottle had disappeared and there was nothing left but a rainbow of wax. I know I was high, because I remember thinking it was one of the most fascinating things I'd ever seen.

"I think I'm stoned," I said finally, and Lyndley started laughing.

"You think?" she said, and we both laughed until we couldn't laugh anymore.

She took the one candle stub she had left and stuck it in the top of the bottle and said, "Voilà."

And then I fell asleep. When I woke up, Lyndley was sitting in the chair looking out the window. She reminded me of those pictures you see of the captains' wives gazing out to sea, searching for a mast on the horizon. The room was finished. It looked good. In the half-light of sunset and the glimmer from the candle, she looked beautiful. Not that she wasn't always beautiful, but the sun was lighting her hair, and it glowed golden and red around her like a halo on an angel or something, which is not a way you'd ever picture Lyndley normally. It took a moment for the stoned sleep image to fade.

"Oh, my God, what time is it?" I said, snapping back to reality and bolting up from the mattress.

"It's not that late."

"May's waiting for the ephedra," I said.

"She knew you'd be a while."

"She'll pull up the ramp."

"No she won't. She's bluffing," Lyndley said.

"No way. May doesn't bluff."

I scrambled around the room, messing things up, trying to find the little bag of herbs that Eva gave us.

I found it, gathered up the rest of my stuff, and headed toward the ladder.

I looked back. "Are you coming?"

"I'm going to stay here for a while."

"You told Eva you were staying on the island."

"I changed my mind."

"Why?"

"It's nice here. . . . I want to stay."

I could tell she was lying.

"You can't sleep here."

"Why not?"

"Because you'll get in trouble."

"Who's going to tell? You?"

"No, but it's not a good place to be."

"What are you talking about?"

"It's the docks."

"The docks are safe enough."

I saw Jack's boat pull in then. It sat low in the water, loaded with lobsters, probably from Canada, where there were more of them these days. I watched from the window as he tied up. He looked up then, flashed a smile. He was shirtless and very tanned.

The smile was intimate. I could feel my face go red with it, which really made me mad, and then I felt Lyndley behind me, and I immediately knew that the smile was meant for her.

He was standing next to a man with a clipboard, pointing to the hold, negotiating a price for his catch. An offer, a shake of the head, and then the man went down and took another look in the hold. Jack held up his index finger rolling his eyes, indicating that he was going to be a minute. The man turned, catching a cleat, ripping a huge hole in the back of his pants. Jack's eyes went wide. A quick "what should I do?" look at Lyndley, and she put a "don't say anything" finger to her lips, and Jack tried then to keep a straight face as the man ambled back to him, totally oblivious. There was more discussion and finally a handshake. Jack and Lyndley kept looking at each other as the man calculated the numbers. Then Jack signed the receipt, the man got out his checkbook, and it was a done deal.

"You're going to get caught," I hissed at Lyndley as Jack started toward the boathouse. I was trying to be the voice of reason, but I sounded more like a demon from some weird cartoon.

"Not unless you tell."

"Pregnant, then, you're going to get pregnant."

"I haven't gotten pregnant yet."

"One time. You were just lucky."

"I've been seeing him all year. Besides, I'm using birth control. I'm not stupid, you know."

But I was stuck on her first sentence. "You've been seeing him all year?"

"He's been driving down to school . . . on weekends."

I stared at her.

"I didn't want to tell you because I knew you wouldn't like it."

Major betrayal.

"We're in love, Towner. He wants to get married and go to Canada."

She didn't get it. Everything she said was only making things worse. It wasn't that she'd been seeing Jack that was bothering me so much, it was that she hadn't *told* me she'd been seeing Jack.

"He wants to get married," she said again, as if that would help.

"That's the oldest line in the book." I was aiming for one of Eva's clichés, but I ended up channeling Cal.

It was a direct hit.

"You're not going to tell me you believe in that happily-ever-after crapola?" I had to keep it going.

"Why wouldn't I?" She was trying to be defiant, but her voice was already weakening.

"Why buy the cow when you can get the milk for free?" I didn't mean to say more, but the momentum of anger was carrying me. It was so very easy. I didn't have to use Cal's foul language; all I needed were Eva's old bromides. With just a few well-aimed barbs, I'd managed to propel Cal Boynton into the room as if he had walked up the stairs himself, spewing his profanities and accusations. My aim was dead-on.

"You should come home," I said, knowing by the look on her face that I'd taken this way too far and feeling bad about it.

There were footsteps downstairs then, and she flinched. Then Jack called hello. His voice was bright and happy, a sharp contrast to the mood I'd just created.

"I'm not going home," she said. She was trying to be happy, too, but the spirit had gone out of her. I had taken it.

I wanted to tell her I was sorry. I wanted to cry and hold on to her. But I didn't want her to stay here with him. Something about Cal's accusations the summer before had stayed with me. Some part of me, a small, strange part, thought maybe he was right. That maybe my sister was what he said she was, a whore. I tried to erase the thought. But she knew what I was thinking. "I'm not covering for you, if that's what you think," is what I finally said.

"No one asked you to," she said, going for toughness, but her voice was flat. She could not have read my thoughts any more clearly if they'd been printed on the wall.

I went down the stairs just before Jack headed up. The tide wasn't high enough for jumping, or I would have gone out the window. I hid in the shadows so he wouldn't see me. Then I got into the Whaler. I could hear them talking from above. I watched them silhouetted in the frame of the window.

"What's the matter?" I heard him say to Lyndley.

"Nothing," she said as brightly as she could, "everything's fine." He went to her then and kissed her.

Her arms hung limply at her sides. She didn't kiss him back.

It was growing dark when I got back. Lyndley had been right. May hadn't pulled up the ramp. She *had* been bluffing.

I was obviously in a bad mood. Neither May nor Beezer asked where Lyndley was, so I didn't have to lie. No one liked to talk to me when I was in one of my moods, and mostly they just let me be.

Lyndley had been right on both counts. May hadn't pulled up the ramp, and I didn't have to cover for her. But I would have. If it had come to that. *I* was the one who'd been bluffing.

In late August, Cal pulled Lyndley out of Miss Porter's. There had been an "incident" at the yacht club he'd been sailing for, and he'd been thrown off the team. He was devastated. He started drinking in the daytime. He made a phone call to Lyndley's school and called the headmistress some terrible names. He blamed her and the school for the corruption of his daughter. By the time Eva called the headmistress, the damage had been done. Even if they'd wanted to take Lyndley back (and there were some implications that she hadn't been the easiest student to discipline), they didn't want to deal with Cal Boynton. . . . It was over.

Eva was livid. Nothing she could say would change their minds. Finally Eva called someone she knew at Pingree School and secretly enrolled Lyndley for the fall term. Then she put Lyndley into May's protective custody and left for Florida, where the Boyntons lived. "Don't let her off this island," Eva said, "and keep that ramp up."

Living in captivity should have put a serious crimp in Lyndley's style. She had been playing house with Jack at the boathouse for most of the summer without getting caught. It should have bothered her. But she seemed resigned to her fate. She seemed almost relieved.

I apologized every way I could. I told her I hadn't meant anything I'd said. We didn't fight about it. She told me that she understood. That I was right.

I was really starting to worry about her.

Eva didn't look too good when she came back from Florida.

"Cal's moving the family to the West Coast," she told May. "He's sailing for San Diego."

They'd sold the house in Florida, and he'd paid Eva back the money he owed her, which meant that she no longer had any leverage over Cal.

"Is Emma going with him?" I could see that May still held out hope.

"Yes, he wants his whole family together out there." Eva pulled an airline ticket out of her purse, putting it on the table between them. It was obviously for Lyndley.

"No way," May said.

Eva pulled out another letter, written in Emma's hand.

May read through the letter once, then a second time. "She's willing to give up custody?" May asked. I could tell that it was something she never expected.

"I talked her into it," she said. "It wasn't easy."

"Will she stick to it?"

Eva shrugged. "It doesn't really matter. I've already spoken to my attorney," Eva said. "The letter will never hold up in court. Not if Cal protests it, which of course he will. . . . If Emma were willing to tell all the facts, then maybe we'd have a chance."

"That will never happen," May said.

We all knew that something was going on. Even Beezer had been listening at locked doors, but he couldn't hear anything, so he finally gave up. Eva and May were good. They had locked themselves in the kitchen so they couldn't be heard, putting rooms between them and us to block the sound, the butler's pantry on one side and the back porch on the other. I had been able to get onto the back porch, though. I'd picked the lock. Once I was inside, I hid behind the coatrack so they wouldn't see me.

I didn't dare move until they had finished talking. May sat at the table for a long time after Eva left. Finally she got up and started making sandwiches for everyone, really bad sandwiches with peanut butter, which Beezer was allergic to, and with pickle relish, which made me gag.

I ended up telling Lyndley what I'd heard—selectively. I told her that Cal wanted her to come to San Diego but that her mother had written a letter saying she could stay with us. I told her she would be switching schools, and although she seemed suspicious about it, I think she liked the idea of staying—but it was getting increasingly difficult to tell.

Still, she was agitated. She pressed me for more details about San Diego. I ended up telling her that Cal had been fired from the Florida team. She was worried about that part, I could see, but when she thought about it, she tried to make the best of it. "San Diego is a better club," she said, thinking maybe that alone could make things better and Cal happier.

I didn't tell her any of Cal's demands. I acted as if he had signed the letter, too. She had no reason to think he wanted her to leave here, since he'd given her permission to stay this past year.

I felt a little bad about what I left out, but I knew I couldn't tell her. After that I had to make my mind as blank as possible, because she was a reader, too, and I didn't want her to get really suspicious.

"Is my mother all right?" Lyndley asked several times before I finally answered her.

"She's fine," I said, again making my mind blank, willing myself to not think about Emma, so Lyndley couldn't read my thoughts.

But it didn't work. Not for long. There were too many closed-door conversations between May and Eva. And no one except Eva was allowed on the island.

"What's really going on?" Lyndley demanded one night. She hadn't slept. I could see the circles under her eyes.

"I told you."

"Maybe you told me some of it, but you sure as hell didn't tell me all of it."

I shrugged my shoulders. If there were more to the story, I said, I hadn't heard it. She knew I was lying.

All the lawyers said the same thing, that the letter Auntie Emma wrote turning custody over to either

May or Eva would never hold up in court. Not if Cal really wanted Lyndley back. And Auntie Emma would agree to give Lyndley up only if no one disparaged Cal in any way. So they were in a no-win situation. In the end May and Eva decided to go to court in spite of it all, if it came to that. They figured they might have the time and money enough to make it inconvenient for Cal. If luck were with us and if Cal did start winning for San Diego, he wouldn't have time to be going to court constantly to fight for custody, especially if the venue were Massachusetts. Plus, Eva had more money than Cal did. So May and Eva assured their lawyer that they were in it for the long haul.

"Get ready for the fight of your life," was his response.

Lyndley would be seventeen in less than a week—they figured if they could hold off the court date for a year, they had it made. Because once she turned eighteen, there would be nothing Cal could do to get her back if she didn't want to go. She would finally be free.

A few days later, Lyndley cornered me again. "Tell me the truth this time," she said, "the whole truth and nothing but."

I caved. I told her everything. I'd been so guilty about not telling that it was like a dam had burst or something, and it all poured out of me.

And it helped. We weren't exactly close anymore, but I could tell that she trusted me again.

When the date on the ticket came and went, Cal started calling Lyndley on the island ship-to-shore. I was in the kitchen when May intercepted one of his calls.

"What do you want?" she said to him.

"I want my daughter back."

"Get used to disappointment," was her reply.

"You tell her that her mother needs her. Tell her if she doesn't come out here herself, I can't be responsible for what's going to happen."

"Be more specific with your threats," May said. "I'm tape-recording this."

May turned off the radio after that. But I saw a shadow moving down the hall and knew that Lyndley had been listening the whole time. Two days later Jack dropped off a letter addressed to Lyndley. It sat on the kitchen table unopened until May asked me what was going on.

I took it upstairs and put it on Lyndley's bed. She didn't touch it. The third day was our birthday. I opened the letter.

"I'm leaving for Canada the day after your birth-day," it said. *"Marry me."* Taped to the letter, wrapped up in tissue, was a ring. It was silver, with a small diamond in the center of a simple setting. He had probably spent a month's lobstering money to buy it.

Lyndley was looking out the window at the Boynton house. I had read her the letter, and I was waiting for her answer. The same way Jack might have waited if he'd been here to ask her himself.

I looked out the window to see what she was staring at. The house needed work. Its wraparound porch was half gone—Cal had removed it last summer to replace some rotting boards, then never got a chance to finish the job.

"It's going to fall down," she said, still looking at the house.

"Maybe."

"What if he kills her next time?" Lyndley asked, remembering her mother's broken jaw. "And I'm not in San Diego to stop him."

"You weren't there to stop him this year," I said by way of encouraging her.

She smiled then. "When did you start believing in all that happily-ever-after crapola?"

"I don't know," I said, meaning it. "Today, maybe."

I had her packed by midafternoon.

By five o'clock we were socked in by fog. Eva radioed to say she couldn't get out of the harbor. She had four bags of groceries for May to cook for our birthday dinner, and she was stuck on dry land.

Part of me was relieved that Eva wasn't coming. The birthday dinner that Eva and May cooked us every year was a great tradition. But every year Eva did a lace reading on our birthday, and tonight I was afraid of what she might see.

The fog would lift eventually, and when it did, I would get Lyndley to Jack. I didn't want anyone standing in the way.

May did her best to put together a birthday celebration. She reverted to sandwiches, because it was all we had on hand. But she did make a cake with one huge candle in the middle of the buttercream icing.

After dinner was over, we sat around. No one knew what to do. We were accustomed to Eva running our parties. But Eva wasn't here.

After a while Beezer got up and did the dishes. May stayed at the table, watching us. We kept glancing at the fog, which was getting thicker by the minute.

"If I didn't know better," May said, "I'd think there was someplace you'd rather be."

"No," I said, too quickly.

"This is great," Lyndley said. She walked over and kissed May's cheek, which was something I'd never seen her do. "Thank you for this lovely party."

May smiled. "You're welcome," she said.

"Let's play a game," Beezer said as he came back into the room. He'd started for the Monopoly board when May held up her hand, remembering something.

"You're forgetting our tradition," she said. She opened the top drawer of the sideboard and pulled out a piece of lace.

"You're not a reader," I said.

"Just because you haven't seen me do it doesn't mean I can't," May said.

"Read me first," I said, doing anything I could think of to keep her from reading Lyndley.

May held the lace in front of my face. I tried to clear my mind, to keep from thinking about Lyndley or Jack or anything that was about to happen. I held my breath.

The image formed quickly in the web of thread. Everyone saw it. Everyone except Beezer. May would later claim she saw nothing, but I knew better. I watched as her expression changed.

The image was of Auntie Emma. Badly beaten, her face and eyes cut.

Lyndley gasped. May dropped the lace.

We sat in silence for a long time.

"What did you see?" Beezer asked.

"Nothing," May said. "Absolutely nothing." She got up and put the lace away. "It's getting late," she said, dismissing us. "You look tired."

Lyndley and I walked to our room in more silence. She didn't want me to know she was crying. "Why won't she leave him?" she asked.

"I don't know," I said, opening the door.

I pulled up the shade and looked out. For a moment I could see the lighthouse beam from Marblehead Neck. Just a flash of green, but it was there.

"It's lifting," I said, pointing to the beam.

She turned toward the window.

"Synchronicity," I said.

"What?"

"The fog is lifting. It's a sign that everything's going to be okay," I said.

She tried to smile.

We couldn't get Lyndley off the island until high tide. I had already moved the Whaler to Back Beach and tied a long line to its bow. I figured if the tide was turning high and the rocks were covered, I could put Lyndley in the boat and tow her out, with me on land walking the rocky perimeter of the island, dragging the line along until she was safely past the point. Then

I would throw her the rope, and Lyndley would pull it in, letting the Whaler drift out toward the Miseries. She wouldn't start the engine at all until she was past the barrier islands and no one could hear her leaving. She could get to the docks by midnight.

The house was dark when we let ourselves out. We closed the screen door slowly so it wouldn't creak.

We walked in silence, taking turns carrying her suitcase, crossing the baseball diamond. We passed the abandoned car where I'd found Lyndley and Jack what seemed like such a long time ago now but was only last summer. We passed Lyndley's house, with the pieces of the porch still lying in a pile by the steps, rotting now. Lyndley didn't look at the house or at the porch but kept her eyes on where she was going.

Though it was hard work, the plan was successful. I had such calluses on my hands from the ropes that I had to keep them in my pockets for days so no one would see them. Ultimately I'm sure everyone figured out that I helped Lyndley. They knew there was no way she could have escaped all by herself.

If the waters at Back Beach didn't exactly part for us, they didn't rise against us either, though in retrospect maybe it would have been better if they had. I pulled the rope along the rocks as far as I could, the dogs watching me as I worked. When I got past the point, I threw the rope far into the water. It landed somewhere to her port side, and she pulled it in. She stood in the boat, and for a minute we just looked at each other, but then the boat got wobbly and she had to sit down. She waved to me then, and I watched her for as long as I could. I watched her drift past the point, the way I had planned. I didn't watch her out of sight, partly because I was crying too hard and my eyes were starting to blur, and partly because of what Eva had always told me, that it was bad luck to watch people until they were out of sight.

I didn't find Jack's ring until the next morning. It was right there in plain sight on my bedside table where Lyndley had left it, but it was dark when I got back, so I didn't see it right away. I ran down the stairs and went through the cabinet where I had seen May put the ticket Cal had sent to her. I pulled the whole cabinet apart before I realized that the ticket was gone.

Eva went to San Diego to get Lyndley back, but it didn't work out. She came back alone.

Fall to winter . . .

May took Lyndley's departure hard. If she had been somewhat reclusive before, now she was showing the first real signs of agoraphobia. When she managed to go into town, she would get so agitated she'd have to come right back. She couldn't breathe, she said. Not with all those people around.

It got cold early that year. Beezer, who was already in boarding school, wrote letters expressing his concern that I wasn't in school at all.

Eva came out and tried to talk May into coming to town for the winter, saying she would give us her entire third floor as an apartment. From there May could go up on the widow's walk and keep an eye on the island. She didn't have to come down until spring, Eva said only half kidding, trying her best to say something, anything, to convince my mother. May refused. Eva asked me to come—ordered me to come, in fact— but I didn't dare leave May. It was true that I hated my mother, but even I could see that she shouldn't be left alone out here. She was hardly sleeping. She had taken to burning her lamp both day and night. She had stopped taking her vitamins. She wasn't shouting orders at me all the time, and she had even stopped making sandwiches.

In October the Department of Social Services came out to the island. Someone had tipped them off that there was a child on the island who wasn't attending school. Homeschooling was illegal in Massachusetts at the time. I always figured it was Cal, but in retrospect I realize that it might have been Eva who called them. May got angry and wouldn't talk to them. She left them in the living room with me. I didn't know what to say. I kept thinking about what Eva would do in such a situation. I offered them tea.

Then one day, later in the month, May came downstairs as if everything were fine. She made cereal. She told me she had decided something. She had decided that I should go live with Eva. "You can come back in the summer if you wish to," she said, "but you should go to live at Eva's now." As an afterthought she added, "And when Beezer comes home for vacation, he should stay in town with you."

And just like that, May gave the rest of her children away. As if she'd finally remembered what had worked for her once before when she was overwhelmed by having had two babies instead of one. Give one away had been her answer then, and even with all the heartache and trouble that had caused, she had decided that it had been a good solution then and it was a good solution now. May packed up my belongings, and I found myself at Eva's before I even knew what hit me. She told Eva she would join us as soon as the weather turned cold, and Eva believed her, I think. But I didn't.

A week later Beezer sent us a letter. He said he was thinking about coming home and maybe going to public school with his friend Jay-Jay. His tone was light, but I could always read his subtext. He was as worried about May as I was. Eva wrote back immediately and told him it was a bad idea, that even if he did come back, his school plan wouldn't work out. The LaLiberties lived up in Witchcraft Heights. The Witchcraft School was out of our district, so he wouldn't get to go to school with Jay-Jay. She told him that things were going fine and that he should *stay put.*

Eva enrolled me at Pingree. After all, she had already paid for Lyndley's spot, so it made sense. I was too late to sign up for bus service, so Eva hired a driver to take me to school every day. The day I started school was the day the hurricane hit. We were evacuated by noon, and by the time the driver got back to Salem, he had to turn around to retrieve me and bring me home. I spent the rest of the day up on the widow's walk, freaking out that May was still on the island. I had no idea whether my mother even knew that a hurricane was coming. I was the one who listened to the radio—either Beezer or myself, May never did. I tried to send her an SOS, then some other signals in Morse code, but the rain was so heavy you couldn't have seen the light even from the coast guard station on Winter Island, let alone from our place. I stayed up on the widow's walk until the winds got really bad, and Eva made me come in. She told me she expected May to come in any day now. She was sure of it. But it never happened.

I kept to myself at school. November first came and went. By then even most of the fishing boats had stopped going out, but my mother never showed up. To distract me Eva gave me a job in the tearoom. And the dancing school. In November, I got an invitation to a cotillion at Hamilton Hall. In the past I'd always thrown the invitations away, and I did the same this time, but Eva fished it out of the garbage and sent an RSVP. When I hadn't seen May's light for two days and wouldn't come down from the widow's walk for most of the weekend, Eva decided she'd had enough. She got a lobsterman to take her out to the island to fetch May, the same way she had with Lyndley, but again she came back alone. I could tell that Eva was upset, and also that she didn't want to worry me. It was Veterans Day, I remember, because we had the day off from school.

"She never had any intention of coming," I said, seeing the truth, knowing that May would rather give us up than leave her island, ever.

"It's not that simple," Eva said, reading me, but I wasn't having any of it.

"It is too that simple."

"For God's sake, Sophya, have some compassion."

"It's the same thing all over again." I was unable to sit, I was so agitated.

"What do you mean?"

"Like with Lyndley."

"What about Lyndley?" She said the words slowly, as if she were trying to find out how much I knew.

"She gave away Lyndley, and now she's giving away Beezer and me."

"What are you talking about?" Eva stared at me.

"What's happening to Lyndley, what he's doing to her." My skin crawled when I thought of that night in Lyndley's room. "None of it would be happening if May hadn't given Lyndley away in the first place. Everyone knows what he does to her!" I was crying uncontrollably as I said the words. I couldn't breathe.

Eva held me for a long time. "It's going to be okay," she said.

I didn't see how.

She took me to a therapist in Boston. The doctor put me on a mild antidepressant. Eva had hoped I would talk to him. I couldn't seem to do it.

"Tell me about your sister," he would say. But I couldn't do it. I could tell Eva, but it wasn't the kind of thing you could tell to a stranger. After six sessions I refused to go back.

She gave me a job helping with the dancing lessons instead. She was trying to keep me busy. The fact that she was expecting me to go to Hamilton Hall and behave like a lady was part of that plan as well. I learned to follow the leads of the most tentative dancing partners. Eva bought me long gloves that extended up past my elbows, and she taught me to tuck the hands of my gloves up when I ate dinner, leaving just the sleeves, and to eat chicken à la king while sitting at a crammed banquet table without moving my elbows and without dropping any peas on my formal dress. When I asked what I should do if they served something besides chicken à la king, Eva just laughed and told me that would never happen, "not in a million years," she said.

A few weeks before the cotillion, I got an invitation from a girl at Pingree to ride to the dance in a small bus her parents had rented for the occasion. I hardly knew the girl; the only thing I remembered about her was that she was really preppy-looking and liked to say "fuck" a lot, just for the shock value. I told Eva I thought it was ridiculous, since the bus was leaving from Beverly Farms and I could walk to Hamilton

Hall from our house, but Eva said I was missing the point. She made me accept the girl's "kind invitation" in writing and had her driver chauffeur me all the way to Beverly Farms and drop me off so that I could take a crowded, smelly bus all the way back to Salem.

The dance wasn't terrible, even if it was from another century. Each girl had two partners going in, one on each arm, and one of my escorts was a kid I knew from the Pleon Yacht Club in Marblehead. Each time the orchestra took a break, they threw felt hats into the audience with the band's name embroidered across the brim, and boys tried to catch them to give to the girls they liked. And even though the kids hated the music, they liked the hats. They fought one another for them, jumping into the air to catch them as if they were at a baseball game or something.

During one of the breaks, someone hid the conductor's stick, and the dance stopped while the chaperones searched for it and interrogated the kids. The guys went outside to smoke, including both of my escorts, and I decided it was a good idea considering the Spanish Inquisition that was going on inside. We stood in the park across the street, and a kid with a madras cummerbund lit up a Marlboro and started his own inquisition about Cal and how he was doing in San Diego.

Up to that point, no one had gotten the connection. To the sailing boys who knew about him, Cal was a local hero, the kind of man they could hope to become if they were lucky and everything went their way. "He's probably the best sailor in the world," the kid said in closing. "And he's rich. He owns that whole island, for God's sake."

"He doesn't own the island. My mother's family owns the island," I said with a little too much edge.

"Same difference."

"I saw his picture in the paper," one of the girls said dreamily.

"He looks like Paul fucking Newman," the Rental Bus Girl said.

I could feel my muscles tense.

One of the girls was shivering. "How long are they going to make us stay out here?"

"Until they find the perpetrator." The Cummerbund winked at me.

"Which gives us some time," the Yacht Club Kid said, with a side glance at the Cummerbund, who pulled a silver flask out of his jacket pocket and stood there passing it around.

"I'm going home," I said.

"What?"

"No way."

"You can't go home. The bus won't be here until eleven."

"I'm not waiting until eleven o'clock for a bus to drive me when I only live six blocks away."

"Party at Towner's house," one of the boys said.

"I live with my Great-Aunt Eva."

The Rental Bus Girl shot me a look.

"Party at Towner's great-aunt's house," the boy declared.

"Eva will be asleep."

"Trust me, you don't want to party there," said one of the other girls.

"Yeah," said the Rental Bus Girl, "Eva Whitney is fucking Emily Post."

"Excuse me?!" The Cummerbund raised an eyebrow. "Did you say her great-aunt is *fucking* Emily Post? I didn't even know that Emily Post was still alive."

The girl started to giggle as if she thought it was the funniest joke she'd ever heard. "You know what I mean."

I left before anyone could concoct an alternate plan that included me. I realized halfway down the block that my coat was still inside, but I didn't want to go back for it because I was afraid I wouldn't get away so easily the next time. Instead I tucked the hands up inside the gloves and worked the long sleeves up as high as I could get them to cover my arms. As I turned the corner, I could hear the orchestra tuning up, and I saw the kids file back inside.

I walked by the house, but Eva was still awake, and I didn't want to go in yet, so I just kept going. As I walked along, I started to get really angry with May for letting this happen: for putting me in this situation and making me live in Eva's house and go to cotillions. And angry because Beezer was gone for good, wasn't he? Because after boarding school was . . . what? Prep school, then college? Going, going, gone. I was starting to realize how much things had changed and how quickly. We'd probably never all live on the island together again. In the blink of an eye, our whole world had changed, and none of us could make it go back to the way it was. Lyndley was gone, my brother was gone. And my mother, May, was depressed or crazy or just plain didn't care.

And then I started getting this really crazy idea. I started thinking that maybe I *could* change it, if I acted quickly, that maybe it wasn't too late if I went home right now, tonight. If I called Beezer and told him to come home, he would. I still had that much power over him, although it was fading quickly. I went to the pay phone on the dock and tried Beezer at school, but it was lights-out already, and they wouldn't answer the call. I figured it didn't matter. He'd be home for Thanksgiving in a few days, and when he got to Eva's and found out I was on the island, he'd get himself over there, and everything would be all right again. I knew him. He'd get there somehow. Even if he had to take a helicopter, my brother would do it.

And so I found myself at the boathouse where the Whaler was put up for the winter, and I checked the tank, and it actually had some gas left, and it was a pretty calm night, so I shoved the boat into the water and got into it, ruining my dress in the process, but who cared? If I was ever going to go home again, tonight was the night. It couldn't wait.

I pushed the boat off, and it drifted into the harbor. The tide was dead low, the moon almost full, but there wasn't another boat anywhere around, so at least no one was going to ask me any questions or try to stop me.

I figured I'd waste some gas starting her up, but it was easier than I'd thought. I picked up the gas can. It was about half full. There were no swells, and with the moon so bright it was easy to spot the rocks. I knew I'd be fine if I didn't do anything stupid, if I didn't fall in. I remember Eva telling Lyndley once that a fifty-year-old had a 50 percent chance of surviving a fifty-yard swim in fifty-degree water. It was one of the reasons you weren't supposed to swim if you fell in. You were supposed to just stay there, using as little energy as possible, and wait until someone rescued you. If you started to swim, you'd force all your blood to your extremities and away from your vital organs. You'd die a hell of a lot faster that way, and that was in fifty-degree water. This water hadn't seen fifty degrees since early October.

When I got out of the harbor and away from the shelter of land, a cold wind rippled the water, and I noticed that there were some swells, too, although they weren't very bad and it wasn't very far to the island, so I wasn't worried about them. Still, the whole thing seemed sort of strange and out of place to me. The stars had the brightness of winter to them, and I remember thinking that even though I'd stayed out on the island in previous winters and seen these same skies, I'd never actually been *on* the water this late in the year. We took our boats out early, right after Columbus Day. Even if it stayed warm, the float had to come out by Veterans Day, because that's when the boatyard closed down for the season, and the boatyard workers are the ones who did all the work. The only boats running this late in the year were the big boats out of Gloucester. And a few of the lobster boats.

I was almost to the island when I got the joke. It was a great cosmic kind of joke, and I got it in a flash. And then I started to laugh. I laughed so hard I had to cut the engine, because I was afraid I'd fall out of the boat if I didn't sit down until it passed.

What was it Eva said? *You can't go home again.* That was the joke. It wasn't figurative, though, or metaphorical. It was literal. When I got close to the island, I realized that the float was gone. The ramp was there, hanging high above the water, just the way it was every night I could remember, when May pulled it up. But the float it connected to was gone. It was pulled out of the water for the winter as it was every year by Veterans Day, but for some reason I hadn't remembered that. It's what Eva had been worried about when she went to fetch May and why she went out there when she did, because once the float was pulled out, May couldn't get off the island until spring except by helicopter, which she would never do. I knew it; we'd been talking about it just last weekend. But what I'd forgotten was that if May couldn't get off the island, I couldn't get onto it either. The only way on was Back Beach, but not in winter waters. It would tear a boat apart this time of year. Here I was making this grand gesture, trying to go home again, but my Aunt Eva was right when she said you can't go home again. And for some reason, now I found it really funny.

I sat in the boat, the engine turned off, looking at the island, which was just a few hundred feet away but might just as well have been a million miles away for all the good it did me. I knew I should start the engine and head back to town, but I couldn't move. I couldn't go forward and I couldn't go backward. I just sat in the boat in my party dress, laughing my ass off.

Jack thought the boat had broken down or something. He was coming from the back side of the island, where his father still kept a few traps. He'd been hauling them out for the winter, and the boat was full of them, a maze of little boxes. He hadn't wanted to come out that night—he told me that later—but his father had been nagging him for weeks, and he was tired of hearing his father's voice. He just wanted to get it over with, so he could get some peace. Because the moon was so bright, Jack saw the Whaler right away. I don't think he realized it was me until he pulled up alongside.

I saw him take in the dress, the gloves. He didn't ask what I was doing out there, didn't even ask about the engine. Instead he grabbed an arm and pulled me aboard, tying up the Whaler to the back of his boat, shoving his jacket at me. He didn't greet me. I could tell he was pissed off. In fact, he didn't speak to me at all for a long time, and when he finally did, it was to ask me, "Are you just stupid, or do you have a real problem?"

I wasn't sure which was the correct answer, so I didn't say anything.

Summer again . . .

The following summer I did go back to the island. It was a decision I made with Eva and with my shrink. May was doing better, and so was I. She sent me a letter saying she hoped I'd be out for the summer, that she was looking forward to it. Beezer didn't come back. He got the opportunity to attend a science camp at Caltech. Everyone, including May, agreed he should go.

Things weren't the same between May and me. But they were tolerable. And she was all right. The depression that had hit her so hard was gone now, and I started to wonder if maybe she really did know what was best for her. That maybe, unlike the rest of us, May knew her own limitations and worked within them.

In early August, Lyndley arrived. She wasn't scheduled to come. She just showed up out of the blue, saying she missed me and wanted to spend our birthday together. She seemed happy. She'd been accepted at two art schools, RISD and CalArts. Lyndley told me that Cal and Auntie Emma were insisting on CalArts. They wanted her to stay close to home.

I had been seeing Jack since Christmas, since the night of the Hamilton Hall dance. It happened with the inevitability of a dream. He didn't even seem to like me at first; he just seemed angry at me, probably because I looked like my sister, and I know how much Lyndley had hurt him. Everyone knew. As Jack and I got more involved, I told myself it didn't matter, that it was okay because Lyndley had been the one to break it off with Jack. She had made the decision.

I'd been hauling traps with Jack all summer, which is how I began not coming home for days at a time. We'd work three days here, then four up in the Maritimes, just over the Canadian border. He had three hundred traps there. Plus another three hundred behind our island and over by Baker's. Jack's father was sick. "From the drink and from the drink," was the way Jack put it, referring to years of fishing and years of frequenting the waterfront bars. His liver was shot. He had bad arthritis. He couldn't fish anymore.

Jack had tried to get his brother Jay-Jay to take over the local traps, but Jay-Jay wasn't interested in lobstering. He got seasick. So Jack hired me. Although I was officially living on the island with May, most of the time I just stayed on the boat with Jack.

The week Lyndley came home, Jack and I had been up in the Maritimes, stopping back by the Isle of Shoals, camping out on a beach there, because by then we both needed to get off the boat. By the time we got back, I was ready to spend a few days on the island, just to be on dry land. It was past midnight, and May wasn't expecting me for another day at least, but the lamp in the kitchen was burning. I knew that Beezer was out in California. It was late, and I was hoping like hell that May wasn't waiting up for me.

But it wasn't May. It was Lyndley who was sitting at the table in the kitchen. She hugged me for a long time. "I missed you so much," she said. "I didn't think I'd ever get back here again."

"God, look at you," she said. "You got so pretty this year."

"I thought you were going to CalArts."

"Forget CalArts," she said. "I'm not going anywhere near CalArts."

She slept in my bed with me, said she didn't want to be alone. I lay there all night, looking out the window, trying not to disturb her, until the sun rose in the reddest sky I'd ever seen.

She was carrying Jack's graduation picture with her. It fell out of her pocket when I went to pick her jeans up from the floor where she'd dropped them. It was wrinkled and worn. I owned the same picture, although mine was in better shape.

I was on the radio with Jack when Lyndley came down for breakfast. She looked thinner than I'd seen her, older, although it was only a month before our eighteenth birthday.

"Who were you talking to?" she asked me.

"Jack."

"My Jack?"

I stood up and got her some cereal. I could tell she wanted to know what was going on, but I didn't want to talk about it yet.

"Did you tell him I was back?" she asked. It was a tentative question. She wasn't sure how he would feel about it.

"Not yet," I said, as if it were some big secret. It was, but not the kind she thought.

I cut up some strawberries for the top of the cereal, because I knew they were her favorite.

"Happily-ever-after granola," was what she said. But she took the strawberries and three whole spoonfuls of sugar. She finished the entire bowl. And then she did something strange. She took off the silver earrings, the ones I'd picked out in Harvard Square. She slid them across the table to me.

"What are you doing?" I asked, suspicious.

"What's mine is yours," she said, and that's how I knew she knew. She held my gaze for a long time, then picked up her bowl and went to get more cereal.

I left the earrings on the table between us. I had no idea what to do. Lyndley came back to the table and ate a second bowl of cereal as if nothing unusual were going on.

Finally she finished eating and took both our bowls to the sink and washed them with salt water. She used a dish towel to dry them, so they wouldn't get all streaky from the salt. Then she actually put them away, which is something I'd never seen her do.

"It's a really nice day," she said. "It's going to be hot."

The sky still had traces of red.

"I'm going to go down and check the house," she said, getting up and walking out. It was a tradition, checking the Boynton house, seeing how it had fared over the winter, and we usually did it together. But this year she didn't ask me if I wanted to come along. And she didn't take back the earrings either.

I never told Jack that Lyndley was back. It seems odd now (with all that's happened) that we never had that conversation, but it's true.

It was dusk by the time he arrived, and it was already choppy from the impending storm. I was on the dock waiting for him when he pulled in. I didn't even let him tie up the boat but jumped in, which wasn't very smart, because the ocean was already churning. I think he had wanted to stay on the island, at least for a little while.

"Get me out of here," I said.

He knew I was upset. He probably figured I'd had a fight with May or something. That was a pretty

common occurrence these days, fighting with my
mother. When she wasn't distracted, the two of us were
always arguing about something, usually stupid things.
Like who had left the water running or who hadn't
pulled up the ramp. That's how things were going between us. It wasn't the way I'd hoped it would be last
winter, when all I had wanted to do was get back here
to the island, when I was counting the days until I could
come home.

There is a tiny door in the lobster traps they call the
"ghost panel." It is made of wood. I noticed it one day
when we were hauling traps. When I asked about it,
Jack told me the reason it is there is to let the lobster
out in the event that the lobsterman never comes back
for his catch. If he is gone for long enough, the wood
will deteriorate and free the lobster. It's supposed to
be humane. I don't know whether it's a relatively new
invention or if traps always had them. Or maybe they
weren't necessary back in the day when all the traps
were made of wood.

At the end of that last day we spent together, we
hauled up one of the old wooden traps, one of the
few Jack still used. I looked for the ghost panel, but
I couldn't find it. Jack already had the trap rebaited
and was ready to toss it back, but I was obsessed with

finding that panel. I was staring at the trap from every angle, looking for a way for the lobster to get out.

"What are you doing?" Jack finally asked.

That's when I told him I didn't want to see him anymore.

He almost laughed, it was so out of the blue. But when he looked at me, I was crying. He'd never seen me cry before. I am not someone who cries easily.

"I can't keep seeing you," I said. He could see I meant it.

"What the hell is going on?"

I couldn't tell him. I didn't want him to know about Lyndley, not yet anyway. I needed to know he was upset about me, and I thought if I told him about her, he wouldn't care so much about the breakup. I don't know what kind of logic I was using; it was just a feeling I had.

His face went red at first, and then slowly the color drained out. I froze in place, expecting a blow. I'd seen white rage before, never on Jack, but on Cal plenty of times. White rage is an unmistakable emotion. I really expected him to hit me. But I was wrong. He didn't hit me. He just stood there for what seemed like forever, staring at me.

"Not again," was what he finally said. His words were ice.

For a minute I didn't know what he meant, "Not again." We had never broken up, never even really had a fight. "Not again" was not an appropriate response.

Then, in a flash, I got it. It was totally appropriate. Whatever I might have wanted to believe, I knew that my instincts had been right not to tell him that Lyndley was back. Jack had been in love with Lyndley since the moment he'd met her. I was just a substitute, the closest he could get to what he really wanted, which was my twin. If I'd been honest with myself, I would have realized that I'd known it all along. I just hadn't wanted to think about it. The blow he dealt me was to the heart, and it was much worse than anything physical he could have done to me.

Angry, Jack slammed the engine into forward, gunning it to full throttle.

As we came around the windward side of the island, by the rock cliffs off Back Beach, the boat slowed, almost imperceptibly at first. I looked up. The sky was brighter than I remember, although to the north it was all clouded over, and it was black and blank-looking as if a whole part of it had been erased. I almost said something to Jack then, almost warned him not to slow down here because the currents and the chop could easily catch you and you could lose your boat on these rocks. I ran to the bow of the boat and leaned over, looking for shadows where the rocks would be. "Don't stop!" I yelled, climbing out onto the bow. I could see the dark silhouettes of the rocks just below the surface. We could smash to pieces here, the way so many boats have. I started to yell at him again, but the look on his face stopped me. He was looking past me at something on the cliff.

My eyes tracked his. I blinked in disbelief. On top of the cliff, about a hundred feet up, was Lyndley. She was barefoot and wearing my nightgown, the one Eva had given me for Christmas, the white one with the lace on it. Her hair was blowing, and so was the gown. She looked like a goddess from some Greek myth. A wave of jealousy hit me hard. Not just because she was standing there so beautiful, with Jack looking up at her like that, but because the entire scenario seemed so completely staged. She must have been standing there for a while just waiting for us to see her, for the wind to be right and for the boat to appear in her range of vision. It was so calculated it was ludicrous, and I couldn't believe Jack would actually be stupid enough to fall for it. At that moment I hated my sister. Utterly and completely. I wanted her to die. I wanted her to fall off the cliff and smash into a million pieces.

The air was thick with the humidity of the storm that was still on the horizon but rapidly moving toward us, making it heavy and black and impossible to breathe.

She was leaning forward, into the wind, like the figurehead on an old Salem ship, the lacy gown billowing out behind her, illuminated by the sliver of the waning moon, the stars and their doubles reflecting from the black sky down to the even blacker water. Her face was perfect and expressionless, like an empty canvas she hadn't yet filled in, leaving us later to paint in our own impressions of what we saw that night. Her whole body tilted forward into the wind at an impossible angle, and just as I realized that the angle couldn't hold, it broke free, obeying the laws of gravity but shattering those of perspective, and she began a long and silent fall into the cold, black ocean below. She flipped over headlong only once, then folded her arms across her chest as if she were already dead, piercing the black water like a needle, never even making a ripple. And she was gone forever. Just like that.

I heard Jack gasp, and the sound jolted me back. We stood staring for what seemed like an eternity, expecting her to surface, to come up at least once, but it didn't happen. Then I was in the water, diving. I heard Jack on the radio, shouting "Mayday! Mayday!" into the static. I gasped for breath, went down again. He blasted the horn, a three-blast distress call, then shined the search beam into the water, trying to help me. Then I heard the splash, and I knew he was in the water, too.

I dove again and again, but the ocean was empty. I couldn't get to the bottom. I came up a third time, exhaled completely, then took a huge, bursting breath and went down yet again, as deep as I could, letting the air out as I went, so I could reach the bottom rocks where I knew her body would be. I felt the rocks sting my legs as I scraped against them, pulling myself along, willing my body to stay down. Then, suddenly, the ocean was not empty anymore but seemed filled with everything anyone had ever lost—an anchor, a bottle, an old lobster trap. My lungs hurt, first from holding my breath, now from their own emptiness. Every part of me wanted to surface, but I knew that if I came up, I would never go back down again.

There is a point where the life force overcomes the will and the body simply breathes itself. It just happens. It hurts like hell when you take a breath of seawater, but the hurt goes away quickly, and then you feel the flow of water and hear the music of the spheres. You are pulled, literally, toward the light, and I remember registering it, realizing that it is true what all those near-death-experience people write about. I remember smiling a bare-toothed smile, the cold water freezing it in time forever.

As we broke the surface, I could see that May was already in the water, swimming toward us. The light I'd seen was not my near-death experience but the searchlight from Jack's boat, and it was his hand that had dragged me back to life. It was horrible. It was as bad and painful as it had been beautiful a minute ago, and now Jack was trying to smother me, his mouth over mine, breathing me, trying to keep us both afloat until help arrived.

May pulled us both to shore and was standing over us, so concerned about me. I was trying to tell her, trying to make her go back for Lyndley, but I couldn't get the sound out. Every time I tried to speak, I gagged and threw up salt water, then gagged again. The pain in my lungs was worse than anything imaginable. He should have let me go, should have let me die with Lyndley. There was no pain in the dying, but the coming back to life was unbearable.

"Be still now," May was saying to me, holding my head in her lap, brushing my hair off my face. I could see Jack, kneeling, coughing, a few feet away. *Tell her*, I was trying to say. *For God's sake, tell her Lyndley is still down there.* May was a strong swimmer. I realized now that I had been wrong worrying about her. May was stronger than I ever knew. She was the only one of us who was strong enough to save

Lyndley now. But she couldn't save her if she didn't even know she was down there. I tried to tell her again and again. But no words came either from Jack or from me.

I watched powerless as Jack heaved and collapsed, exhausted, sobbing into the sand.

PART FOUR

Out of the chaos and the swirling of pattern, the images will begin to emerge. The first will appear at the still point. These are the Guides. The Lace Reader must use the Guides to move past the still point and beyond the veil. Beware of images that emerge at this place. They are not real. The Guides are tricksters. They will show you their magic and invite you to linger. If they are able and the Seeker is vulnerable, the Guides will fool you into believing that they themselves are the answer. Their egos are great. The Reader must resist the urge to allow the Seeker to rest here, no matter how captivating the images seem, or how true. It is the Lace Reader's job to move the Seeker past the still point to the real truth, which lies not within the veil but just beyond.

—THE LACE READER'S GUIDE

Chapter 21

Rafferty and Towner sat together on the porch like an old couple on a cruise ship, blankets over their legs, deck chairs pulled up tight against the rail of the old Victorian fixer-upper Rafferty had bought his first winter here and regretted ever since.

"Taking the cruise to nowhere"—that's what Towner called sitting here like this. It had become her main occupation since she got out of the hospital. It was prescribed. Rest, the doctors said. When she felt strong enough, she could swim a little, as long as it was in salt water. That last part had been Rafferty's idea, not Towner's. He knew she was a swimmer—all the Whitney women were—so he'd asked the doctor about a little swimming. Good idea, the doctor said. So far Towner had not gone anywhere near the water.

She'd been in the hospital for three weeks, the first on a vancomycin drip. It was a bad infection. Postsurgical, they said. With complications. They hadn't defined the complications, but they were there. Complications were a given in Towner's life, and they were what had worried Eva most about her grandniece. There was something inevitable about these recent complications—not about what was happening but about Towner's reaction to it all. Eva's words kept coming back to him: *There are many ways to kill yourself.*

In the weeks that followed the infection, Rafferty read everything he could find on twins and bereavement. Twins were something special. Lose a twin at any age and you lose part of yourself. Half of you dies. Even people who didn't know they were twins, who had lost a twin in the womb or been separated at birth, walked around all their lives with feelings of separation and grief, as if half of themselves had been lost and could never be found again.

Ever since he read Towner's journal, the image she had created of Lyndley's suicide kept playing through his mind. It was classic survivor's guilt, if you thought about it. Suicide was almost impossible to get over. Rafferty's roommate at Fordham had committed suicide, a fact made much worse because it wasn't talked about, because the Catholic Church considered suicide not only a crime but a sin. In some ways it had felt like sin. At least to someone left behind. It engendered the same sick feeling you get when you've done something from which you can never truly recover. Like sin, or a low-grade virus.

Rafferty had been the one to discover his roommate. The image had never left him. Unlike Towner, Rafferty had never tried to kill himself, not directly. But the possibility was always there. Like the virus. Once you were exposed, it stayed with you forever, just waiting for you to weaken. You never knew what day your resistance would be down and the sickness would get its shot at you.

Rafferty visited Towner at Salem Hospital. He stopped there most days on his way home from work. They didn't talk much but sat on the roof porch looking out toward the harbor. When it was time for her release, it seemed natural to take her to his porch, where the view was better and he could keep an eye on things.

She couldn't go back to California, not yet. She didn't want to go back to Eva's, and he sure as hell didn't want her to. So he offered her his daughter's room. Only for a few weeks, he said, when he heard her hesitation. Until she was stronger.

She liked his daughter's room, seemed to feel comfortable surrounded by the souvenirs of a life that had nothing to do with her own: a poster of Tupac Shakur over the dresser, Beanie Babies suspended from the ceiling in a makeshift hammock.

"How old is your daughter?" It was one of the only questions Towner ever asked him.

"Leah is almost fifteen," he said.

She would have turned fifteen while she was vacationing up here this summer, if he hadn't changed the dates of her visit.

"What would you think about coming a couple of weeks later?" he had asked Leah when he'd called her last week. "We could take the boat up to Maine."

"The big boat or the little one?" she'd wanted to know.

"The big one."

"Okay," she'd said. "Whatever."

His ex-wife had been all over him for changing the date. And for not taking it up with her.

"You can't just keep changing everything," she'd said.

"I don't keep changing everything, I just changed this one thing. Leah didn't seem to mind."

"The things you don't know about children could fill a book."

Rafferty thought she was probably right. "I'm on a case." It wasn't an explanation, not really, but it was all he had, so he went with it.

"So what else is new?"

"A murder case."

There'd been a long pause when he said the word. "I thought you moved up there to get away from murder cases," she'd said finally.

"I moved up here to get away from a lot of things."

It had been a direct hit, and he knew it. He hadn't meant it, not really. It was habit.

"You can't just go changing things," she'd repeated. "What if I made plans?"

"So this is really about you."

Click. He'd gotten used to the hang-up. It was the way most of their conversations ended. And it was usually because of something he'd said.

He'd felt bad about the whole thing for maybe an hour. Rafferty knew that Leah probably did care that he changed things around. But he also knew that to his daughter this wasn't a vacation, it was a "dutation." Leah had given it that name herself. Part duty, part vacation. She was clever with words, his daughter. He'd been a little insulted when she came up with the word, even if it was an accurate description of their time together. They were awkward with each other. It was as tough for her to come here as it was for him to have her. Not that he didn't love her. He loved her a lot. But the guilt of leaving her behind had been too much for him. When he'd left New York, she'd wanted to come with him. She didn't like the man her mother had left him for, she'd said. "I just want to be with you."

"Your mother would never allow it," had been his response. It was true, of course, but it wasn't an answer.

She hadn't asked him again. It wasn't her nature. He'd counted on that. Just as it wasn't her nature to question the change in vacation dates. She didn't ask questions. Which was a good thing, at least in this case. The last thing Rafferty wanted Leah to know was the real reason he had changed things around. He didn't want her to know he'd fallen for Towner Whitney.

Most nights Rafferty made dinner for the two of them. Pasta mainly, because it was something she would actually eat. She liked ice cream, too. Sometimes the ice cream truck made its way into the Willows, and he would walk down to the little beach to get some for her. Other nights, if he was working late, he would stop by the Dairy Witch on his way home. She liked anything with jimmies—the chocolate ones, not the rainbow sprinkles.

"What are you looking at?" he asked her. Her gaze was distant most of the time. He had asked the question before, usually without getting any answer.

"The lights," she said. She was looking toward May's window. "She usually has only the one light burning," Towner said, pointing to the two lights that shone in May's window again tonight.

One if by land and two if by sea, Rafferty thought. He stopped short of saying it out loud.

It surprised him that she had noticed the lights, the detail. He took it as a good sign.

That she didn't seem to notice Jack's boat leaving the harbor seemed a good sign, too, if for a different reason. Towner's night with Jack LaLibertie was the elephant in the middle of the room that neither of them talked about. Not that they talked about anything, really. But they definitely didn't talk about Jack LaLibertie.

He had to admit he was relieved when her eyes stayed on May's lights and did not track Jack's boat heading for the Miseries, where most of his traps were located, then turning off its running lights and taking a hard turn to starboard and the back side of Yellow Dog Island.

They didn't talk much. That was the truth of it. If they had, he might have asked her about Jack. He definitely would have asked about the journal. Or was it a book of short stories? Rafferty didn't know exactly how to categorize it. The stories he had heard from Eva seemed to overlap and twist in Towner's version. He knew she was filling in the gaps of her own history, that it was somehow therapeutic; that's what she'd told him when he'd asked if he could read it. Yes, he could read it, she'd said, if he thought it would help with his case against Cal. But she didn't want anything to do with it.

He'd read it over and over. Each time it raised more questions than it answered. It had instructor's notes scrawled across the bottoms of the pages. The class she wrote it for was taught by a BU professor, though Towner had never enrolled as a student there. Rather, it was part of her reentry program her last year at McLean.

Rafferty had been able to fact-check that much. But the course instructor was long gone. The course title, Introduction to Fiction Writing, didn't do much to explain it either. The instructor may have believed that Towner was writing fiction; there certainly was a good amount of fiction involved. But there were facts, too, facts a more normal person might not want to share with the world.

He would have asked her about Lyndley, about the love triangle, and about Towner's conclusion that it was Lyndley whom Jack really loved, and not her. It was too personal and too painful for him to ask about, yet he couldn't help reading it over and over again, trying to get a handle on it, trying to figure out the questions he would ask, should ask, if the time were ever right.

This was the part of the journal that was the hardest for him to take. And how he knew he was in trouble. The part he kept reading over and over wasn't the part about Cal, it was the part about Towner and Jack.

Rafferty had known everything there was to know about Jack and Towner long before he'd met her. Not because Eva had told him but because Jack had told the story in AA meetings. Not just once but many times.

He knew how they'd met and how Jack had put up with things he never should have put up with because he was in love. How he'd gone to the hospital every day in hopes that she would speak to him. How, after she got out, Towner had pretended not to know him. *Not to even know me!* Jack had almost cried when he said it. Rafferty had felt sorry for Jack, sure, but he'd also judged him for it, deciding that Towner had probably never loved him, not really.

But Rafferty had changed his mind about that, both because of recent events and because of the journal. After reading her journal, Rafferty realized that at least at one time Towner had been in love with Jack LaLibertie. Probably she loved him still.

It was because of Jack LaLibertie that Rafferty had stopped going to the Salem AA meetings. Not because Jack was there—no, he wasn't likely to show up at AA anytime soon. Jack had fallen off the wagon long before Towner had come back to town. The reason Rafferty had stopped going to the meetings was that everybody knew about Towner, which made Rafferty feel guilty as hell. He had good reason. At one time, before Jack had started drinking again, Rafferty had been his sponsor.

"Check your integrity, Rafferty," Roberta had said to him the last time he'd gone to a meeting in Salem. The room fell silent. It was what everybody wanted to say to him and didn't dare.

Things got even worse for him at work.

Every part of Rafferty's cop's brain knew that what was happening to him was a bad thing. And other people had been starting to notice.

The chief had warned him. "Don't corrupt the case just because you've got an itch."

"Fuck you," Rafferty had replied.

Towner had been in the hospital for three days before Rafferty arrested Cal for her assault. He could have done it sooner—the chief had been pressuring him to, in fact—but he knew that Cal would probably be out within twenty-four hours. If he waited until 4:00 P.M. on Friday, the arraignment wouldn't take place until Monday morning. At the very least, Cal would spend the weekend in jail. It wasn't much, but it was something. And it gave Rafferty a chance to interrogate some of the Calvinist followers without Cal's ever-present supervision.

The interrogations proved fruitless. If anything, the Calvinists were more dogmatic than their leader. Or just plain brainwashed.

Rafferty had one other idea, but it was a long shot.

At the arraignment he asked the judge to allow no bail, explaining that Cal was a danger to the community, citing his beatings of Emma Boynton as evidence, beatings that had left her blinded and brain-damaged. He brought in the medical and court records to support his claims.

Cal's attorney had of course anticipated this, and he countered by producing Cal's spotless record for the last thirteen years and his community-service commendation from the mayor of San Diego.

On the day of Cal's hearing, the courtroom was packed.

First the chief presented some complaints against Cal from the local merchants whose businesses the Calvinists had interrupted and from some mothers who stated that Cal's exorcism practices included corporal punishment that bordered on abuse.

Rafferty then took over, telling the judge that Cal was a prime suspect in the disappearance of Angela Rickey, who was allegedly carrying his child.

Cal's attorney countered by telling the judge that Angela Rickey had left the Calvinists, as agreed, to go home to her parents' house to have her baby.

Rafferty said that Angela had never returned home to her parents and was not likely to do so.

Cal's attorney showed a sworn statement signed by Cal Boynton that stated he had never had sexual relations with Angela Rickey.

Rafferty said that Angela claimed that the baby she was carrying did indeed belong to Cal and that she insisted on having the baby even though she wasn't certain how Cal would feel about it. Clearly, Cal had not been pleased. Rafferty also pointed out that Cal had both means and motive. "Fathering a child would be bad business for a man who has made so much money preaching celibacy."

Cal asked to say some words on his own behalf. In a performance that was half sermon, half sales pitch,

Cal likened himself to John Newton, who wrote the hymn "Amazing Grace." Like Cal, Newton had been depraved and unrepentant, a sinner of the worst kind, Cal explained—a slave trader, in fact. And like Cal, Newton had found his great deliverance at sea. The day of his conversion was not unlike Cal's own, and like Newton, Cal had gone on to become an evangelist minister. "Saved by God's grace and intervention," Cal said.

"Who among us does not believe in redemption?" Cal implored, turning to his congregation—the lawyers, the judge, the Calvinists, and several townspeople who had come to attend the arraignment.

"Who among you will cast the first stone?" Cal continued.

Several members of the council of churches sat along the back row. The Presbyterian minister muttered to the Methodist that *he* might cast a stone, if he thought he could hit Cal on the head with it from way back here. It was meant to be funny. The Presbyterians were the sect most offended by Cal's practices and by his adoption of the Calvinist name, a name that had long been associated with their brand of Protestantism. Not that they wanted the name, mind you; the Calvinist label had been a PR nightmare for the Presbyterians, an association they'd worked hard to live down over the years. They weren't likely to benefit in any way from the kind of press Cal was inspiring.

"I'd like to throw a stone or two." A woman rose to her feet. Her red hat and purple dress stood out in a sea of grays and browns.

Another Red Hat got up to stand with her. "Let's make it a boulder," she said.

The judge motioned the women forward. Five more Red Hats joined them as they walked to the front of the courtroom.

"Good morning, ladies," the judge couldn't help saying. Red and purple was a color combination he didn't see that often in the courtroom. He knew who they were, though: His wife had been threatening to start her own Red Hat chapter ever since she turned fifty.

"Your Honor, we would like to say a few words pertaining to the dangerousness of Calvin Boynton." The group had appointed Ruth as official spokesperson, and Rafferty had spent an hour coaching her.

"Proceed," the judge said.

"As many of you know, we were regular customers of Eva Whitney's tearoom," Ruth said. "We have reason to believe that Eva's disappearance was no accident." The woman continued without taking a breath before the judge was able to tell her that her information didn't pertain to this case. "We witnessed the ongoing harassment of Eva Whitney, not only of her business but of her personally. He threatened her on many occasions."

"That is a damnable lie!" Cal said, jumping up.

"Sit down, Mr. Boynton," the judge commanded.

"What kind of threats did he make?" the judge asked.

"He threatened to burn her at the stake, for one," the Gulf War mother who'd attended Eva's funeral said. Rafferty noticed that she had gotten rid of her pastel hat and was now sporting a bright red one.

"Excuse me?"

"He called her a witch, and he threatened to hang her or burn her or drown her, all on different occasions."

"He threatened to kill her, Your Honor," a third Red Hat offered. "One day when he didn't know we were in the tearoom."

"And how did Ms. Whitney respond to these threats?"

"Well, she called the police, naturally."

"This is true, Your Honor," Rafferty said. "We have many reports of such harassment. At the beginning of April, Eva Whitney took out a restraining order against Cal Boynton." Rafferty presented a copy to the judge.

"She told us," the Gulf War mother said, "that if anything happened to her, it would be Cal Boynton who did it."

"She was found all the way out by Children's Island," another Red Hat said. "Everyone knows that's where they dump the bodies."

A few years back, another body had been found out by Children's Island. It was a murder case that had just been solved. And an association that everyone had. Like Eva, and maybe like Angela, the woman had been missing for a while before her body had turned up out by Children's Island.

"Eva never left the harbor on her swims." Ruth took over. "She was eighty-five years old, for God's sake. She never could have made that swim."

Cal's attorney pointed out that there had been an autopsy on Eva. There had been no sign of foul play.

"There had been no sign of anything," Rafferty interjected. "By the time we found Eva, her body had been picked apart by lobsters. We had to identify her by her dental records."

The judge held Cal for thirty days. "If you want me to hold him longer, you're going to have to get me a body."

He wasn't talking about Eva. He was talking about Angela Rickey.

As Rafferty left the courtroom, he walked over to the Red Hats.

"Good work, ladies," he said.

"Do you think it helped?" the Gulf War mother asked.

"Very much."

"What about the other girl . . . this Angela?" Ruth wanted to know.

"Do you think he killed her, too?" the third Red Hat asked.

"I'm not sure what I think," Rafferty said. He had a bad feeling about what had happened to Angela. All he knew was that he had to find her. And fast.

As the crowd thinned out, Rafferty realized that he was probably the only person in town who didn't think that Cal had murdered Eva Whitney. Rafferty had let public opinion achieve his goal, which was to get Cal off the streets, at least for a little while. But he didn't think for a minute that Cal had actually killed Eva. The reason was simple. If Cal had done it, he would have been smart enough to drop the body inside the harbor, where Eva usually swam. The fact that Eva was found "where they dump the bodies" was the one thing Eva had done wrong in her plan to stop Cal Boynton. The Children's Island thing was meant to stand out. And it did. But to Rafferty it stood out for all the wrong reasons.

The swim was a good idea, but Eva had taken it too far. Besides, she was a Whitney. Any one of the Whitney women could have made that swim. At any age.

Rafferty told Towner that they were holding Cal. He didn't tell her the rest of what had happened. He figured it wasn't something she needed to know.

He wasn't sure what he believed about Angela. He wasn't wrong about the child. And he wasn't wrong about the motive. He only hoped he was wrong about his growing feeling that she was either already dead, or soon to be.

Rafferty couldn't do much about Angela. But at least he could keep an eye on Towner. That's what he told himself anyway. What Towner needed was R&R, and so he did his best to take care of her. He cooked. They sat outside and watched the boats.

Tonight they sat on the porch looking out at the ocean. "Is Leah a sailor?" Towner asked. It was race week in Marblehead. She was looking out over the harbor at a line of spinnakered sailboats.

The question was so far from his thoughts that it took him by surprise. "What?"

"Does your daughter sail?"

"Yeah," he said, "a little."

It was one of the only times Towner had spoken all evening. He should answer her if only to continue any form of conversation. "The boat she wants me to buy is a Scarab."

Towner nodded as if she understood. "The need for speed," she said. "She'll grow out of that. Tastes change."

"Is that true?" He was hopeful.

"Definitely," she said.

Tonight Rafferty offered pasta, he offered to grill some steaks, but nothing seemed to appeal to her. He was running out of menu options. He was tired.

"I'm not hungry," she said.

He stood up from the deck chair and stretched his legs.

"Then I'm going for a run," he said.

"Now?" She seemed surprised. He'd been yawning all evening.

"Yup. And after that I'm stopping at the Willows for a chop suey sandwich."

"You and your chop suey sandwiches," she said.

"You want to come along?" He always asked. She never said yes, but he kept asking.

"I'm tired," she said.

"Ice cream?" He tried one more time. Ice cream was something she would always eat.

"I'm all set."

Rafferty made three loops to Derby Street before he slowed down. With each turn he ran past Winter Island. Cal might still be in jail, but the rest of the Calvinists were just as dangerous as he was.

Rafferty ran until he tired himself out. On the cut-through path to Willows Park, he finally slowed to a walk. He was pouring sweat. He passed neighbors sitting on porches, kids playing street hockey. Down on the beach, a neighbor's kid stopped smoking weed and hid his stash behind a rock. At the end of the walkway, another neighbor called to her dog.

"Sorry," the woman said to Rafferty as she put her dog back in compliance with Salem's leash law. Rafferty tried to smile. Being a cop put an automatic distance between him and everybody else in town.

Someone fishing on the end of a pier pulled in a striper. It waved through the air like a pendulum, catching the red of the falling sun and painting it across the sky.

The Harleys were lined up just across from the midway, the leather-clad bikers behind them in full costume. Accountants and dentists, Rafferty thought, but no, there were Hells Angels, too. They made a pilgrimage to Salem twice a year, thousands of motorcycles. Salem closed the streets for them. It was impressive. When they rode into town, you could hear the roar of the engines way back on Highland Avenue long before you could see them. People lined the streets in lawn chairs just to watch them roll in.

The bikers rode in the Heritage Parade, too. And they rode on Halloween. Behind the witches. Right between the preschoolers and the marching band.

Roberta spotted him before he saw her. She stood sipping her Diet Coke, admiring the row of bikes. When she saw Rafferty, she turned the other way.

Rafferty stood in line for a chop suey sandwich, then took a seat between the band shell and the dock. As soon as he sat down, the band went on break.

Perfect, he thought.

But it was probably a good thing. With the band quieted, the sounds from Winter Island would echo over the noise of the midway, and he figured Towner was safe. He could make it back to the house in less than two minutes if he had to, and that was much faster than anyone could get to her.

But the Calvinists didn't seem to be preaching tonight. When Rafferty passed on his run, the hangar was dark. Instead a group of them were proselytizing down here. One of them wore a sandwich board with the same printed message on both sides: JESUS IS HELL-BENT ON SAVING THE HELLS ANGELS.

The bikers weren't biting, but some of the local witches took the bait. They argued back and forth, throwing words and phrases at one another.

"Go back to Derby Street!" the Calvinists yelled at the witches, who had set up a booth to sell Celtic jewelry.

"Oh, go jump in the ocean!" one of the witches yelled at the true believer they called John the Baptist. But John wasn't doing his ocean baptisms tonight. Instead the robed disciple had made his baptisms portable. He carried a bucket and a huge sponge, more suited to a student car wash than a soul-saving mission. Rafferty thought he should change his placard and offer a free Harley wash with every conversion. Some of the bikers had traveled a long way to be here tonight, and their bikes were very dusty.

In the last few weeks, Rafferty had run background checks on most of the Calvinists, particularly the robed ones and the women who reportedly had gone after Angela the first time. John the Baptist's real name was Charlie Pedrick. He wasn't from Jerusalem, as he had insisted when Rafferty had questioned him. Actually, he was from Braintree. Diagnosed with schizophrenia in his late teens, Charlie'd had his share of run-ins with the law. But not since he was "saved."

In a controversial ritual that Cal named "pharma-copeia exorcism," mental patients were encouraged to throw their medications into the harbor. They then endured a purification ritual not unlike the kind that took place in a Native American sweat lodge. In his endless stealing of doctrine from other faiths, Cal had even called this ritual a vision quest. It seemed appropriate. After two days with no food and little water, not one of these former mental patients failed to have a vision of some sort. Likening it to his time lost at sea, Cal directed his followers to listen for the voice of God and let that voice direct their lives.

Among those women whose belief systems favored such things, there were three Virgin Marys and two Joans of Arc. The voices that Charlie Pedrick had heard during his own vision quest had informed him that he was the reincarnation of John the Baptist.

Rafferty had been told about the ritual when he arrived in Salem, but he hadn't really taken it seriously until he saw the orange prescription bottles floating in Salem Harbor one morning. He'd spent several hours fishing them out, then made his first arrest of Cal Boynton. For littering.

———

The two groups were in front of the casino now, and things were really heating up.

"Take your pagan idols and go home!" one of the Calvinists shouted.

"Free enterprise!" one of the witches yelled back. She pointed to the side of the booth where the name of Ann's store was prominently displayed on the license. "Freedom to get a business license!"

Freedom to eat my dinner, Rafferty thought. "Hey, take it down a notch," he said. "You're giving me indigestion."

The Calvinists took this as an invitation to turn their venom on him.

"God save your immortal soul!" John the Baptist yelled at Rafferty. "And the woman you live with in sin!"

"Redheaded harlot!" yelled one of the Calvinists.

"Unrepenting demon!" yelled another.

A fight broke out on the sidelines. One of the Virgin Marys took a swing at one of the witches.

"All right," Rafferty said, putting down his sandwich and standing up. "Enough."

The park went quiet. People held breath, turning, waiting to see what he was going to do.

Then he saw the fear on the faces of the Calvinists. It surprised him. He'd never known them to back down from any kind of confrontation. But it wasn't him they were looking at—it was something behind him. Rafferty turned to see a woman all in black, her arms raised. Voice deep, eyes steeled at the Calvinists, she began her incantation.

"'*Gallia est omnis divisa in partes tres . . .*'" she chanted, in a voice so deep and rich it seemed not to come from her but from somewhere else entirely. It was a voice that lifted the gulls into the air and left them suspended and riding on the wind.

The Calvinists froze.

The witch took a breath. Then she pointed an accusing index finger at the group and lowered her voice again. "'*. . . quarum unam incolunt Belgae.*'"

It did the trick. The Calvinists scattered and slid out of the park like tiny balls of mercury.

Everyone stared at the looming figure of Ann Chase in full witch regalia. She was impressive.

"And another thing . . . !" she yelled after them in her now normal-pitched voice. Then she giggled, breaking the spell. She wiped her hands together as if washing the whole scene away, spread her robes behind her, suddenly every bit the lady, and sat down on the bench next to Rafferty.

"Very nice," Rafferty said. "Let's see, the nearest I can remember from high-school Latin is that you were reciting a passage from *Jason and the Argonauts.*"

"Caesar's *Gallic Wars*," she said. "But you're close. Saved your sorry ass, though, didn't it?"

"At least my dinner," he said, laughing.

"I saved you and you know it." Ann laughed, too. "And again I ask . . . what kind of weak, lily-livered god are they worshipping if they're afraid of a few witches?"

"They weren't afraid of a few witches, they were afraid of you. Hell, *I* was afraid of you."

"Really?" Ann seemed delighted.

"You bet."

They sat in silence for a minute.

"So what are you doing down here all dolled up?" Rafferty wanted to know.

"Just checking on my girls," she said, gesturing to the booth of witches that had had the confrontation with the Calvinists. Now they were celebrating their giddy victory, flirting openly as they helped the bikers try on pentacle necklaces and charms. The bikers were all too happy to have such attention from the pretty young witches.

"Should we be worried about them?" Rafferty asked, looking at the bikers.

"They should be worried about me," Ann said. She raised a hand and waved sweetly at the toughest-looking biker, who wilted a little in her presence. "That's right,

Mama's here," she said, continuing to wave politely, but with a protective sweep. "Be afraid," she said in sweet singsong. "Be very afraid."

"Hey, I wouldn't mess with you," Rafferty said. "You're liable to send me to the Gallic Wars."

"You got that right."

"One question," he said. "How come you didn't put a real spell on that John the Baptist character?"

"How many times do I have to tell you?" she said. "We don't do black magic. You're getting witches confused with satanists. Or voodoos."

"'Voodoos'? Is that the Latin terminology?"

"You know what I mean."

"You mean the ones with the dolls and the pins."

She nodded and made the "on the nose" sign with one hand while grabbing what was left of his sandwich with the other.

"Help yourself," he said.

She laughed. "I don't do mean spells. It's against my religion. I do a great business in love spells, though," she said. "In case you'd be needing one."

Rafferty's response was hard to read. It fell somewhere between a grunt and a grumble. Ann noticed him watching Jack's boat disappear behind the Miseries on its way up the coast.

"She didn't sleep with him, you know."

"What?"

"Towner. She didn't sleep with Jack LaLibertie."

"Is that your psychic opinion?"

"That's what she told me."

Rafferty looked surprised.

"She seemed to think it was important to clarify that point," Ann said.

Rafferty didn't respond.

"Maybe I'll say a few words for you when I get back to the shop," Ann said. "For free."

"Don't do me any favors," he said.

"If she were in love with Jack LaLibertie, she'd be staying with him, not you. Did you ever think of that?"

"Yeah. Well. Maybe."

"You've got it bad," Ann said.

Rafferty laughed. It was an understatement.

In reading the lace, there is no wrong answer. Even so, it is easy to receive wrong results, simply by asking the wrong question.

—THE LACE READER'S GUIDE

Chapter 22

Rafferty didn't go home until he was sure Towner had gone to bed. In the morning he left early to catch the men's AA meeting in Marblehead.

When he got to the station, there were three messages from May.

He took his coffee into his office, shut the door, and phoned her back.

"I just called the hospital," she said, "and they told me Sophya was released a week ago. My sources tell me she's staying at your house."

"And?" He wished May had never gotten herself a cell phone.

"And I want to know why."

Rafferty reached into his drawer. "I had an extra room. I offered."

"I can protect her better out here," May said.

"I doubt that."

"She needs protection."

"I have more guns than you do," he said, only half kidding.

"You can't watch her every minute."

"Neither could you," he said. "And besides, Cal's in jail. Did your sources tell you that?"

"Temporarily," she said.

It seemed to stop her. But only for a moment.

"It's not going to work," she said, as if deciding something on the spot.

"What?"

"You two."

That one stopped *him*.

"Opposites attract," she said.

"So?"

"So you're not opposites. . . . You're the walking wounded, both of you. Neither of you is capable of handling any kind of relationship."

Rafferty wondered how May knew so much about him. Was she a reader, too, or had Eva told May his history? Either way he didn't feel like discussing his lack of relationship skills with her. He was trying to think of a clever retort when she went on.

"When you two break up, and believe me you will, you won't just split apart like normal people. You'll send each other flying."

"I'll take that under advisement," he said, and hung up.

He reached over the desk to put the phone back, catching his cup with the cord, spilling coffee all over the files.

This wasn't going to be a good day.

The chief was coming in as Rafferty was leaving.

"I'm going to Portland again," he said. "To ask around."

The chief nodded. "Good idea," he said. "Then I'll see you tomorrow."

"I'm off tomorrow."

"Right," the chief said.

He stopped at the house to tell Towner he was going. She wasn't there. He started to panic. Then he caught sight of her out the window heading uphill from the harbor. She was wearing cutoffs and his daughter's bathing-suit top. Her hair was wet. She'd been swimming.

She looked like a different person. Younger. Healthy, almost.

"Hi," she said.

"I stopped to tell you I have to go to Portland."

"Portland, Maine?"

"Yeah," he said. "You want to come along?" As soon as he said it, he regretted the words. He was on a job; it wasn't a good idea. Besides, he couldn't take another no.

"Yes," she said. "I think I do."

Every Reader of lace must learn to exist within the empty spaces that form the question.

—THE LACE READER'S GUIDE

Chapter 23

A ngela Rickey's parents lived just north of Portland in a town that was a dull blend of trailer parks and run-down factory housing. Every building faced the river and the long-defunct paper mill that occupied the only prime real estate in town. The brick factory slumped like a hammock in the middle, with some failed attempts at renovation at both ends. The trailer park where Angela's family lived was just past the factory, at the back end of a parking lot that was shared by an Agway and the local Masonic hall. In the middle of the park, a half-finished on-ramp (part of a highway extension meant to connect the town with I-95 and the tourist dollars) cast a long shadow across the trailer that belonged to Angela's family.

Towner waited in the car while Rafferty went inside.

It was a short visit. They hadn't seen her. They hadn't heard from her. Rafferty knew that it was a long shot—he'd been up here before—but it was worth a try.

"She'd better not come back here," her father said. "She owes me money."

Her father had put out the money for beauty school. He'd told Rafferty that several times before.

"If she thinks I'm supporting her and a kid . . ." He didn't finish the sentence.

"If you hear from her, you need to call me," Rafferty said.

"What kind of trouble is she in this time?" the old man asked.

"She's not in any trouble," Rafferty said. "But she might be dead."

It stopped him. It was a cruel thing to say, but it stopped him.

Rafferty dropped Towner off at the Public Market, then went over to Congress Street to the beauty school Angela had attended. He asked questions. Had anyone seen her? No. Did she have any friends in town? No. Yes. Well, maybe. There was this one girl, they said,

Susan something. She worked over in the Old Port in a shop that sold products made from hemp. Rafferty thanked the woman, left his number. "If you see her, you call me right away."

He walked down Congress and over to the Old Port. He found the hemp shop. Susan was no longer there, and no one recognized Angela from her photo. Rafferty showed Angela's photo to a few more merchants up and down the cobblestone streets. Then he drove back to the Public Market and parked his car on the second level, taking the walking bridge over to the loft, where Towner sat eating a blueberry scone.

She held it out to him. "Bite?"

"Thanks, but it's past noon. I want lunch," he said.

They walked down the long flight of stairs from the loft to the shops. He couldn't help noticing that she took the stairs much easier, that she no longer held the handrail as she descended. There was something lighter about her step, and there was definitely something lighter about her mood.

"What do you feel like having?" Rafferty asked, looking around. "You can get pretty much anything in this place."

"You pick," she said.

He looked around. There were booths with cheeses and breads, and several serving chowder and other soups. He turned to her. It was time. "I like soup, do you like soup?"

She stared at him.

"Two of my many talents," he said. "Lies and deception."

A smile started in the corners of her mouth. She tried to stop it but found she couldn't. It spread across her face. Then she started to laugh. "Son of a bitch," she said.

Driving south, Rafferty got a speeding warning on Route 95.

"I should give you a ticket," the young state trooper said. "You were going twenty miles over the limit, but hey, professional courtesy, right?"

Rafferty smiled and thanked the kid, then stuffed the warning into the glove compartment with all the parking tickets he couldn't remember to pay.

As they pulled into the driveway, they spotted the dog, tied up to the newel post on Rafferty's front deck, a bowl of water upside down beside him. He'd obviously been trying to escape. His eyes were wild.

"That's one of May's dogs," Towner said, jumping out of the car.

There was a note tied to the dog's collar. "'My name is Byzantium,'" Towner read.

The dog bared teeth and growled. Nonplussed, Towner sat down on the deck, not looking directly at him but bringing herself down to his level. She sat for a long time, gazing out at the harbor, as if it were the most natural thing to be doing on such a day. When his breathing slowed, she reached under his muzzle and began to stroke his neck. "Hello, Byzy," she said, her voice soothing. Finally she looked at him. He went down slowly, as if hypnotized, and rolled onto his side. She stroked his stomach. "Good puppy," she said.

Rafferty had been sitting in the driveway with the door open. Now he got out of the car.

"Why do you think May sent him?" Towner asked.

"To torture me, I expect," Rafferty said, and sneezed.

"This isn't a good idea," Towner said.

But Rafferty couldn't help thinking it might be. May was right—he couldn't watch her every minute. He'd actually feel better knowing that Byzy was there. "It's okay, he can stay," he said. "As long as he doesn't eat my shoes."

Towner laughed. "What do you think he *does* eat?" she asked. "I mean, besides rabbit and rats."

"Purina something-or-other," Rafferty said, grabbing the upside-down water bowl and taking it to the hose to fill it up. He put it down in front of the dog, who started to drink.

"He looks like Skybo," she said.

Rafferty remembered the name. Skybo had been her first dog, the one Cal had killed. He'd read that in her journal, and Eva had told him about it as well. Skybo had been her friend and protector. So the fact that this dog looked like Skybo gave them an immediate connection.

Rafferty started up the stairs, sneezing twice as he passed the dog, who growled as he walked by. "Hey, buddy, we're on the same side," he said, and Towner laughed again.

"Down, boy," she said to Byzantium, and he obeyed.

Rafferty didn't put the car in the garage. He knew he would be going to Crosby's for kibbles in a couple of minutes. He'd have to remember to buy some Benadryl. Then he was going to bed. He needed a good night's sleep. For the last couple of weeks, ever since Towner had gotten here, he hadn't slept much at all.

Rafferty took two Benadryl and slept until noon. He woke, finally, to Byzy's low growl. He cracked his door. The dog sat nose pressed against the slider, looking out at the harbor and growling at the boats heading in and out. Rafferty could hear the water running in the bathroom. Towner was brushing her teeth.

He turned on the electric kettle, made himself coffee in the small French press Leah had given him last Christmas. He ran his cup under hot water, warming it. Then he opened the slider and stepped out onto the deck. "Come on," he said to Byzy, "you can get 'em better from out here." The dog hesitated, then stepped outside.

Rafferty sipped his coffee. He squinted to see what had captured the dog's attention. At first he thought it was the boats heading out for the day. Or the huge ship coming into the harbor to drop coal at the power plant. Then he noticed something else. . . . The moorings were moving.

He stood up. There were about twenty of them, right off the docks between the Willows and Winter Island, moving slowly and methodically along the shoreline. Rafferty looked again and realized he was looking not at moorings but divers' buoys. They were searching for a body.

Ignoring Byzy's whines, Rafferty shut the dog back inside. Still carrying his coffee, he walked down the hill to the docks. It could be anyone. Probably some boater who got drunk and swam for shore. God, he hoped it wasn't a kid.

He could see the police cars on the bluff. The chief stood talking to one of the divers.

"What's going on?" Rafferty said.

The chief dismissed the diver, then turned to Rafferty.

"I tried you yesterday on your cell," the chief said. "It happened as soon as you left. We got a tip. From Cal. He's convinced that Angela Rickey is at the bottom of Salem Harbor."

"Cal confessed?" Rafferty asked. It was an unlikely scenario.

"Not exactly," the chief said.

"What does that mean?" Rafferty wanted to know.

"It wasn't exactly a confession. But it might be almost as good if we find a body. He said he saw her dead. He told us where to look."

"That sounds like a confession to me."

"Not exactly," the chief said. "He said that God had sent him the information. In a dream."

Rafferty looked down the harbor toward Winter Island. He could see the Calvinists lined up on the shore of Waikiki Beach watching the whole thing. A few of them were kneeling. There was an element of badly staged theater to it all.

"He's fucking with you," Rafferty said.

He knew the kind of pressure the chief was under. The merchants were furious about the Calvinists, who were interfering with the witch business and driving the tourists up the coast. Just yesterday the Chamber of Commerce demanded that Cal's group be relocated to a campground in Cape Ann. In the chief's position, Rafferty might have done the same thing.

"Isn't it your day off?" the chief replied.

"Right," Rafferty said. "It is."

Towner was coming down the path with Byzy on leash. She was wearing a bathing suit.

"I'm taking him swimming." Towner smiled. The dog followed at her heels, eager for any adventure.

Rafferty thought quickly. He'd had enough of the whole thing. Like the chief said, it was his day off.

"I know a much better place to swim," Rafferty said, "if you two are up for a boat ride."

Sometimes the Reader must turn the lace in many different directions and gaze at the piece through varied light before the images begin to appear.

—THE LACE READER'S GUIDE

Chapter 24

Rafferty and I stop in Beverly for lunch at a take-out lobster shack that's run by a friend of his. He brings the food back to the boat.

He feeds Byzy a clam, which the dog spits out on the deck. It wedges itself into the gap between the planks. Rafferty goes on hands and knees to retrieve it, finally heaving it over the side. "That's what I get," he says, laughing.

"I think Byzy prefers rabbit," I say.

"Of course he does."

Before we get under way again, Rafferty goes up to the docks and across Route 1A to a little grocery for supplies. He brings back a bag of food and puts it in the galley. He pulls out a dog treat.

Rafferty lets me take the wheel and steer us out of the harbor. I am used to lobster boats. This one slips to port a bit, but it handles well. And it moves. He has done a great job restoring it. By that I mean it doesn't smell like bait.

We head toward the Miseries, and then he directs me past them and out toward open ocean.

"Where is this place?" I ask.

Rafferty points to the horizon. "It's out there," he says.

"Really?" I am intrigued.

It's a beautiful day. Byzy sits on the bow like a figurehead, fur blowing back. When we slow, he comes over to see if we're eating anything. When he sees we're not, he heads back to the bow and barks at seagulls.

"Funny dog," Rafferty says.

I smile.

Rafferty's island is straight out to sea, past the Miseries, past Baker's. It looks like something you'd find in Polynesia, narrow sugar-sand beach sloping to a small hill. I recognize it immediately. I've been here before. When we were kids, we used to play pirates on this island.

"It's not on any of the maps," Rafferty informs me. "It doesn't have a name."

I don't know why I don't tell him I've been here before, but I don't. We came here a few times, Beezer and Lyndley and me, but it was always a little too far to go and a difficult place to land—because it's so rocky, it's hard to get to shore. You can't even drop anchor here very easily, because beyond the rocks the bottom smooths out and becomes as slippery as ice. An anchor dropped here will drag out to sea with nothing to catch onto. You'll leave your boat, and when you come back, it won't be there. It will have drifted off and disappeared into the blue.

It happened to Beezer and me once. At first I didn't believe it. I thought it was Lyndley playing pirate tricks on us, and I told Beezer so, which only made him cry and get more scared when I was actually trying to be reassuring. "I wish you wouldn't say things like that," he said. I wasn't sure which thing I'd said to make him so distraught, but we found the boat anyway, behind the island, and it wasn't very windy that day, so I was able to swim out and retrieve the Whaler, no harm done. So I don't know why he took it that badly, but he never wanted to go back to No Name Island after that. That's what we called the place, No Name Island.

I can tell that Rafferty's been here a number of times. He's got a system. He has brought rope with him, a lot of it, which he has attached to the bowline. Then he wades in and climbs up on the bluff about twenty or thirty feet and ties the line around one of the only existing trees on the island.

He comes back to the boat to get me, but I'm already in the water, handing him the bags with the food. As soon as I get to shore, he lets the boat drift out until the line goes taut. He gives me a hand, and we climb up the eroded bluff together.

On the far side of the island, you can't see anything but open ocean. It's one of the only places from here to Rockport where you actually look straight out to sea and not at the protected bay that leads up to Cape Ann. It is wild and windswept, and its lack of vegetation makes you feel as if you could be anywhere, from the surface of the moon to Treasure Island or the Blue Lagoon.

Byzy and I swim while Rafferty collects driftwood for a fire.

Later we sit on the beach facing out to sea, watching the sun drop. The fire is dying down enough to cook, and I watch as Rafferty piles on some seaweed for steaming and throws several ears of corn on the fire. Then he pulls out cheese, crackers, and a huge steak. He loves this place. He tells me he's never seen anyone else here. "Not another living soul," he says, and hands me a lemonade.

We eat steak and corn. Three plates, one for each of us. Byzy hunkers over his, gulps.

Afterward we watch the sky streak and then go dark. The moon comes up above the water. Rafferty notices that I'm shivering and puts his jacket over my shoulders. His jacket is old. It smells of the ocean.

Byzy burrows into the sand and starts to snore.

"This island doesn't have a name," Rafferty says again, as if I missed it the first time, or because I didn't react. "That sandbar over there has a name—they even named that, but they never named this place. It slipped through the cracks," he says, happy that something, anything, could slip through the proverbial cracks.

"Maybe it doesn't really exist," I say. "Maybe we're the ones who have slipped through the cracks."

He looks startled at first. Then he starts to laugh. Not loud, but genuine. "You're an interesting woman," he says. "You walk that line."

"What line is that?" I ask, knowing very well what line he's talking about. The line that by its very definition is not a line but a crack. One I slipped into a long time ago.

He thinks before he speaks. "The one between the real world and the world of the possible."

"Poetically put," I say.

"Sometimes the real world is much crazier," he says.

I can tell he means it. Something has happened out here today. "How's the case going?" I ask. The question sounds too much like small talk, and I can tell he doesn't want to talk about it, so I don't press him for an answer.

"Let's not talk about that tonight," he says.

The moon is almost full. It carves a path through the darkening water, and for a minute I think of Lyndley. My eyes tear up. I don't want him to see it, so I turn away until the tears recede.

Rafferty gets up. He walks to the water. He leans over, scoops some water, looks at it, then lets it fall through his fingers. Then he puts his hand to his mouth and tastes the salt. I can see him make a decision.

"Let's swim," he says.

It surprises me.

We swim for a long time. He's a strong swimmer, not one who flows with the water but one who is strong enough to power through it. He swims with his head out; he must have worked as a lifeguard during his summers on Long Island. Lifeguards always swim with their heads out of the water, always on the alert, keeping an eye on the victim. It's different when he sails. Sailing is to Rafferty what swimming is to me.

There is magic in the water tonight, phosphorescence. Every stroke we take leaves a sparkling trail.

We're both tired when we get back to shore. It's a beautiful night. We fall asleep in the sand.

I awaken to the sound of Byzy up on the hill, baying at the moon. He is actually howling, the way I've heard the island dogs do when the moon is waxing and almost full. The moon is overhead now, so I know it has to be after eleven. I climb to the top of the bluff, to the center of the little island, and perch myself on a small outcropping of ledge with views all around. From up here you can see the curve of shoreline, the mouths of several harbors. I can make out the party boat heading in on its last run of the night, its draping string of lights making it look more like the Golden Gate Bridge than a boat. We are not close enough to hear the music; it's just the visual, lights moving slowly, floating strangely right above the water, a ghost ship.

I remember the first time I saw the Golden Gate Bridge. There was a man I was dating for a short period. His family had a house in Sonoma County, and we drove up the coast to see it. For some reason, as we were driving across the bridge, he told me how many people kill themselves each year by jumping off that bridge. We broke up shortly afterward.

I let Rafferty sleep. It's not as if I have anything press-
ing, and I know he doesn't sleep much. I'm glad he
suggested this day. If I had my way, I wouldn't go back
to town at all. I'm much more comfortable out here.

Rafferty finally wakes up and comes looking for us.

"What time is it?" he asks.

"I don't know. I just saw the party boat heading in."

"Midnight," he says. "I guess we'd better get going."

I nod, but I don't get up.

I can tell he feels the same, that going in is the last
thing he wants to do. He sits down next to me. Neither
of us moves.

"Why is it," he says finally, "that it all looks so pretty
from out here?"

"It *is* pretty," I say, "even from in there it's pretty.
It's just the people who make it ugly . . . sometimes."

"Not all of them," he says, his eyes holding on mine.

I don't look away.

I'm not sure who kisses whom. It's the most mutual
kiss in the world. It is perfection in compromise, in cooperation. Nothing can follow it. Anything else would
be a letdown. We're both old enough and smart enough
to realize it.

"What about Jack?" Rafferty says.

"There is no Jack," I say.

I watch him make the decision. He has decided that he will believe me. Then he takes my hand, and we walk together back to the boat.

We don't get home until after two. Rafferty and I fall asleep together on top of his bed, my head in the crook of his shoulder. I shift, roll toward the open window, and his arms come around me, muscles taut even in sleep. He sleeps peacefully, not the way you would expect from him. When I shift, he moves to fit.

I wake at first light to discover the lace in the window. I didn't see it last night. If I had, I never would have come into this room. But I see it now. It catches me in its swirls and pulls the breath out of me as if the air itself were only part of the thread, the part that creates the negative spaces so that the pattern can exist. I see the pattern clearly only as I am pulled into it, into the world behind the world. It is a place I know, a place I'm terrified of. It is the still point. All movement freezes in this place; the breath pauses on top of its wave, neither cresting nor falling, as if the whole ocean had frozen solid. I will be paralyzed and trapped here until it thaws to release me, and there will be no thaw until the lace shows me what it has pulled me under to see. I hold my breath. The wave stops, but the rhythm of it remains, as regular as waves on sand.

I see the gun. I hear the crack as the shot flies. I smell the powder. I feel the bullet pierce my side, not physical pain, exactly, but the cut of it, the creation of the divide. The rhythm of the wave changes then, not wave at all (I realize now) but breath. I don't know it is breath until its rhythm alters, shortens. I feel Rafferty's arms around me then, tight, tighter, and I hear his breath, feel it as it comes, gasping now. He has been hit. The blood is warm, pooling around us. The shot has pinned us together, fusing us. It is a killing shot. It is meant to be.

"No!" I scream, jumping up, tearing the lace from the window. I cannot have this, I will not. Not him.

His instincts take over. He is out of bed and at the window, pushing me away from it, out of the line of fire.

We hit the floor hard. It takes him a minute to realize we are both okay.

"Cal," he says.

"No," I say.

He heard it, too. I know it as he says it.

He looks outside. Then he sees Byzy, staring at us from the other room. If there had been a shot, the dog's reaction would have been different and much more agitated.

Rafferty tries to clear his head. He spots the lace on the floor. "I saw Cal . . ." he starts.

"It was a dream."

"He was here."

"No," I say.

He rubs his temples.

"You were dreaming," I say. I gesture to Byzy, who is staring at us. "If there had been a shot . . ."

Rafferty holds up his hand, already getting it. He sits back on the bed. "God," he says. "It seemed so real."

I will not look at him. If I look at him, I'll never be able to leave. And I must leave. I have seen it in the lace. The bullet went though him and into me. I felt the life go out of him, and I was alone. We were still attached, still fused, but he was dead.

Put your hand together with mine as if you're praying, Lyndley used to say to me. *Then run your thumb and index finger across both of them. . . . That's what dead feels like.*

No, not Rafferty. Please, not him.

He reaches for me, tries to draw me to him.

I twist away.

"This was a mistake," I say.

"It's okay. It was a dream."

"No." I pull back. "Not that. This." I point to the bed, to us. "This was a huge mistake."

I can see the hurt on him, a lot of hurt. But no real surprise. Rafferty is more psychic than he knows.

I only realize that now. In some deep psychic place, he already knew that it would come to this.

"I'm sorry," I say. I do not look at him. I cannot look at him again or I won't be able to leave. If I stay, he will die. I have seen it in the lace. The bullet will fuse us together, but the man I love will die.

The realization of my own feelings stops me. But only for a minute. I know what I have to do. I fumble for Byzy's leash. I clip it to his collar and pull him up.

"Where are you going?" Rafferty asks.

"I'm sorry," I say again. I drag Byzy to the door and down the steps.

I look toward town and Eva's house. The only place to go. It seems so far from here that I'll never make it. When I get there, I'll make the call and get myself to California. I'll do what I did once before. I'll get as far away from here as I can without falling off the edge of the earth.

PART FIVE

If the question is right and the Seeker is prepared
to receive, the answer will be immediate.

—THE LACE READER'S GUIDE

Chapter 25

Rafferty hung up the phone and looked at his watch. Leah was coming in at three. He had time.

He'd been smart for a change and talked directly to his ex. "Would you mind if we went back to the original schedule?" Rafferty had asked. There must have been something in his voice that got to her, because she didn't hang up.

"You mean tomorrow?" she asked.

"I mean as soon as possible."

"Yeah, I guess. That is, if it's okay with Leah," she said, then added, "The only problem is, we've already made plans for the week before Labor Day. I'll have to change them if she's coming back early."

"I don't want her to go back early," Rafferty said. "Hell, I don't want her to go back at all."

"You sound strange. Are you okay?" she asked.

"I've been better," he said.

He hadn't told the chief that Towner was leaving. She wouldn't be back for the trial, wasn't going to testify against Cal when the time came. She'd told him she wanted to drop the charges. He'd told her it was impossible. That *she* hadn't filed the charges, the state had. She said she wouldn't testify. The only hope they had of nailing Cal now was if they found Angela's body. Rafferty didn't want to hope for that.

They'd all agreed that he should turn over the case to a new guy, a young kid who'd just been promoted to detective. Rafferty had gotten too close, the chief said. The chief didn't know the half of it.

Rafferty packed the files in a box for the new kid, taking out some of the more personal stuff about Towner, filing those old manila folders back in the archive room where they belonged. If the new guy was going to dig that deep into the case, he'd have to do it himself. It wasn't much, but it was the only thing Rafferty could do for her. He cleaned his coffee cup and straightened his desk. He knew he was wasting time. He wasn't anxious to tell the chief that the assault case against Cal Boynton was all but finished.

The chief came through the door and stared at Rafferty. "It's over," he said, as if reading Rafferty's mind. The chief's look was incredulous, he was amazed.

"I was going to tell you," Rafferty said. "Towner's going back to California. She's not going to testify."

The chief looked at him strangely. "I'm not talking about Towner," the chief said.

"I don't understand."

"Come with me."

Rafferty followed the chief to the lobby. Standing at the desk, talking to the desk clerk, was Angela Rickey. The bruises on her face were healed. She was dressed in maternity clothes that were almost fashionable.

"What the . . . ? Where the hell have you been?" Rafferty said.

Angela turned to him. "I was in New York City visiting my friend Susan," she said. "Someone called from Maine and said you were looking for me."

"That's the understatement of the century," the chief said.

"The whole town thinks you're dead," Rafferty said.

"I came as soon as I heard."

The desk clerk spoke up. "She wants me to tell her where Cal is."

"He's in jail under suspicion of murdering you."

All of a sudden, she didn't look as well.

"I need to see him." Her voice was shaky.

"I told her he's not here, but she doesn't believe me," the desk clerk said.

"He's up in Middleton," said the chief.

"I need to see him," she said again.

Chapter 26

Jack told Jay-Jay he wouldn't be back. He didn't tell him the other part, that May had fired him. Rafferty might have figured out that Jack was running girls for May's new Underground Railroad, but his brother Jay-Jay didn't have a clue. Jay-Jay thought he was hanging around in the hopes that Towner would come back, which was also true.

"You know I love you, Jack," May had said. "But you're becoming a liability. You're a drunk. I have to end this."

He'd already sold his slip. The only reason he was still here was to meet with the guy and get the check. He'd sold the traps last week, when he knew he was really going.

He saw Eva's boathouse door open. Saw Towner leaning over to start the Whaler. There was a dog in the bow, a big hulking yellow thing with huge teeth.

Jack ducked inside the cabin; he didn't want to see her. Still, he kept an eye on her as the boat passed.

She looked better. Thank God. He never would have touched her if he'd known about the surgery. Shouldn't have anyway. She couldn't drink. Never could. The notion that he might have caused her to get sick was something he thought about every hour he was awake. She could have died. Almost did, according to May, though May had no idea what had happened between them that night, no idea it might have been his fault.

He'd taken advantage of her the way you hear about at frat parties. Hadn't used a roofie, nothing like that, but she had been . . . how do you say it? Impaired. He hated himself for it. As soon as he touched her he'd hated himself. But it hadn't stopped him. She was just lying there, eyes distant, not looking at him. Some deep part of him, some sick romantic part, had thought if he just kissed her, she would wake up and come back to him. It hadn't worked. Then, for some even sicker reason, he thought he should do more. The more he touched her the further she went, until her eyes, still open, were dead-looking and far away. She wasn't there at all.

She didn't love him. Not anymore. She loved the other guy. Maybe she'd never loved him.

There was a woman up in Canada. Someone he'd been seeing for a long time. He couldn't commit to her.

And she wouldn't commit to him either, because of his drinking. "You're going to die," she'd said to him. "If you don't stop, you're just going to drop dead one of these days, and I don't want to be there to see it."

He watched Towner head out of the harbor toward Yellow Dog Island. He wished they could go back and change things. Wished he had killed Cal that night in the car, the one time he got the chance.

He wished he could kill Rafferty now. No, that wasn't true. Rafferty was a nice guy. A much nicer guy than he was. Which is what made it hurt even more.

Fuck. He had to stop drinking. He knew it. He could feel his fucking liver when he touched his side. It was huge.

He started to cry. He couldn't stop.

He'd raped her. That was probably a fact. Maybe she wouldn't call it that, if she even remembered it, but that's what it was. He'd raped her, and he'd almost killed her. All he'd wanted was for her to come back to him. And what he'd ended up doing was the same thing as Cal. He was as bad as Cal Boynton. Worse, maybe, because he knew the horrible history of what Cal had done.

The real truth was that he had spent the better part of his life hoping for something that would never happen. Hoping that Towner would come back and see him and know him the way she once had, and that they would live happily ever after the way some part of him had always believed they would. She'd once believed the happily-ever-after crapola as much as he had. He was certain of it.

What he'd wanted that night was to wake her with a kiss and have her see him as her prince—her fucking prince, for God's sake, how stupid did that sound? He wanted her to see him as a prince, when the fact was she couldn't see him at all, not anymore. She hadn't been able to see him, or even look at him, since the day she'd jumped off of his boat and tried to drown herself, and he'd jumped, too, all heroic, actually believing he could save her.

Chapter 27

Angela had insisted on seeing Cal. The police escorted her to Middleton.

When she came out, she was wearing his ring, the one he let his followers kiss. It was huge on her finger. She held it like a treasure.

"We're getting married," she said, her eyes full of tears. "We're going to Las Vegas and getting married as soon as he gets out of there."

"Which should be sometime tonight," Cal's attorney said.

Neither Rafferty nor the new detective said a word on their way back.

She wanted to be dropped off at Winter Island. "To tell the congregation the good news," she announced, beaming. "I also need to get my stuff."

The new detective was waiting for a reaction from Rafferty, but none came. As soon as they got back to the station, Rafferty left for the airport to pick up his daughter. He'd had enough.

Chapter 28

May stood on the float watching the Whaler pull into the channel. The dog was in the bow, a figurehead. From a distance she was back in time, watching Towner and Skybo come around the barrier island to the docks. At this moment Towner didn't look any older than that.

Time was having its way with May today. Towner had called, saying she was bringing back the dog, saying it would be cruel to take him with her to Los Angeles where she didn't even have a place of her own to live.

"You could buy a place," May had suggested. "You have plenty of money now."

They didn't fly dogs in the summer, Towner informed her. It was too dangerous. By the time Towner could have him shipped to L.A., Byzy would have turned wild again. It would be cruel, she repeated. He belonged on the island.

May realized that meant Towner would not see Byzy again. Only in thinking that did it strike her that in all likelihood she herself would never see Towner again. It was hard to bear, but that was the truth of it. Unless May changed. Unless she could leave the island and travel three thousand miles. She wanted to, and in this moment she thought that it really could happen. People changed; things were possible. But as soon as the thought became real, May realized that the reasoning behind it was not. That she could no more leave this island and travel to Los Angeles than Towner could come back to her.

Her heart skipped. She teared up. But she didn't cry.

Towner needed to get away from this place. It wasn't safe. Sometimes running away was exactly what you should do. The only thing you *could* do. She knew that Eva wouldn't agree, that Eva thought all of Towner's problems could be solved if she only moved back here, but Eva had been wrong. If there was one thing May had learned from working with abused women and this new Underground Railroad, it was that sometimes the only thing you could do was run away and never look back.

Chapter 29

May ties up the Whaler as we pull in.

Byzy is pacing in the small boat. Tipping it wildly. A few of the other goldens (who have been sleeping in a pile at the top of the dock) are standing now, straining to see what's going on. They jump around, excited to see him.

It's too much. His whole body is shaking as he tries to hold himself back until I release him.

"Go," I say when I can't stand it anymore. He runs for them then, not knowing there's anything final about this visit, not having any idea he's not coming back with me. The dogs jump and wrestle one another in reunion, playing, rolling around.

"You're leaving tonight," she says.

"Yes."

I look up, catching sight of Auntie Emma in the vegetable garden. She looks up, too, feeling my presence. My hand goes to my heart. I see May notice. For a moment I don't know where I am. I can't speak; it's all too much for me. Then, finally, I pull myself back.

"I came to say good-bye," I say.

I look around the island. I see the women who make their homes here. They are walking back and forth doing the chores of daily living. This is their life now, all of them working together. Living together.

I look up, and I see Auntie Emma walking back to the house with her basket of vegetables for tonight's meal. I can picture it. All of the women and children cooking together, sitting together at May's big table. An odd sense of longing overtakes me.

"You can stay here," May says. "You've always known that."

We both knew it wasn't true. Still, I was glad to have the words.

"I can't."

She nods.

For a moment it is all I want. All I've ever wanted, I realize. Everything has changed, and nothing has changed. And yet the only way to make it stop is to leave this place.

I know that I should go up and say good-bye to Auntie Emma, but I just can't do it. For some reason the sight of her gets to me—walking back to the house with her vegetables in the basket, moving forward into what is now her life. It is too much to bear. And I can't make myself go to her. May can read it on me. All this emotion. She can tell it has immobilized me. And I can tell that she understands. "Will you say good-bye for me?"

She nods and says, "When the time is right."

We stand in another kind of silence.

"I don't expect you'll be back," she says, "now that Eva's gone."

"No," I answer.

She hugs me. It is out of character for May to do this and for me to allow. We hold on to each other for a long moment.

"Take care of yourself," she says as I finally pull back. And I can tell that it really matters to her.

Byzy is sitting at the top of the dock, just looking at me, with his head cocked, wondering what's next. What will our next great adventure be? I realize I have to leave now if I'm ever going to do it. I turn and walk toward the Whaler.

"Sophya?" May says.

I turn back for just an instant and say, "Yes?"

I can tell she thinks about it for a second time, maybe even a third, before finally deciding to say it. "I couldn't have loved you more if you *had* been my own daughter," she says.

Chapter 30

Open ocean. Fog. Hand shaking with the vibrations of the motor. Judging the distance by the echo of gulls. Judging direction by the air. It wasn't foggy a minute ago, but that's the way it goes in this part of the world. Fog doesn't roll in here. It drops in patches—not like a blanket, like a feather pillow. It can smother.

I can't breathe for the thickness of it. No, that's not it. I'm hyperventilating.

I couldn't have loved you more if you had been my own daughter.

Hands tightening, going into spasm, hyperventilation.

I am smothering. Dying.

No paper bag. Nothing to breathe into. I cup my hands. Useless.

I look in all directions. There is no place to go.

I cut the engine. Peel my hands off. Sit, putting head down between the knees. Then I remember the Stelazine. In case of emergency, break glass.

I swallow it dry. It sticks. I swallow again. Cough.

I couldn't have loved you more . . .

I find myself standing, rocking the boat crazily. Force myself to sit.

This is the fog from the dream. I squint my eyes. I expect to see Eva or Lyndley, expect to be led. But there's nothing.

I sit low in the boat. I'm afraid of standing again. Afraid I'll do it without knowing. I don't trust myself.

No sound now. No birds. No air. Only the pattern on the water, a dark lace.

Then, for a moment, I think I see the sea horse.

My first instinct is to look away, but I am dying. I feel like I have in fact died.

Just get back to the house. The plane. Just get to the plane and get back to California.

I start the engine. I cannot move.

I am pinned. Unmoving. Cal is here. Cal is on top of me. Cal is suffocating me. Then the shape-shift and the face changes. This is not Cal. It is Jack.

I am crying. Just let me get back. Please. Just let me go.

I put the engine in forward. Then I see the body parts. Floating in the water up ahead of me. An arm, a leg, a torso. Life-size, it seems, until I come upon them. Then no, not life-size, tiny. Plastic? No. Ceramic. Religious. Ceremonial. I've seen them in L.A., on Olvera Street. I follow the trail of floating *milagros* until the fog clears and I can see the curve of Salem Willows dead ahead. I make myself think. I make a list. Get to L.A. Call Dr. Fukuhara. Get help. I can do this. I have to believe I can do it, or I'll die right here. Get to L.A. Call Dr. Fukuhara. . . .

I couldn't have loved you more if you had been my own daughter.

Chapter 31

Angela took down the *milagros* and wrapped each of them in toilet paper, winding them, then placing them inside pieces of her clothing for protection, one in a sock, one double-wrapped and placed into a running shoe.

She folded the black lace mantilla and threw it into the trash. Cal hated lace. He wasn't fond of the picture of the Virgin either, but she left that up. When they got back here, she'd be living in Cal's trailer; the next person who lived here might think it a pretty picture.

She had stopped to tell the rest of the Calvinists the good news. That she was going to have the baby, Cal's baby. That he'd finally admitted the baby was his. That they were going to Las Vegas to get married.

"Reverend Cal would never go to Las Vegas," Charlie Pedrick said. Angela refused to call him John the Baptist even though she'd heard a rumor that he was trying to legally change his name.

"Reverend Cal hates Las Vegas," one of the women agreed. "That and San Francisco."

"You can get a marriage license any time of the day or night in Las Vegas," Angela explained.

"I will pray on it," Charlie said.

You do that, Angela thought, and started moving her things into Cal's trailer.

John the Baptist called a prayer meeting. Fine. They could do what they wanted. Let Charlie call a prayer meeting; she had a lot to do before Cal got here. She had to get both of them packed and ready to go.

She filled her backpack, throwing in a change of clothes for Cal and his best Armani suit for the wedding. She thought about calling her parents and telling them the good news—her mother, not her father. But there wasn't time. She had to find out the ferry schedule. She had to get airline tickets.

She took Cal's wallet and some credit cards, then remembered she didn't have any underwear for him. It was odd choosing underwear for Reverend Cal. She grabbed his comb, looked for his toothbrush. She didn't know what else of his to take.

The backpack was heavy as Angela stepped off the metal stairs to the grass below.

They were all waiting for her—Charlie, the women, and some of the others, the ones Cal referred to as his bodyguards.

"What's up?" she said, thinking it would be nice if one of them could at least help her with the backpack.

"I just have one question," Charlie said.

"What's that?"

"Could you please recite the Lord's Prayer for me before you go?"

"You're kidding, right?"

He smiled at her.

"He's kidding." She turned to the others for confirmation.

A nervous shiver ran through the crowd. No one spoke.

"Come on. You don't need me to recite the Lord's Prayer for you. You know the Lord's Prayer."

"I do. I was just wondering if you did," Charlie said.

"This is ridiculous," Angela said.

"She doesn't know it," one of the women said.

"She doesn't know the Lord's Prayer."

"Of course I know it."

"Please recite it."

"No, I won't recite it, this is ridiculous. And Reverend Cal isn't going to like it when I tell him how you're treating me."

"I prayed on it, and the Lord answered. . . ." He leveled his eyes at Angela. "Reverend Cal would never set foot in Las Vegas," he said.

"Well, he's going there with me. Tonight."

"I don't think so," Charlie said, stepping in front of her.

"Your baby does not belong to Reverend Cal," one of the women said.

"Your baby belongs to the devil," Charlie said.

Angela laughed at that. "Right," she said. "The devil."

Some part of her still thought they were kidding.

"She has the mark," one of the women said. Another of them fainted.

This couldn't be happening. Angela's eyes darted, searching for an escape route.

Charlie grabbed her quickly, slamming her face into the side of the trailer. Angela reeled, saw the blood.

"Name yourself, demon!" Charlie roared.

One of the women picked up a rock and heaved it.

Angela dropped the backpack and took off down the other side of Waikiki Beach toward the rocks and town.

"Get the witch!" one of the bodyguards shouted.

"Get her!" Charlie ordered.

Roberta saw everything from the booth. She got on the phone quickly, calling Rafferty first, then, when she couldn't get him, she called 911.

Chapter 32

The fog clears as I enter the harbor. The *milagros* disappear, and the water goes deep blue. The air is warmer here. I can see Derby Street.

Just get to the house.

I see two police cars in the parking lot at Winter Island as I pass.

Instead of slowing, I speed up. It's getting late. I have to make that plane.

As I pull into the channel toward the boathouse, I notice the Calvinists out at the end of Derby Wharf, halfway into the harbor by the tiny lighthouse. They scramble over the rocks that surround the wharf, looking for something.

Two of them sit in front of the boathouse.

I should put the Whaler away, but I don't want to go near them. And I can't wait for them to move. Instead I

tie up and leave the Whaler at the dock. When I get to
the airport, I'll call May and tell her to have someone
pick it up.

I feel sick. Bad idea, probably, taking the pill on an
empty stomach. Or at all. But I am here. I am safe.

As I walk up the street toward the house, I see more
Calvinists. Searching in doorways, behind the Custom
House.

I cross the street, trying not to look at them, keeping
my eyes leveled. All I have to do is get my bags and call
the cab. I'll relax when I get to the airport.

My hands shake as I unlock the door. I lock it
again behind me, go to the kitchen for a piece of bread,
put my head over the sink and gulp from the faucet.

Behind me glass shatters.

I stiffen, waiting for another sound. I hear the thump
of a body as it hits the floor.

Someone is in the house.

Cal.

I start for the door.

"Help me!" a voice cries.

This is a female voice. One I have never heard in life
before, one I recognize only from my dreams.

I reel around to see Angela Rickey. She stands
there shaking and terrified. The bruise I mistook for
a birthmark has faded now to just a shadow across
her right cheek, and new bruises have formed, one

across an eyebrow and another, bloodier one where one of her eyeteeth has been pushed through her upper lip.

"They're trying to kill my baby." She's crying now, trembling, trying to make me understand.

"Cal?"

"No." She shakes her head urgently. "The others."

I look in the direction she's pointing, toward the park, and I can see the Calvinists lined up on the sidewalk. They watch the house, waiting. They look like Hitchcock's birds gathering on the jungle gym at Bodega Bay.

"They think I bewitched Cal. They think our baby is the devil!"

"This is Cal's baby?" I say weakly. I realize I should have known. It was the one detail everyone was keeping from me.

A hand over a mouth. Smothering. *Don't move, don't make a sound.*

I throw up. Right on the floor in the middle of the pantry. I see the cracked blue shell of the Stelazine still undissolved.

They're crossing the street now. There are more of them than before. A torch is lit, then more lit from the first.

There is noise. And chanting. "Get the witch!"

Angela starts to cry.

I grab the phone, dial 911.

"Oh, God." Angela freezes in place. She's staring out the window, still as death.

The 911 operator picks up. "What's the nature of the problem?"

"I have Angela Rickey here. She's pregnant and she's been beaten."

"Stay on the phone," the 911 operator orders. "I have your location."

I can hear her in the background giving directions to the cruisers.

"They're on their way," I say to Angela.

She is sobbing.

"She's hurt pretty bad," I say.

Angela sobs harder. "My baby," she sobs.

I see them crossing the street, torches blazing. Traffic stops for them, creating a jam of onlookers. I see the looks of amusement from the tourists. They think they're watching one of the pageants they've seen over and over again in this city.

"Get the witch!" they chant.

The tourists think it's Bridget Bishop, or one of the other reenactments. They are trying to do their part tonight as well, trying to engage the hysteria, to show they're comfortable with it. Getting their children involved, too. "Get the witch! Get the witch!" they cry.

A woman stops her car, gets out to watch with her children, sitting them on the hood so they get a good vantage point as the Calvinists push by them across the street and into the yard.

"They're coming." Angela's voice climbs an octave. She's moving all over the room now, unable to stand still anymore.

She goes to the window and yells for help. The crowd applauds.

The torches bob endlessly, nightmarishly forward.

"Please," I say to the 911 operator. "They're coming!"

"The cruisers are on the way," she says.

"Oh, God, oh, God!" Angela moans.

"Make sure your doors and windows are locked," the operator says. She's well trained, trying not to sound alarmed.

Sound of footsteps on wood, as the first Calvinist ascends the front steps.

"They're on the porch!" I yell toward the phone as I scramble to make sure everything is locked. Using all my strength, I push the hutch in front of the window Angela broke.

"Get the witch!" It's louder now. I am reading them. It's inside my head.

This can't be happening. This must be a dream. Or a hallucination. I have to fight to stay here. Part of me is already going away, distancing myself from the inevitable. I am going under.

For a minute I can stand back from it and just watch it happen. This is not real. It is too much out of time to be real. It is not real, and at the same time it is very real. Hyper-real. Every detail stands out and lingers as if in slow motion.

Kill her! Kill her!

In this place the scene has become simple and universal. What we are seeing is history repeating itself, one scene superimposed over the other. We are both here and back in old Salem at the same time, with the real Calvinists, the first ones. There is a feeling of impending doom here, and when I look at Angela, for just a moment, I see her in the drab brown Puritan dress, her hair tied back and covered. And we are back in history in the days when they came to get you because you were a woman alone in the world, or because you were different, because your hair was red, or because you had no children of your own and no husband to protect you. Or maybe even because you owned property that one of them wanted.

Every part of me fights to pull myself out of this scene. To create the distance of the divide. It is not real. I am not real.

But Angela is real. That is the one truth to the scene, the only thing I know for sure. And all my life I have remembered this. Standing here, out of time, with this woman, whom I realize now that I recognized from my own dreams the moment I saw her standing at the tearoom door, coming first to Eva and now to me for help.

The voices are still inside my head, chanting. *Kill her!* I push them away, struggling to hear the voice of the 911 operator. "I have a car in your area," she says. "Can you get to a secure location until we can reach you?"

"I think so," I say. Mind racing, settling on the widow's walk, figuring it's the only place they can't get to. If we get up to the widow's walk and sit on the trapdoor, no one can push it open from below. I used to do that when I wanted to be alone. There's only the narrow ladder leading up to it, and only room for one person to climb. One person can't get enough leverage to push the trapdoor open.

"The widow's walk," I say to the operator, so she'll know to tell them where to look. "We'll be up on the widow's walk."

"Go!" she says, and we run.

They're blocking traffic as they cross the street, still coming. There must be fifty of them. So many. Not just men but women, too. Angela's eyes are desperately searching the crowd for Cal. She keeps saying he will save her. Over and over, this is what she says. But Cal is nowhere in this. He is still in jail. And while she waits for the rescue that I know will never come, the mob is beating down the gardens, trampling them as they surround the house.

I see their faces. They are at the windows.

Another shattering of glass. A change in the air, olfactory, a smell remembered from another time and place. The smell of summers and sun on the wood of the dock at the Willows or maybe at Trani where Jack is filling up the boat before we head out for a day of pulling traps together. And me lying on the deck getting some sun on my back before we go, letting him do all the busywork. Still tired from last night, happy. Drifting and dreaming while he fills up the gas tank.

I loved this smell then, the smell of gasoline. It was such a pleasant smell to me that it now takes me a moment to break from its hypnotic spell and realize it's in the room with us here, that someone has poured gasoline through the broken window and is soaking the floor with it.

A popping sound as someone throws one of the torches through the opening. A larger explosion, and the room fills with flames. And the chanting changes on the spot. They are good at improvisation, these

Calvinists, able to change their chant to suit their circumstances. "Get the witch!" morphs into the older, more historically correct "Burn the witch!" And then to an even shorter chant, the one I heard in my head just moments ago: "Kill her! Kill her!"

I glance outside at the watching crowd that has suddenly gone quiet. Some look confused, no longer certain what they're seeing. Is this theater? Is Salem getting so good at their special effects that they actually have the budget to burn down a real house? I watch as one man, the only one in the crowd who gets it, runs across the street to the corner by the Hawthorne Hotel and pulls the red fire-alarm box.

"The house is on fire!" Angela screams, starting up the stairs toward the widow's walk. I grab her.

"No!" I yell. "Don't go up!"

"Get out of the house!" the operator says. She's still with us, I realize now, but it's the wrong idea. If we step outside the house, they will kill us. From outside I can hear the sound of sirens, but distant, too long to wait for. The streets are completely crowded with spectators. Horns blaring. Some of them getting out of their cars now, trying to get a closer look.

"The cellar!" Angela says, starting toward the door "There's a tunnel in the cellar!"

I follow her down into the blackness, closing the door behind us against the smoke. I know that this is the right move to make—there's a bulkhead down there, behind the house, and I'm thinking maybe we can get out that way. They won't see us back there, maybe, and we can somehow sneak past them. But there aren't any tunnels left that I know of, not anymore. Beezer and I had looked for the tunnels when we were kids. We'd spent long hours searching— whole days, even. The tunnels were here a hundred years ago, weaving a web of deception under Salem Common, keeping the British tax collector at bay. Maybe they remained later, during the Underground Railroad, the last stop on the way to Canada and freedom. It would have made sense for May's new Underground Railroad. But the tunnels had all been filled in. That's what Eva had told us anyway, when she'd had enough of our searching or when she felt bad that we weren't finding anything, or maybe when she just decided that we should play outside and get some fresh air for a change instead of hanging out in her basement all the time. Eva told us the same thing our teachers had told us, that the city of Salem had filled in all the tunnels at the end of the last century. They were sorry about it, too, when World War II came, and even sorrier during the Cold War, because the tunnels would have been a good place for an air-raid shelter, and the city wouldn't have had to spend good money to build its own.

Angela is groping along the back wall, clawing at it. "I know it's down here somewhere," she says. "That was how Eva got me out of here the last time."

So that was it. It must be true. The tunnels must have been how Eva made Angela "disappear." They were the reason Cal and his followers thought Eva was a witch. What was it Rafferty said? They saw Angela go into the house, they had the whole house surrounded, but Angela never came out again. When she finally showed up again, she was on the island with May's girls. Until Rafferty brought her back. May was angry at Rafferty for helping Cal, but she didn't get the point. The point was that Cal was scared of both Eva and May. He believed his own accusations about them. He didn't know about the tunnels. What he believed was that, with the exception of his ex-wife, all the Whitney women had magical powers.

They have the house surrounded now, the same way they did that night. I can see the sandal-clad feet outside the high basement windows. There is no way to get out the bulkhead exit now. They are standing on it. Holding it closed. We can see their figures, like shadow puppets lit from behind, their profiles projected across the basement walls by the headlights of the few cars that are still able to pass on the streets, the ones not stuck in traffic.

Angela pushes on the wall again, giving it everything she's got, almost knocking herself out before I stop her.

"What are you doing?"

"I know it's here!" she says. "Behind this wall. There's a whole room in there. Eva hid me there the last time. Until she could get me out." She is hurting herself. She coughs. It is damp and smoky in here—damp and smoky, with the vague smell of mildew. . . .

And I think of the Realtor looking at the wine cellar, inspecting the water on the floor. That's where it had to be. The wine cellar. I had always wondered why Eva had a stocked wine cellar put in when she didn't drink at all. The secret door is on the wine cellar's wall. It has to be. The slats and cross-hatchings must be a way of disguising it. The liquid on the floor wasn't spilled wine or a leaky pipe. It was the salt water that was making the flowers mildew. The tunnel was tidal.

"Where does the tunnel come out?" I say, just to double-check, to make sure I am right in my hunch. But I'm already pretty certain. I'm moving toward the wine racks. Even as I'm asking the question, I already know the answer.

"The boathouse," she says.

I move my fingers slowly along the wall, feeling for the cracks, the world behind the world: spiny wooden racks, a lattice of wood and bottles, dust. I'm looking for what is different. What does it say in Eva's journal? "Look for one of two things: something that enhances the pattern or something that breaks it."

It's getting too smoky to see. I feel along the spiny racks, reading them with my fingers, like Braille. And then my fingertips find a small slice across the grain of the wood. Small as the blade of a razor. I follow the tiny crack with my fingers as it moves three bottles up, cuts ninety degrees, goes four bottles across, then heads back down the wall. I have found it. It is real.

It's a secret Alice in Wonderland door, smaller than me, the right size for a person the year it was built, maybe, but not anymore. I reach in between the bottles at the same height a handle should be, and I find a small lever. I push it down. It engages. I can hear the cylinders turning, but the door doesn't open. It is locked. I feel around, looking for the thumb turn or a keyhole or something, one hand in my pocket already searching, trying to find something to pick it with. Then my fingers hit the smooth, round plate where the key should be but isn't. My heart sinks. It's a keyed dead bolt.

It's getting harder to breathe. I call out to Angela, but she cannot hear me over the building noise of the approaching fire.

It smells of old wood and horsehair plaster as the fire burns through the walls of the tearoom above us. The heat seems to drive the mold spores into the air. I can smell the lavender from the flowers that Eva had drying on the racks next to me, the ones I forgot to throw away.

And then I remember the combination. From the house inspection. And from the Realtor's telling me it was half the problem. Mildew in the basement, from the drying flowers. Hung upside down like a distress flag.

"Who in the world would dry flowers in a basement?" It annoyed me when she asked the question, as if she thought Eva were stupid or senile. But I had to admit that I'd wondered about it, too. Who in the world *would* dry flowers in a basement? The answer was, no one. No one who knew what they were doing anyway. Eva wouldn't. And it becomes another thing that breaks the pattern, that stands out—the flowers, of course. Eva was nothing if not consistent. The key to the dead bolt was in the drying, moldy flowers.

I grab the bunches one by one, pulling them off the hooks, shaking them the same way Beezer shook the bells that last Christmas we were children. I shake each bunch slowly, deliberately, as if I'm expecting one of them to have a different tone.

Above us a timber crashes through the floor, shaking the house to its foundations. Angela jumps back from it.

"What are you doing?" Angela is freaking out. "We need to get out of here now," she says. She thinks I'm losing it, standing here shaking flowers while the house is falling down around us. She's afraid that what she has heard about me is true. I'm beginning to think she's right, because I'm not finding the key. She's pulling at my arm now. Wanting to head back up and maybe go out the same way she came in. But it's already too late for that. The whole floor above us is on fire. Angela pounds on the bulkhead, pushing her body against it, screaming at the onlookers, shouting at them. Either they don't hear her or they choose not to hear. Then she collapses on the floor next to me in tears. "We're going to die!" she wails.

I pick up the last bunch of flowers, barely able to see it now with the smoke closing in. I shake it hard, and the key falls to the floor. I feel for it, my fingers closing around it, running my other arm along the door until it finds the dead bolt. Slowly, carefully, I put key to lock and turn it clockwise until I feel the click. The door springs open.

"We're in," I say, grabbing Angela's hand, pulling her, half standing, half crawling, until we're inside, closing the door behind us against the inferno that is now the cellar.

Angela knows the room. She moves along the far wall until she locates a flashlight. The light is dim. At first I assume it's because the batteries are bad, but it's not the batteries, it's the smoke.

This place is more cave than secret room, its hollowed-out earthen walls reinforced with the wooden frames of old ships. Cobblestones line part of the floor, then stop abruptly where the builders ran out of them and couldn't steal any more from the streets of Salem.

There are treasures here as well: A piece of ivory— the carved handle of a knife, its blade rusted and disintegrated to a pile of red dust. The knife sits on top of a spice box, the kind I recognize from the houses of old Salem, its wood warped from water damage. There's an ancient wooden bed in the corner, with sleep-tight ropes instead of a box spring. And there's the chinoiserie, a lot of it, stolen probably when my grandfather's forebears turned to privateering. Probably too recognizable or too hot to ever bring upstairs and display.

Except for some of the chinoiserie, most of the stuff left in this room is broken. I notice that. Everything else was eventually taken upstairs and assimilated. The items left behind are not functional. Except for the bed. The bed was left here for the people who waited.

There is a sense of waiting in this room. And a sense of fear. Both are palpable. We are fearful now, of course, but it's more than our fear that resides here. This is the room where the slaves waited for their freedom. The last stop on their trip north. They waited here, never knowing if they would get out or if they would die trying. Trusting the abolitionists, who were the same blood and only a few generations removed from the people who owned the ships that brought them here to be sold into slavery in the first place. Trusting the untrustworthy. Having no other choice. Hoping that it has come full circle, as all evil must do before it meets its final end.

There is fear in this room. But there is also hope. I can see it. The hope is over there, on the far side of the room in the small black opening that leads downward toward freedom. The hope is in the tunnel.

"We can't stay here," I say, seeing her sit down on the bed. Seeing how tired she is.

"It's high tide," she says, knowing the mistake she has made. "We can't get out of here until the tide is low. At high tide the whole entrance to the tunnel is underwater." She wants to sleep, she says, leaning back on the bed. "Just for a minute. I'm so exhausted," she says.

She's right about the tides. You can smell the water from here. But you can smell the smoke, too, and that smell is stronger. It isn't exhaustion that's making Angela so sleepy. It's the smoke.

"Come on!" I say, pulling her up. She wants to wait. She wants to see if they'll rescue us. But the room is filling up with smoke. Already it is having its way with her. She thinks her judgment is clear, but it isn't. We can't wait to be rescued, if anyone even tells them we're inside the house. If they come to get us, they will go up toward the widow's walk. Where we told them we'd be. Even if they check the cellar, they will not find us. No one knows about the tunnel.

"Come on," I say again. "We can't stay here."

The rats are ahead of us in the tunnel. I try not to look at them. They scramble down the sides, all going the same way, moving away from the smoke.

Except for the scratching sound the rats make, it is silent. When we stop to rest, the smoke catches up with us.

As we move farther from the burning, it gets easier for Angela to breathe. "Maybe we can wait," she says, encouraged a little by it. "When we get to the end of the tunnel . . . maybe we can wait there until the tide goes out."

"Maybe," I say, trying to give her hope. But the smoke is right behind us. There is no waiting here.

I can feel the water on our ankles. I take the flashlight from Angela, shine it dead ahead. I can see the opening to the tunnel get narrower, higher, as the water deepens around us.

"How far to the end?" I ask.

She either can't or doesn't want to make that call.

"Estimate," I say.

"I don't know. . . . Fifty yards, maybe?"

"Half a football field?"

She nods. "I think so."

"Is it straight or does it curve?"

"Straight," she says, "but we can't . . ."

We are waist-high in the water now. Ahead of us the rats have stopped. There is only a foot of tunnel height left. A half-moon crescent of air. The rats have given up. They cling together on its edge as close to the water as they can get. They have come as far as they can. They have reached their end.

Behind us the smoke curls up and creeps slowly forward.

"I'm not going in there," she says. "It's suicide to go into that water."

But then she sees the smoke. Stealthy, creeping forward.

"We don't have a choice," I say, looking at the rats, making her look at them.

I can see my own history in her eyes. She has heard the stories about me. She thinks she has just made a big mistake, that she has just turned her life over to a crazy person.

I see her think about it. "I can't make it," she says, crying. "I can't swim that far underwater."

"I can," I say.

We're up to our chests. Too close to the rats. She looks at them and then at me. She knows I'm her only choice.

"Don't swim," I say, "don't paddle." She nods at me. "Don't even kick your feet." She nods again.

I show her how to do it. How to breathe and exhale. The way you do for long dives. Getting all the air out first so that you can take that one deep breath that will sustain you.

"God help me," she says, still a believer.

"God help us both."

We exhale everything. Taking one bursting breath, I push her down into the water. And then under.

I grab her by the hair. That's the only way to do it. Make her go limp and grab her hair. Holding it in my teeth so both hands are free. Feet alternately scissoring and pushing off against the bottom or sides of the tunnel. Propelling us slowly forward.

It seems hours, years, an eternity, maybe, in this blackness. I am aware of her under me, or alongside. Limp deadweight, letting herself be pulled along.

My lungs ache. Time shifts.

The blackness is everywhere. I haven't touched wall for a long time now. Or floor. Maybe the tunnel has widened. *Keep moving,* I think, *keep the rhythm.*

I'm losing sensation, of the water, of its coldness.

We are lost. All around us there is nothing but the empty blackness, vast and stretching endlessly in every direction. I realize for the first time what doom really feels like. Not the fantasy—the reality. Not the end of a painful life but the endless nothingness.

Angela was right. This is suicide. It's Lyndley's plunge. The jump from the Golden Gate Bridge. The swim to the moon. This is the death I always thought I wanted, the death I've been trying to find my way to every day since I was seventeen. It's mine now, finally, if I want it. The nothingness is all around me.

And there is a moment where I let go. I begin to die. It would be so easy. To rest here with the shells and smooth stones. I've been here once before, and it was perfect. Peaceful. But not now. Not anymore. Because it's not what I want anymore. It's what Lyndley wanted, not me. I do not want to die in the water, and I do not want to die in the tunnel. I try to want it. But I can't. I have to save Angela. And her baby. And, as I am just beginning to realize for the first time in my life, I have to save myself.

Angela's hair starts to slip out of my teeth. I grab for it, catching the tangles in my fist, unleashing everything that's hidden. Like May's hair, Angela's hair holds secrets. It is a gill net, catching the magic as it drags, now releasing it back one treasure at a time: the *milagros*, the veil, the picture of the Virgin Mother. All caught in the lace net of her hair, all leading the way.

As I push her in front of me, I see the lace web of hair and, through it, the luminescence. The sea horse swims ahead of us, into the web of light. It is the sea horse I first saw in May's hair as a child. This symbol is mine, I realize now, and I follow it into the web, spotting something in the distance . . . and I see . . . a faint green glow. Then, as my hand moves back in its stroke, Angela's hair falls out of the way, and I realize that the glow remains. We have found the opening to the tunnel. We are swimming toward the light.

We surface in the boathouse. Under the dock. I push Angela out in front of me to open air. We gasp for breath.

***

I manage to help her upstairs to the loft. She sits on the bed, rolls onto her side. "Are you all right?" I ask her.

"I think so," she says, though I can tell she's not. She turns again, moans.

"I'll get help," I say to her, opening the loft window to light my way. She manages to nod.

There is a pay phone on the docks. I start down the stairs when I see the robed disciples. Sitting on the other side of the canal, on the bench where the old men usually congregate. The old men have left that bench empty. They have gone up to see the fire, like everyone else in town. In their place are three robed figures looking toward the boathouse. Then, as I glance across the water at the opposing pier, I see more of them. Moving down from the house. Torches still blazing. The mob. Lighting grass, buildings, anything that will burn.

I run back up the stairs. Angela is on her knees.

"He will come for me. I know he will," she says.

"Who?"

"Reverend Cal."

"Cal is in jail," I say.

"No he's not, he got out. He should be here. Reverend Cal will come for me. We're going to Vegas. We're getting married."

"Get up." I try to help her off the bed.

"He should be here by now. They said he'd be here."
She is staring out the window, scanning the crowd.

"Reverend Cal will come. He promised."

"Get away from the window!" I grab her and pull
her back.

Angela starts to cry. My eyes trick me. I see . . .

*Lyndley standing in the same spot. Crying. Our first
summer together. We are thirteen years old. We keep
saying how happy we should be to be teenagers, that
everything is going to change for us now and how
good it is going to get, but everything has changed
already, this summer. And it is not good for us. It
is horrible. I can feel her pain. Horrible things have
happened. Things I can't say or even think about.
They happened to Lyndley, but I felt them, too; in
some dark twin place, I felt every beating. I knew
every time Cal came to her bed. She could handle
things, she said. And I believed her. She could handle things as long as we were together, as long as she
was on the island and we were together. That's what
she said, but she was wrong. She couldn't handle
things. She couldn't handle them any more than I
could.*

We have to tell someone, I said.

He said he'd stop. He promised.

———

I am jolted back to present by the sound of more fire engines, from all the adjoining towns, answering the alarm call that Salem has sounded.

The torches are moving forward. There are fires now, on the street leading down from Eva's house. A back lot. A shed.

They are moving toward us.

They are all races, all religions. They are flashbacks. They are hallucinations. The angry mob: the farmer whose crops have failed, the neighbor with the still-born child. They are all the people who have ever been hurt enough or angry enough with their lot in life to go looking for someone to blame.

"What are we going to do?" Angela turns to me.

As if I had the answer. As if I have ever had any answers.

And then I see it. The answer. It is immediate, and it is all around us. It's in the glint of moonlight shining golden off the roof of the Custom House. I think of Hawthorne and the stories he wrote, sitting at his desk over there. Even after he left this town, he couldn't get away. It was Salem he wrote about.

And I think about Ann Chase. And what she said about the Calvinists the night of Eva's funeral. "I wouldn't want their god," she said, "if their god isn't powerful enough to make them unafraid of us. What kind of weak, lily-livered god is that?"

And my mind flashes back to Ann and the first spell we ever saw her do. Lyndley and I sitting in the harbor off the pier, spying from the darkness. Giggling as we watched Ann and her hippie friends lifting their arms to the full moon and dancing around at the end of the pier. Performing their love spells. And us just laughing and laughing, because although we couldn't hear them, they looked so damned silly, like true believers, out there dancing around like that with their hands raised up to the full moon and the future loves of their lives all still ahead of them. And I remember thinking that even though they were older than we were, they were so young and so very naive and believing. Because the world doesn't work like that, not even for true believers.

"What are we going to do?" Angela sobs as the Calvinists get closer.

"We're going to give them what they expect."

She watches as I raise my hands to the full moon.

"Put your arms up," I say to her, and she does it.

I'll pit my God against your god any day, I say to the Calvinists. It's not their god I'm praying to, and it's not one of Ann's goddesses either. The God I'm praying to is neither male nor female. My God is the one who exists apart from all of men's agendas, the God who takes you away when there is no possible place you can go.

"Please," I pray.

Angela and I stand with our hands in the air. Our hands are lifted to the light, which I thought was the light of the full moon yet which I now realize is not one light but many. The many lights are moving toward us now in formation, hanging just above the water like tiny UFOs.

The Calvinists see them, too. And it stops them, just like that. The robed men, the ones who were wading across the water, are scrambling out of the way. And I watch as the formation shape-shifts yet again and turns into the lights from the top of the Golden Gate Bridge.

"*Trust your gift.*" I hear Eva's voice in my head. . . . And then I start to laugh.

Angela sees the success of it, but she doesn't get the joke. It's not just that our prayer has been answered but that it has been answered so immediately and so thoroughly and with a sense of elegance and irony that only the real God could provide. Because when I asked for help, God sent me the symbols of my own demise. First the moon. Then the Golden Gate Bridge. But I was wrong about what I was seeing, I realize now. The images were never wrong. It was only my interpretation that failed. The treasures in the water were not symbols of my death at all but of my survival.

And then the sound cuts through the silence, the requisite blast—as the Golden Gate Bridge morphs into the party boat and the party boat makes its turn into the canal between the boathouse and Derby Wharf. The Calvinists scramble back onto the banks and out of the way of the huge boat full of drunken revelers and loud music and everything the Calvinists are repenting for as the party boat pulls into port.

"Jump!" I say.

We jump into the water below as the boat passes, putting it between us and the Calvinists, blocking their view. We jump just as the other robed men arrive at the back side of the boathouse, the smarter ones who walked instead of swimming from one pier to the other. They break down the doors and rush up the boathouse stairs, only to find that we have disappeared, confirming their belief in our powers, making them fall to their knees and beat their breasts and pray for deliverance from the likes of us.

No one sees us jump. The captain of the boat is too busy trying to dock. The revelers are all looking past us, up toward town and Eva's house, wondering at the flashing lights, the fire trucks, and the smoke that has turned now from black to white as the firefighters finally begin to contain the blaze.

We don't look back. Instead we swim together, Angela and me. At the mouth of the harbor, I find a small dory. It takes all my strength to get her into it, and she collapses against the hull, panting, exhausted.

The moonlight cuts a path directly toward Yellow Dog Island, lighting our way. It's a beautiful night, one of the last warm nights of the summer. Clear here in the harbor, but foggy out in open ocean. The island lies just behind the fog bank. The full moon is visible through the filmy vapor, a diffused beacon lighting a path directly to Back Beach.

The magic is with us. The tide is high, the moon right. We float into Back Beach on the tides, in a sea of sparkling phosphorescence.

I tell her to stay in the boat. A few of the dogs come out of their caves to see what's going on, but they don't approach.

"They won't hurt you," I say. "I'm going up to get May."

She nods, trusting me. She is barely moving, but I can see some blood in the boat and a lot of water. The baby is coming.

I run up the beach, taking the new path, avoiding the part where the ocean is starting to erode the cliffs, beginning to take back its own.

At the top of the path, I turn left, away from Auntie Emma's house with its fallen porch and toward the distant lights of May's house at the far end of the island.

I cut across the baseball diamond toward the dirt road, passing the stone kennel on my right, the rock spires from which Lyndley jumped standing like a castle fortress on the left.

I can see the old car, wisteria vines growing through its broken windshield, curling around the antenna.

And I'm stopped by something, a presence. He is leaning against the car. I almost don't see him, unshaven and in jeans and T-shirt. But his presence is unmistakable. A shiver runs to my feet. I stop dead.

"Sophya," he says, stepping in front of me, blocking my way. His tone is one of authority. The way he says it makes me realize now why I changed my name, why I had to. I couldn't stand to hear my own name spoken. Because of how he said it, sibilant, snakelike. Sophya was a name that could be whispered in the night. Real quiet, so that no one else could hear it. Quiet enough so it didn't even wake my mother.

I am standing at the horizon where all the lines meet. All the lines of perspective I've drawn off of every surface in my life. It is the still point. Every thread runs from this point, and every thread runs back to it.

We have been here before. I know what is coming. When the dogs begin to appear, it doesn't surprise me at all.

There is Byzy standing on the rocks; behind him are the others. I count ten, then twenty, then more. They move from their hiding places softly, silently. Cal doesn't even see it happening until they are surrounding him. When he does finally see them, there is terror on his face, but there is also recognition. We have been in this still point together before, Cal and I. Cal on the boat he stole from San Diego. Dehydrated and dying. Lost at sea. And me lost here on this island at the same point somewhere in time. We shared the same vision, the same hallucination. We have both seen this same ending. And we both know that I am the maker of this lace. We both know that everything that happens from here on out is up to me.

The dogs are closing in on him now. The same way the robed men closed in on us. Quietly moving forward. The dogs' eyes are glowing, teeth bared.

"You came to get Angela," I say.

"Yes," he says. "I came for her."

"You can't have her," I say.

As I say this, the dogs make their move. They are on him before I have a chance to speak another word. Tearing at his clothes, his flesh. And just like in the dream, I know that I can stop them. This time I know the word. But this time what is different is that I don't know why I would want to.

And then Angela appears. Moving toward Cal, trying to get between him and the dogs. "Stop!" she yells at them, but it only makes them more fierce.

"Get out of the way!" I yell at her. She doesn't move. And I can see in her eyes what May saw that night in Auntie Emma's. It's what made her unable to pull the trigger and stop all this, what made her miss the opportunity she'd been given.

For whatever reason, Angela loves Cal Boynton. She loves him enough to die for him. "Please!" She is crying now. Trying to get close to him.

One of the dogs turns on Angela, biting her forearm. I see the blood come.

I am disgusted. By her as much as by him. All the anger of my childhood pours out, and for a moment I think they *should* die together. That they deserve each other. They deserve this end. But there is a fourth person here. And I can see her face. She is here with us. My sister. I can see her young, and I can see what she will grow up to become, what she wants to become if she is given the chance this time around. And I owe her that chance.

"Stop!" I yell, knowing that the word Angela used was right, but that the word has to come from my lips. And knowing I have to mean it. "Stop!" I yell louder, meaning it this time. The world goes still. The dogs lean over on their haunches as if they've stopped in freeze-frame and are waiting for someone to restart this film.

Angela falls back now, sobbing.

Cal is on the ground between us. He is bleeding badly.

"I knew you would come for me," Angela says, starting to move forward. Then, seeing the blood, she stops. As if cut in two, she doubles over with the first pain of labor.

Cal struggles to get to his feet, dragging himself toward her. My eyes freeze him in place.

"I'm okay," Angela says, holding up a hand. She leans back against one of the rocks for support.

And I can see that he loves her, too. He wants to help her. I can see it in his eyes. But as much as he wants to, he does not move. He can't. When he finally speaks, it is to me. But he doesn't say what I think he's going to say. He doesn't tell me that I'm possessed or a temptress or that everything that happened was my fault.

"Forgive me," he says, his voice soft. It is not a command this time. It is more like a prayer.

Blood pools around his feet.

He steps forward then. Toward me. His arms are outstretched. There are tears in his eyes.

I stand still as a statue. I hear Byzy growl, but he doesn't move. He won't move until I tell him to, and the others won't move without him.

My mind is blank. I feel Cal reach for me, feel his arms come up, and then there's a cracking sound, and I can feel my ribs break as I fall backward under him onto the rocks.

We are fused together.

And then I see May. Standing there, the rifle in her hand. The other women are with her. They move in, circling Angela, and I see one of them take her by the arm and lead her back toward the stone kennel, the closest building. Angela is crying. It's a low, animal sound, composed equally of grief and birth. The women have enveloped her the same way they enveloped the frightened woman with the children the first day I was here.

"Call the coast guard," May says. "Tell them we need the medevac helicopter."

May puts down the rifle. Using all her strength, she rolls Cal's body off me.

The moans from the stone kennel merge with the sound of my own blood in my ears. The moans turn to the wails of a woman in labor. My life is flashing before me. With each of Angela's moans, something flows out of me. Breath and blood. With every moan something slips further away. I am dying.

They are all here. All the women. Auntie Emma is here, along with the others. Women from my past, teachers, friends. And then, through the crowd, I see Eva. Sitting off to one side, on the same rock Angela just left. She is working on something. Looking down at it. What is she doing? And then it comes to me. She is working on the piece of lace. My lace. The one she sent to me before she died. She is trying to finish it.

I fight for breath. Darkness is everywhere. The fog is coming down. Covering the moon and stars. It is so cold.

And all the time Eva just keeps working. Passing bobbin over bobbin. I want her to look up, to look at me, but she won't do it. She just keeps weaving the lace. She is doing it for me, I realize. But she can't help me.

Not this time. I want her to look up, because I want to tell her that, because I know it, even if she doesn't. This time my help can't come from Eva. It has to come from someone else.

I hear the sounds first, tiny farting sounds. It annoys me, it's out of place. Then I see the sandals. And I look up. She is coming through the crowd, parting it. She is smoking a joint. And I think how much like Lyndley this is, how self-centered, that she would be smoking a joint and fooling around even as I lie here dying. Stealing focus from me as usual, the same as she always did. She is wearing the bedspread. Not as pants the way she meant to, but draped across her shoulders like a huge shawl that's too long and dragging on the ground behind her, pulling debris and small pieces of grass, getting dirty as it drags. Her hair is long and tied back in a braid.

"Lyndley," I say.

"Towner," she answers, as if this were nothing unusual at all, me lying here on the ground dying like this. She leans over to get a better look at my situation, taking a deep drag off the joint. And then I know what she is going to do. She is going to blow the smoke at me. I'm dying, and she's going to blow smoke in my lungs and try to make me get high with her.

"Relax," she says, and I realize there is no way out of it.

I feel her lips on mine. I can't move away. I feel the smoke as it moves down my windpipe, burning, stinging.

I reach out to grab her arm, but she is gone again. I squint my eyes to see her, but the moon has come down. It is descending on us too fast.

The fog clears then, and I realize that once again it's not the moon but something moving that I see. And then I hear the sound, as it catches up with the light. It's not the moon, and it's not the party boat either. It brings the wind with it as it descends, and my vision clears. The wind from the helicopter blades has blown off the fog.

I watch Lyndley turn and walk away from me and toward the stone kennel. It is time. She looks back and smiles and then goes inside to take the chance that was stolen from her so long ago.

I try to say her name, but I can no longer recognize my own voice.

"Who is Lyndley?" I hear one of the women from the Circle ask May, as she hears me say my sister's name. The paramedics swarm around me. The woman's voice is tiny, afraid.

"It's not Lyndley," May says to her. "It is Lyndsey. . . . Lyndsey was Sophya's twin sister."

"Is she here?" The girl is looking around. She sees the shadow as it passes. Her eyes follow mine.

"No," May says. "Lyndsey is not here. She died at birth."

She did. I know. And I don't know. It is true and not true, both at the same time.

I am dying. And at the same time, in the stone kennel, my sister, Lyndley, is finally getting her chance to be born.

The dogs run for cover then, all the dogs except for Byzy, who won't leave my side until May grabs his collar to keep him from biting the paramedics as they take me away from him, putting me first onto the stretcher and then the helicopter.

PART SIX

As each piece of lace is finished, it is cut free from the pillow and he ld up to the light, and for the first time its delicate pattern is revealed. The cutting of the lace is done with great care and ceremony. The women gather in a circle, holding their breath as the lace maker cuts the delicate linen threads. One is reminded of midwives, of birth, the cutting of the umbilical cord, such is the delicacy, the anticipation. When finally the lace is cut free, there are murmurs of delight and admiration. This is a moment of great joy for these women, who have come so far together.

—THE LACE READER'S GUIDE

Chapter 33

I was at Mass General for six weeks. One of my lungs collapsed from the rifle bullet, which went through Cal and into me. I had six transfusions.

Beezer and Anya came home from Norway. They were there most days, as was Rafferty, who actually tried to bring Byzy in to see me. But he was turned away at the door. Instead he stood outside and made me look out through the window to the sidewalk below, where he had Byzy on a leash, and I could see even from there that Rafferty was already sneezing. He said he did it for Byzy and not for me, because the damned dog kept swimming to town to look for me and kept getting himself arrested by the dog officer and put in the pound. He said he needed to show Byzy that I was all right, so he would go back to the island and stay there. "And stop being such a pain in the ass all the time."

May came once. To talk to the doctors. She told me that Angela had a baby girl. "She named her Linda," May said, looking at me. The doctors had told her what I thought, that Angela's baby was my sister, Lyndley. "Interesting choice of name," May said. "Don't you think?"

Both Angela and her baby are gone from this place. Not north this time, but south to some friends May has made in Georgia, people who will help her, part of the Underground Railroad. She is not in danger from the Calvinists anymore. But she couldn't stay here.

The Calvinists are gone, too. The group dispersed when they learned of Cal's death. But they would have broken up anyway. It was either disappear or be arrested on several counts of arson. As well as attempted murder. They have left town one by one, dumping their robes in trash cans around town or on park benches. Disappearing into the vapor, never to return.

I am seeing three different psychiatrists as well as a researcher from Harvard who is doing his doctoral thesis on precognition and has taken an interest in my case. To the best of my knowledge, no diagnosis has been made. Dissociative disorder is certainly part of it. And survivor's guilt.

May and the doctors have helped me fill in the gaps. My twin sister, Lyndley, was born dead. Her real name was Lyndsey, or would have been if she had lived. May has explained everything to the doctors, and I know she is telling the truth, because it resonates on some level the way truth always does. My sister died as a result of a severe beating my mother got from my father, Cal Boynton. We were both born prematurely, but I am the one who survived. Emma has always blamed herself for Lyndley's death. Lyndsey's, I mean. That's what May says. It is not unusual for the abused to blame themselves for everything that happens. By the time we were born, Cal had my mother convinced that most things that went wrong in the world were her fault.

May says that Emma is like the other abused women in that regard. They often blame themselves. The beatings don't start overnight. Most abuse begins slowly. An offhand remark, something derogatory that the woman already believes about herself. It starts with the undermining of already fragile self-esteem. Then isolation. It is a scenario May has seen again and again. It is a gradual process you hardly notice. Until the actual beatings start. By that time the victim is usually so shaky and unsure of herself that she is no longer capable of escape.

There is another specialist coming to town sometime next week. Someone Rafferty found who has written a book on grief counseling in twins. And another who specializes in long-term sexual abuse in children. The best doctor I see is someone my own shrink set me up with, a classmate of hers from Harvard. I started seeing him while I was still at Mass General, and I go into Boston twice a week now that I'm out. Sometimes I take the train. Sometimes Rafferty drives me, and we stop in the North End for lunch or maybe an early dinner and some gelato if he doesn't have to get back to work.

I am grieving. For Eva. For my real mother, Emma, and everything that has happened to her. And for Lyndley. I am asked to sit with my grief, to feel it. It is difficult. It breaks through at times, but I am so accustomed to feeling nothing that even the pain itself feels distanced, as if it were happening to someone else. But I make the effort.

I have taken the house off the market. I cannot sell, not yet. Some of the reasons are practical. One whole wing of it was burned in the fire. It's surprising how little of it was lost, considering the intensity and scope of the fire. About a quarter of the house was gutted, the part with the tearoom in it. I've hired a builder to restore it, someone recommended by the Peabody Essex Museum. They are very interested in restoring the tunnels, if they can talk the town of Salem out of filling them in. I've donated the chinoiserie to the museum. We'll see about the rest. For now Byzy and I are living in the coach house. Going back and forth to the main house as we need something, but sleeping in the little house where it's cozy, more like the caves he's used to.

We have to stay for May's trial. It will be sometime next year, probably in the spring.

I have seen Ann Chase on several occasions. She wants to open Eva's tearoom again, though somewhere else, in some commercial space downtown. She and her girls have started reading lace.

As part of my therapy, I have taken up painting. I sit for long hours at the easel Eva set up for me the year I painted *Swimming to the Moon.* I paint the harbor and the common. Sometimes I try to paint the flowers. If there is one thing that all the doctors agree upon, it is that I have no talent whatsoever. But they urge me to keep trying, convinced that the talent must be inside me somewhere, the same way they believe that Lyndley was inside me. And so I sit.

It is getting cold. Tomorrow is Halloween. All this month the Fright Train has been running from Boston to Salem, bringing the tourists here for what has turned out to be the busiest season for the merchants. People in monster costumes serve mixed drinks to the commuters. I sit and watch them sometimes and think about free enterprise and just how creative it can get. Mom-and-pop haunted houses crop up on every corner this time of year, with no legislation to limit them. That law didn't pass. It failed for the same reason that Rafferty says the Calvinists would have ultimately failed if they hadn't done themselves in. It failed because Salem is a town of tolerance—religious, social, and even economic. Maybe it doesn't achieve perfect peace. Such a thing is difficult to imagine in today's world. But in the end Salem is a town that doesn't take itself too seriously, because it learned early on, way back in the 1600s, what can happen when you do.

The limos are already lining up in front of the Hawthorne Hotel. The Witches Ball is tonight. It is formal, and I understand from Ann that it is a beautiful event, the highlight of their social season.

Across the street on the common, there are three thousand pumpkins, all carved and lit up, lining the pathways or sitting on tree limbs. It is something to see. A couple of days ago, the weather got too warm—it went up into the eighties for a day or two—and Rafferty was worried that the pumpkins would rot and not last until Halloween, when his daughter would get a chance to see them. But then it got cold again, so he need not have worried. He told me his daughter wanted to get a lace reading, that she's always wanted one. She doesn't know about Eva and what happened to her; she just saw Eva's sign once on one of her trips up here and thought it would be fun to have her fortune told.

I think about Jack a lot. He has moved away from here, to Canada, where he always wanted to live. And I think about Eva. I even think about Cal, and I wonder about forgiveness. I know it is what must happen. Every book I read tells me that. As does Dr. Ward. All forgiveness is self-forgiveness. That's what he says. But I do not yet know how to forgive. Or who, in the end, really needs to be forgiven.

Beezer and Anya are staying around for a while. They're still living in Cambridge, but they come out here a lot to help out. She is nicer than I believed. They want to have children. May is thrilled at the thought. She wants to be a grandmother. She says she'll be better at it than she ever was as a mother, and Beezer says that's not far to go, but I don't know. May was a good mother to Beezer; she gave him what he needed. And she was a good mother to me when my own mother couldn't be, when she was too weak and wounded to act as a mother anymore.

I don't know if Emma knows what has happened. Or if she even recognizes me as her daughter. Sometimes I think she does, but I can't be sure. It is enough for me that I recognize her. That she is still alive and, I would say, finally happy in her world as she understands it. We are given gifts, I realize. Small ones and big ones.

I have finally read my journals. And the book Eva wrote: *The Lace Reader's Guide.* Pulling apart the pages and finding her faint hand. Each page reveals another secret, like when we were kids and we used to make disappearing ink out of lemon juice and then hold it over a lightbulb to be read. I am doing my best to restore it, laying my handwriting over hers. Its gaps mimic my own, and I work at filling in the pages the same way I work at filling in my own history. Slow going. A lingering process. Good work for the long winter that is coming.

I notice one curious thing as I work. As my pen moves over Eva's and the words on the page grow darker and easier to read, my image of Eva begins to grow dimmer. It is as if the two have somehow traded places, one moving into the foreground as the other fades back.

Still, I do get visits from Eva on some occasions. Today I was taking something inside, up the old staircase, and I ran into Eva coming down. She was dressed for her swim, in a beach robe and a bathing cap, a towel slung over her shoulder. She still does this; she goes for her swim. It's the only time I see her. She doesn't speak anymore. And her image is very faint. As she passes me, she smiles as always and then does something else that she always does. She checks her pockets as if she's looking for something.

I put the things away in Eva's room. My room now. I'm a little tired. I decide to lie down for just a minute on the canopy bed, for a quick sleep and maybe a dream. I don't worry about the dreams anymore; the nightmares have stopped. Propped against the other pillows is the lace pillow that Eva sent to me before she died.

I pick it up to move it to the bedside table, so I can lie down. And I think of Eva checking her pockets. I remember the pocket on the lace pillow; I checked it before. I checked it the day I got the pillow, expecting to find a note, surprised when there wasn't one. I check it again now, thinking maybe I missed something that first time, that this is what Eva is trying to tell me when she keeps checking her pockets. But the pocket is empty. And then I see her again in my mind's eye. Checking her other pocket. One, two. Everything in twos. But traditionally these lace pillows had only the one pocket. I know that. It is something I have learned. Still, I turn the pillow all around, and under the gathering on its opposite end I find the second pocket. Inside is the little set of scissors I recognize from childhood, the ones Eva used to cut off my pigtail. I also find the note.

> *Dear Towner:*
>
> *I'm doing it. I'm swimming to the moon. I will finish what your sister started so long ago. I can't think of any other way to help you out of your downward spiral but this—I will swim to the moon. I will do for you what your sister ultimately could not. I will take your place.*
>
> *Live a long and happy life. . . . And trust your gift. It is true.*
>
> *Eva*

I cry for a long time. When I finally wipe the tears from my eyes, I pick up the scissors and cut the lace free from the pillow. I hold it up to the light, turning its crazy patterns and looking at it from all perspectives, seeing each of its imperfections.

And then I say back to Eva the same words she said to me so many years ago, when she cut my braid. Maybe it wasn't true then, or not lastingly true anyway. But it is true now. The words I say back to her are the same words she said to me that day so long ago: *The spell is broken. You are free.*

Acknowledgments

I'd like to thank the following:
 – Alexandra Seros for years of help and friendship.
 – My agent, Rebecca Oliver, for believing and making it all happen. Brian Lipson for having the vision. The Endeavor Agency.
 – Laurie Chittenden for being such a champion of this story. Laurie Chittenden and Clare Smith for great notes and inspiration. All of the great people at William Morrow/HarperCollins. And a special thanks to Lisa Gallagher for reading the manuscript at Heathrow Airport.
 – My mother, June, for her prescience and gift of second sight that told me to keep writing. My father, Jack, who always believed in the good guys. And good dogs. And me.

– Pal and Pal: Whitney Barry and Emily Bradford for reading and commenting on numerous drafts, for their unwavering faith, and for their incredible gift of *The Lace Reader*'s garden.

– The Warren Street Writers: Jacqueline Franklin and Ginni Spencer for five years of support and suggestions.

– Diane Stern for all her help.

– Kelley and Hall for their PR expertise.

– Tami Wolff and the Deer Island APS English class for my first reading.

– Rema Badwan for generously sharing her vast knowledge of the publishing industry.

– Jim McAllister for checking historical accuracy and Salem trivia.

– Early editing: Tom Jenks for notes on point of view. Ed Chapman and Norma Hoffman for their editing expertise. Also, Laura Vogel and Ruth Greenberg.

– And the readers: Mandee Barry, Mark Barry, Susan Marchand, Donna Housh, Ed Trotta, Marcia Goodstein, Dottie Dennesen, Andy Postman, Jeannine Zwoboda, Carol Cassella, Gloria Kelley, Jocelyn Kelley, and Megan Hall.

. . . and last but not least, to Byzy, great warrior and super pup.

Author's Disclaimer

The Lace Reader is a work of fiction. Still, the sense of place is very real, and many of the locations do exist.

However, a few of the locations are fictional extrapolations of real places. Yellow Dog Island does not exist, but its geography and topography closely resemble that of the real Children's Island, where I once worked. Eva's house is a compilation of one that we considered buying in Salem, the one we ended up buying, and my grandmother's house, which was not in Salem but in Swampscott. Eva's gardens were inspired by the gardens at the historic Ropes Mansion.

Cutting the lace free is something Ipswich lace makers do not do, since the threads are wound around pins. If you cut the actual thread used to make the lace, it would unravel the lace and ruin the piece. Eva invented the technique of tacking the lace to the pillow in order to hold the work in progress securely in place. This was done with a sewing needle and a separate thread that could later be cut.

I have taken some liberties with the time frame of the book. It is loosely set in 1996, but I have combined Salem details I found interesting from other years in the same decade: the pumpkins in the park, the progress on the *Friendship,* and so on. In general, when historical events are cited, every effort was made to present them as accurately as possible, provided that in doing so the integrity of the fictional narrative was preserved (i.e., this is a novel, not a history book).

My apologies to Roger Conant, who was never in danger of being removed from his podium for lewd behavior and would no doubt have been appalled at the thought.

Oh, and I've never seen any rats near Salem Harbor (or anywhere else in Salem, for that matter).

To Learn More about
The Lace Reader

P lease visit www.LaceReader.com for a schedule of author events, general news, background information about Salem, Eva's method of lace reading, and discussions, or to send us your questions and comments.

HarperLuxe

THE NEW LUXURY IN READING

We hope you enjoyed reading
our new, comfortable print size and found it
an experience you would like to repeat.

Well – you're in luck!

HarperLuxe offers the finest in fiction and
nonfiction books in this same larger print size and
paperback format. Light and easy to read, HarperLuxe
paperbacks are for book lovers who want to see
what they are reading without the strain.

For a full listing of titles and
new releases to come, please visit our website:

www.HarperLuxe.com

SEEING IS BELIEVING!